BREAKOUT

THE ROSWELL LEGACY

GARY CLOSE

Breakout: The Roswell Legacy
Published by Maple Tree Press, LLC.
Copyright Gary L. Close, 2014

Second Edition

ISBN 978-0-9907185-0-5 e-book

ISBN 978-0-9907185-2-9 softcover

TABLE OF CONTENTS

AUTHOR'S NOTE

There are some things that need to be said here. First I could not have written this book but for the support of my wife, Linda. Without her encouragement this series of books would still be floating about in my heard unwritten and unknown. How do you adequately say thank you to that? I'm still trying to figure it out.

About lawyers. I have many good friends who are lawyers. Of special note is Federal District Court Judge Elizabeth Dillon who helped me through some very dark days indeed. She also encouraged this book to the point of reading the very first draft. For her help and work I am grateful. Another attorney friend is former Virginia Delegate John J. Butch Davies III who proved his mettle when the chips were down. And finally former law school classmate John Buckley who acted as a beta-reader for me -- thank you John for your many helpful suggestions.

About typos. I hate them. The book has been edited and reedited but the pesky varmints seem to appear at the oddest places. My apologies in advance.

About this book. At one level it is science fiction and a legal mystery combined. At another level it is about much more. I leave the latter interpretation to you.

About Reviews. Authors live and die by reviews. Good, bad or indifferent they all help. I encourage you to leave a short review on the Breakout Amazon page or on Goodreads. You can keep up with Breakout and its sequel on the face book page of the same name.

Sit back, strap in, and enjoy the ride.

"THE NSA HAS BUILT AN INFRASTRUCTURE THAT ALLOWS IT TO INTERCEPT ALMOST ANYTHING."

--EDWARD SNOWDEN

PREFACE

The Chinese satellite disappeared after thirty-six days. There were no indications of malfunction. One second it was fully powered, fully functional—hurtling around the earth's surface on a standard polar orbit. The next second it disappeared. While suspecting the United States as the author of the satellite's destruction, Chinese scientists and engineers were not certain of what had happened to erase it from their radar screens.

Given what they had learned they were not certain of anything.

At first technicians monitoring the data thought the satellite's stealth detection system had malfunctioned. While over the American East Coast on the first day the satellite detected one object in the atmosphere arcing from the planet's surface and beyond polar orbit in a matter of minutes.

It was astonishing.

At day fifteen the satellite picked up another object again moving vertically through the atmosphere of the American East Coast. The information of the object's existence punched its way back to earth. Not only were technicians able to determine the location of the object's launch but they could extrapolate, after a day of tracking, the object's final destination.

Mars.

Chinese leaders now understood that the United States was conducting a secret aerospace program with technology unheard of otherwise.

Data transfers made during the satellite's existence were tracked down and erased. Technicians were told in no uncertain terms of the value of forgetfulness.

But the People's Republic had channels and backchannels unknown to any one person. A state that monitors one billion people has built into the system multiple layers of bureaucracy, information gathering, information storage and information dissemination: known but unknown, known but forgotten, forgotten but functioning.

And knowledge, like water, finds a way.

BOOK ONE:

EARTH

CHAPTER 1

"WHEN I SAW WHAT WE WERE REALLY DOING IN CULPEPER I COULDN'T JUST LET IT GO. I THOUGHT IF I STARTED WITH (PAUSE)...IF I SHOWED WHAT WE WERE CAPABLE OF IN TERMS OF SURVEILLANCE THEN THE PUBLIC WOULD BE MORE ABLE TO ABSORB THE ACTUAL PURPOSE OF THE NSA. " -- TRANSCRIPT OF EDWARD SNOWDEN'S STATEMENT TO 929 OPERATIVES, MOSCOW AIRPORT, RUSSIA, JULY 2013.

--- EXCERPTS FROM THE NSA PRESIDENTIAL BRIEFING PAPERS ON THE ROSWELL INCIDENT

ZIJUAN/BEJING-- MINISTRY OF STATE SECURITY (MSS) (FOURTH BUREAU)

Cho Tsing lit another cigarette from the tip of the one he had just finished and sucked hard until a satisfying rush of unfiltered smoke curled its way into his lungs. He leaned back in his chair and exhaled: one cigarette in each hand. With eyes closed, and in a well-practiced move, he ground out the used butt into an over-flowing ashtray on his desk, scattering flecks of gray ash onto the mahogany surface.

He was on to something--and it was massive.

Dressed in a western business suit, Cho could have fit into any American or European business office like one of the 300 or so million other Chinese who had modernized during the past decades. But unlike his compatriots who dressed in western fashion and tried to mimic western culture as much as possible, Cho had in fact obtained, five years earlier, a degree in Electrical Engineering at San Diego State University, living, as it were, in the heart of American excess.

Tall and thin, the twenty-six-year-old Cho still hungered for the wide open atmosphere of America-- admiring and despising it at the same time. Conflicted as he was, obsessing as he did with all things American, he often thought it odd that something so removed physically from his life in China would bedevil him so. But late at night, streaming Lady Gaga on his I-Pod, deep in his gin, he knew the real reason for the fascination and repulsion, the real reason for the torment because it faced him every month like clockwork. Every month he did something so disgusting, so horrifying, he could hardly believe it was he who did it. And, hard as he might try to resist, in the end, like a dog nosing about a rotten carcass he always came back to it. God help him but he did. And he hated the thing he had become.

The horror started in San Diego -- after a four week blackout of which he knew nothing -- and then came the first episode. He remembered the shock and terror as the compulsion drove him to do what it was he did so reluctantly but so efficiently. So, he got out of San Diego as fast as he could with hope that the episodes would end, only to find that they merely followed him to Beijing.

Today, however, all the self- examination, all the anger at his dark secret melted away as he read the reports on his desk and smoked cigarette after cigarette. Cho had discovered an odd sequence of transmission reports in the mass of material he routinely read. At first the material meant nothing. Then a pattern emerged. And after running some computer simulations, he came to a startling conclusion. A massively important conclusion. The Americans were routinely launching, or tracking launches, outside the planetary orbit of earth, although insofar as he understood the present level of American technology, there was no chance that what the material indicated was in fact happening. And yet, it did happen, routinely and effortlessly.

Leaning forward, he punched a button on his desk phone for a direct scrambled line to his superior in the Fourth Bureau. It was a bold thing for a junior technology analyst to do but Cho wanted to go back to America. He wanted to confront his demons there. Whatever had changed him began in San Diego, in America, and he wanted it to end. He wanted to learn more about what it was he had just discovered-- a desire almost as strong as the first stages of an episode itself.

Two hours later, having finished outlining what he had discovered, Cho found himself being stared at by the porcine director of the MSS Fourth Bureau with disconcerting intensity.

"This is all very interesting," Director Rong said. "The facility mentioned in the documents you found is outside Washington. Correct?"

"Yes," Cho said.

And with that Rong outlined his plan. Go to America with a Dragon Team and find out what the documents meant. Because Cho said he wanted to go back to America, Rong insisted the young analyst repay Rong by carrying out a side job for Rong -- investing the director's money surreptitiously in the Western stock market.

"Invest wisely," Rong warned. "The team is there to make sure you do and that you come back. As to what you have found in these reports," here he pointed to the documents Cho had regarding American space activity. "You will produce on that as well. I send you because you understand that there are other, more personal, considerations here," he concluded, shooting a sly smile in Cho's direction. You have two missions. One for the state. One for me. Don't fail in either."

Cho felt a cold coil unravel in his gut, fear or anticipation; it did not matter, for the first time in years he felt a real mission called him: and it called him to a furtive clash in the night of his soul where he imagined his episodes originated.

BOULDER, COLORADO, USA

Iraq-Afgan War veteran, Captain John Weir, thirty-two, did not like Boulder, Colorado. It was an attractive town but he hated the smug, self-righteous atmosphere that seemed to rise from the very pavement of the streets. And, he especially disliked Pearl Street, which was packed with every imaginable type of millennial weirdo sitting on the sidewalks or meandering down the street and all of them, it seemed to Weir, trailed a heavy cloud of marijuana smoke behind.

The disorder of it all bothered the farm boy from Kansas. There the fields were in squares, the roads straight, the men short-haired and the work hard but honest. Here was something else. He maneuvered around a dread- locked young Caucasian sitting on the pavement chanting with arms outstretched. Ahead he saw his destination: *The Black Dog.*

Just as he reached for the polished brass handle of the pub's entry door, he heard a voice behind him.

"Captain Weir?"

Weir turned and saw an older man, late 50s, dressed in blue jeans and a blue work shirt. His erect bearing, trim waistline and buzz-cut hairstyle said to the world, unlike his clothing, a military or para-military background. The older man reached in his pants pocket and pulled out a small, black plastic device.

"Do you have an authenticator?" he asked.

Weir fumbled in his pocket and pulled out a similar device which he had been given that morning. Without a word, both men exchanged authenticators. Then, as if by cue, the two exchanged devices again. A small circle glowed green in each indicating a trace DNA match.

"Very good, Mr. Smith," Weir said. "I guess you're who I'm supposed to meet."

"So are you, Captain Weir, so are you," Smith replied. "Let's go inside."

Weir looked around the pub as he entered. It was crowded with a mixture of college students, businessmen, and tourists. The interior itself gleamed with polished brass and old wood. Along one side of the room stretched a wide, old-fashioned, ornately carved bar. Behind it, young bartenders tried to keep up with the press of customers. The other side of the room was lined with booths. In between ran a line of tables. On a wall, a large chalkboard listed the brews available.

Weir found it mildly annoying that so few national brands were displayed on the board. Typical Boulder, he thought, no Pabst Blue Ribbon.

As if reading his thoughts, Smith interrupted the inspection. "You like Boulder?"

"It's too trendy," Weir replied. "I mean, look at what we had to walk through. Every politically correct nut case between Denver and the Front Range is here."

"Ahhh!" Smith exclaimed. "Do I detect a political conservative?"

"No, I'm not much on politics, I just don't like flakes."

The two took a booth and placed their orders. Smith resumed the conversation, "Well how about the base? You like working there?"

Weir gave the man a long stare. Now we get to why I'm here, he thought.

"Listen Mr. Smith, or whatever your name is, I want to make it clear that normally I wouldn't even acknowledge a question like that," Weir said flushing. "But this morning, my superior gives me an authenticator and tells me to meet a Mr. Smith at the *Black Dog*, a Mr. Smith who has the highest security clearance. And, my superior tells me this Mr. Smith has a project going that could be very helpful to my career. So, I'll answer your question, but I don't like even discussing 'the base' as you call it, here or anywhere else."

"I appreciate your reluctance to talk about it," Smith said. "That's your training and I'll respect it. I just want to know if you like working there." Smith took a sip from a newly arrived beer mug.

"Yes, I like working there."

"How about your wife? Does it bother her you can't talk about your job?"

"No. Not really."

"Your kids?" Smith asked.

"Well, you know, they're really too young to understand much beyond the fact that I work for the Army and that I leave in the morning and come home at night."

"What about later?"

"When they get older?" Weir responded. "I'll use the usual cover. Office work for the Army. Quarter Master Corps or something like that. Look, I understand security. My wife does too and it doesn't bother either of us. I take it by your questions that this is a black project."

Smith nodded. "This is an extreme black project. And it's long term."

Weir lifted his mug to swallow his beer and give him time to think. Weir knew what Smith meant by using the term *extreme*. There were black projects like the development of the stealth bomber and then there were "extreme" black projects which exist on paper, satellite photos, and even on the ground, but do not officially exist at all, and these were high priority, usually dangerous, and extremely good for one's career.

"Yes?" Smith asked.

"You said this was an extreme black project, was that just a phrase or…?"

"So you've heard the term before," Smith chuckled. "Yes, it's an extreme black project with all the implications the terminology implies."

"Can you tell me where I'd go?" Weir asked, judging the new information he had gathered.

"East Coast," Smith responded flatly. "That's it at this point. Once you've accepted I can brief you further."

"How long is the assignment?"

"Well, let's just say it's long term," Smith explained. "That's the nature of the project when it's extreme."

"Compensation?"

"It is very good. Your salary scale will be supplemented by hazardous duty pay and in addition extreme projects have their own supplement. In effect your take home salary will double. Also, I am authorized to tell you that after six months your rank will advance to Major."

Weir jumped internally at that. He'd felt for some time that his career had stalled. This would kick it back on track.

"OK, I'll do it," Weir said.

"You surprise me Captain. What about your wife?"

"Rebecca will agree," Weir explained. "Her parents live on the East Coast. She's always wanted to get closer to home. I assume you'll have some papers for me to sign."

"No, Captain," Smith responded flatly. "There are no papers. There are conditions, but they'll be conveyed verbally and your acknowledgement will be verbal. But understand that once you are in the project, once briefed, you cannot withdraw from the conditions. And enforcement is also, as we call it, extreme."

Weir was surprised at the lack of paperwork. However, he'd already signed away his life a long time ago and he was sure the Army had drafted the waivers and pledges to be all encompassing. He also knew what extreme enforcement meant and he was very surprised by that. He'd only heard of it once before. Extreme enforcement meant you disappeared – no one ever asked any questions. Not even family members.

"Do you want to withdraw your acceptance?"

"No."

Later that evening he told Rebecca who at first was angry that he had made the decision to move without consulting her, but when he told her where they were going to, her anger faded. Culpeper was only an hour's drive from her parents' house in Leesburg.

Sitting in a non-descript dark colored van a block away from Weir's house, Smith listened to Weir explain the move to his wife. Smith was pleased with Weir's carefully worded explanation of where they were going and why. Rebecca Weir's positive reaction was entirely predictable. Not only did the move take her closer to her family but it removed them from the neighborhood where Weir had just concluded an affair with a neighbor's wife. Of course the affair became public, Smith had learned during his preliminary background check, and Rebecca Weir had threatened divorce. But they had apparently patched things up and Smith thought the affair plus the location of Rebecca's family would seal the deal, and as a result he had recommended Weir for the position in Culpeper. Satisfied that Rebecca Weir would go along with John Weir's rather hasty decision to accept, Smith nodded to the driver next to him. The van pulled away from the curb. Inside, Smith, the driver, and two other men relaxed. Smith liked Weir. He would have hated to use extreme enforcement on Weir and his wife if she had balked at his snap decision. *And then there were the kids. It could have been a messy thing, really.*

Yes, thought Smith, Weir's quick decision did surprise him. And he learned from the surprise. *Weir was not entirely predictable. And in this business, that can either be good or bad – but it needed to be remembered.*

PENNSYLVANIA TURNPIKE, CENTRAL PENNSYLVANIA

Ed Wood looked at his sleeping wife, whose strikingly beautiful face was illuminated by the instrument panel lights inside the car. Although they had been married thirty-four years, Ed still thought himself lucky to have found a woman like Pat to be his wife. Her fifty-four years of life had been kind to her. She looked all of ten years younger. Ed, on the other hand, had friends tell him, in moments of honesty on the golf course, that he looked like he'd been rode hard and put down wet. It was said as a joke, he knew, but it was also true, not that he cared, but every time he looked in the mirror he wondered what it was that Pat saw in the beat-up face that looked back at him.

They had three children who were all off and on their own. Ed's dry cleaning business had expanded and was thriving. Pat was enmeshed in tennis and gardening.

Up until three months ago, they had lived the ideal, middle-class American dream. Norman Rockwell stuff, really.

Then it had all changed on that trip to Erie. As he had many times before, Ed sifted through the vague patterns and memories to create some meaning to those four weeks.

And that was the most frightening part of it all. His last memory was driving to Erie, Pennsylvania for a few days to visit his sister. Four weeks later, he and Pat were in their car parked by Lake Erie outside Jamestown, New York. And in between neither he nor his wife could remember anything.

Well that's not exactly true, he thought. They both remembered things – but things that did not make any sense.

My God, he thought, are we going crazy? But he reasoned as he had many times before, both he and Pat could not be going crazy at the same time, about the same thing, with the same consequences. *And that was why they decided to take another trip. This trip.*

Pat moved in her shoulder harness seat belt, then yawned and blinked her eyes open.

"Are we out of Pennsylvania yet?" she asked.

"No, but the next exit is Breezewood. We'll get off the turnpike there and take 270 South to 81."

"How long?"

"Probably four hours."

"Just about dawn."

"Yes"

They rode in silence as Ed negotiated his way through a cluster of traffic. After he passed the last truck he looked back at Pat and was shocked to see tears glistening in her eyes. Pat wasn't the one to cry, not even at weddings.

"Pat, you ok?"

"No. I'm not ok," she snapped. "I've prayed about this -- and I ask God to help us -- but I don't see anything happening. I've asked Him to stop what's happening to us but it just goes on and on. And

I have to ask for what purpose? Why would He allow something like this to happen to us? Why won't He answer when I pray?"

"God doesn't always answer the way we want Him to," Ed said.

"That sounds like something one of those televangelists say, and it's pretty lame," she replied bitterly.

"Nevertheless."

"Ed, why can't we just forget about all this?" Pat asked. "Why can't we just turn around?"

"We've been through this before, Pat," he reminded her.

"I know, I know." She wiped another tear away. "But I don't feel good about doing this anymore. Let's just get back to our lives. What's left anyway."

"You say that now," Ed replied. "But you know we can't. How many times have you had nightmares about it and then, what about the cravings? We can't forget every time you or I have the urge to eat….well, you know."

This only made her face scrunch up in a rictus of disgust and Ed understood why. It was the most horrible part of what had happened to them. Again, Ed asked himself, are we going crazy? And again he thought of the science fiction story he had read as a teenager where colonists were forced to eat slugs to survive

No, we don't eat slugs, Ed thought grimly, nothing as revolting as that. No, we eat crickets. Just the thought of crunching down on a kicking cricket made his mouth water. He licked his lips as he pictured the cricket cage they packed away in the trunk.

Crickets were easy to get. Furthermore, most pet stores could bulk order them for you. Ed found that out real quick. And Ed found that a handful of crickets a day could tide him over to the next day. The same with Pat.

Yeah, I don't eat slugs, but a cricket, Ed thought, a cricket is nice and dry and best of all you get the texture of its legs on your tongue it you eat it just right. Even so, he still remembered the re- vulsion he had experienced the day he first saw Pat with a cricket in her mouth – one leg dangling between her lips--a revulsion that soon disappeared when the craving led him to the back yard to catch his own little dark treat. It hadn't taken him long to figure out that the lost four weeks and the cricket eating must be connected; a theory

Pat was quick to accept. It was either that or believe the two of them had fallen into some sick food perversion.

And it didn't help to learn that many people around the world eat insects. That was ok for them, but for Ed it was a sick and ugly reminder that something happened to them that month away.

"Ed?" Pat's voice broke into Ed's thoughts.

"Yes."

"Do you mind if we stop in Breezewood for a bite to eat?"

"No. I had the same idea." He took the exit.

Breezewood existed as an exotic neon jungle of businesses catering to motorists coming off or going on the turnpike-- a fluorescent island in the center of rural backwater darkness. As he and Pat exited the car in a fast-food parking lot, Ed absently fingered a plastic ball point pen in his pants pocket. It was the same pen he found in the car after he and Pat woke up in New York.

Someone, during those missing four weeks, had dropped the pen on the rear seat. Somehow, Ed knew then, the pen could lead them to the answers he craved as much as he craved the squirming treats in his car trunk.

Ed pulled it out. Down the side he read "2ⁿᵈ National Bank" in bold green letters and numbers. Underneath in smaller print the green letters glowed sinisterly in the artificial neon night: "**Culpeper, Virginia**."

UNIVERSITY OF TAMPA--FLORIDA

Nineteen-year-old Leotie Thunder walked absently down University Drive. It was early evening, and a warm, slight ocean breeze carrying the hint of sea water drifted across the campus. To her left she could see the brutal towers of downtown Tampa, but to her right danced the Italianate turreted heart that beat at the center of the University. She loved the building's old world ornate charm. Once a luxury turn of the century hotel, it now acted as the University's center. In the early evening she liked to amble around the building, taking in the essence its designer so obviously wanted observers to absorb. Every unnecessary curve, every Victorian gingerbread swath of turned wood, every onion-shaped dome of which there were too many, it seemed, to count, all said to the world through the ages that beauty was valuable for its own sake -- or perhap for humanity's sake.

So different, her 19- year- old mind perceived, from the glass box monstrosities that rose like alien occupiers across the Hillsborough River to her left in downtown Tampa. They angled 20 or thirty stories high, blocking the sun, blocking the night sky with their bulk and brightly lighted offices--blocking human interaction with the world itself she mused absently more than once. So brutal, they seemed to block the very concept of human emotion and warmth.

The university building she stared at was so stunning, so different from her home in Arizona. There, beauty came from red rocks and blue skies. Not from man-made objects like this mound of turrets and whimsy.

Leotie loved to walk the University grounds but her wanderings often made her feel so lonely. It had been a hard transition from the reservation outside Flagstaff to this booming metropolis. Her father, a full-blooded Cherokee transplanted to the non-Cherokee reservation by the winds of chance, landed when casinos were just opening on reservation lands.

He made a fortune. He became a Mormon.

And he wanted his daughter to see a world he only experienced from the outside. His American-Indian accent and narrowed life experience telling him every day he did not belong to the world he worked and succeeded within. He had decided Leotie would have better. And so he sent her east to this private school in the Florida south, Southern but heavily influenced by the New Yorkers who migrated down to attend the same school.

She stopped to look upward at the stars. A muted version of what she would see at home but nonetheless a connection to the Arizona desert. And again, she pondered what it was she was meant to do as only someone her age can ponder with a clarity that emanates free from responsibility, free from the care and the wounds that cascade with time.

Then in the distance she heard music. The reggae beat instinctively drew her. A crowd milled about while in the center she saw four or five students playing instruments. The rhythmic lyrics burst out across the green campus.

"They're good don't you think?" She heard a deep voice ask from behind.

Leotie turned to see a young man, older than a freshman, but not too old to stand out on a campus full of coltish students. He was tall, thin, with close cropped blond hair and his clothing looked appropriately preppy for the school. He moved quickly to close the gap between them.

"What?"

"The tunes. They're good," he said.

Leotie stepped back. Something about him made her uncomfortable. He was no student, her instincts told her.

"Yeah, I guess they're pretty good." She turned to walk away.

"Hold on. What's your name?" he asked.

"I've got to go," she said and started to walk swiftly towards the group around the band.

"Hey! Wait! Aren't you in my English class?" he asked.

"I've got to go. See you around," she said over her shoulder. She turned one last time to see him standing alone watching her, his hands hanging loosely by his side, an intense look imprinted on his features. She gratefully slipped into the crowd.

For the past week Leotie had felt watched. She could not pin her sensitivity on any one thing but childhood experience in stalking desert wilderness creatures created in her a sixth sense all hunters develop. Stalking instilled stealth but stealth required an uncanny ability to perceive the very essence of an environment. The young man emanated something other than casual conversation, something deeper and more calculated, now that Leotie consciously thought about the encounter. Like the nervous deer on the field, she tested the air about her, looking at every face, every movement, to see if it signaled something more sinister. She noted nothing but remained alert.

Leotie listened to the music. Deeper in her soul, she listened to her sixth sense. It told her, though she tried to ignore it, that a new hunt was on, and she the prey.

CHAPTER 2

EFFORTS AT CONTAINING INFORMATION ABOUT THE ROSWELL SPACE-
CRAFT HAVE PROVEN EXTREMELY DIFFICULT FOR THE UNITED STATES
GOVERNMENT. ORIGINALLY, THE JUSTIFICATION FOR SECRECY CENTERED
ON THE IMPACT THE EXISTENCE OF SUCH A VEHICLE WOULD HAVE
ON U.S. - SOVIET RELATIONS, IT BEING SUSPECTED THAT THE CRAFT
HAD ORIGINATED IN THE SOVIET UNION UNTIL INVESTIGATORS REALIZED
THAT THE TECHNOLOGY INVOLVED FAR EXCEEDED HUMAN CAPABILITIES.
PRESIDENT TRUMAN, RECOGNIZING ITS VALUE FOR U.S. DEFENSE EF-
FORTS AND AT THE SAME TIME THE GREAT THREAT SUCH TECHNOLOGY
WOULD SEEM TO POSE FOR THE SOVIET UNION, APPROVED AND ADOPTED
THE MILITARY'S FIRST RESPONSE TO NEWS OF THE CRAFT'S DISCOVERY.
(SEE EXECUTIVE ORDER DS 0002 AND GENERAL MAXWELL'S LETTER TO
PRESIDENT TRUMAN DATED AUGUST 30, 1948) THUS, GOVERNMENTAL RE-
SOURCES WERE TASKED TO DENY THE CRAFT'S EXISTENCE. INITIALLY SUC-
CESSFUL, CONTAINMENT EFFORTS ARE INCREASINGLY INEFFECTIVE. TWO
FACTORS HAVE CONTRIBUTED TO THE INFORMATION LEAKAGE: FIRST, THE
GROWING "ALIEN ABDUCTION PHENOMENON" THAT HAS FUELED INTEREST
IN ALL THINGS OF EXTRA-TERRESTRIAL ORIGIN; SECONDLY, THE GROWTH OF
COMPUTER TECHNOLOGY AND THE RISE OF THE INTERNET AS A MEANS
OF COMMUNICATION. ALTHOUGH IN THE PAST IT WAS RELATIVELY EASY
FOR GOVERNMENT AGENTS TO CONTROL INFORMATION DISSEMINATION AT
CHOKE POINTS IN THE MEDIA, INFORMATION TECHNOLOGY AS IT IS NOW
CONSTITUTED MAKES INFORMATION CONTROL IMPOSSIBLE.

--- EXCERPTS FROM THE NSA PRESIDENTIAL BRIEFING PAPERS ON THE ROSWELL INCIDENT

CULPEPER COUNTY COURTHOUSE

Mordecai Binford's secretary poked her head around the door jam,   "There are two people out here to see you. They don't have an appointment."

"Are they defendants?" Binford asked. As the county's prose-cutor, this was always a piece of information he needed. She pulled back and closed the door behind her. He heard a muffled conversation before the door opened again

"No. They wouldn't say why they are here – only that they needed to see you."

"Tell them I'll speak to them in a minute," Binford told her, rubbing his eyes. She shut the door again.

He'd been pouring over the budget for his office for what seemed hours. When he was elected to the prosecutor's position ten years earlier, he had thought being the county prosecutor was about what went on in court, about keeping the community safe, *and there was that.* But it took money to hire assistants. It took diplomacy to get the cooperation from the police and sheriff's departments, both of which worked with him but not for him. The difference meant politics. The need for money meant politics. The desire to get re-elected meant not angering too many people while at the same time prosecuting their friends, family or coworkers. And that was politics whether he wanted to admit it or not. And then there were the times when he had to say no to trying a case because there just wasn't enough evidence. Say *no* to the outraged parents whose three-year-old daughter had been molested by a scumbag predator who covered his tracks far too well for the court system to assign guilt. Say *no* even though Binford knew the babysitter's dirt-bag boyfriend did it, say *no* even though chances were he'd molest again. That sometimes could be the worst part of his job. Knowing in his heart, in the center of what made Binford, Binford, knowing that he stood as the gatekeeper to the criminal justice system and that there were times when the law just did not support placing a charge. The law. In the end he served the law. Not the people. He knew that but it did not make the process any easier-- especially in a small community like Culpeper.

But today there was something else bothering Binford.

Recently the prosecutor felt he had been drifting: drifting into mediocrity, drifting professionally, drifting personally. And he didn't like it. Binford had always wanted to make a difference in the world. He wanted his work to count for something other than a paycheck. But he was settling. He knew it and he didn't like it. He hoped someday he would find whatever purpose it was that he had been put on earth to serve. So far, he hadn't a clue--but it wasn't for lack of searching. His wife Kate had seen him struggling and offered the only encouragement she could.

"You're already doing what you were meant to do," Kate had said to him more than once when he confided his doubts to her. "Every day, with every decision you make, you protect me and the kids. You stand at the wall. This is where God wants you. I believe that."

But hearing that from her wasn't enough.

Inwardly the prosecutor shrugged, adjusted his wire-rim glasses, and then pushed all doubts to the back of his mind. The mundane called.

"I'm ready. Show them in," Binford said into the desk intercom.

When the two visitors entered what immediately struck Binford was the couple's haunted glances about the room. He'd seen the look before, usually in the eyes of rape victims. Otherwise the two presented themselves as a prosperous, upper- middle-class couple in their fifties. Using an old salesman's trick, Binford took note of their jewelry and accessories. A good suit without a good watch or, in the case of a woman, expensive jewelry, indicated either a lack of resources or a tightfisted attitude towards money.

In this case the man wore a Rolex watch, and the woman a pearl choker with matching earrings and bracelet. Her wedding band flashed hypnotically in the afternoon light streaming through the window.

Definitely buyers, Binford thought as they introduced themselves as Ed and Pat Wood.

"I understand you are not involved as defendants in a case?" he asked, being extra careful not to cross any ethical boundaries by contacting a defendant without a defense attorney present.

"That's correct," Ed Wood answered. "We're here to do some research for a book. I'm a freelance author and I'm exploring an idea I have."

"Well, if I can help you I will," Binford said. "Is the book about criminal justice?"

"No. No. Nothing like that," Wood smiled slightly. "Actually, I write travel books. You've probably seen the genre on coffee tables. I pick a particular geographic area and highlight all the points of interest. For example, around here there seems to be a great deal of civil war history. So I'll highlight that. But people are interested in other things as well."

"Such as?" Binford asked.

"Well that's why we're here --because every place is different. What I do is ask people in an area if there are places or things unusual or outstanding around the community. So," Ed asked awkwardly, almost desperately to Binford's way of thinking, "does anything come to mind?"

"The Federal Reserve just outside town is interesting," Binford said almost instantaneously, startling even himself with the readiness of the answer. But then the prosecutor rationalized internally, the place just looked creepy.

"Really? How so? " Wood asked, his eyebrows arched in surprise at the ready answer.

"First, because most of the facility is underground," Binford explained. "Secondly, I guess, is because access is extremely limited. I've driven past the facility but I've never been inside. "

Wood jotted down notes. "Any other unusual installations?" he asked without looking up.

"Well, there's the Warrenton Training Center."

"What is it?"

"I'm not sure," Binford said. "It has something to do with the Army. There are a lot of radar domes and antennas there and it's surrounded by a barb wire topped fence, so my guess it's high security in some way or another."

The conversation drifted on but later, after the Woods left, Binford reflected that their interest had waned greatly once he left off the Federal Reserve and the Warrenton Training Center. He got the impression that there was much more to the couple's visit than what they revealed.

Two days after the meeting with Binford, Ed pulled his car over onto the gravel drive of a rest area where oak trees shaded picnic tables. The wayside stop was usually empty at this time of day. And that suited Ed and Pat just fine. Neither wanted company for this stop. No sir, Ed thought as he pulled under a tree, the gravel crunching richly, seductively, in the autumn heat, no sir, we will be dining alone today, thank you very much.

"I need to eat," he said. He was tired but more than that he was ravenous.

"I do too," Pat replied with an eagerness which Ed, even though he felt the same, found repulsive. We're getting used to it, he thought with a shudder.

"I'll get the container," Ed said. He unlatched his seat belt, opened the car door and moving quickly he opened the trunk and lifted a blanket over the right wheel well.

Early on, Ed had learned that his little treats liked the dark. Being stored in the trunk took care of that preference. But Ed liked to be sure, so he'd covered the cage with the blanket.

Just seeing the long black bodies of the crickets made Ed's hands shake slightly. He lifted the wire cage out of the trunk to return to Pat. In his eagerness to get back he left the trunk open.

Once back in the driver's seat, he opened the cage at the top and reaching inside, he trapped two squirming crickets in the palm of his hand--their legs kicking spasmodically across his gently curled fingers.

His mouth began to water.

Ed pulled the handful out and gave it to Pat. Without even an acknowledgement she crammed the contents into her mouth.

In his own excitement Ed didn't notice the moans coming from Pat as the cricket bodies crunched between her teeth.

He reached back into the bait cage and lifted his own squirming treat out. An excitement, almost sexual in nature, flooded through him as he shoved the kicking black mass into his mouth.

After their feeding frenzy, and really that's what Ed always thought of it afterwards, the two sat quietly in the car, appalled at what they had become. With the craving satisfied, they were left with only disgust. And yet, Ed thought, I don't ever throw away that damn cage.

Love and pride coursed through Ed as he looked as his wife, stony faced, tears sliding silently down her face. She was strong, he thought. How many would have fallen apart by now? But not Pat. She may cry, but she had stuck it out while they had probed the cause of their malady.

And, he thought, as he settled back in his seat, they had learned a lot. Culpeper was the seat of a postcard southern county where, in the old part of town, large houses flanked tree-lined streets and neighbors sat on the front porch in the cool of the evening. But there was another side to the town and the county. The interview with the county prosecutor had been very helpful. It did indeed seem strange that two facilities like the Federal Reserve and the Warrenton Training Center were located in such an out of the way place One facility here, ok, he had thought. They were, after all, not far outside Washington. But two? That *had* seemed odd.

But it was both Ed and Pat's reaction to the Federal Reserve that had convinced them they were onto something.

The Federal Reserve sat in the side of a small mountain, or large hill, just east of the town. Later, he had learned the eroded prehistoric volcano cone was called Mt. Pony. The facility was visible from the road, a concrete and glass structure, covered in vines, peeking out from the hillside with the remainder buried behind. As Ed and Pat drove on Germanna Highway near the town's outskirts Ed had felt vaguely uncomfortable. Then as Mt. Pony reared up in the sky he had felt an electric shock run through him. Pat, too, had reacted strongly to the sight of the mountain. She unceremoniously vomited onto the car floor.

He had pulled over and stumbled out of the car before he too fell to his knees and retched onto the gravel roadside shoulder.

Memories surged forward in his mind as he had crouched on his hand and knees, gravel grinding into his knees, memories that still swirled and shifted but always revolved around fear, and cold, and isolation.

Somehow they had managed to get away from the sight of the mountain.

And then the research began. They focused entirely on the Reserve. Ed spent hours at coffee shops trolling the internet but found little to help. And now they sat in a car eating dusky treats like animals. He had hit a dead end. It was time to switch up the game, he decided.

"We have to get inside the Federal Reserve." Ed said quietly, brushing a cricket leg from his shirt.

"I know," Pat replied.

"I don't want to but I don't see any other way," he said as if to convince himself.

"I know," she said again with a shudder.

WARRENTON TRAINING CENTER

"This way, Captain Weir," the young corporal said as he led the way down the highly waxed hallway of the Warrenton Training Center.

It had been a whirlwind month for Weir and Rebecca. Smith, or whatever his name was, had not told him all the perks that came with the job when they talked at the Black Dog, the first having been the sale of their house. A third party bought it the day they listed it. No haggling. No delay. Next, the military moved them at no cost to a brick rancher in Remington, Virginia.

He got orders yesterday to appear at the Warrenton Training Center and meet the director --which was where he was now.

Weir still didn't know exactly what he was supposed to do there, but, as the corporal clicked down the waxed floors ahead of him, he had a feeling that he was about to find out. And whatever it was, Weir thought, it probably would be as strange as the training center itself.

Weir had heard of the training center but he'd never seen it before. He was shocked at the seeming lack of security. The facility sat alone in a remote part of Culpeper County, yet only a barbed wire-topped fence separated the center from the occasional farmer outside, while at the entrance a lone guard house regulated traffic. Before entering the facility, a small cast-iron sign, the type usually used for historical site markers in Virginia, read "Warrenton Training Center, NCS, U.S. Army, Station C, Admission by permit only, Guard Port Ahead."

Perhaps, Weir thought, the fence and the guard were adequate, but when you considered that the center was the largest facility for encrypted communication in the U.S. intelligence community, there was certainly not the degree of security he would have expected. And that was strange.

As Weir walked down the institutional green cinder-block hall, he glanced out a side window where, stretched across a large open field, perhaps 30 to 50 antennas of all different shapes and sizes jutted into the clear blue sky. He noticed two white microwave domes. The antennas could have been built in the 1950s for all the technological sophistication they showed. The domes gleamed white. The juxtaposition of the two technologies, one obviously human in its steel towers and rusted bolts, the other alien in its clean octagonal textured surface, jarred Weir in some unexplainable way. He looked away.

The corporal stopped and opened a side door.

Weir stepped inside and saw a room that looked more like a lawyer's office than the headquarters for the drab institutional facility he had just traversed. A woman, in her late 40s, with a conservative grey suit, looked up from her desk unsmilingly.

She nodded to the corporal who shut the door. Weir sat on a burgundy leather couch and looked around the reception room. Across the room two leather chairs flanked a mahogany, round side table. On it a brass lamp glowed dull amber. His eyes wandered to the rich tan plastered walls. At first, they looked to be the typical trophy walls of someone who had worked his way up to power and prestige, the "I love me walls" as he had heard them called. Usually such walls were covered with certificates of achievement-- but this wall was different.

The photographs on the wall were of a man with one President after another. No certificates or degrees announced educational prestige. Apparently the photographs said all that needed to be said.

Weir's inspection was interrupted by an office door opening to frame a portly man dressed in civilian clothes: a dark suit, white shirt, and a red stripe tie, the same man in the photographs.

"Weir, good to meet you, Ford Allen Sims," Sims stepped forward and grasped Weir's hand as he rose. The action flustered Weir slightly. He was rising to his feet to salute but Sims grabbed his hand before he could accomplish the act.

"You all settled in?" Sims asked as he ushered Weir into the office and shut the door behind them.

"Yes, well, there are boxes to be unpacked but, yes, we're settling in."

" Good. Good. Kids adjusting?" Sims asked settling into his chair behind the executive desk which dominated the room.

"Yes." Weir replied shortly, irritated by this too-casual attitude. In Weir's opinion, Sims was acting more like a Baptist deacon than a military superior. It offended Weir's sense of decorum.

"Good," Sims said, abruptly abandoning the preliminary chit chat as he opened a file and leafed through it. "Mr. Weir, this is what is known as an extreme black project. The way we work here is that you will get eased into your duties. If things don't work out, as sometimes happens early on, you can move on without knowing any more than you have to. There is a facility in Culpeper that we operate in conjunction with the Warrenton Training Center called the Federal Reserve. Your primary responsibilities will be there as head of security."

Suddenly, deliberately looking Weir in the eyes, Sims' whole demeanor changed and Weir saw the razor sharp steel within the man.

And the coldness.

"Let me emphasize to you, Captain, that this project is of the utmost importance to the security of the United States," he said. "It is important that you understand this. There is no project – no other project – that is more vital to this country."

"Yes sir," Weir responded automatically.

"This is a high-security operation," Sims continued. "You'll understand why when you learn more about the project. But what I want you to understand now is that there can be no room for error in our security blanket. None. It will be your job to make sure there are no breaches at the Federal Reserve. Do you understand what I am saying?"

"I assume you mean that anyone who violates security protocol inside or outside the facility will be prosecuted fully," Weir replied.

Ford Allen Sims' smile turned wolfish.

"'Prosecuted fully' is a good way of putting it," he said coldly.

It was the first time since his deployment in Iraq that Weir had seen such flat empty eyes in anyone who was still alive.

TAMPA--COURTNEY CAMPBELL CAUSEWAY

There it was again! Leotie looked in her rear view mirror. In the clogged traffic heading to the beach, she saw a black SUV with tinted windows six to ten cars behind her in the stacked traffic stopped at a light, a car she had first seen just off the campus grounds. A black SUV in Tampa stood out like a Hawaiian shirt in Flagstaff. It didn't belong. After first seeing the vehicle, she began tracking its progress behind her. Sometimes she deliberately slowed to allow traffic to pass. The car never passed. It moved when she moved. She turned. Six cars behind it turned. She slowed. Six cars behind it slowed.

Leotie frantically called her best friend Judy.

"Hey! What's up?" Judy's voice boomed inside Leotie's vintage aqua Volkswagen Bug.

"It's happening again," she replied. "Someone's following me." Leotie fretted as the SUV disappeared behind a truck only to reappear again directly to her rear.

"Who? Where?" Judy asked.

"After I crossed the Campbell Causeway, I noticed a black SUV behind kept following me."

"Call the cops, Leotie," Judy replied.

"And tell them what? No. I just wanted to tell you in case something happened."

Leotie kept dodging and weaving in the traffic. Behind her the black vehicle kept pace.

"I've got to go. I'll call you again." Leotie said, pushing the end call button, drowning out Judy's frantic protest.

Since the encounter at the reggae concert on the university campus, Leotie watched her environment cautiously. Twice after the concert she'd seen the man approaching her on campus but had dodged into a building to avoid him each time. She shared her suspicions with Judy Levine, her roommate, and just as she had on the phone, Judy's advice had been to call the police. Advice Leotie consistently rejected. The police could not be trusted on the reservation and she did not expect things to be any different in Florida. No, she told Judy, she had to take care of it herself. But how?

The red tail lights of a pickup truck stopping ahead jerked Leotie to the present. She stomped her brakes to avoid rear-ending it --a squeal smoking out from under her tortured tires. In the rearview mirror she quickly located the suspect SUV. It had advanced beyond the box truck and now sat two cars behind her. Through the tinted window she detected two shadowy figures. She flicked her eyes ahead and with shock saw a second black SUV gleaming in the bright Florida sun.

Leotie fumbled with her phone and speed dialed Judy again.

"Judy! I'm hemmed in!" Leotie shouted into the phone as soon as the line connected.

"Calm down Leotie. What's going on?"

"There's the same car behind me and now a black SUV is in front of me!"

"Drive away!"

"I can't. Traffic is stopped."

"I'm going to call the cops if you don't," Judy said.

"No. No. What could we tell them? I don't know anything right now. They'd just think I was hysterical. Anyway, the last time I tried to talk to the police, the cop tried to get me to go out with him. What a creep."

"Just don't hang up on me. Put the phone on speaker and talk to me if anything happens."

When traffic inched forward the two SUVs kept pace with Leotie as cars merged to get around the wreck ahead, the reason for the slowdown. An ambulance approached the scene from a side road, followed by a police car.

"Pull off the road and stop near the police," Judy advised her. "You don't have to talk to anybody. See if that shakes them."

Relieved Leotie took a right onto the side road shared by the police car. She parked and watched in her rear view mirror for the other SUV. She saw it pass by and disappear down the road.

Leotie's hands shook. Somehow, she had to find out what was happening.

"Unbelievable!" Major Lloyd Smith banged the dashboard of his SUV in frustration as he passed by the intersection Leotie had used to get off the main road.

"I say we just get it over with and grab her wherever we find her next time," Sgt. Nigel Swinson said craning his neck to see Leotie's Volkswagon. Four times now she had dodged the young man and he was ready to move on to the next target.

"Think Swinson," Major Smith said shaking his head ever so slightly in the negative. "We can't afford to make a mess here."

"Who would care?" Swinson asked. "She's just some little bitch fresh off the Rez."

"You mean the reservation?" Smith asked mockingly.

"Whatever, man. We should have picked her up two weeks ago but nooooo," he exaggerated, "she's somehow special. Can't leave a mess. Can't mess her up. I'm done with it. I say we just grab her today and get the hell out of here."

"Well that's probably why," Smith said archly, "when we're in the world, you call me 'sir'."

"Whatever, dude."

"Don't push your cover too far Swinson. I'm not liking the tone."

"Keep to character. Don't keep to character. What the hell?" Swinson looked over and saw the expression on Smith's hardened face. "Um…Major…sir."

"Better."

"She's still a bitch," Swinson said. "I never have problems hooking up. What's got her so spooked?"

"If you were her and knew what we were gonna do, you'd be spooked too. Sometimes targets just have a second sense about things."

"So we try again?"

"Oh, yeah, Swinson, we keep on until we get her." Major Smith's mouth compressed grimly into a razor-thin slash.

CHAPTER 3

THE UNITED STATES AIR CORPS RETAINED JURISDICTION OVER THE INITIAL INVESTIGATION OF THE ROSWELL CRAFT. THIS WAS THE RESULT OF ACCIDENT RATHER THAN BY PLAN. BECAUSE IT WAS THE AIR CORPS THAT FIRST OBTAINED THE POSSESSION OF THE CRAFT AND RETAINED IT AT WRIGHT-PATTERSON AIRFIELD, IT WAS THE AIR CORPS THAT DIRECTED ITS USE.

THE TECHNOLOGICAL AND BIOLOGICAL DATA COLLECTION BEGAN IN EARNEST SIX WEEKS AFTER THE INITIAL DISCOVERY DURING WHICH TIME MANPOWER AND RESOURCES DEVOTED TO THE CRAFT GREW GEOMETRICALLY. (SEE PROJECT ANVIL MEMORANDUM 11678-13-48 DELINEATING THE PROJECTED BUDGET FOR FY 1948-1952. APPENDIX IV PG. 419). IT SOON BECAME APPARENT TO PRESIDENT TRUMAN THAT PROJECT ANVIL, AS THE ROSWELL CRAFT INVESTIGATIONS WERE CALLED AT THAT TIME, WOULD SOON GROW TOO LARGE TO KEEP HIDDEN WITHIN THE AIR CORPS BUDGET. BESIDES THE TECHNOLOGICAL INVESTIGATIONS OF THE CRAFT'S STRUCTURE AND PROPULSION SYSTEMS, VARIOUS TEAMS WERE EXAMINING THE BODIES OF THE CREW.

PRESIDENT TRUMAN DECIDED TO PLACE PROJECT ANVIL UNDER THE DIRECTION OF THE CENTRAL INTELLIGENCE AGENCY. THIS WOULD PROVIDE SUFFICIENT COVER FOR MASSIVE EXPENDITURES EXPECTED SINCE ALL INTERNAL CIA EXPENDITURES RECEIVED ONLY CURSORY CONGRESSIONAL OVERSIGHT AT THE TIME.

THIS DECISION PRODUCED THE FIRST OF SEVERAL CONSTITUTIONAL CRISES THAT DEVELOPED AS A RESULT OF PROJECT ANVIL. THE AIR CORPS REFUSED TO RELEASE THE JURISDICTION OF THE CRAFT. (SEE GENERAL MCMULLAN'S LETTER TO PRESIDENT TRUMAN, SEPT. 16, 1950). WHEN PRESIDENT TRUMAN ORDERED HIS DISMISSAL AND COURT MARTIAL, THE JOINT CHIEFS OF STAFF REFUSED. (SEE GENERALLY APPENDIX V PG. 1-253). INTENSE NEGOTIATIONS ENSUED BETWEEN THE MILITARY AND THE CIVILIAN GOVERNMENT UNTIL A COMPROMISE WAS REACHED THAT DELINEATES CONDUCT AND JURISDICTION OVER THE ROSWELL CRAFT AND ITS INVESTIGATION TO THIS DAY, PLACING THE CRAFT AND ITS COROLLARY PROJECTS UNDER THE JURISDICTION OF THE MILITARY THROUGH THE DEPARTMENT OF DEFENSE. HOWEVER, THE PRESIDENT IS ABLE TO APPOINT THE DIRECTOR OF THE PROJECT WHO REPORTS DIRECTLY TO THE

EXECUTIVE BRANCH. THE ARRANGEMENT BECAME THE GENESIS FOR THE CREATION OF THE NATIONAL SECURITY AGENCY (NSA) IN 1952. THE NSA IS A SEPARATE AGENCY WITHIN THE DEPARTMENT OF DEFENSE AND, OF COURSE, THE NATIONAL SECURITY ADVISOR REPORTS DIRECTLY TO THE PRESIDENT, BYPASSING ENTIRELY THE SECRETARY OF DEFENSE AND THE JOINT CHIEFS OF STAFF. (SEE THE JOINT MEMORANDUM OF AUG. 15, 1951 FROM THE JOINT CHIEFS OF STAFF TO PRESIDENT TRUMAN OUTLINING THE AGREEMENT. APPENDIX V).

PRESIDENT TRUMAN, WHILE OBVIOUSLY NOT HAPPY ABOUT THE AR-RANGEMENT, USED IT TO HIS ADVANTAGE FOR DEALING WITH GENERAL DOUGLAS MACARTHUR WHO HAD BEDEVILED TRUMAN SINCE TRUMAN HAD TAKEN OFFICE. TRUMAN DEMANDED AND RECEIVED A COMPROMISE, BEING THE ASSURANCE FROM THE MILITARY THAT GENERAL MACARTHUR COULD BE DISMISSED WITHOUT OPPOSITION FROM THE JOINT CHIEFS. THIS WAS RELUCTANTLY AGREED TO BY THE MILITARY AND GENERAL MACARTHUR WAS SUBSEQUENTLY FIRED BY THE PRESIDENT.

--- EXCERPTS FROM THE NSA PRESIDENTIAL BRIEFING PAPERS ON THE ROSWELL INCIDENT

CULPEPER – BEFORE THE FEDERAL RESERVE

Shivering in the cold predawn air, Ed wished for the hundredth time the he had worn a sweater over the army surplus camouflage shirt. Although the temperature was well above freezing, it being after all, only late September, his breath still came out in small explosions of white vapor.

Ed wiggled forward on his stomach to the edge of the wood line and parted the foliage. In front of him ran a shallow drainage ditch for a small county public road and on the other side the Federal Reserve compound, surrounded by a chain link fence, spread across and up the side of Mt. Pony.

As Ed had approached the small round-topped mountain through the woods and fields on the outskirts of town he did not think he could carry through with his plan. Upon seeing Mt. Pony he vomited all the contents of his stomach -- and dry-heaved at intervals afterwards. Nonetheless he remained determined to finish his mission, whatever that was, he thought grimly. Because, in reality, Ed had no idea what he was going to do. He just knew he had to learn as much as he could about the building and the mountain that affected him and Pat so strongly.

Ed scanned the hillside in front of him looking for any activity. In the early predawn light it was hard to make out much in the way of details. Ed shifted his weight and reached back to a side pocket in his combat pants for a pair of Gen II Ghost Hunter night-vision goggles, then awkwardly slipped it on, fumbling with the head straps.

I must look like some cartoon alien with these things, he thought.

And the bug-eyed instrument did transform Ed's middle-aged, mild-mannered face into something other worldly. The green and black grease paint on his face added to the effect.

The night goggles changed the landscape for Ed as well. Now the compound was as bright and sharp-edged as if it were the middle of the day. He noted a guard moving about within an observation post but otherwise the facility looked deserted.

Ed crouched low and sprinted across the open road, throwing himself into the weeds at the edge of the compound perimeter. Nervously, he peeked up at the guardhouse only to find the guard staring intently towards Ed's position while picking up a telephone.

Great, Ed thought. Now what do I do? It was unlikely the guard would leave his post. He had probably just called in for instructions. Ed decided that the guard would, more than likely, be told to sit tight and watch for anything unusual. Perhaps someone else would be tasked to investigate further. Or maybe, the guard didn't see him at all.

Either way, Ed decided, it was time to move.

Crouching low, and calling upon the woodcraft of his youth, he began working his way up the hill paralleling the chain link fence. The bramble on the edge of the wood was a combination of broom sage and wild blackberry bushes.

Ed stepped gingerly around the blackberry when he could see it, and when he didn't, it tore his clothing with long, gripping thorns.

After a hundred yards of climbing, Ed came to the spot where the fence made a right angle to turn away from him and ran along the top of the slope.

Ed followed the fence to the midway point before stopping. He sat down with his back against a rock outcrop.

Below Ed, the compound spread out as if a map. Although Ed had gotten a good look at it from the road, the bird's-eye view he got from his new vantage point was much better, the land inside the fence having been mowed and, except for a few flowering dogwoods or ornamental bushes, clear of trees and brush.

The top third of the compound, that closest to him, presented a green sweep of grass. The entrance portal and parking area were contained in the compound farthest from him.

After surveying the area intently and seeing no signs of movement, Ed removed the night-vision goggles and replaced them with a pair of binoculars he had carried with him in a small knapsack.

He scanned the area in detail, and seeing nothing he settled back, having decided to wait for a while before scaling the fence. *Because he wasn't ready.* Not yet. Maybe in a little while, he thought. Ed had learned a long time ago that sometimes the best thing to do was to wait. Wait until it was time to strike, and then strike quickly.

He leaned back against a red oak and continued to scan the perimeter.

As a boy, he had hunted. Not with a gun, but with a bow. The corn fields of Ohio had kept the white tail deer fat and happy. But as fat and happy as they may be, deer were still a wary and worthy adversary. Ed had learned often the best way to hunt and see his prey in advance was to sit and wait. Deer and wild animals in general did possess acute senses, but they were not perfect.

The best hunt scenario for Ed, as a boy, had been when the prey was distracted by some other activity. Then the kill was usually easy.

He hoped, if he waited long enough, something would happen in the compound. *Then he would scale the fence. Then he would be ready.*

If on the other hand no distraction presented itself he would move at dawn, that in and of itself was often a distraction enough in hunting. Perhaps it would be enough here. Of course, Ed thought, I don't really know what I am hunting – except maybe my sanity. And Pat's – he thought grimly.

As it turned out, he didn't have too long to wait before a five-vehicle convoy consisting of three minivans and two passenger cars appeared and turned into the compound sally port. In the predawn light it was hard to see the make of the vehicles, but Ed was certain they were civilian.

This is it, he thought, his stomach tightening.

Quickly he stowed the binoculars and night goggles in the knapsack. He paused – then decided to leave the pack; he buried it in some leaves at the base of another rock outcrop. Drawing his 9mm Ruger, he worked a round into the chamber. He carried four more clips loaded with 16 rounds each. Ed did not plan to use the gun – but given the events of the past two months, he was taking no chances.

Once inside the compound grounds, he didn't have any idea what would happen. But he was damn sure of one thing, he wasn't eating anymore crickets and, if that meant following someone inside, that is exactly what he intended to do.

With that thought Ed crouched, slid the gun back into the drop-leg tactical holster, and moved toward the fence, fairly certain that it was not electrified since there were no warning signs. Furthermore, he did not see any insulators. Still, just to be sure, Ed broke off a dried sprig of grass and gingerly touched the wire mesh and feeling no tingle touched each of the three strands of barbed wire. No tingle. Ed dropped the grass and tenderly touched the fence with his fingertips. Feeling nothing he deftly mounted the fence and worked his way over the barbed strands knowing that fences, such as this, always looked more forbidding than they really were.

He dropped lightly to his feet and ran, crouching low, over the green field. Below, he saw the five vehicles drive past the guard house.

Ed decided speed was better than caution. He sprinted to the concrete compound building while hearing automobile motors switching off and car doors slamming.

Moving quickly he jogged along the building wall. Thumbing the safety off, Ed unholstered the gun and carried it low to his side. Then he peeked around the wall corner.

About 50 yards away, people were disembarking the minivans. Between Ed and the group were several dogwoods. Ed decided to use the trees as cover, not that they concealed very much, and get closer.

He crouched and sprinted to the first tree about ten yards downhill. Just before he reached cover, a searing punch to his lower back slammed Ed to the ground.

Groaning involuntarily, Ed reached around and felt a sickening wetness--but not as much as he would have felt if the bullet had not hit the bottom of his Kevlar vest. He rolled, fearing a second blow from his attacker.

The dirt kicked up next to his face, throwing debris into his eyes. He lurched to his feet and stumbled toward the tree cover.

The pain in his back grabbed him in waves.

Ed fell to the ground a second time--this time his left thigh buckling from an unseen blow. And this time there was no protective Kevlar--flesh took the full impact.

He rolled under the camouflage of the tree and aimed the Ruger in the direction from which the blows had come, squeezing off two rounds blindly into the darkness.

The raw power of the sound had shocked Weir.

He had heard guns fired plenty of times. You weren't in the business he was in and not be intimately familiar with weapons of all kinds. In fact, by the sound of it, Weir figured he'd just heard a 9mm pistol being fired. But in the predawn stillness, the two shots Ed Wood fired seemed to sound more like two cannons firing off rather than just two rounds being expended.

Actually, Weir was just as surprised by the man's tenacity as he was by the sound of the gun being fired. Most men would have dropped after the first shot. Weir couldn't believe his eyes when he saw Wood get up after being hit. The return fire from Wood spoke of an exceptional physique or an exceptional will. Weir had seen both attributes before, under fire, and it had always amazed him: the way a spectator is amazed and awed by the brute power a bull displays in a bull fight.

But, ultimately, the bull dies. And, Weir knew, Ed Wood would eventually lay motionless on the ground.

Weir didn't think Wood could move again but he decided to wait before approaching the dogwood where the man fell.

UNDER THE DOGWOOD TREE - FEDERAL RESERVE COMPOUND

Ed felt sick. Soul sick. He had failed both himself and Pat.

Once or twice he almost passed out from the pain radiating down his back and leg, but willed himself back from the watery darkness that threatened to overwhelm. He knew the second shot had hit his femoral artery. He was bleeding out despite his best efforts to pinch off the blood vessel with a belt wrapped around his upper thigh.

Bastard was just waiting for me to bleed out, he thought vaguely. But, he was going make sure somebody was going to pay. Somebody had done something to him and Pat and Ed was pretty sure that whoever it was he was right here. And by God, that sumbitch was going to pay.

So Ed held on. And he thought about Pat - and her eyes – and her hair – and the way she smelled on their first date. And the way she ate crickets.

Somebody was going to pay.

But, as the seconds stretched into minutes, Ed felt the pain spread and with each minute he felt the darkness creeping closer.

And then, behind the pain, came numbness. Ed's hip burned like fire, but his leg, where he'd been hit, was numb. He tried to move it and couldn't.

The murky black inched closer. It was hard to hold on. Then seeing something move by the building he gathered himself for one final effort.

When he saw movement again, he squeezed off another round and a dark shape hit the ground. Released by that final effort, a bursting dam of liquid blackness swelled upwards, threatening to pull him down into the inky depths lurking beneath, but he fought back. There was, he thought, something else he needed to do. Something else knocked at his consciousness.

It knocked until it burst through the walls of sanity.

"Oh, no." Ed whispered, because at that instant he remembered. He remembered the cold and the loneliness and the hopelessness in that other place, that other place where death hovered in a stinking cloud of funk wherever he went.

And there was nowhere to hide.

Then, with the horror of that other place gathering in his mind, Ed slid almost thankfully into the insistent, dark, cold pool. Cold, yes. But it promised forgetfulness.

The round, fired from almost point blank range, took Weir squarely in the chest, and he fell, gasping liked a hooked fish, realizing that he should have waited a little longer. Rolling onto his stomach he got up on his hands and knees and reached under the camo jacket to feel where the round went, exploring the smooth edges of an entry hole. He felt no blood – and decided that he would live. Wearing the Kevlar vest had been a good idea.

He heard feet pounding towards him. It was Johnson, Clatterbuck, and Martinez – his backup team, guns at the ready.

"You all right, Captain Weir?" Johnson asked in his Boston accent.

Weir shook his head and lurched to his feet "Get him inside," Weir gasped. "I'll be in shortly. I want to see where he crossed the perimeter."

Weir waited until they had dragged the lifeless body into the compound building before turning. He stepped gingerly over the slick blood trail in the grass and walked slowly towards the fence line where Wood had crossed. It had been a strange night, he thought as he trudged up the hill.

First, Weir had been given instructions on the arrival of what were termed "transports." They were coming in vans, he was told. He was to keep their path of travel clear of Reserve personnel.

And, they were going to level three.

Level three. Now that was a mystery wrapped in a black box. Weir was in charge of the compound's security, but level three was off limits to him, a secure compound within the compound itself. In time, Sims told Weir, he would gain access. In time. Well, Weir thought, he could wait. The few people he'd met who had access to level three gave him the creeps.

Then there had been the call from Sims a couple of hours earlier. Expect an intruder he was told.

Weir had wanted to take out the intruder before he even crossed the fence. Sims had nixed the idea.

"Let's see how he does. Let him get as close to the compound buildings as seems prudent before you neutralize him," Sims said. And Sims was adamant that Weir was not to interfere with Wood if he did not cross the fence.

"This is a first. We want to observe him a bit longer," Sims had said.

Weir hadn't asked for an explanation of that cryptic comment and Sims hadn't offered one.

So Weir had let Wood breach the fence. He had tracked him across the compound field. But, when it looked as if Wood was going to have contact with the "transports," whatever the hell they were, Weir had decided that it was time the game was over and he had taken out Wood or, as Sims put it, neutralized him.

The only thing Weir hadn't expected and that apparently Sims hadn't known was that Wood had been armed.

Weir decided it would be a good thing to remember that, although Sims and his organization had good intelligence, it wasn't infallible. Or, and Weir knew this was just as probable, Sims' intelligence was very good and he had deliberately withheld that one fact from Weir – for whatever reason. And that, too, was something to remember. Weir didn't like it either way.

Weir stopped when he got to the fence where the intruder had crossed over. The light was good enough now so that he could see where the rust of the metal mesh had been disturbed by the man's boots.

Weir looked through the fence into the forest gloom. And, for a moment, he had the feeling that the fence was more for keeping people in rather than out. Shivering, he turned back toward the compound building: it was going to be a long day.

TAMPA UNIVERSITY

"Come on, Leotie!" Judy pulled her roommate's arm in a half-hearted attempt to pull Leotie off the bed and onto her feet. "You've got to live a little. Let's go!"

It had been two weeks since the incident on the causeway. Although Leotie remained suspicious, even she was starting to wonder if all her concerns had been over nothing. Now Judy wanted someone to go with her while she hung out with a new friend from her Algebra class. Judy's best argument so far had been along the lines of "he's really cute!" Of course, Leotie knew the fact that he was cute meant it was important for Judy and that Leotie should come because of that quality alone, not that Leotie should in anyway notice his "cuteness" or "non-cuteness." Leotie had learned that Anglo girls were like that. They never said half of what they meant. On the Rez, things were more direct.

"I don't know, Judy," Leotie replied. "I've got an English paper due next week."

"Next week!" Judy exclaimed. "That's, like, a year away! Come on! Did I tell you he was really cute?"

Leotie let herself be persuaded. Besides the lack of suspicious activity, she was curious about sailing. Judy's friend promised a day on his 32-foot sloop and Leotie had never before sailed.

And, it was a beautiful Florida fall day, hinting of the warm salt water, full of promise and adventure.

They drove to the marina where Judy spied her friend, Hugh, picking his way across a debris-strewn dock. She pointed out the tall, well-built, twenty-something man who flashed a brilliant smile at the two. Leotie noticed that he moved with the grace of a cougar. Fluid and powerful.

"Hey, Judy!" Hugh waved. "Tide's going out, come on, let's hurry!"

Hugh helped them settle in the cockpit at the rear of the boat. They sat and watched as he cast off and motored out to the aqua-blue sea. A slight swell met them as they left the harbor. With little fanfare Hugh unfurled the foresail and mainsail.

Leotie was fascinated with the ease with which their new-found friend pulled lines, tied knots and steered the craft, all at the same time, seemingly nonchalant until the wind shifted, at which he would pounce to tighten a luffing canvass or turn the rudder. She allowed herself to relax and contemplated the shifting clouds, settling into the rhythm of the swells as the sloop cut through the water. Again, Leotie wondered whether her suspicions over the past few weeks had been nothing more than paranoia. Nothing had seemed out of the ordinary, but then she had stayed away from long jaunts and kept herself to the dorm or to her classes so that there would be little chance of a stranger entering her life.

In fact, she realized, Hugh was the first stranger she'd allowed near her since the incident on the causeway. And she didn't even know his last name. She shifted her gaze from the bright white clouds to examine Hugh. He and Judy were deep in a flirtatious disagreement over the relative merits of the original Oreo cookie versus the double-stuff version. Leotie gathered that Hugh preferred the original Oreo.

She thought that odd. Everyone she knew liked the thicker filling. Only her parents preferred the original. She looked closer at Hugh and realized he was older than either she or Judy. If you got past the good looks, she thought to herself, and the white, Billionaire Boys Club deck shoes, he did look more like a grad student than a freshman. And the powerful lithe body under the Henley tee shirt was more appropriate for someone in his late twenties than the stick-figure boys in her algebra class.

Suddenly Leotie's senses went on full alert. There was something profoundly wrong with Hugh. Wrong age, wrong clothes, wrong in his attraction to Judy. His friendly banter, her intuition told her, was nothing but the bored sparring of someone with another agenda, the chatter of someone marking time for the main event.

"Hey, I know a great little Cay we can anchor off," Hugh said.

"And do what?" Judy asked with a sideways glance.

"Take a dip in the water. Explore the island." Hugh replied.

"That's all?" she asked.

"Hey! That's all *I* had in mind."

"Judy, I've got to go back pretty soon," Leotie interrupted.

"No worries," Hugh replied quickly. "We can tie up, jump in the water, and be out of there in no time. It'll be awesome."

"Comon, Leotie, chill," Judy pleaded. "Just a little side trip. It'll be fun."

They sailed another hour out into the Gulf of Mexico. An abandoned oil rig jutted ragged on the horizon.

"The Cay is just on the other side of that rig," Hugh said.

As they neared the skeletal iron and steel structure, Leotie saw a sleek looking power boat resting easy behind. Languidly it started up and motored towards them.

Hugh didn't say anything as the strange craft neared. Leotie searched in vain for their destination on the other side of the rig.

"Judy, do you see an island *anywhere?*" Leotie asked desperately.

The deep throb of the speedboat's engines drowned out any reply.

CHAPTER 4

IN 1957 NSA ANALYST, HENRY KISSINGER, AUTHORED A MEMO REGARDING THE POTENTIAL RAMIFICATIONS OF CONTACT WITH A TECHNOLOGICALLY SUPERIOR SOCIETY BY ONE LESS ADVANCED AND, HIS THESIS BEING THAT HUMAN HISTORY WAS REPLETE WITH EXAMPLES OF THIS COLLISION, SUGGESTED THAT THE NSA SHOULD DEVOTE MORE RESOURCES TOWARDS STUDY OF THOSE UNEQUAL CONTACTS. HE ARGUED THAT THE UNITED STATES SHOULD BE PREPARED TO MEET THE ALIEN CIVILIZATION IF NOT WITH TECHNOLOGICAL PARITY AT LEAST WITH SOCIETAL PARITY. THIS CAN ONLY BE ACHIEVED BY FIRST ANALYZING PAST HUMAN CONTACTS OF A SIMILAR NATURE AND THEN MANIPULATING SOCIETAL INSTITUTIONS TO REDUCE THE NEGATIVE ASPECTS OF SUCH CONTACT. (SEE APPENDIX XV, PG. 39 FOR THE OCT. 22, 1957 MEMO "SOCIETAL PREPARATION FOR EXTRATERRESTRIAL CONTACT: AN ARGUMENT FOR HISTORICAL ANALYSIS AND PROJECTIONS; BY H. KISSINGER"). THE MEMO WAS APPROVED AND EVENTUALLY ADOPTED BY PRESIDENT EISENHOWER AS THE BASIS FOR EXECUTIVE ORDER DS 929.

****

IN 1963, PRESIDENT KENNEDY WAS PRESENTED WITH THE INITIAL RESULTS AND RECOMMENDATIONS OF THE NSA JOINT COMMITTEE FOR HISTORICAL – SOCIETAL ANALYSIS AND TRANSFIGURATION. THE SHORTHAND REFERENCE FOR THE COMMITTEE WAS AND IS GROUP 929 IN RECOGNITION OF EISENHOWER'S EXECUTIVE ORDER CREATING THE PROGRAM.

****

BASED ON THE CONCLUSIONS AND RECOMMENDATIONS OF GROUP 929, PRESIDENT KENNEDY BEGAN A PROCESS OF SOCIETAL CHANGE IN THE UNITED STATES, AND AS A CONSEQUENCE THROUGHOUT THE WESTERN WORLD, CREATED SPECIFICALLY TO STRENGTHEN THOSE CHARACTERISTICS THAT WOULD HELP EARTH CULTURE ABSORB CONTACT WITH A TECHNOLOGICALLY SUPERIOR CIVILIZATION. THE CIVIL RIGHTS MOVEMENT HE PROPOSED, AND WHICH PRESIDENT JOHNSON, A SOUTHERNER, PUSHED THROUGH CONGRESS, IS A DIRECT RESULT OF THE CONCLUSIONS AND RECOMMENDATIONS FROM GROUP 929. IN FACT MUCH OF GOVERNMENTAL-INITIATED

SOCIETAL CHANGES IN THE UNITED STATES CAN BE ATTRIBUTED TO THE
RECOMMENDATIONS OF GROUP 929.

****

SURPRISING AS IT MAY SEEM, THE STEADY RISE IN SCIENCE FICTION AS
A LITERARY AND FILM GENRE IS A DIRECT RESULT OF MANIPULATIONS
BY THE NSA THROUGH GRANTS AND OTHER MEANS OF SUPPORT. THESE
EFFORTS ARE AN ATTEMPT AT MAKING THE INEVITABLE CONTACT AS
PALATABLE AS POSSIBLE FOR THE CITIZENS OF THE UNITED STATES.

****

WHILE THE NSA REMAINS FOCUSED PRIMARILY ON THE TECHNOLOGICAL
ASPECTS OF THE ROSWELL CRAFT, FULLY 40% OF THE AGENCY'S BUDGET
IS DEVOTED TO SOCIETAL MANIPULATION AND CONTAINMENT AS OUTLINED
BY GROUP 929 RECOMMENDATIONS.

****

GROUP 929 HAS NEVER DISBANDED. IT REMAINS A SEPARATE RESEARCH
AND PROJECT DIRECTORATE WITHIN THE NSA. ONE OF ITS MORE CON-
TROVERSIAL RECOMMENDATIONS, AND AT PRESENT ITS MOST SENSITIVE,
IS BEING CARRIED OUT IN THE HORSE COUNTRY OF NORTHERN VIRGINIA,
NEAR WASHINGTON D.C.

**--- EXCERPTS FROM THE NSA PRESIDENTIAL BRIEFING PAPERS ON THE
ROSWELL INCIDENT**

MIAMI, FLORIDA

Cho Tsing lit a cigarette and looked with disgust at the taco in
front of him. The ground beef filling turned his stomach. He'd forgotten how much beef and fat figured into American cooking. While
some American cooking at least made the horrible meat tolerable –
the Hispanic-inspired meals he'd seen so far only added to its worst
qualities. He just wanted to hit someone. Anyone. He was angry
at the mess in front of him. He was angry at the mess in which he
found himself entangled.

Cho quelled his rebellious stomach and forced himself to shove
the greasy combination of corn shell, meat and spice into his un-
willing mouth. Lettuce and tomato sauce squirted out of the shell,

dribbling down his chin and onto his lap. He ate what was before him, cleaning the debris field in his lap.

He took a drag from his cigarette as if that, somehow, would make his meal more palatable. He hoped the nicotine would help calm his nerves.

So far, Cho thought, lunch is right in line with the entire mission.

Rong's tracing of the Dragon Team's flight plan across the globe two months earlier seemed laughable to Cho now. In fact the entire episode was absurd, particularly since Rong had promised the Dragon Team's assembly within a week.

It had, in fact, taken a month.

Who knows, Cho thought, perhaps all the delay was just cover for Rong, the grubby little pig, to get his money. Cho knew this much – he was in Miami for only one reason. And that reason sat in the Bank of Honduras in Coral Cables. Or rather, he thought, three million reasons sat in the bank and he was there to get them out, place them with a lawyer to hold in a trust account, and get on with his real mission.

And his real mission? That was simple really. Why *did* he kill? Why did something that horrified him so much become an overwhelming obsession each month? The blood lust so strong he lost control, lost all rational thought, lived only for the next blood spray. Despair racked Cho as he dredged up snapshots from the past. What *happened* to him in San Diego?

And then there was the other mission. Why did all of that data he mined from his cyber-sleuthing lead to Virginia? What could be so important about a place like Culpeper? And why was he so insistently drawn by the place? He'd never even been to Virginia, much less heard of the little town.

Were the two missions somehow connected? Could the universe be that random?

As he finished the first cigarette, Cho thought distractedly, even his personal mission for Rong had become more complicated than either he or his superior in Beijing had contemplated. Cho had never expected it would be so hard to get cash out of a bank without the American government knowing. Having never paid taxes in the United States, Cho realized too late that he was unaware of all the forms and procedures the IRS created to track down money. Homeland Security regulations required another layer of bureaucratic hurdles to overcome. And the drug infested atmosphere of Miami made it worse. Every large transaction was scrutinized by every governmental agency in existence – or so it seemed to Cho.

In addition, the IRS- mandated1099 form required a valid social security number. He had "acquired" a social security number through the efforts of the Dragon Team. But, neither he nor the leader of the Dragon Team, Xia Zin, wanted to create a paper trail which would lead whoever might follow it back to a dismembered body in LA.

So now Cho sat in a greasy Hialeah Cuban restaurant waiting for a man named Roberto to help him retrieve the cash. Cho tapped out another cigarette.

"Wang Lee?" A Spanish accented voice asked in English.

It startled Cho. First, he had to decipher the mangled English. Then he had to remember his identity was now Wang Cho. No, Lee, Wang Lee, he corrected himself silently.

"Yes. I am Wang Lee," he said as he was joined by a slight, short figure dressed casually in white cotton pants and a garish untucked shirt. The man's hair was jet black, long, combed back from his forehead, and gathered in a bobbed pony-tail.

"Bueno!" The man sat down opposite Cho. "I am Roberto." His eyes glinted darkly in the fluorescent lights.

"You are the one I was told to see about a financial transaction?" Cho asked.

"Yes. I am the one," Roberto replied, staring at him so hard that Cho was relieved when the waitress returned. Curiously enough, however, this time when she looked at him, her dark Latino eyes flashed with interest, while before she had only seemed bored.

Cho wondered what had transpired to create the change.

"So, you need help with a financial thing," Roberto stated.

"Yes. I and my partners have some money held in the Bank of Honduras. You know the Bank?"

"Yes. It is in Coral Gables. I know it. You cannot withdraw the money?"

"I can. But I do not wish the DEA to know about it."

"Ah. The police. Many in Miami do not wish the others to know their business. It is ... how do you say ... rude. Impolite."

"My associates have told me you know how to do such things."

Roberto's white teeth flashed against his dark face as he smiled in a way that made Cho shudder inside.

The waitress returned with a bottle of beer. Next to it she set down a plate of three hard boiled eggs and a small bottle of hot sauce.

Roberto peeled an egg as he spoke.

"This thing you want. Do you need it to happen quick or is this a matter that we have time on?"

"It must be quick."

"Then it will be hard."

"What does that mean?"

Roberto sprinkled hot sauce on the egg and bit off the white and red stained portion. "It means it will cost," he said.

"How much?"

Sprinkling hot sauce on the remainder of the egg and popping it into his mouth, Roberto acted as if he had not heard Cho's question. Cho was beginning to get frustrated at the Cuban. Americans were a mystery enough, and Cubans, with whom he had never dealt before, even more so. The silence between the two drew taut.

"How much will it cost?" Cho asked again.

"I'm deciding how much." Roberto sprinkled sauce on the remainder of his second egg. "You want the money in small or large bills?"

"It doesn't matter."

Roberto seemed to consider the answer before replying, "I can do it for forty percent."

"Forty is too high."

"Nevertheless, that is how much it will cost. No one can do it cheaper. I have a contact at the bank. He can help smooth it out."

"How?"

"My contact. He will show the transaction to go to a business already here in Miami," Roberto said, suddenly becoming more loquacious. "It is legitimate, but it will go to the business as a business loan. You understand, that they can write off the loan on their taxes. The forty percent is to pay me, my contact, and the business for its help."

"What do I do?"

"Nothing. You walk in. Get the money. And then meet me at this place." He slid a post card across the table. Cho recognized it as a card often given out by hotels. He turned the card over. On it was written "Port of Miami – Slip 14."

"We meet there to get paid," Roberto said. "At the Trinidad Star. A freighter tied up there."

"How do you know you will get paid? I could just leave with the money."

Roberto laughed.

"You don't know Miami. I have friends everywhere. They help me when someone tries to hurt me. But come, must we speak of unpleasantness? To what end? You are not going to cheat me. I am not going to cheat you. This is business."

Cho was at a loss. He did not trust the man who, in all probability, was busy cheating him. At the same time, he needed to get Rong's money as quickly as possible so that he could get to Virginia.

"Ok. Let's do it." Cho said.

"Bueno!" Roberto said brightly before sliding another egg into his mouth. While chewing he reached into his shirt pocket and retrieved a pen. Then, taking a napkin, he wrote "Alfredo Tomas" on the napkin and slid it over to Cho. The letters were well formed and uniform, the penmanship surprising Cho. It spoke of someone calculated and exacting. Not the personal characteristics Cho gleaned from his brief conversation with the Cuban.

"You will ask for this person," Roberto went on. "He is an officer in the bank. He will know what to do. You must wait two days for me to set everything up."

"You want me to get the money in two days." Cho calculated in Chinese then translated to English. "On Wednesday. Get the money on Wednesday."

"Yes, Wednesday. In the afternoon."

"Why not tomorrow?" Cho asked.

"Please. It takes time. What is the difference in one day? No one could do it quicker. And, when you meet me at this place," --here Roberto tapped the postcard-- "you must bring all the money."

"Why do you care if I bring it all?" Cho asked.

"I trust you, my companion. But my friends, they do not trust. They do not trust me and they do not know you. They will want to be sure that they get the correct amount and since I charge by percentage of the total that is what they will want to see. The total amount."

"When do I meet you?" Cho asked, tired of the whole business.

"You go into the Bank at four in the afternoon. Then, you drive straight to Port of Miami. Take U.S. 4. It is quicker and exits onto the port. Let me see. It should take you an hour. Meet me at five-thirty. It is the main slip. On the river. Here, let me write the directions down on the napkin. Also, the money will be in a briefcase. The briefcase will be locked. Do not tamper with it. If you do, my friends will not be happy. They will think you are cheating them and that would be a very bad thing."

Suddenly, Cho had a sickening feeling that he was in over his head in this whole mess.

CULPEPER COURTHOUSE

The dead bodies lay in a tumbled heap in the tall yellow grass. Binford was actually surprised at the strangely casual way dead bodies often seemed to fling themselves across whatever landscape they were in. The effect was more disconcerting here because he had actually known these two, although he was at a loss as to why the well-mannered couple that had shown up in his office two weeks earlier had willfully thrown themselves onto the ground in the entangled heap that had been Mr. and Mrs. Wood.

Binford looked at another photograph from the stack in his hand. It showed an overview of the crime scene. The bodies looked small and insignificant in the tall broom sage field. A border of woodland framed the background.

Binford flipped to another photo which showed the same crime scene but from a different angle.

"You say you were given these by the FBI?" Binford asked Sheriff Tucker Ray Carter, who sat across from him. The sheriff was a big man, 54 years old, salt and pepper flat top, tall, broad and obese enough that it was all that he had been able to do to squeeze himself into Binford's office chair. He shifted uneasily in the confinement.

Binford laid the stack of photographs down and flipped through the pages of the written report which was typically repetitive and full of law enforcement lingo. Why, Binford had often wondered, why couldn't a report just call someone by their given name rather than by "subject" or, even worse, by some random number assigned earlier in the report, forcing the reader to flip back and forth between the front and the body of the report to figure out who was "subject one," "subject two," and "subject three."

"Well Sheriff Carter, don't get me wrong. I'm always glad to have you here, but why are you presenting this to me rather than the FBI? That's how it's usually done, isn't it?"

Binford's question was only partly theoretical. He'd dealt with the town police, the county sheriff's office, and the state police. Only rarely had he had any contact with the FBI, since they investigated federal violations and he prosecuted violations of state law only. Rarely did the two meet. As a result he wasn't sure if having the sheriff act as go between was normal operating procedure or not.

"Hell's bells, Mordecai," Carter said shrugging his massive shoulders, "who knows what is normal with those boys. I got this package in the mail this morning. It's the first I heard of anybody being found dead. In my own county, damn it. You'd think they'd at least have the decency to call me before they work up the scene."

"I thought you said you did talk with someone." Binford said. He took off his glasses and cleaned them with his tie.

"I did. After I read the report I called the contact person," Carter spat out the last two words, "to find out what the hell was going on. But he didn't add anything to what's already there."

"That would be Mr. Weir, I see," Binford said, putting his glasses back on and scanning the front page of the report. "Well, it says here it was a murder-suicide. Have you any reason to think differently?"

"If you wanted to kill somebody and leave no suspects around, murder-suicide is the best way," Carter suggested. "It's nice and neat."

"But, do you see anything in the report that leads you to suspect something other than a murder-suicide?" Binford asked impatiently.

"No. But it's their report and who the hell knows if they know what they are doing. Let me tell you, Mordecai, them boys with the FBI are a bunch of prima donnas. The only cases they take are the ones we already worked up and then ask them to take over."

"Right, for enhanced punishment," Binford added tonelessly.

"Damn straight. Other than that they ain't worth a bucket of warm spit. Now they say this is a murder-suicide, but I say murder-suicide is a tricky case to work up. This is only a few days old. How can you come up with a conclusion that quick?"

"Well, the bottom line is the bodies were found on federal property and that makes it federal," Binford told him. "We're out of it as far as I'm concerned."

"I don't give a damn about federal property. Two people were found dead in my county and I sure as hell want to know why. And so should you."

"Ok. Message received, Sheriff." Binford leaned back in his chair and fumbled with his glasses again. "You want me to call over and get some more information?"

"I think if you do, we might at least get to look at the crime scene. The crime scene that sits in my own damn county but I ain't even laid eyes on yet. Yeah, give 'em a call. Maybe we'll get an invite."

Having gotten what he wanted, Tucker Ray Carter left shortly afterwards, leaving Binford alone in his office with time to think. To Binford, the issue was simple. Any criminal act on federal property was in the jurisdiction of federal law enforcement, under federal law, in federal courts. Period. He'd learned this early on when some kids had vandalized the National Cemetery in town. The cemetery, which had been created after the Battle of Cedar Mountain during the Civil War, was run by the federal government. One night, after some kids spray-painted swastikas on a few tombstones, the town police had charged them under a state statute. However, since the vandalism occurred in a federal enclave, the state courts lacked any authority to hear the cases, with the result that the kids were charged, prosecuted, and convicted in the federal courts in Charlottesville. The state charges were dismissed.

With this in mind, Binford concluded that this entire exercise was futile. However, since the sheriff, who was an elected constitutional officer just as Binford was, wanted Binford to make a few calls, he'd do it. Call it professional courtesy. And, Binford thought wryly, smart politics. A healthy working relationship between his office and the sheriff's department was a good thing. A bad relationship, a bad thing. A pretty simple rule to Binford, but one that was often lost to others.

With that in mind, Binford dialed the number for Weir listed at the top of the report and left his name and telephone number on the voice mail. He'd wait for Weir to get back to him.

Binford reviewed the report, which said, in essence, that the two bodies were found on the entrance road to the Warrenton Training Center. The man had been shot several times. She once to the head. The suicide note left by her seemed to seal the murder – suicide theory.

Binford remembered then the hollow look in both the Woods' eyes, as well as the fact that he'd mentioned the Warrenton Training Center. It was an eerie feeling to have spoken to the two only a few days earlier and now to see their bodies heaped on the ground.

His secretary interrupted Binford's musings.

"Mr. Binford. There's a Mr. Weir on line two. He says he's returning your call." She looked at him expectantly from the doorway.

"Ok." He grabbed the telephone and in doing so chose one of two paths at an unseen fork in life's thoroughfare. Unbeknownst to Binford, it was a perilous path paved with despair and sorrow.

WARRENTON TRAINING CENTER

Weir sat in Ford Allen Sims' office nursing a hammering headache. While in Colorado, he'd forgotten what the humid environment of the east coast did to his sinuses. To touch his forehead was agony. Between that ongoing agony in his head and the hassle of dealing with Sheriff Carter, the week was turning into one real disaster.

Add to that the horror that was Ed and Pat Wood, an episode that he replayed over and over again despite his best efforts to compartmentalize the whole affair. To take the memories and tuck them away under the categories of "work," "needed to be done," and "needed to be forgotten." The trick had worked well enough for him during the worst fighting in Iraq and Afghanistan. Here, it didn't seem so effective.

And the home life wasn't working out real well either. Rebecca claimed he had been distracted and short with her and the kids since they moved to Virginia. Last night they'd had a real yelling match. It was the kind of fight that dug deep and clawed the soul. He knew it even as he had spewed invective.

Worse, the kids had seen it all.

When he and Rebecca finally went to bed, exhausted in their anger, a hard silence fell upon them. Finally, he could not stand it any longer and moved to the couch. It had been a first for the two of them since Colorado.

The most awful part of it was that Weir knew Rebecca was right. He hadn't been himself since taking the job at the Federal Reserve. Who the hell could be straight, Weir said to himself, when he had to do the things he had done.

The Ed Wood incident, as Sims had called it, had shaken Weir more than he realized at the time. And now he'd had to pose as an FBI agent to Sheriff Carter. Weir had done a lot of undercover work but he'd never lied to a United States law enforcement officer. *Never.* And somehow it had felt like treason to him. However, Sims had quickly reminded Weir what real treason was and real treason according to Sims was disobeying Sims' orders.

Now that self-important Sheriff wanted to view the "murder-suicide" scene personally. Sims had assured Weir that a report in the mail was all that was needed for local law enforcement.

But Sims hadn't figured on Sheriff Carter's tenacity. And then there was the county prosecutor who, although he didn't say much, gave Weir the impression that he too, was perhaps more than what Sims had bargained for. But it was Sheriff Carter he had to deal with now and it was Carter who had proven the hardest nut to crack.

"I don't give a hound dog's crooked hind leg about federal jurisdiction." Carter had said to Weir over the telephone. "The people of Culpeper County elected me to protect them and by God, I'm gonna find out why two people are dead."

"Weir?" Sims' voice broke Weir from his thoughts.   He got up and slumped into his superior's office.

"So, how is Sheriff Carter?" Sims asked. He sat on the edge of his desk. Weir noticed that Sims wore Argyle socks. The crisscross pattern clashed with his dark blue pin-stripe pant leg.

"Carter is a very persistent man." Weir said.

"Ha!" Sims barked out a single laugh and jumped off the desk. He stood and walked towards the room's single window.

"Ha! Very good. Persistent, is he?" He bounced up and down on his heels.

"Sheriff Carter is an incompetent fool," he said bluntly. Turning towards Weir he smiled slowly. It was not a pleasant sight. "Show him the site. Cooperate."

"Cooperate," Weir responded doubtfully.

"Within reason."

"What does that mean?"

"It means within reason. You have your directive. I shouldn't have to spell out every tactical move you make to carry it out. Now get out."

CULPEPER COURTHOUSE

The old county courthouse had a certain dignity in Binford's mind that no modern structure, no matter how elaborate, could ever retain. In fact, there was something uniquely human about older buildings that seemed to strike a chord within him, something which modern buildings, straight-lined and cold, never did. People did not seek shelter in those hard steel and glass structures. People merely visited modern buildings to conduct their business and leave as quickly as possible. All this Binford had thought or felt in a vague way many times. But perhaps it came to him most strongly while in the Circuit Court room in Culpeper.

The courtroom was large and high ceilinged. The judge's bench, made of heart of pine and painted white, sat high in the room with a flanking platform on either end for the clerk and bailiff to sit. Between the two sat the judge and behind him hung five large oil paintings of former judges. History, warm and humid, seeped out of every corner of the old room.

During lulls in court, Binford often found himself admiring the simple but elegant architecture and furnishings, which was precisely what he was engaged in doing when the judge's question to the Commonwealth jolted him into the present.

"I'm sorry, Your Honor, I did not hear the question," Binford said. The courtroom had through the years gained a reputation of poor acoustics, a reputation that had often been enhanced by Binford's momentary lapses.

"Does the Commonwealth have a preference for what date to set the arraignment?" the judge asked again a little louder, and having been assured that it had not, directed his attention again to the defendant and his attorney leaving Binford free to slip into another session of introspection until the Judge asked, "Does the Commonwealth have any other matters?"

Binford answered automatically. "No, Your Honor."

"Very well, court is adjourned." The judge stood.

"All rise," the brown uniformed county bailiff ordered loudly. The few people in the nearly empty courtroom stood. Binford gathered his file and court calendar. When he looked up, he was surprised to see a grim-faced Sheriff Carter striding towards him.

The sheriff rarely entered the courtroom. His deputies acted in his stead as bailiffs for courtroom security.

"Sheriff?" Binford said as a greeting.

"We need to talk." Sheriff Carter replied tersely.

"My office?"

"Suits me."

They marched silently to Binford's office and, after shutting the door, Carter got straight to the point. "Mordecai, I'm just a country boy. And there's a whole lot I don't know. But I sure as hell know one thing. That fellow Weir ain't a federal agent and those people didn't die where he says they did."

"Who are you talking about?" Binford asked, thrown off by the abrupt announcement.

"That couple that died over at the Training Center."

Memories of the bodies, tangled like barbwire on the ground, crowded into Binford's mind.

"Right. The Wood couple."

"Yes sir. Those people from Ohio no more died on the federal property than I did. And that fellow Weir, or whatever the hell his name is, knows it."

"All right Sheriff, then *what* did happen?" Binford asked, slightly put off by Carter's assertive manner.

"Well, I met up with Weir just like you set it up. I drive there in my car and that was the first thing that was wrong."

"What do you mean?"

"Hell, Mordecai. I couldn't even drive up to the building. When I go out there, the first thing I see when I come around the curve is Weir sitting in a car at the entrance. He stops me. I'd never seen him before, only talked to him on the phone, so I thought he was a security guard. Like I said, he stops me. Tells me I got to leave my car there and ride with him and some goon in the back seat. I don't got much choice, do I? It's his dog run, not mine. So, I leave the car and get in with him. We drive out to the main building. You ever been there?"

Binford shook his head no.

"Well, it sits out in the middle of a big ole field. I mean a hundred acres or so," Carter said, shifting his bulk in the office chair, "and that field is full of antennas. Big ole towers. Anyway, the road is probably a good three-fourths of a mile long. Now that's a long way to ride a car in and not say a thing. That Weir fellow, he don't say a damn thing. Just sits there and drives, nervous as a cat in a dog pen."

"So anyway we go inside. I got to check my gun at the door. Me, the damn Sheriff of the county, got to check my gun. I almost left, but figured I'd gone that far I might as well see it thru. So we go into a little room they got there. Then he starts into his top secret routine. That's when I know Weir is as much of an FBI agent as I am."

"What do you mean?" Binford asked.

"Let me tell you, Mordecai. Them FBI boys know they're God's gift to every two-bit sheriff around. And they know that everyone else knows it. They just assume you're gonna kiss their butt for even talking to you. I ain't ever seen an FBI agent not act that way. They're so arrogant they just assume we're all in awe of 'em. Like they're Moses coming off Mount Sini or something. They don't ever think of going into the kind of routine this Weir fellow did."

"OK." Binford had seen the same attitude at the Attorney General's Office in Richmond. Real power assumed dominance. Pretenders always tried to display their power.

"So after he stops flashing his badge and quoting federal statutes and what not, we finally get to the business at hand," Carter said, leaning forward, his ample stomach bulging against the brown shirt of his uniform. "That boy don't know the first thing about crime-scene investigation. They never did a ground sweep. They never did gun powder analysis of the hands. Hell, he didn't even have a good explanation as to why two of 'em were piled up on each other."

The image of the tangled bodies leapt back into Binford's mind's eye again. "What do you mean, Sheriff? How does the position of the bodies have anything to do with it?" He asked.

Carter leaned back in his chair with a satisfied gleam in his eyes, "That's something most folks don't know. Mordecai, I've worked sixteen murder-suicides and this is the first one I've seen bunched up like that. Usually, the shooter can't bear to see what he done, so he usually walks off a little way and does his-self. That FBI boy," he continued, spitting out the words with disgust, "didn't even know that. He just swallows air like a horny toad and says something about national security not allowing him to disclose their reason for not looking into it anymore."

This seemed to fire up the sheriff to new levels of disgust.

"And I tell you something, Mordecai. Them there bodies weren't found out on the entrance road like the report says. No, sir. Who ever heard of a lover's spat in the middle of nowhere, on a dirt road, at the entrance of an army facility. Hell, no. It usually happens at home, in a hotel room, in a car. Not like that. Not out for God and everyone to see."

"Well, Sheriff, it's hard to say how people decide where to commit a murder-suicide." Binford said warily, knowing from experience that it was a good idea not to be too confrontational when the Sherriff got wound up.

"No, Mordecai. You ain't been in this business long enough. No sir. I've seen it all before and I'm telling you this ain't right." Carter said.

"So what do you want me to think, Sheriff? That someone is posing as an FBI agent at the Warrenton Training Center? That the medical examiner's report," Binford pulled the report from a pile on his desk, and adjusting his glasses, read, "from Atlanta, Georgia," he looked up for emphasis and continued, " is a fake? I can't go that far."

"I didn't say that." Carter hedged. "I just said this don't smell right to me."

"What do you want me to do?"

"Nothing. Not yet. Just let me know if anything funny comes up. I know you ain't buying it, Mordecai, but I'm telling you this whole thing stinks like a skunk in the middle of the road.

"You've got to admit, Sheriff, there isn't much more than instinct making you suspicious. That's not much to hang a theory on, especially the one you're trying to sell."

"No. I got more than that. I almost forgot." Carter freed himself from the chair and reached into his back hip pocket. He pulled out two photos and tossed them onto Binford's desk. They landed face up. Both showed empty fields with a tree line in the distance. Binford recognized one because of the bodies in the foreground. The other he had never seen before.

"What are these? I mean I recognize this. It's the murder scene. Where was the other photo taken?"

The Sheriff smiled, "Right where that Weir fellow told me the bodies had been found."

Binford examined the second picture closer. He looked again at the crime scene photo supplied with the FBI report.

"You must have taken this picture from a different angle," Binford said. The tree line of the two photos was different.

"Don't think so, Mordecai. There's only one tree line that matches the distance shown in the FBI picture and that's it." Carter said.

"Can't be, Sheriff. These are two different fields. You check this with all the crime scene photos?"

"Hell yes," Carter said. "This is the photo that mostly matches the picture I took."   Binford held the two pictures in his hands and looked from one to the other.

"These are two different fields," Binford said almost to himself.

Carter nodded his head slowly. "Why the hell do you think that Weir fellow tried to get my camera? Good thing I took the picture just before I left rather than when I got there."

Binford started to get a prickly feeling on his neck.

"These are two different fields," he said for the third time.

"Like I said, Mordecai," Sheriff Carter replied, "something ain't right."

Tampa Bay Times, Section B-1

Tampa--Two Tampa University students Leotie Thunder, 19, and Judy Levine, 20, have been reported missing by the Tampa Police Department. The pair was last seen at classes on campus last Thursday. Police emphasized that at this time foul play was not suspected. Friends had noticed over the weekend that the pair went missing and had reported Thunder's and Levine's absence to University Police on Monday.

"Often we find that students take off to the beach for a week then show up, no harm done," said Police spokesman Tom Alexis. "We just want them to report back to the University so that we know they are alright. No one is in any trouble. This is just a routine safety check."

Police ask that anyone with information about the pair contact the department at the Tampa Police website.

CHAPTER 5

SOON AFTER THE ROSWELL INCIDENT, ALIEN CONTACTS OCCURRED THROUGHOUT THE UNITED STATES. UNDER THE DIRECTION OF THE NSA, REPORTED ALIEN ENTITY (AE) CONTACTS WERE MONITORED AND ANALYZED EXTENSIVELY. UP UNTIL 1972, THE NSA TOOK COUNTER MEASURES TO DISCREDIT CONTACT AND ABDUCTEE STORIES. IN 1972 THE NSA MOVED FROM BEING A REACTIVE TO A PROACTIVE AGENT.

THE APOLLO XVII LUNAR MISSION WAS THE CATALYST FOR THE CHANGE. DURING THE MISSION THE APOLLO COMMAND MODULE (CM) WHILE IN LUNAR ORBIT, RECEIVED A HIGH SPEED COMMUNICATION BURST. THE MESSAGE WAS IN LATIN.

(SEE ALAN TOLIVER'S PAPER PRESENTED IN 1978 ENTITLED "THE USE OF LATIN IN ALIEN-HUMAN CONTACT", AN ANALYSIS IN WHICH HE ARGUES THAT THE USE OF THIS SO-CALLED "DEAD" LANGUAGE POINTS TO SIGNIFICANT GAPS IN ALIEN KNOWLEDGE OF HUMAN HISTORY AND SOCIETAL STRUCTURE. CITE: LLNSA 0.13972.A139, PP. 36. HOWEVER HE ALSO ACKNOWLEDGES THAT LATIN IS KNOWN BY SCHOLARS WORLD-WIDE, UNLIKE OTHER LANGUAGES. FURTHERMORE, IT IS NOT SUBJECT TO THE SORT OF CURRENT SLANG THAT ALLOWS FOR MISUNDERSTANDING. THE READER IS DIRECTED TO SEPARATE PAPERS REGARDING THE AE TEXT AND THE ANALYSIS OF IT.)

IN RESPONSE TO THE MESSAGE, AND UNDER THE CONTROL OF THE NATIONAL SECURITY ADVISOR, A DIRECT LINK WAS SET UP BETWEEN THE UNITED STATES GOVERNMENT AND THE AE.

IN ESSENCE, THE UNITED STATES WAS TOLD THAT NO FURTHER HUMAN ACCESS TO THE LUNAR SURFACE OR ANY ORBIT OF THE MOON WOULD BE TOLERATED. SECONDLY, IT WOULD SERVE ALIEN INTERESTS IF THE GOVERNMENT WERE TO COOPERATE IN HUMAN ABDUCTIONS. HOWEVER, WITH OR WITHOUT U.S. GOVERNMENT HELP, THE AE PROGRAM OF ABDUCTIONS WOULD CONTINUE.

GROUP 929 WAS GIVEN THE ISSUE FOR POLICY FORMATION. AFTER HEATED DEBATE, GROUP 929 RECOMMENDED COOPERATION, WHICH PRESIDENT NIXON SUMMARILY REJECTED.

DURING THIS PERIOD OF COMMUNICATION, REPORTS OF RANDOM ALIEN CONTACTS CEASED. THE AE RESPONSE TO PRESIDENT NIXON'S DECISION WAS THE RESUMPTION OF ABDUCTIONS, WITH THE RESULT THAT

PRESIDENT NIXON, APPLYING THE SAME STRATEGY HE HAD USED WITH THE USSR, THREATENED NUCLEAR RETALIATION IF ABDUCTIONS CONTINUED.

ALL MILITARY INSTALLATIONS WERE ORDERED ON A NUCLEAR ALERT STATUS. HOWEVER, WITH NO FOE TO CONFRONT, THE FUTILITY OF RESISTANCE WAS APPARENT AND PRESIDENT NIXON SOON ORDERED A STANDDOWN OF MILITARY PERSONNEL.

BY ACCIDENT, SINCE ALL OF THIS OCCURRED DURING THE YOM KIPPUR WAR OF 1973, MANY POLITICAL OBSERVERS THOUGHT THE NUCLEAR ALERT AN OVERKILL RESPONSE BY THE UNITED STATES TO THE FIGHTING IN THE MIDDLE EAST. IN FACT THE ALERT HAD NOTHING TO DO WITH THE ISRAELI-EGYPTIAN CONFLICT, BUT THE HOSTILITIES PROVIDED A GOOD COVER FOR THE ACTION.

GROUP 929'S RECOMMENDATIONS WERE ADOPTED AND IMPLEMENTED.

--- EXCERPTS FROM THE NSA PRESIDENTIAL BRIEFING PAPERS ON THE ROSWELL INCIDENT

MIAMI: PORT OF MIAMI

It was early morning and John Howington watched as forensic personnel collected evidence around the sprawl of bodies on the pier slip. Where a ship had been berthed in the Miami Harbor, only empty water glimmered in the seemingly perpetual tropic sun of South Florida

A team of photographers were also working over the pier. Howington made sure he wasn't in any of the photos by keeping an eye on their location and standing discreetly out of the way.

Howington's big frame hid the growing spare tire around his middle but, at 43, Howington was still in good physical shape. He had to be in his job. If Columbia was the capital of cocaine production, Miami was the capital of cocaine distribution for the East Coast. The Drug Enforcement Agency (DEA) was the federal government's first line of defense for cocaine and heroin distribution. Howington was in charge of the DEA's drug interdiction teams in Miami, which meant that he was on the front line of the front line. Howington had learned early in his career that drug lords didn't play by the rules – either in Mexico, Columbia or in Miami. Fortunately, in this brutal underworld, he found his big frame and weight had more than once come in handy in intimidating a snitch or a suspect.

Here though, he reflected, no one had been interested in intimidation. Only killing. And a lot of it.

Eleven bodies lay in pools of black congealed blood. In Miami that scene was not unusual. Down on the docks lives were cheap. Money bought everything. And illicit drugs controlled it all.

No, eleven dead was not that unusual.

The fact that they were *Chinese* was unusual. Being in charge of drug interdiction meant Howington spent more time at a desk and less time on the streets, but the fact that the dead were Chinese--or at least Asian-- was enough to bring him down to the scene personally.

He guessed they were Chinese. They sure as hell were Oriental. And as far as Howington knew, this was the first time Chinese drug runners had shown up in Miami. Howington was afraid this just might mean that Chinese-sourced fentanyl was making an entrance through his jurisdiction. He would have none of that. Fentanyl was 10,000 times more potent than Morphine and 100 times more potent than Heroin. Just touching the stuff could kill an ordinary person. Too many had died already from a deadly mixture of the two for him to stand by and let the Chinese crave out a new trade route into the United States. Not on his watch --no sir.

Directly there was no evidence of drugs, but all the hallmarks of a drug deal gone bad were present to Howington's way of thinking. And then there was the tip his office had gotten of three million dollars being transferred out of the Bank of Honduras.

Howington had his sources of information. He'd heard that there was a Chinese male in touch with the local Cuban mafia for a contact to withdraw money outside normal channels.

It had sounded to him like some sort of trade scam until this morning when he heard about the bodies.

"Hey, Thacker." Howington said.

"Yo. Here, Captain," a wiry, short uniformed African-American cop answered.

"Hey. Come here. I need a favor."

"Hell, you always need something, Howie." The local Metro-Dade Police Department tolerated the DEA. Howington and Thacker, that is Howard Thacker, a senior police lieutenant for the department, had struck up an informal working arrangement through the years. He helped Thacker. Thacker helped him. In the process they had formed a friendship as well.

"What I usually need you ain't never gonna have," Howington said with a well-practiced exaggerated leer.

"Man. You're so old they ought to lock you up for taking indecent liberties with life."

"Yeah. Well, you're so ugly the doctor slapped your momma when you were born."

"Don't start on me, Howie."

"What do you make of this?" Howington said smoothly changing the subject and nodding towards the bodies.

"Drug deal gone wrong," Thacker said with a shrug. "We're calling in the drug dogs right now to see if there is any trace scent."

"What about the fact that they're Asians?"

"How do you know that? Could they be they're some type of Indian from South America. I've seen some from Brazil that you'd have thought were Asian."

"Yeah. Well, what if I know they're Chinese."

"Why? You know something I don't?"

"Let's say I'm pretty sure they're Chinese."

"If that's so, then it might be anything. Smuggling? Maybe they jumped ship trying to get away. Who knows?" Thacker said.

"How about if I tell you that I think they might have been hooked up with big money coming out of the Bank of Honduras?" Howington said.

"You do know something."

"I think I might."

Howington looked out across the sparkling water of Biscayne Bay towards the glass and concrete towers of downtown Miami and saw the glint of the metro gliding across the elevated rail to Biscayne Station, all the while debating whether to ask the favor. Then, figuring, what the hell, I got nothing to lose, he asked.

"I need you to round up The Rat for me," Howington said.

"The Rat!" Thacker exclaimed. "Dude, you are scraping the slime off the bottom now. We don't even use him. Who knows when he's lying. If I was to use him on a case, even as a CI, the DA would have me up on charges."

"Yeah, I know," Howington agreed. "But he's the one who set up the money. Or so I've been told," Howington said.

"You share everything you know with me?" Thacker said.

"Of course, my friend."

"Now you're being a smart ass."

"Can you get him?"

"As a matter of fact, I can squeeze him a little if you want."

"Don't squeeze him. I need the truth and I don't want him lying to get out of the squeeze."

"Ok. I'll set up the meet."

The two walked together across the hot pavement and stopped in front of the body of a man, eyes glazed, whose jet black hair was tied in a greasy pony tail.

"How long till they finish?" Howington asked, indicating the group of police and forensic technicians hovering over the site.

"Couple more hours."

"Sun's gonna start cooking the evidence." Howington observed sardonically referring to the bodies.

"Lieutenant!" A police officer dog-trotted over to Thacker, "Thought you might want to know this. We started running IDs on the victims here. First one just came back."

"So?"

The young officer glanced at Howington.

"Go ahead. We're cooperating." Thacker assured him.

"Right. It seems one Ren Xi Peng is dead in Los Angeles. Been dead about a week."

"So?" Jones said.

"Well, the man over there," officer pointed to another body lying face down, "had Peng's ID."

The group started walking over to the body of the man.

"How do we know this man here isn't Peng and the guy in LA is an imposter?"

"This is the first one ID'ed, Lieutenant, but seems like this Peng was an American-Chinese second or third generation. Lots of connections in LA. His family there identified him. And something else. Peng's wallet had been taken. Probably the same one we have here."

Thacker looked meaningfully at Howington, "Remember, friend. We have a deal."

"Never doubted it, my friend." Howington replied. "Set up the meet. I'll keep you in the loop." The DEA agent turned to walk away when he felt Thacker grab his arm.

"Hold up bro," Thacker whispered as he fell in step with Howington.

"This is going to be good. I can just tell it."

"Yo. You be careful when you mess with our Rat friend. I can't prove it but two years ago he got involved with Jack Hawkins, you remember him?"

"Undercover officer from Tampa temporarily assigned for drug interdiction in Miami, right? The dude who got wacked over in Hialeah?"

"That's him. Listen, Howie, I think Hawkins got too close to something The Rat had going --next thing you know there's a hit out on Hawkins. Never could pin The Rat with it -- but I just got a bad feeling about him and anything he's connected to. People seem to die when he's involved."

"Point well taken," Howington responded gravely.

MIAMI -LOBBY OF THE EDEN ROC

Howington walked up the steps and through the turnstile doors fronting the *Eden Roc,* one of the premier hotels on the Miami Beach oceanfront. Newly renovated, it gleamed in the aqua-blue Miami sky, its sun-splashed white stucco walls climbing twenty stories above him, a place, he absently noted, far beyond his means.

Howington stepped into the main lobby dominated by an elegant oval sunken lounge, filled with couches and chairs arranged for conversation, while overhead the suspended ceiling soared thirty feet above the floor, supported by gold-tinted plastic and chrome columns. A shaft of light angled through the windows to shatter and sparkle around the room.

Howington looked for The Rat among the hustle and bustle of people arriving and departing. Having been told by Thacker that he would be in the lobby, Howington searched for the informer, finally spying him on a stuffed beige chair sipping from an espresso cup. "Ah, Mr. Howington," the Rat said as he approached. "Sit down--please."

The Cuban's dark flashing eyes, olive complexion and jet black hair contrasted sharply with the white Guayabera cotton shirt and gold chain around his neck. The Rat lived in the twilight world of criminality and snitching for the police – federal or Metro Dade. Like some creature of the jungle, Roberto survived in his biological niche between law enforcement and the underworld of theft, pimping, and drugs. With one foot in either principality, none claimed him as its own but each recognized his value as a conduit of information about the other.

Nevertheless, Howington fully expected to be present when Roberto's water-bloated body would be pulled from the Miami River. One snitch too many and Roberto would end up with a bullet in his head if he were lucky or a slit throat if not.

"Would you have something to drink?" Roberto raised his long slender fingers and caught the eye of a waitress.

"Two more espressos por favor," he said.

He turned to Howington having dispatched her with a wave of his hand, "So, I understand you want some information."

"Roberto, you surprise me," Howington said sarcastically, "I'd expect to meet you at the Bayside or maybe at the Lincoln Mall, not here. What kinda scam are you up to this time? You run into money or what?"

"No, no," he smiled slightly. "You misjudge me. I am a man of business, yes? I have many friends. Sometimes they help me. Sometimes I help them."

The waitress returned with the espresso. Howington took the tiny coffee cup in his thumb and forefinger and sipped the thick strong coffee heavily laced with sugar.

"Sometimes you get paid," he said. It was an accusation--flat and foul in the refined atmosphere in which he found himself, but Howington didn't care. He wanted to dirty the place up a little, make it more in line with the business at hand.

"Yes. Sometimes. It's business." Roberto replied with a shrug, refusing to be insulted.

"I understand you know something about the shooting down on the dock."

"I have heard of it."

"No. I hear you know more about it than most."

"I might. What is it you need?"

"Why are the Chinese coming to Miami? Are they opening up a new supply?" Howington didn't need to elaborate on the terminology. Everyone in The Rat's circle knew there could be only one "supply" – drugs.

"You're information is good."

"What? They're Chinese or they're opening up a new supply?"

"Both."

Howington digested this information. It made no sense for the Chinese to supply all the way to Miami. If they were opening up a new route they'd come through LA or San Francisco. Not Miami.

"Who killed them?"

"That I do not know. But I have heard that there was a Columbian ship docked there that night."

"The money?"

" I'm sure there was money."

"I hear you helped set it up."

"No. I do not know anything about the money."

"I hear you set it up. Don't mess with me Roberto."

"Where did you hear that?"

"Thacker."

"Oh, well. If you had only said that at first. I never know when you federals and the Metro Dade are working together."

"Thacker set the meet up," Howington said flatly.

"Means nothing. Means nothing." Roberto waived a hand as though brushing away a fly. "I did help them get the money."

"How much?"

"Three million."

"Where did it come from?"

"Who knows?" Roberto replied. "They don't say. I don't ask. It is not polite."

"Did they get the money?"

"Of course! I always keep my business straight."

"Sure you do, Roberto." Howington sneered, igniting fire in the Latin eyes, although Roberto maintained the slightly bored expression he had assumed since they began to talk. It gratified Howington to see something true emanate from the snitch, even if it was veiled anger.

"What do you know about the unfortunate Chinese Officer Howington?" he asked.

This was the tricky part with The Rat. To keep him talking you had to give him something. God knows what he did with it. But that was the unspoken deal.

"We don't know much," Howington admitted. "But they all carried false IDs. Seems they all traced back to Chinese-Americans from L.A." Howington decided to hold back on the fact that so far every one of the poor bastards in L.A. were dead or missing.

"The newspapers. They say that eleven died," Roberto volunteered. "But they are missing two. There were thirteen of them."

Howington was surprised. He thought all had died. "Did you meet with any directly?" he asked.

"No. I did not meet them directly, I only learned of this." Roberto said, sipping his espresso. "There is one more thing."

"Yes?" Howington's interest jumped at this. The Rat rarely volunteered information and with this second opening Howington knew he was being played while at the same time a beneficiary of whatever game The Rat was into.

"I hear the Chinese were only here for a stop. They were headed for Washington or Virginia. Maybe both." Roberto politely dabbed at his mouth with a white linen napkin.

"For drug runners, they sure were loose at the mouth," Howington observed.

"I do not vouch for this. I only say that I heard it," Roberto said with a sly smile. "But sometimes when one drinks with a pretty girl, one talks a little too much. No?"

Howington leaned back in the overstuffed chair and lifted the espresso cup to his lips. His eyes wandered across the room and halted upon a group of well-dressed, brown-skinned women who spoke excitedly in Spanish, their hands fluttering in the air like so many butterflies. The diamonds and gold glittered from their fingers and wrists in a strange dance of lightning flashes and dull yellow gleams.

The whole atmosphere was Miami in its essence. The blending of Anglo and Hispanic cultures. The extravagant wealth. The undercurrent of violence and crime. The glitz of plastic and chrome. To Howington's Midwestern tastes, it all seemed somehow alluring and yet decadent at the same time.

Howington knew The Rat only volunteered information for his own purposes. And Howington knew that the Rat lied as easily as he told the truth. But somehow during this encounter, he sensed that he was hearing more truth than usual. Remembering Thacker's warning, Howington reminded himself to remain cautious and suddenly he felt adrift, unsure who was in charge of the interview. He knew his agenda. He did not know The Rat's. Inexplicably, in that instant, Howington in a deep and fundamental way intuited that he was in over his head. Dangerously so.

"Why would Chinese drug runners take three million dollars and go to Washington?" Howington asked. "Or Virginia, for that matter?"

"Who can say? You better than someone like me. But it would seem to be an angle--as you police often say--worth following."

It was obviously a setup, Howington knew it was a setup, but God help him, he couldn't resist the trail presented even as he knew he was being manipulated --like a rabbit knows something is amiss just before the snare jerks the slipknot tight.

After Howington left, The Rat remained seated and lazily sipped a second espresso. The caffeine and sugar raced through his body like electric arcs. Finishing, he set the delicate porcelain cup ever so gently on the table in front of him and ambled into the rear pool and garden area. Palm trees waved in the ocean breeze as he threaded his way under them, through the flowered garden, and up onto a wooden boardwalk that paralleled Miami beach. As he walked, he looked out across the blazing white sand to the gently lapping turquoise ocean surf.

Anglos are stupid like the fish, he thought to himself. They always think in a straight line – one thing at a time. Throw a lure in front of them and they only can think, do they strike or not? Make the lure attractive enough and they strike. Like Howington is going to strike. The stupid Anglo.

If Howington had thrown a lure to me like I did to him, I would have laughed, Roberto thought. Whether you strike depends on whether there are better lures in other places. And, whether they have barbs.

But the stupid Anglo would not think like that. The Rat stopped in front of the *Fountain Bleu*. In the water he could see nearly naked feminine torsos glistening in the hot sun and salt water, flitting in and out of the gentle blue that seemed to dance ever so softly on the white beach.

The Anglos he knew he could discount, but the Chinese, although merely naïve, were a different matter. In fact, he recognized a soul mate in the one they called Xia Zen. But they did not expect the double-cross so quickly and so violently.

It had been so easy. That first Chinese man he had met and the others brought the money to him, on the dock. Here The Rat allowed the smallest of smiles to cross his darkly tanned face. On the dock. No one in Miami would walk on the dock at Port of Miami with three million in cash. No one. Especially if you were aware that others knew about it. He realized that they would come together for safety – that was predictable. And you could always buy a crew for a little wet work. Then all it took was a few guns equipped with silencers and scopes. The crew paid off and in international waters the same day. And, most importantly, the money in his hands.

Of course, there are always unexpected surprises. The two that got away – that had been a surprise. He had appointed six rifles to six crew members, figuring two shots per crew member would be clean and neat. But one of the crew members, the stupid Nicaraguan, had been high on dope and missed his shots. Not once, but twice.

So, two got away -- Cho and the other one. Ran off between steel-walled cargo units stacked on the pier.

The crew had looked for them in the tangle of cranes and debris without success. No matter, he'd set the DEA on them. That ought to keep them out of Miami and away from him. Three million dollars. It was a sweet deal.

He turned back towards the *Eden Roc*. The surf looked good. He thought he would take a swim, then go on down to the *Bash* for a couple of drinks. If he didn't meet some cash-starved model there, he'd go over to *Madonna's*, a strip joint where companionship came a lot cheaper there than at the *Bash*.

Besides, at the *Bash* you had to pretend you almost cared about whoever you picked up. At *Madonna's,* everyone knew it was a straight business transaction--simple and true.

Until the money ran out, it was going to be a good life, Roberto thought absently.

CULPEPER: BEFORE THE WARRENTON TRAINING CENTER

Sheriff Carter scooted down lower in the brambles and brush.

"Damn," he muttered when his back was raked by a blackberry branch. He leaned forward to pull away from the offending thorns only to have the spiked stem lodge itself more firmly in his flesh.

He was determined to ignore the pain so that he could concentrate on the entrance to the Warrenton Training Center. For the better part of a week, old man Barlow had let him use the field to observe the entrance road to the facility. "Never did like them damn government spooks," Barlow had muttered between his remaining tobacco-stained teeth. "Go ahead, Sheriff, and if you need a good chew or sip of liquor come on up to the house."

Carter had guessed Barlow would help him out. He'd arrested Barlow a couple of times through the years when he had come to town to raise a little hell, but the old man had never held it against him. He knew Carter had a job to do and never begrudged him the right to perform it. Not like some of them no-good dope dealers or skyscraper Richmond lawyers, Carter thought to himself. They were a damn nasty bunch. Lied to you easily as food goes through a goose.

Of course, he knew dopers weren't the only criminals who lied easy-like. No, sir. That there Weir fellow was a damn sight better at lying than any dope-dealer or Richmond lawyer. Carter proved that to himself during the past week.

First, after he'd seen Weir come and go out of the training center two or three times, and had set one of his deputies to following him, the fellow had gone right to the Federal Reserve. And then from there to his house in Fauquier County. Weir must've taken him for a fool to lie like that.

Well, others had made that mistake and lived to regret it. Carter had learned to cultivate the stupid county-boy image – helped him get votes in rural Culpeper County. But, it didn't hurt when others thought you too stupid to count the fingers on your hand. It made 'em sloppy, especially the fancy-firm lawyers, and when Carter hit, they never knew what happened.

And, Weir had been sloppy. All it took was a couple of calls to find out that the FBI didn't know who the hell Weir was or that a murder-suicide had not been investigated on the ground.

In the computer files – yes. In the computers, there was a record of the investigation. But the local office – the one that was listed as having conducted the investigation didn't know a damn thing about Weir or the murder-suicide.

You weren't the sheriff of a county for thirty-one years and not have a few tricks and make a few contacts along the way. Even with the FBI.

Carter had had a gut feeling about Weir and it had proved true. Now he was trying to figure out what was going on at the training center.

He knew it was a sort of spook central for the NSA. Everyone in Culpeper knew about it. After all, someone had to mow that grass and clean the toilets and that sure as hell wasn't going to be the spooks that worked there.

So through the years, the community had built up a common pool of information about the place. And Carter hadn't been elected sheriff six times without getting to know just about everyone in the county. So it didn't take much to find several people who had worked there in the past.

Hells bells, he even knew who worked there now as a grounds-keeper: Peanut Lightfoot. Peanut hadn't had any scrapes with the law. But his brother, who was called Footsy, because he liked to press it to the floor in his short-bed pick up – especially when the police were trying to pull him over, had seen the inside of the jail once or twice.

But Carter had always liked Peanut and he'd never treated Footsy with anything but respect so the whole family regarded him as a distant uncle. And, that was the sort of thing that had been a secret of Carter's success both at the ballot box and during a criminal investigation. Treat people with respect, especially those who usually didn't get much otherwise, and they would do the same to you. And, since criminals swim in the same water, they usually know what was what. More so than the church-going, hard-working folks that voted for Carter.

Peanut had told him that usually on the third Friday of the month, "a whole butt load" of cars and trucks came to the Warrenton Training Center.

Carter wanted to see those mother-loving cars.

He wanted to know why Weir was impersonating an FBI agent.

But most of all, he wanted to know how Ed Wood and his wife died.

It was his duty. He was the damn Sheriff.

BRANDY STATION – CULPEPER

Cho turned the electric switch and the powerful four-cycle engine between his legs throbbed into life.

In America, anyone walking or riding a bike stood out as something to take notice of, while a motorcycle, on the other hand, barely warranted a glance. An additional bonus was that the helmet and visor concealed Cho's Asian features without advertising the fact that it was a mask he wore. A hard and visored mask, but a mask nonetheless.

Cho twisted the handle throttle, kicked the transmission and the sleek Honda bike rocketed forward. He leaned onto the curve that took him from the gravel driveway onto the paved road.

Gravel kicked behind him as the rear tire grabbed the blacktop. Cho sped down the country lane leaning into the wind pushing hard against him. When he crouched low and kicked the bike into a higher gear, the roadside clutter became a blur and Cho, once again, experienced the exhilarating fusion of machine and human in an envelope of speed and adrenaline.

In many ways Cho was glad to be rid of the Dragon Team. He had never cared for the deadly quiet Special Forces operatives whose eyes looked more like the eyes of a dead man that those of living flesh. Cho had no doubt that any them would have killed him on orders without a second thought. That Cuban in Miami had the same eyes.

So it had been a relief, once the shock wore off, when the double-cross on the Miami dock had occurred. He'd never trusted the Cuban, but Cho didn't think anyone could have taken on the Dragon Team and bested them.

Inside the jet-black visor helmet, Cho grimaced. They had already decided to take out the Cuban on the dock -- their own double cross but then it didn't go that way. When the storm of bullets took them by surprise, he'd dropped the two briefcases full of money in the scramble to get away. Cho didn't care. He'd never liked Director

Rong or his money or his greed. Cho only used the money as a means to get where he wanted and what he wanted was right here in Virginia. Almost like food, the very idea of the place attracted him and each day the attraction grew stronger and more insistent. Why?

Cho down shifted and leaned into another curve in the road. He and Xio, the Dragon Team leader, had left Miami the same night of the shooting. Two days later they had been in a safe house in Fairfax County preparing to move to Culpeper.

Every little American town has at least one Chinese restaurant. Culpeper had three. Usually, someone had relatives in China. And usually, or so Xio had told Cho, those in America responded well to swift and violent threats to their remaining family in China.

It had taken all of one day of frantic phone calls between the local proprietor of the Canton Restaurant and his relatives in Guangzhou, to give Cho and Xio a cover as new workers in the business, as well as buy both men new motorcycles.

Cho had been pleased to find out that the mighty arm of state security reached even to the outskirts of Washington, DC. Soon, and very soon he thought with pride, it would reach beyond the orbit of the Earth itself. He stopped the bike and dismounted.

"Now what the hell is this guy doing?" Sheriff Carter mused as, ignoring the brambles that scratched and punctured his skin as he squatted to avoid detection, he adjusted the binoculars for a clearer view of the motorcycle rider in front of him.

He'd heard the big rice-burner for a minute before it passed by the entrance to the Warrenton Training Center, and then, turning around, returned. Now the rider had taken off his helmet and was looking intently at the field of antennas that was visible beyond the tree line at the Center's entrance.

Carter noted the make of the cycle. Then he mentally jotted down the license plate number, figuring he would run it when he got back to the office.

Carter watched the man as he paced back and forth in front of the entrance nervously smoking a cigarette. The man was apparently interested in the field of antennas beyond the trees. He turned and looked towards the spot where Carter was sitting. The man walked back to his bike, flicked the finished cigarette to the ground, and pulled something from his jacket.

By his activities, Carter surmised the mystery motorcycle rider was taking photographs with his cellphone of the entrance.

Now this is damn funny, Carter thought to himself, as the man slid the cell phone back into his jacket, turned and began walking towards Carter's hiding place.

Realizing that things might get interesting, Carter pulled his .357 from his holster. Most Sheriffs carried clip-feed pistols – like 9mm Rugers. But Carter liked a revolver. He didn't have as many rounds as a clip – only six in the pistol cylinder – but it was a rule for him not to get in the position where he needed more than six rounds. And he wanted the six rounds that he *did* shoot, if it came to that, to count. If you got hit with a .357 you weren't getting up anytime soon. In fact, you probably weren't ever getting up.

Well, this sum-bitch was gonna find out real quick what a .357 could do if he pushed it, Carter thought. The potential of action brought a surge of anticipation to the sheriff who readily admitted he was a man of action rather one to contemplate the whys and where-fores. Waiting and watching ran counter to everything that made up who and what he had come to be. Carter knew it and was proud of it. Although he didn't really want a confrontation, another more primitive part of him did – it would be a relief to all the inaction of the past week.

Crouching on one knee, ready to spring if necessary, Carter slowly cocked the hammer back and held the gun barrel up at the ready, as the motorcycle rider continued to approach, as announced by the leaves crunching under his feet. And yet, he couldn't have seen him. No, dressed as he was in camo gear, it seemed clear to Carter that the intruder was seeking an observation point and, in the process, was about to literally step on him.

The crunching leaves stopped just on the other side of a vegeta-tive tangle that hid Carter and the sheriff heard knee joints pop as the man crouched. Leaning forward, Carter pushed away the vines and placed the muzzle of the .357 just inches from the stranger's nose, whispering, "Freeze, you sumbitch."

At the same moment the sound of sliding gravel and car doors opening drew the attention of both men. Carter, his decades of experience screaming at him through the adrenaline of the moment, sensed that the Asian was as anxious at not being detected as was Carter. He motioned with the gun for the man to get down.

"Stay quiet or the last thing you'll ever hear will come from this hog leg!" Carter whispered.

Men in black military uniforms milled about the motorcycle. Carter saw one, who appeared to be in charge, point in the direction of where he was hiding.

"Looks like we might get company," Carter muttered. He jerked his gun to add emphasis, "You go first. Do anything funny and I'll shoot you in the leg and leave you for them. Comprende? Move it."

The two wriggled their way through the tangle of vines and scrub trees until they reached a well-trodden animal trail.

"Ok, buddy," Carter snarled at his prisoner, "You in front. Take off and I'll shoot you. If I don't kill you, they'll get you. If I miss, you'll get lost and they'll still get you. Understand?"

Although the fellow made no response, it was clear that he understood all too well what Carter meant, which was, Carter thought, a bit odd in itself but nothing he couldn't figure out when they got back to his office.   But as they made their exit, Carter thought about the odd coincidence that all of the past hour's activity focused on the same spot where the Wood couple's bodies had sprawled in the weeds. The only problem was, Carter didn't believe in coincidences.

CHAPTER 6

EXECUTIVE ORDER 002 APPROVED BY PRESIDENT TRUMAN AND RE-EX-ECUTED BY EVERY OTHER SITTING PRESIDENT, WHILE EXTREMELY CON-TROVERSIAL, HAS BEEN CRUCIAL TO THE ENTIRE UNITED STATES EFFORT AT CONTAINING AND CONTROLLING THE ROSWELL INCIDENT. E02, AS THE DIRECTIVE IS CALLED, DECLARES THE COUNTRY IN A STATE OF MILITARY EMERGENCY AND SUSPENDS ALL CONSTITUTIONAL PROVISIONS IN THE IN-TEREST OF NATIONAL SECURITY. THERE MUST, HOWEVER, BE A FINDING, BY THE PRESIDENT, THAT E02 IS PUT IN CONTROL BEFORE THE PROVISIONS OF THE DIRECTIVE ARE ENFORCED. THE PRESIDENT MUST CERTIFY THAT THE NATIONAL SECURITY INTEREST IN ALIEN TECHNOLOGY AND COMMUNICATION IS ENGAGED BEFORE E02 CAN BE IMPLEMENTED.

THE COUNTRY, THEN, OPERATES UNDER TWIN SYSTEMS OF LEGAL AND POLITICAL CONTROL. IN MOST MATTERS, E02 IS NOT INVOLVED. HOWEVER, BECAUSE THE COUNTRY IS DECLARED TO BE IN A STATE OF MILITARY EMERGENCY, AND HAS BEEN SINCE 1948, THE PRESIDENT NEED ONLY CERTIFY THAT ALIEN INTERESTS ARE INVOLVED IN A PARTICULAR SITUATION AND THE FULL POWERS OF E02 ARE APPLIED.

THE PATRIOT ACT AND ITS PROGENY IS A SHADOW PARALLEL SYSTEM CREATED TO GIVE LEGITIMACY FOR E02 ACTIVITIES. GROUP 929 SUGGESTED THE ADOPTION OF THE PATRIOT ACT AS MEANS OF CREATING A LAYER OF PROTECTION AND CAMOUFLAGE FOR GROUP 929 ACTIVITIES IN A WORLD DOMINATED BY UNRESTRAINED INFORMATION DISSEMINATION.

E02, IN BROAD TERMS, AND TO LESSER EXTENT THE PATRIOT ACT, SUSPENDS ALL CONSTITUTIONAL PROVISIONS AND PROTECTIONS AND EMPOWERS THE PRESIDENT OR HIS APPOINTEES TO EXECUTE WHATEVER MEASURES ARE NECESSARY TO PROTECT THE NATIONAL SECURITY. WHILE E02 HAS NEVER BEEN RATIFIED BY THE CONGRESS OR REVIEWED BY THE SUPREME COURT, IT IS THE OPINION OF THE ATTORNEY GENERAL, GIVEN THE EXTRAORDINARY CIRCUMSTANCES OF THE ROSWELL CRAFT AND THE SUBSEQUENT ALIEN CONTACTS, E02 WOULD, IF NECESSARY, WITHSTAND CONGRESSIONAL AND JUDICIAL SCRUTINY.

THE PATRIOT ACT OPERATES UNDER A SIMILAR REVIEW SYSTEM.

PRESIDENT TRUMAN AND EVERY PRESIDENT SINCE HAVE MADE E02 FINDINGS.

OBVIOUSLY GROUP 929'S RECOMMENDATIONS FOR ALIEN CONTACT AND COOPERATION COULD NOT HAVE BEEN IMPLEMENTED WITHOUT THE LEGAL FOUNDATION CREATED BY THE E02 FINDING.

IN 1978, PRESIDENT CARTER GRANTED PERMANENT E02 FINDING STATUS TO GROUP 929. GROUP 929 OPERATES UNDER THE EXECUTIVE POWERS CONFERRED UPON THE PRESIDENT BY THE CONSTITUTION AND THEREFORE MAY INVOKE THE FINDING STATUS, AS IT IS CALLED, AT ANY TIME. GROUP 929, BY ITS VERY NATURE, MUST AND DOES EXERCISE E02 POWERS ON A REGULAR BASIS. IT IS BECAUSE OF THIS SPECIAL MISSION THAT PERMANENT STATUS WAS CONFERRED ON GROUP 929.

THIS GRANT OF POWER IS SOMETIMES EXERCISED BY FIELD AGENTS WHO MUST ACT ON THE SPOT. TO GUARD AGAINST IMPROPER EXERCISE OF E02 POWERS, EVERY E02 INCIDENT MUST BE REPORTED AND RE-VIEWED BY THE GROUP 929 E02 REVIEW COMMITTEE. IN TURN, THE NATIONAL SECURITY ADVISOR IS TASKED WITH OVERSIGHT OF GROUP 929 E02 FINDINGS.

THE PENALTY FOR AN IMPROPER EXERCISE OF E02 POWER BY A FIELD AGENT IS SWIFT AND SEVERE. SUMMARY EXECUTION ORDERED BY THE PRESIDENT UNDER THE POWERS OF E02 IS RARE BUT NOT WITHOUT PRECEDENT.

--- EXCERPTS FROM THE NSA PRESIDENTIAL BRIEFING PAPERS ON THE ROSWELL INCIDENT

CULPEPER COUTHOUSE

"Damn it. Binford, there's gotta be a way to cuff 'em on this thing," Sheriff Carter said kicking the grass impatiently.

The two men were standing in the small courtyard that separated the courthouse from the Sheriff's office and jail annex, a grassy square surrounding the Confederate war memorial, scattered with cast iron and wooden benches under the arching shade of old maple trees. Sinking down on one bench, Mordecai Binford stretched out his legs, dug his fists into his khaki trouser pockets, and stared up at the old brick courthouse.

"Sheriff, you tell me," he grumbled. "What has this Wang Lee done? To be exact, what do you suggest we charge him with?"

"All I know is that you're the attorney, Binford, and I'm expecting you to find a way to hold 'em till I can find out what the hell he was doing over at the Training Center. Are you seriously telling me there ain't something we can't charge him with? You telling me I gotta come up with something – me who ain't ever gone to college, much less law school?"

"Cut the crap, Sheriff."

"Hells Bells, Binford, we can't just let him go."

"It's not illegal to drive a motorcycle on a state highway," Binford said impatiently. "You said he was properly licensed and the last time I checked it's not illegal to take pictures there – you've done the same thing yourself. And besides...."

"That was during an investigation." Sheriff Carter interrupted.

"It doesn't matter," the prosecutor continued. "It's not illegal to walk in the woods. It's not posted. Fact is, Sheriff, you're looking at a false arrest. You've at least got to have probable cause to execute an investigative detention and you're way beyond that. Way beyond."

"Look, Binford. All I want to do is hold him a little," the sheriff protested. "Jam him up some. See if he'll talk."

Binford pursed his lips and watched a woman in an out-of-date floral pants suit waddle down the street with two kids in tow. "You say he parked the cycle in the road."

"Yeah"

"Any cars come by?"

"Just the vans."

"They stop?"

"Yeah."

"Well, the best you got is impeding the flow of traffic."

"Hell, I could've come up with that," Carter growled.

"Well you didn't," Binford snapped.

"That's it?" Carter asked.

"That's all you got."

"I can't hold him on that," Carter complained.

"It's the best you got."

"Smith is the magistrate," Carter said disgustedly. "Maybe I can get him to set a high bond. That could give us some time."

"The Judge is here today." Binford said.

"Damn!" Carter exclaimed. "So much for a day or two behind bars." Both men knew, under Virginia law, a person who has bond set by a magistrate is to be brought before a sitting judge for bond review expeditiously-- meaning within hours if not sooner. And the two knew, without speaking of it, that there was little chance a judge would hold anyone on the motorcycle driver's charge no matter how high the original bond.

"It's the best we got, Sheriff." Binford said matter-of-factly. Secretly, he kinda liked to twist the sheriff's tail every once in a while.

"Maybe it we get him under oath, in front of the judge, he might slip on something."

"OK, I'll be around. Let me know when he's ready for the hearing," Binford concluded.

"Right." Carter marched off to his office. Binford watched his brown uniformed bulk bounce up the Sheriff's Office entrance stairs and disappear inside. No doubt, he thought, Carter was overreacting, but then again, the sheriff had a nose for investigations. And, it sure *did* seem strange that he would show an interest in the exact same spot as Carter, especially since the Warrenton Training Center was out in the middle of nowhere.

Binford leaned back on the bench and looked at the red brick courthouse. The building was really composed of the two parts. The older two-story tin-roofed structure had been built in 1870 and it exhibited the grace that public buildings of that age possessed. Tacked on to the rear, like a wart, was the three-story, flat- roofed addition of 1970. For the hundredth time, Binford shook his head at the alien monstrosity attached to the beautiful Italianate 1870 building. The clash between the two structures struck a chord of deep unease in Binford. Like the awkward merger of the two architectural styles, there was something profoundly wrong with this murder-suicide investigation. Besides the false photos in the report and Weir's misrepresentations, the fact that the motorcycle rider showed an interest in the Warrenton Training Center could very well be indicative that there was some merit to the Sheriff's suspicions. Yes, sir. The sheriff might just be on to something.

Binford looked forward to listening to what this motorcycle rider would testify to once on the stand.

FEDERAL RESERVE - CULPEPER

"Find out who this Chinese national is." Sims said on the telephone, his terse tone telegraphing to the new security chief that he was none too happy. Weir had noticed Sims' attitude towards him had taken a precipitous drop after Sheriff Carter began nosing around.

"My interviews indicate he left the area with Sheriff Carter." Weir said.

"Yeah, well, you need to do better than that," Sims sneered.

"I think he's working with Carter," Weir added, "although I'm not precisely sure how."

"Ha. Working with Carter. Ha." Sims barked out a laugh. "Look, Weir, you're not performing to standard. You haven't handled Carter so as to satisfy his overblown sense of duty. You lost the motorcycle rider in the woods."

Weir wanted to protest the last accusation, particularly since it was not entirely correct. He *was* in charge of security for the Federal Reserve, *not* the Training Center and as such was not responsible for "handling" Carter. However, he had learned long ago in the military the best response to criticism by a superior, whether warranted or not, was to salute and say, "Yes, sir."

"Yes, sir." Weir responded.

"Don't give me that "Yes, sir" crap Weir," Sims snarled. "It doesn't work with me. I want results."

"We'll find the subject, sir."

"Great guns, man!" Sims exclaimed-- "I've already found him. I want to know who he is!"

Weir felt a dangerous anger begin to loosen within. This was the second time Sims had been less than honest with him. Instead of sharing information and God knows where'd he got it, he'd tested Weir first and, in the process, belittled him. Weir didn't like to play games. You were on the same side or you weren't – you didn't withhold information from your own people. Period.

"Where is he?" Weir asked.

"Carter has him locked up," Sims continued. "Somehow I don't think that bodes well for your theory on the two working together. Apparently the sheriff was able to convince a magistrate to set a cash bond on this guy. He's set to have a bond hearing this afternoon."

"A bond hearing? What the hell is that?" Weir asked.

"Talk to the legal eagles. I don't really care," Sims said dismissively.

"Is it open to public?" Weir asked.

"Why do you think I'm telling you about it?" Sims demanded in a voice thick with sarcasm.

"You want me there."

"Of course," Sims paused. "Don't mess this up."

"What do you want me to do?"

"Sit there and record every word they say."

"How much time do I have?"

"You should be there now."

"Wait a minute. Won't Carter and Binford know who I am?" Weir asked.

"So what? They know the subject was seen by our security in front of the Training Center. You're merely following up on the incident this morning. After all, you *are* an FBI agent. And in case it's failed to register with you, the FBI *is* interested in terrorism. Like I said, don't blow it. Report to me personally immediately after the hearing."

"Ok."

"And Weir, one more thing to put a little fire under your butt, I've been informed there is an EO2 finding in this matter."

Weir felt his stomach twist. He didn't say anything.

"Did you hear me?" Sims barked.

"Yes, sir."

"Watch and report back to me. Understood?"

"Yes, sir."

"Go," Sims ordered and cut the connection.

Weir replaced the phone on its cradle. He knew from his orientation at the Federal Reserve that an EO2 finding was serious. He could get burned – anyone could get burned. All the rules were suspended. Completion of the mission was paramount. Nothing stood in the way of an EO2 finding. Not life. Not liberty. Not happiness. Nothing.

CULPEPER GENERAL DISTRICT COURT

Binford bounded up the back stairs to the second floor of the General District Court room. It was a habit he had formed in college when he ran three miles a day. Now, although he didn't run anymore, he refused to plod up the stairs one at the time. To plod was to surrender to middle age and he wasn't ready to surrender just yet.

Puffing his way to the top of the landing, Binford opened the door to the courtroom, nodding to the bailiff and went to stand to the left of the judge's bench, a position from which he habitually took note of who was sitting in the audience.

It was a typical end of the day collection of people in the room. On the right wall sat a number of prisoners in shackles, their fluorescent orange jumpsuits clashing with the somber suits of the attorneys and the brown uniforms from the sheriff's department.

The courtroom was nearly empty. A scattering of people, most likely friends or relatives of the prisoners, sat randomly in the gallery.

None drew Binford's attention except for the Sheriff to whom he nodded.

"Wang Lee." The bailiff called, seeing Binford arrive in the courtroom.

Cho Tsing responded to the called name and positioned himself in front of the Judge's bench to be joined by Binford and the sheriff who whispered, "That FBI puke Weir is here. Back in the corner--"

Binford turned to look back at the gallery where he singled out one figure in the rear, a man whose arms were crossed firmly over his chest. He was wearing jeans and a blue work shirt. Binford did not recognize him. He turned back to the judge.

"Mr. Lee?" Judge Bell asked the prisoner.

"Yes. Yes, sir." Cho responded.

"I note a slight accent, Mr. Lee. Can you speak English? Do you need an interpreter?"

"No, sir. I can speak English," Cho answered quietly.

"Good." Judge Bell began shuffling papers in front of him. "Let's see what Mr. Lee is supposed to have done to draw the attention of the Commonwealth's Attorney *and* the Sheriff." Judge Bell looked up at Binford and Carter. "Gentlemen, good to see you in our court," he said with a hint of amusement.

"Let's see…" The judge began looking at the warrant and criminal complaint. An expression of surprise crossed his face. His eyes swiveled to look at Binford.

"Mr. Binford, am I missing something here?"

"No, sir." Binford answered.

"I see," Judge Bell said.

"Your Honor," Binford said, "the Commonwealth might be agreeable to amending the bond downwards. May I *voir dire* the defendant?"

"Well, Mr. Binford. I'm glad the Commonwealth *might* consider reducing the bond from fifty thousand dollars," the judge said sarcastically. "Mr. Binford is allowed to ask you a few questions, Mr. Lee, and then we'll look at your bond."

To those unfamiliar with criminal law and procedure, nothing seemed out of ordinary, but a $50,000 bond on a traffic violation was unheard of – as was Binford's *voir dire*.

Voir dire, meaning to speak the truth, is a common legal procedure that allows one side to ask questions of the other. In a bond hearing, the prosecution is allowed to ask the defendant about his background. In theory, this allows the commonwealth and the court to make a more informed decision about the defendant's propensity for flight or violence. That impacts how much bond is appropriate: the more serious the crime, the higher the bond, and the greater the risk of flight, the higher the bond.

Of course, neither consideration was really at issue in a traffic infraction. Binford and Carter knew this. The judge knew it. Weir didn't. Neither did Cho.

And so the questioning began. Cho was bewildered. This morning he had been on top of the world – speeding down the highway on a motorcycle, certain he was close to unlocking the secret of the transmissions he had first learned of in the now far-distant China with Miami nothing but a bad dream.

The judge's attitude was puzzling to Cho. He seemed more amused than anything else. Cho knew the American justice system was pathetically weak but surely any criminal proceeding required a stern demeanor.

What Cho could not remember in his cover story he made up.

Then, just when he thought he could not come up with another answer, the judge told him he was released, and he was promptly unshackled, led back to the jail, given his clothes in exchange for the orange jumpsuit, and provided with the keys to his motorcycle. What had just happened, he wondered, as he sped to his safehouse. Clearly, he needed instructions. And even more, he needed a cigarette.

"Good job, Mordecai," the Sheriff said to Binford on the courthouse lawn. The two had just left the courtroom and walked outside to discuss the bond hearing.

"The judge released him," Binford said heatedly. "There is no way any kind of secured bond was going to stick on a traffic ticket."

"Hells bells, Mordecai, I know that. Don't get so riled up. Just wanted to buck you up a little. That's all. We got some info on the guy. That's what I needed. Now I'm gonna pay a visit to a certain Chinese restaurant here and find out more. And I'm gonna send a wire to California and see what gives on this guy. Visiting relatives my ass, Chinese don't give a damn about their relatives that don't live with 'em, excepting maybe ma or pa back in China."

"What about the FBI agent?" Binford asked.

"Weir?"

"Yeah. What about him? Why's he interested in our guy?"

"Why the hell was I up there at the Training Center, Mordecai? There's something wrong at that place. And ain't it interesting that the Chinese fellow takes pictures of the same place where Mr. and Mrs. Wood are supposed to have off'd each other?" Carter observed.

"Yeah, well, what about Weir?" Binford asked again.

"He's hiding something, Mordecai. And I think Wang Lee, if that's his name, either knows what it is or wants to know – just like me."

MIAMI: FEDERAL BUILDING

"Jackpot!" Howington said as he read the email from the Washington DEA field office and, after forwarding it to his deputy, Stu Stover, opened a new window on his computer screen in order to search for Culpeper on Google Earth. Stover read the email on his mobile phone, then looked at Howington's work on the computer screen.

"You think this is the same guy?" Stover asked.

"Damn straight. The Rat said he was off to Virginia. All the other bodies traced to LA. Now we got some sheriff in Virginia doing a criminal check on a "Wang Lee" from LA. Five to one we find the guy in a city morgue – or missing."

The power of the DEA to track criminal records and criminal record checks was a poorly-kept secret. Throughout the United States, law enforcement agencies could access the criminal records of just about anyone, with the FBI providing the clearing house for information, and the DEA, as a federal agency, having total access to all FBI criminal records. In addition, it monitored record checks and matched them via computer to its own data base of subjects. Drug running was a multi-state, multi-national operation and the monitoring system helped DEA agents stay on top of who was going where in the twilight world of crack and heroin and meth. All Howington had to do was put in a request to monitor any criminal record check originating in Virginia and directed to LA.

He had to wade through about seventy-five when the hit before him appeared. The oriental name was a kicker. He was sure this was it.

"You want me to get the requesting agency on the line?" Stover said.

"No," Howington said after a pause. "No, we don't know what this is. I don't want to tip off the locals just in case."

Howington didn't have to explain to Stover that the "just in case" meant just in case the locals were in on it. With the money as good as it is in the drug business, it was easy to buy off whole police departments in the backwoods counties. He and Stover had seen it before and he knew they'd see it again.

"No. We'll operate out of the Washington field office," he continued staring at the computer screen, tapping a pencil against his front upper teeth, a nervous habit he had formed in elementary school and never been able to shake. "I don't want to close in too fast."

"Why the hell would the Chinese want to start a drug operation out of Miami?" Howington mused, "Isn't LA or Mexico easier?"

"Maybe they figured we'd never expect them coming in from the east coast." Stover said.

"Maybe or maybe there's more to this than drugs."

"Like what?"

"You know much about Chinese history, Stu?"

"No."

"Well, interestingly enough, the West introduced and marketed opium in China in the nineteenth century."

"So?"

"So maybe the Chinese government wants to return the favor," Howington said. "The British used the drugs as a way to weaken Chinese society. Then it was much easier for them to get trade concessions."

"They don't need any trade concessions," Stu said. "Everything in Wal-Mart is stamped with "Made in China"."

"No. You don't get it. How does a militarily inferior power take on a stronger country? Especially a country like the United States which you think is illegitimate?" Howington asked.

"Come on, Chief. This is just a drug deal."

"You go for the underbelly," Howington persisted. "Stu, we're going to Washington. I want in on this. It's got national security written all over it."

"When do you want to leave?"

"Now. You get the tickets. We'll try to catch a flight this evening."

Later, Howington wondered whether this might be the ticket to get of the Miami field office and get into the Washington Office.

Tampa Bay Times Section A-1

University of Tampa--Over two hundred students gathered in a candlelight vigil Tuesday night to mark the disappearance of University students Leotie Thunder, 19, and Judy Levine, 20.

The two women have been missing for almost a week. Police say that no leads have developed in the case. At first police treated the incident as one of many instances of freshmen taking off for a week to party at the beach. After the missing students' parents protested what they termed as the police department's lax attitude towards their daughters' predicament, police upgraded the case to suspected foul play.

The University Women's Student Action League also criticized the department for what it termed "paternalistic tendencies" in its handling of the disappearance.

"Two independent women decide to take a week off. What business is it of the police?" asked Joycie Myers-Stratten. Myers-Stratten is the chapter's faculty advisor.

"We take every missing person report seriously," Tampa police spokesman Tom Alexis said in response to the criticism. "But the fact is that in almost all cases the missing students reappear."

"My daughter would never stay out of touch for so long," said Henry Thunder of his daughter, Leotie. "There is something wrong."

"Judy always skypes her mother every day," said Andy Levine, the father of Judy Levine. "The Tampa police need to step up and treat this as the serious incident that it is."

The two freshmen are roommates at the University of Tampa and fellow students report they are also close friends.

While police report no new leads, an employee at the Double A Marina on Old Tampa Bay told the Tampa Bay Times that he saw two women matching the description of Thunder and Levine boarding a sloop with a young man on the weekend they were reported to have disappeared. Tampa police refused to comment on the tip when asked about it by the Tampa Bay Times.

CHAPTER 7

WHAT IS IT THAT THE AE WANT WITH HUMAN BEINGS? THAT IS THE CENTRAL QUESTION THAT LIES AT THE HEART OF ALL INVESTIGATIONS INTO THE ROSWELL CRAFT AND SUBSEQUENT AE CONTACT. OBVIOUSLY PRIOR TO THE ORGANIZED ABDUCTIONS OF HUMAN BEINGS, OUR THEORIES REGARDING AE INTENTIONS AND GOALS VARIED GREATLY FROM THE COMMONLY ACCEPTED EXPLANATION TODAY. (SEE THE SEPARATE "ALIEN INTENTIONS: A HISTORY OF HUMAN SPECULATION 1947-1963," A PAPER DELIVERED TO GROUP 929, AUGUST 23, 1974, BY DR. ABRAM TREEWORTH AND PUBLISHED[23] BY NSA GRANT OF AUTHORITY, 1975.) IN 1979, DR. SIMON ELLIOT PRESENTED A 115-PAGE STUDY OF ABDUCTION RECALL MEMORIES TO GROUP 929. THAT INITIAL STUDY HAS BEEN EXPANDED REPEATEDLY; HOWEVER, ITS CORE THESIS REMAINS THE BEST OPINION OF GROUP 929 AS TO ALIEN OBJECTIVES IN HUMAN ABDUCTION.

IN SHORT FORM, ELLIOT'S THESIS IS THAT ALIEN BIOLOGY IS NOT CARBON-BASED, AS IS EARTH'S, AND THEREFORE EARTH ORIGINATED LIFE FORMS ARE AS SURPRISING AND BIZARRE TO ALIEN MINDS AS THEIR OWN LIFE FORMS, IF KNOWN, WOULD BE TO HUMANS. THERE IS SOME INDICATION THAT HUMANS ARE BEING USED IN BIOLOGICAL EXPERIMENTATION: PERHAPS TO UNDERSTAND THE ORGANIC CHEMISTRY OF EARTH LIFE; HOWEVER, ELLIOT AND THOSE AFTERWARD HAVE POSTULATED A MORE SINISTER PURPOSE. CERTAIN PHYSICAL TRACES OF THE EXPERIMENTATION ON BOTH HUMANS AND ANIMALS WOULD SEEM TO INDICATE BIOLOGICAL WARFARE AS A PRIME MOTIVE OF THE ABDUCTIONS. IT SHOULD BE EXPLAINED THAT ELLIOT AND HIS PROGENY HAVE BEEN VERY TENTATIVE IN POSTULATING THIS MOTIVE FOR ABDUCTIONS.

****

"CLEARLY THE LABORATORY MONKEY IN A BIOLOGICAL EXPERIMENT HAS NO IDEA OF HIS PURPOSE, EVEN LESS HIS COMPATRIOTS IN THE ASIAN JUNGLES." --SIMON ELLIOT

[23]"PUBLISHED" DEFINED AS GENERAL DISSEMINATION WITHIN THE NSA ON A NEED-TO-KNOW BASIS. ALL PAPERS ARE TOP SECRET AND ARE TREATED AS SUCH.

CULPEPER

After talking with Sheriff Carter, Binford was disturbed.

He didn't like making weak arguments before the judge. And clearly the bond hearing was a sham. He didn't like the fact that this situation was forcing him to do things like that. In fact, there was nothing that he liked about this whole mess.

Binford had never been one for conspiracy theories, but Carter's digging had found some bothersome details about the Wood murder-suicide.

First, the photographs of the crime scene didn't match. That was clear. Second, the FBI didn't know a damn thing about an investigation at the Warrenton Training Center. Third, what did this Chinese visitor want with the Training Center? And, why was the FBI so interested that they would send their guy Weir to the bond hearing?

And finally, Binford reflected, if Weir had been legitimate, he would have contacted Carter or himself before or after the hearing, since they were all part of the same law enforcement fraternity. But Weir had scooted out of the courtroom like a scared rabbit right after the bailiffs took Wang back to the sheriff's office for release.

Binford played with his pen and swiveled his leather desk chair to look out of the window. He didn't like this one bit. And worst of all, he suspected that Carter was on to something. Carter liked to act the country simpleton but Binford had come to know Carter well enough to know that most of it was an act. He continued to stare out of the window putting off the decision he knew he would have to make. Somehow, he felt as if he were looking across a darkening landscape, tangled, torn, and simmering with misery. It reminded him all too vividly of the tangle of arms and legs that had once been the Woods, lying in the somber field of broom sage. He remembered their dead eyes staring up at the blue sky.

"Damn," he muttered and reached for the phone, cradling it between his ear and shoulder as he thumbed through his rolodex. He found the name he was looking for.

The receiver rang twice.

"Ops Center. Smith." A heavy male voice spat out the greeting.

"3516 Blondie, "Binford responded as he had been instructed when he got the number.

"Operator?" the male voice asked.

"Binford 20605," Binford responded.

The line clicked, then rang five times.

"Blondie." Binford heard the familiar voice say.

"I need a favor," Binford said.

"Binford? From me?" Catabin asked, disbelief in his voice.

"I think so," Binford said.

"I gotta hear this," Catabin said.

"Is this a secure line?" Binford asked.

"Are you serious?" Catabin asked incredulously.

"I wish I weren't," Binford said.

"Wait a minute while I run a diagnostic."

The line went silent and Binford could hear faint tones and electronic squeals. "It's ok," Catabin said. "You're on a land-line so there's little chance of an air transmission and recovery. I don't detect any taps or bugs in your system, which means it's probably secure. So, what's going on?"

"I need a favor."

"So you said."

"I need you to check on something for me."

"Is this business or is it personal? Cause I'm gonna tell you right now if it's either I can't do it," Blondie said.

"Hear me out."

"OK. For you, but I'm still going to say no."

"Don't be too encouraging," Binford replied. "I might get my hopes up."

"Obviously you're not gonna ask me to borrow the lawnmower. And I'm not with the local county Mounties."

"Hear me out."

"OK, shoot, but I'm still gonna tell you no."

WASHINGTON, DC: DEA DIVISION H. Q.

"Bloody hell," Ian Steele exclaimed, his eyes remaining fixed on the computer terminal in front of him as he deftly clicked on the new information as it scrolled across the screen.

"Bloody hell," he said again slowly and distinctly, his British accent adding emphasis to the expression.

Silent, his mouth set in a straight line, Howington leaned over Steele's shoulder and looked at the information on the screen, while Stover sat, legs out stretched, a Styrofoam cup of coffee in one hand, a moon pie in the other. He alternated sipping the hot black liquid and nibbling the round chocolate and marshmallow snack. Crumbs spilled down his shirt and tie.

"Mary, Mother of ..." Steele began, and then with forced calmness, "...would you mind the crumbly bits? Don't want them clogging up all the electrical equipment. Much less bringing in roaches. Nasty things, roaches."

The three men were in a windowless cubicle office on the third floor of the DEA Washington Field Office. Steele was not assigned to the Field Office but was merely a liaison from the El Paso Intelligence Center (EPIC) for the Washington Office.

EPIC is a clearing house for tactical intelligence related to drug transportation around the world, to which eleven federal agencies contributed, including the Department of Homeland Security.

At the moment, Howington and Stover, through EPIC's intelligence unit at the Washington Division headquarters, were tapping into the wealth of information stored in the main-frame computers in Texas.

The unique feature of EPIC's computer programs was the ability to cross reference and categorize seemingly unrelated information into larger patterns. For example, without human instruction, the program would pull out information on private freight ship movement as monitored by U. S. satellites and coca crop production worldwide in order to identify likely seaborne routes for cocaine delivery. This would be based on separate harvesting estimates provided by the Department of Agriculture and shipping manifests the CIA and the NSA had hacked from private computer systems worldwide. NSA email and phone monitoring also fed into the data base as well as NSA drone feeds from around the world. Without prompting, the EPIC program would access all this information amidst the ocean of other information stored and detect a possible pattern for cocaine transportation -- or whatever. It was presently performing a similar pattern function with the variables given by Howington.

"What are you into, Howie?" Steele asked.

"I'm not sure." Howington replied, tapping a pencil against his front teeth.

And, in fact, the Miami DEA head wasn't sure. The more he thought of his drug-running theory involving the Chinese in Miami the more farfetched it had seemed. But, he had set the wheels in motion for an inquiry with EPIC and he had felt obligated to see it through.

After he and Stu had flown up from Miami International to Dulles, they had rented a car and checked into a couple of rooms at the Radisson in the District before meeting with Steele early the next morning.

Howington had worked with Steele before, and found he liked the lanky, red-headed Englishman almost from the start. Steele was a veteran of the Iraq War, having been with intelligence in the Royal Marines. Afterwards he left the military and settled in London where, after a whirlwind romance with an American graduate student at the London School of Economics, he married. Tired of Great Britain's seemingly inexorable decline on the world stage, he and his new bride decided to set up housekeeping in America. He had never looked back.

Howington liked his "can do" attitude and innate ability to pry order from the chaos of raw data. That and the fact that Howington was an unreserved anglophile had been enough to cement a friendship between the two.

Howington stared with renewed interest over Steele's shoulder at the computer screen which was divided into separates boxes, each showing a different function of the EPIC program's analysis. From time to time the program required Steele to make choices from a set of inquiries. As the program selected a variable that it had coded as being part of the larger pattern, it listed the data in the upper right hand box. As the variables grew the list scrolled upwards in the box allowing the screen operator, in this case Steele, the option of scrolling the variables up or down. Clicking on one would open up a separate box to show the new data and analysis for listing variables.

As a new variable popped into the list, Steele would flick from one or another to review the program's analysis for listing it as significant in the overall pattern. To Howington it all seemed far removed from the dead bodies on the Miami docks.

"It's an empty house," Steele muttered.

"A what?" Howington asked.

"An empty house. We've hit 'em before. Usually turn out to be something the spooks are interested in." Steele offered as an explanation. He noticed Howington's and Stover's blank expressions. "Here, give me that piece of paper."

Stover handed one over to Steele upon which he drew what looked like interlocking boxes. With some disgust, he flicked off a smeared bit of chocolate from the paper's edge, then using the pen as a pointer he tapped the drawing.

"EPIC can only trace pattern. The typical drug pattern is straight forward: supply, transportation, money-laundering. But sometimes we feed information and EPIC picks up a different pattern, like this," he nodded his head to the still running program. "We call it an empty house."

"Why empty house?" Stover drained the last of his coffee and tossed the cup in the general direction of the trash can.

"Well, the program can pick up the outlines of a pattern. Like these boxes. Imagine each as a room. You may know the layout of the house as far as rooms are concerned, but you don't know how each room is furnished or what it's used for. Same thing here. We've picked up a pattern. It's elaborate, but what it all means is beyond us."

"So what happens now?" Stover asked.

"I usually get a call in a day or two from someone over at the NSA."

"Yeah? What for?" Stover said, working a toothpick through his mouth.

"They've got a cooperative agreement with DEA. Anytime we hit an open house, they get an automatic download and notification," Steele replied.

"That already happened here?" Howington interjected.

"Don't know. But before it's finished I imagine the people over at Fort Meade will know all about it. Don't worry. It's not really a problem. More like a pain in the arse because they usually come snooping around trying to track down the leads that we plugged in to generate the empty house."

Howington digested this new twist.

"You mean they're gonna ask you where you got the variables for the program?" Howington asked. "And, you're gonna tell them what?"

"That some washed out DEA agent had a half-ass theory about drugs, the Chinese, and Miami."

"And?"

"And, that obviously EPIC went chasing butterflies."

"They gonna call on me and Stover?"

"Of course," Steele replied, continuing to stare at the blue and green script sliding across the computer screen.

"There's nothing here that says this isn't drug- related, is there?" Howington asked.

"No, not technically. But, believe me, there's a lot more here than some little drug operation. What, I don't have a clue."

"OK. It's still drug-related as far as I'm concerned," Howington replied. "Tell me this. We gonna learn much from this empty house pattern?"

"Don't know. Maybe. Usually they're pretty obscure. This one's got a strange twist for a drug operation."

"Yeah, what?" Stover asked.

"There's a lot of aerospace data."

"So?" Howington asked.

"So," Steele told the two, "I've never seen that before."

The traffic on I-66 West was heavy as Howington and Stover weaved their rental Ford Escort across four lanes of bumper to bumper automobiles, having decided to take a quick look at Culpeper and then return that evening. Steele had agreed to call them when the EPIC program ran its course.

"These empty house anomalies usually take a while to complete," he had told them.

Howington had just passed the National Rifle Association headquarters when his cell phone beeped.

"Howington here."

"Howie, it's Steele."

"EPIC finished?"

"No. Now listen. I don't have much time. You've kicked over a hornet's nest here. Just after you left a couple of NSA suits came over and shut the program down."

"It didn't finish?"

"No. Be quiet man, I've got to get off this line damn fast. Look, I heard one of them talk about extreme action. I got outta there double time."

"You're paranoid."

"Shut up. Meet me in two hours at the Fairfax Government Center. Just drive around a couple of times and park. I'll find you."

"You gotta be kidding," Howington said.

"No, I'm not. And there's something else."

"Yeah."

"Watch your back. They know who you are by now." The phone went dead.

Steele wasn't the excitable type. Howington knew that. But this last call was right out of a Robert Ludlum novel. The NSA after him? Ridiculous. But Steele had sounded a little more than worried and it took a lot to get a Royal Marine excited. Howington decided that the prudent course of action was to play along. After all, what was the harm? And, he had learned more than once as an undercover agent in the DEA that strange things can happen when massive amounts of money, guns, and drugs were involved. He'd survived because he'd been careful. He'd be careful now.

"What's up?" Stover asked and, as soon as Howington told him, they decided to ditch the cheap little Ford for something with a little more power. It took little or no time to find a rental car agency, turn in the Ford, pay cash, and drive out in a black Dodge Durango. Howington wanted something big with power and sporting a four-wheel drive. If they were driving into trouble he wanted the ability to go nuclear if need be. And Howington reasoned, if "they", whoever "they" were, had identified him as the driver of an Escort, the SUV would make it harder to trail him.

Securing the Durango took up most of the time they had. When the two exited the interstate onto the Fairfax Government Parkway, Howington pulled off onto the road shoulder. He and Stover checked their weapons. Both carried 9mm Glock semi-automatic pistols. Howington checked the slide. He removed the clip and inspected the top round for any imperfection that could jam it up. The round looked good. The oil sheen on the gun glinted hot in the afternoon sun. He rammed the clip home and replaced the weapon in his shoulder holster.

Stover did the same.

"Ready?" he asked Stover.

"Let's do it."

Howington reentered traffic, drove past the lake and fountain in front of the building and then turned down the four lane access road where traffic was light, giving him time to look around. Unlike Miami's skyscrapers, the blue glass structure which was the government center squatted down on the landscape, surrounded by oaks and a parking area.

He turned into the nearest parking space and shifted the car into park but left the engine running.

Automatically, he and Stover scanned their respective sides of the car looking for any unusual activity. Cars came and left the parking area but no one seemed to pay any attention to the two men. At 2:15, Howington was ready to leave when his cell phone beeped again.

"Where are you?" Howington demanded when he heard Steele's voice on the phone.

"Where I can see you. You notice anything unusual?"

"No. Now cut the crap. What do you want?"

"Drive up to the front entrance. I'll meet you there."

"What's up?" Stover asked as Howington placed the mobile back in his jacket pocket.

"We drive up to the building and meet him."

"OK. Want a ho-ho?" Stover proffered a chocolate-covered snack cake to Howington.

"Hell, no. I can't believe you're eating." Howington said, not bothering to hide his disgust.

"Suit yourself," Stover replied grinning. He popped the treat whole into his mouth. "Think I ought to save some for Steele?" he asked while chewing.

"You're hopeless." Howington replied. He tried to remain irritated at his associate – then gave in to grin. "Mind the crumbly bits. Might jam the gun," he said in a poor mimic of Steele's English accent. Howington shifted into drive and wheeled the car around the parking lot.

"There he is." Stover pointed out the thin Brit. Steele opened the rear door and climbed in quickly.

"Just drive," Steele ordered tersely.

"You got it," Howington replied.

As the Durango neared the access road to the Center, a white van with tinted windows pulled behind him.

"Uh oh. I got one behind me." Howington said, his eyes flicking to the rear view mirror.

The two vehicles drove slowly towards the access road entrance, Howington keeping his speed steady so as not to tip off his pursuers that they had been spotted.

"I don't see anything ahead," Stover said.

Howington pulled onto the access road and turned left to get onto the main artery.

"They're gonna stop us in broad daylight in the middle of traffic." Howington predicted, "They'll either do it now --or follow us for a while."

"Well, excuse my French, but let's force the bastards to do something," Stover said.

But before they could make a move, two white vans appeared in the access road ahead, and simultaneously they heard the thump, thump, thump of a helicopter rotor somewhere overhead.

"He's gonna ram us!" Steele shouted from the back.

"That's the block," Stover said indicating the two vans ahead.

The impact of the van from the rear flung all three backward, then forward. The van rammed them a second time.

The rotor wake kicked up dust and debris from the road. Ahead the two vans split blocking the road ahead.

"I think they want us to stop," Stover observed laconically.

Howington only had seconds to make his move before he'd be forced to halt. He considered ramming between them but knew it would be futile. If the two had pulled across the road, horizontal to him, he might have been able to plow through spinning them as kinetic energy carried him. These guys knew their business, he thought. By remaining vertical to him they eliminated his most likely counter- move.

"Hang on!" he shouted as he shifted the Durango into four-wheel drive.

The access road climbed up a hill to join the main four- lane artery while, on the left, the road dropped off steeply to a lake and fountain but to the right the land remained level. Between the wood line and curb, a wide swath of landscaped bushes, small trees, and grass paralleled the road.

Howington yanked the wheel right and the Durango popped over the curb plowing through shrubbery and flowers. He heard branches scrape the undercarriage as mulch and grass spewed out from underneath its front wheels, leaving the rear to bump over the curb as the Durango clawed its way through azaleas and dogwood onto a clear grassy area.

"Damn fine driving," Steele muttered.

"What are they doing?" Howington shouted, distracted by the gauntlet of shrubbery before him.

"The block has stopped." Stover told him and Steele added, "So has the chaser," as its door opened and five men dressed in black uniforms jumped out and pointed automatic weapons at the careening Durango.

"Get out, get out!" Steele shouted as the earsplitting whump, whump, whump of lead slapping into fiber-glass and sheet-metal filled the vehicle.

"I'm hit," Stover groaned.

As Howington gunned the Durango to get past the vans and up to the main road more rounds slammed into the rear quadrant of the vehicle and men poured out of the two other vans. They too began unloading on Howington's vehicle. More lead splattered against the steel undercarriage.

"Get out now!" Steele shouted again.

Howington sped past the vans, spewing shredded shrubbery behind before bumping back onto the access road from which he tore onto the main artery, squealing as he crossed oncoming traffic to get to the I-66 interchange.

Howington noticed that the sound of the chopper's rotors were still following the vehicle.

"They following us in the vans?" Howington asked.

"No. Not that I can tell." Steele shouted looking back.

"Stover, how are you?"

"I'm hit. Not too bad. In the thigh."

"Tourniquet?" Howington asked.

Stover examined the blood welling up out of his torn pant leg. "No."

"OK. We've got to ditch the copter." Howington said as he craned his neck to look upward toward the Sikorsky HH-60G Pavehawk overhead. Focusing again on the road ahead he followed the flow of traffic onto the entry ramp for the interstate. "Anybody got any ideas?"

"The metro," Steele said. "Take the next exit. There's a station right there. We ditch the car and take the train back into DC. We can switch lines a couple of times. That'll give us time to think of something else to do," Steele said.

"Sounds like a plan," Howington said approvingly.

"I'm in," Stover groaned.

"In the meantime, turn off your cells and take out the batteries," Steele ordered as he pulled out his phone. Trust me; these things can be tracked even when you turn them off so long as they have a battery. Homeland Security does it all the time."

Howington pushed the Durango through the heavy rush-hour traffic and took the next metro exit. The copter followed but from a distance. The white van did not reappear.

"They're waiting for us to go to ground," Howington said.

At the metro station, Howington squealed to a stop at the crossover entrance and the three jogged in, Stover limping.

Once through the flyover, the three arrived at the line of fare machines. Impatiently each man fed a twenty dollar bill in the machine and out popped the paper ticket with a magnetic strip on the back, then they dashed to the turnstiles and fed the tickets through them, looking apprehensively behind, expecting to see hordes of NSA operatives following. They boarded the first train squealing into the station. Because it was rush hour and everyone was trying to get out of Washington, the east bound metro car was almost empty.

"OK, Steele, what the hell is going on here?" Howington demanded, collapsing onto one the plastic seats, "Who were those guys?"

"I think they're CIA or NSA." Steele told him.

"Oh, come on," Howington said with disbelief. "Why would our own guys be after us?"

"Look!" Steele exclaimed. "First things first. I called Janet and told her to get the hell out of town for a while. You ought to do the same."

Howington and Stover's eyes grew wide at the implication of Steele's suggestion.

"Better do it now while we're still on the metro," Steele said. "They'll trace any cell phone call we make."

Howington measured the import of what Steele was telling them. Whoever was after them would also go after their families. And, not only were these people vicious, but they were well-organized and technologically proficient, which sounded more and more like a government operation and less and less like a drug-running cartel. And, now that he thought about it, the presence of the Sikorsky Pavehawk, one of the military's most sophisticated helicopters, screamed the presence of government power. While Howington could not bring himself to believe that the CIA or NSA was after him, he could not deny the events of the past half an hour nor the bleeding wound in Stover's thigh.

They reloaded their batteries. The phone felt heavy in his hand as Howington called Marcie. He could picture the vintage 1960s wall phone ringing in the bright yellow kitchen in the tidy stucco bungalow they had renovated in Cutler Ridge. The phone rang twice.

"Howie!" Marcie's voice betrayed tension and relief. "Oh God Howie, I'm so glad you called."

"What's wrong?"

"I'm not sure. I think somebody was trying to get in the house. They're gone now."

"Listen," Howington said alarmed and relieved at the same time, "I don't have much time. Tell the kids to be careful. Remember the purple sweater?" Howington asked.

There was a pause on the other end. Then in a quiet voice Marcie answered: "Yes, I remember."

"Ok. I've got to go. I love you."

"I love you. Be careful."

"The purple sweater."

"I know."

Howington pushed the off button and pulled the battery out, a tight knot of anger loosening in his stomach. How dare anyone try to hurt Marcie? In all his years at the DEA the lowest scum of drug dealers had never tried anything like that.

Howington was glad he and Marcie had planned for just such an emergency. They had prearranged many years ago that if Howington ever felt the violence of his job was going to spill over into his personal life that he would give Marcie warning through the use of the code phrase "purple sweater." The code meant she needed to leave town. She'd leave word of her location with their attorney. He'd never had to use the plan until today.

He turned to Steele and asked sternly, "Now, what the hell is going on?"

"When you left, the EPIC program started to run in a direction I've never seen before. Ran right to NSA files--it bloody well did-- I saw all kinds of shit. Then, before you could blink, NSA goons were all over the freaking office. They shut it all down. Removed hard drives. They started removing the bloody computers, yanking out cable, running a comprehensive electronic sweep of the building. I stayed in a side office until I heard some suit talking on a radio and decided it was time to bug out."

"That's when you heard "extreme action?" Stover asked.

"Yeah. Seems something is cooking in Culpeper just south of here. The EPIC program started pulling information on some NSA project down there and that was like pouring water on an ant hill." Steele wiped his mouth with his sleeve and looked out into the underground blackness of the metro tunnel.

"Listen," he continued, "these guys mean business. I've already decided what we've got to do."

"Yeah?" Howington said. "What?"

"We've got to get to Culpeper and find out what the hell is going on down there. That seems to be the center of whatever is going on. Otherwise, we're dead."

Howington followed Steele's gaze into the black beyond the subway window. Howington was alarmed, alarmed because he too had come to the same crazy conclusion.

CHAPTER 8

IT WOULD SURPRISE MANY TO KNOW THAT EDWARD SNOWDEN'S REV-
ELATIONS REGARDING NSA ACTIVITIES BARELY SCRATCHED THE SURFACE
OF SURVEILLANCE NOW CONDUCTED UNDER EO2 AUTHORITY. SNOWDEN'S
LEAKS, WHILE DAMAGING, WERE IN FACT LIMITED BY A PREEMPTIVE
BRUSHFIRE OPERATION. SNOWDEN COULD NOT BE ELIMINATED DUE TO
THE HEAVY PUBLICITY SURROUNDING HIS INITIAL ACTIVITIES BUT OPERA-
TIVES WERE ABLE TO MAKE PHYSICAL CONTACT WITH HIM IN THE COURSE
OF HIS LENGTHY DETENTION AT THE MOSCOW AIRPORT. DURING THAT
INTERVAL, SNOWDEN WAS INJECTED WITH COGNITIVE-ALTERING NANO-
STIMULATORS SO AS TO DESTROY ALL REFERENCES WITHIN HIS MEMORY
TO GROUP 929. (SEE THE SEPARATE REPORT REGARDING THE SNOWDEN
AFFAIR IDENTIFIED AS NSA MEMO 2287300013 FOR A MORE COMPLETE
RECITATION OF THE EVENT.)

MOST DISTURBING ABOUT THE SNOWDEN AFFAIR WAS THE FACT
THAT HE HAD WORKED UNDER THE AUSPICES OF GROUP 929 EVEN TO
THE POINT OF HAVING ACCESS TO THE TRANSPORT FACILITY IN CULPEPER.
IT WOULD APPEAR HE SUFFERED AN EMOTIONAL BREAKDOWN AFTER
PARTICIPATING IN THE PROGRAM THERE. THIS POINTS TO THE NEED FOR
MORE RIGOROUS PSYCHOLOGICAL CONDITIONING BEFORE FULL ACCESS IS
GRANTED TO TECHNICIANS.

**---EXCERPTS FROM THE NSA PRESIDENTIAL BRIEFING PAPERS ON THE
ROSWELL INCIDENT**

NSA GROUP 929 OPERATIONS CENTER—FAIRFAX, VIRGINIA

Weir and Sims drove separately to the Op Center in Fairfax, a
campus of three four-story square, blue cubes of reflecting glass and
steel located on a one hundred and thirty-acre campus of oak trees
and black asphalt parking lots just off the I-495 beltway. A single
driveway provided entrance to the complex from the Georgetown
Pike. Behind the forest barrier an eight-foot tall chain-link fence
topped by four strands of barbed wire provided security in addition
to an entrance gatehouse.

Sims arrived first at Building One, where both were required to present identification before being ushered into a waiting area of polished stone floors and wood-paneled walls. Weir busied himself thumbing through that morning's *Washington Post* while Sims checked his email on the phone. They were cordial but obviously separated by rank and speaking little. A uniformed Lieutenant ushered the two into another much larger windowless room dominated by a long wood table around which sat twelve people, each with a laptop. Behind a podium at the opposite end from their entrance stood a tall thin man, the Group 929 Chairman, wearing a pin-stripe suit with a white carnation.

"Colonel Sims, Captain Weir. Please take a seat," the Chairman pointed to two chairs against the wall near his left side. He smiled as he gestured.

"Gentlemen, I believe we are all here," he said to the rest of the group. "Let us begin." He looked to a middle-aged man near the end of the table but against the wall. He was not one of the twelve and neither Weir nor Sims noticed him when they entered the room.

"Mr. Catabin. Why don't we begin with you since it was your call which led the executive committee to call for a full meeting of Group 929. You should know, I think, that Mr. Catabin's neighbor is a prosecutor in Culpeper County who, two days ago, called about the Warrenton Training Center. Mr Catabin?"

"Two days ago my neighbor Mordecai Binford called me on a secure line at Langley," Catabin began in a clipped Chicago accent, gripping the podium with both hands. "I had given him my internal code for emergencies, primarily because our backyards adjoin each other and we keep an eye out on each other's house. Nevertheless, he called specifically to ask me to check on a federal investigation of the Wood's murder-suicide at the Warrenton Training Center."

Suddenly, the attention of the group was focused on Weir and Sims.

"Binford is the county prosecutor and he obviously works closely with the sheriff of the county, Tucker Ray Carter," Catabin continued. "According to Binford, Sheriff Carter found some indications that the investigation of the Wood's death was manufactured and that perhaps there was more to it than Captain Weir had said to him. Binford told me he had specifically checked with the local FBI office, where he, of course, has contacts, and they knew nothing of the investigation. He told me that the sheriff was determined to find out the truth of the matter and, contrary to outward appearances, was a very capable investigator. In addition, he told me that the sheriff had picked up and briefly held a Chinese national who was also investigating the site of the supposed murder-suicide. The sheriff now suspects the Chinese national is here illegally and has already put an inquiry into ICE regarding his status. Binford asked me to use my federal contacts to find out the truth behind the murder-suicide. He has also concluded that the investigation was not legitimate and suspects that drugs may be at the bottom of the affair. As a result, I told him I would check my contacts and let him know what I found out. He believes I work with Delta Force and that I have connections with federal authorities throughout the military intelligence community. Immediately afterwards, I called my superior at 929."

"Thank you, Mr. Catabin, we will get back to you." The Group Chairman resumed his place at the podium. "Now. Reports?" He looked down the table.

"There has been a significant leakage at the DEA EPIC center," one of the seated committee members said as he shut his laptop. "The EPIC program picked up streams of data coming from our Boulder complex, we are attempting to trace the leak but until then we had to clean the facility."

"I'm sorry, did you say 'clean the facility'? Don't you think that's a little extreme?" a younger committee member demanded. "We've had leakage before. I mean, we didn't have to go to that extreme with Snowden."

"This is larger than any we have had before including Snowden. It wouldn't take long to trace movements back to us." The original speaker replied.

"You mean transport movements?" another questioned.

"Yes," the answer came back flat and hard.

There was an involuntary intake of breath from several in the room.

"That must have been one helluva data dump to be able to trace transport movements," came one comment.

"How is that possible?" another at the table asked incredulously.

"We are still trying to trace the source," the original speaker answered. "Quite frankly with the scope and breadth of the project, combined with the rather porous nature of data accumulation and dissemination, it is not surprising that EPIC will sometimes pick up patterns. But having said that I do recognize that a significant data loss like the one we just experienced is unprecedented. And, just to be clear when I say 'transport movements,' I mean all transport movements." The blank stares prompted him to elaborate, "Terrestrial and non-terrestrial."

The room erupted, "Impossible!" "What?" "No!"

"Right, gentlemen, let's work our way through this," the Group Chairman said in a loud voice. "Continue," he gestured to the speaker who originally broached the topic. "Explain what happened during the clean-out." It was less a request than a stern command.

"Well, we sent a team over to DEA to clean computers when the data dump was detected. One of our team members, a new recruit I might add, started to play cowboy. I think he had watched too many movies. He used the term 'extreme measures' inadvertently while others were listening. One person in particular, Ian Steele, apparently heard the conversation and reacted. He left the building and dodged our personnel sweep. Obviously, he had arranged a pickup from the Miami DEA agents to evade what he thought was an elimination effort on our part. Our new recruit organized a 'Grab and Run' team to pick them all up at their rendezvous point. Gunfire was exchanged. That is what is claimed anyway. We are trying to verify. The DEA group and Steele escaped."

"There was no EO2 finding in this situation," a balding man with bifocals observed. "Why were you rounding up personnel?"

"As I said, we had a cowboy in our midst," the speaker explained.

The Group Chairman nodded and looked at the assembled committee as a whole. "You," he said, pointing at a man with Asian features, "did you have something to add?"

"Yes," he said loud enough to be heard over the side conversations that had started up. "This explains cryptologic reports we have gotten from Signals."

"Quiet people! Go on."

"Our Chinese mainland signals-post has picked up a lot of chatter regarding U.S. aerospace engineering efforts in the last month.

There is also chatter on US launch events not related to NASA. This has been going on for the past month. We picked up on it separate from regular CIA analysis ---and of course understood the true significance of the launch reports."

The low level buzz in the room resumed as the men around the table took in the significance of what was just said.

"In addition," the committee member continued, "there is increased scrutiny of the Martian transit. The implications of that are obvious. Again, we have been monitoring and evaluating how and where this data leakage occurred. It is clearly a second breakout separate from the one at DEA."

"Also, I learned this morning Signals reports strong indications that a Chinese Dragon Team has entered the United States with either Warrenton or the Fed as the focus of interest. That explains why the Chinese national the sheriff holds has such interest in our facilities in Culpeper."

The room erupted for a second time.

The Group Chairman rapped the podium with his empty glass. "Quiet! Now, we are going to deal with this in an orderly manner. Colonel Sims?"

Sims stood with his hands clasped in front of him, "As ordered, we monitored the Wood couple," he said. "They were, after all, the first of the transported to return to the point of embarkation. When Ed Wood entered the transport facility grounds, Weir eliminated him: primarily to prevent contact with arriving Transportees. We were subsequently forced to eliminate Mrs. Wood. Weir staged a murder-suicide on the Warrenton Training Center property, bringing the investigation under federal jurisdiction. Unfortunately our meddlesome sheriff has taken it upon himself to investigate anything in his county regardless of jurisdiction. We are monitoring the Chinese national," he concluded.

"Thank you, Colonel Sims," the Chairman announced. "Now, Captain Weir. No keep your seat. There is no need for you to speak unless you have something to add in addition to what has already been said. The executive committee specifically wanted you here so that you could understand the full scope of the problem. Normally we would move you gradually. But there is no time and truly, Captain, your record indicates you are fully capable to take on your entire compliment of responsibilities." The Group Chair nodded slightly and allowed the faintest of a smile to cross his face.

"I think it is clear why the executive committee has called a full meeting of 929," the Chairman continued. "Let me summarize. There are multiple unexplained data leakages. Our operations in Culpeper are clearly indicated in the leaks. In addition, the Chinese have knowledge of our operations. In fact, they know to look at the Martian Transit. That is unprecedented. They have sent a Dragon Team to investigate. Again, unprecedented. And we have a DEA team on the loose, probably heading to Culpeper. Does that sound correct?" The Group Chair looked around the table. "Fine. Suggestions?"

An elderly man at the far end of the table had remained silent and impassive during the meeting. His long grey eyebrows swept up and sideways, adding drama to his long wrinkled face. When he spoke his deep baritone resonated to the far corners of the room.

"This meets all the criteria of a breakout. In addition it is un-controlled and unpredictable. I don't think anyone in the room can deny that. We have modeled this scenario for thirty years. The re-sult has always been the same. Unless a brushfire operation is under-taken, chaos will reign. Look at Edward Snowden. To a lesser extent Julian Assange. I don't think we have any choice."

A heavy silence stretched out before the assemblage until; final-ly, the Group Chair broke the awful spell of the old man's conclusion.

"Comments?" he asked.

A voice clawed through the curtain of silence. "I agree that this is a serious breach," the younger man who had spoken earlier said. "I don't think we've had one this bad --although the Oklahoma situation comes close," he said referring to the 1995 clean up in Oklahoma City. In that data breakout, 929 operatives had been forced to destroy a federal building before the information leakage was contained. "And," he continued, "as I understand it, no brushfire operation was ordered then."

"True, but this breakout is multi-layered and involves a non-friendly foreign power. Vastly larger in scale," a middle aged African-American sporting a West Point ring pointed out. He stared down at the table and folded his hands.

Another committee member drew in a sharp intake of breath, signaling his intent to speak, "I agree that this is serious but not to the degree to request brushfire authorization. There is already an EO2 finding. Isn't that enough to allow us to deal with all of this? I know the Wood couple is not connected to the Chinese data leak but that clean-up operation is bound up in the entirety of the situation. We can thank our mystery Chinese visitor for that."

"Brushfire is premature," someone else added. "Yes, premature," several said simultaneously. In relief, others nodded in agreement.

The elderly man spoke in a harsh whisper, his baritone reverberating through the fabric of the room, "You can ignore the facts, but they remain nonetheless. This breakout cannot be contained unless drastic measures are used. Half measures always fail. You know this from our past computer mockups. Mark my words gentlemen. *We will have to spill blood.*"

"Alright, enough melodramatics," the Group Chairman declared, his voice going up an octave. "This is clearly a breakout…. but is this a meltdown scenario envisioned when a full-on brushfire operation was formulated as a response?"

"Multiple layers of information leakage," The African-American West Point Officer responded. "Foreign power involvement. A gun-battle at the Fairfax Government Center now being reported on the local news channels. A cowboy DEA agent probably on his way to Culpeper. Knowledge of our Transport Center in Culpeper. The Martian Transit. Given the fact that we are already on the verge of a breakout as it is…this very well may push us into an uncontrolled environment. I'd say this is a meltdown or we are in the precursor to one. This is much worse than the Snowden affair."

It was clear that, although unspoken, all on the committee understood the full implications of a brushfire operation. It was nothing less than a Presidential declaration of martial law coinciding with a fabricated war against whichever country the United States was currently at odds. The point of brushfire was to create as much destruction as necessary to divert attention from the data outbreak. In addition the destruction allowed for mass death with a plausible rationale that did not implicate the NSA or Group 929. Its purpose was to destroy inconvenient knowledge that could unmask the entirety of NSA operations.

"Gentlemen," the Group Chairman said firmly, "I believe before we continue any further it might be prudent for our guests to retire for a short time. If you would be so kind as to leave while we take these matters up? Thank you. We will call you back directly."

Weir, Sims and Catabin left the room through the same door they entered. When the door shut the Group Chairman addressed himself to the group as a whole --with special emphasis directed towards the proponents of brushfire.

"How *dare* you discuss brushfire in front of non-group members?" he began, slamming his hand down on the podium, his eyes flashing. "Are you mad!" A sliver of spittle appeared on his lip, produced by the fury of the exclamation. "You know that protocol requires elimination of any non-authorized personnel who gain knowledge of brushfire. Are you ready to discuss *that*? Sims is in charge of the operation in Culpeper. Shall we lose *him* now? We can lose Weir. I don't care about him. But Catabin shows great promise. Shall we eliminate him? I gave you more than ample opportunity to stop discussions, but no, you had to go back to brushfire." He paused shaking his head, "What can you be thinking? All of you."

While the men and women of the 929 committee debated how to deal with their breakout problem Cho had his own breakout situation in Culpeper. He took the downhill side street to Yowell Meadow Park—walking briskly, arms swinging. The crisp September air felt good against his skin and the sun winked through the still green trees, flickering across his face in patterns of warmth. He closed his eyes and continued walking, only to open them when the terrain leveled and he knew he was at Blue Ridge Avenue. Crossing the busy road, he scurried onto the paved walking trail that traced the park's perimeter. Here he walked with purpose driving his steps faster, exhaling puffs of white breath in the morning air, willing his body to exert itself more vigorously. It was hopeless he knew, but somehow, over the years, he had convinced himself that exercise would help delay an episode.

And, an episode was coming on: strong and heavy, he felt "the Need" gathering inside, twisting itself around his mind, slithering ever so quietly into every thought, ready to burst out and reveal itself to him and to the whole of creation if he let it. Cho had hoped that satisfying the almost insane desire to find out what was happening in Culpeper, first born in Beijing, would somehow take the place of "the need." In fact he had had glimmers of hope that such a thing might have happened when he first saw Mt. Pony silhouetted against the evening sky. The sight of the small mountain had sent waves of electric shock through him so strong that he had had to pull over to the side of the road and was glad that he did as the first wave of nausea hit him and he vomited until there was nothing left but dry heaves.

That was when he knew Culpeper, in some very strange and bizarre way, was tied to "the Need" he had discovered a month after he woke up in that San Diego park.

"The need," Cho thought to himself, picturing the word with quotation marks around it, a word that he always thought of in English instead of his native Mandarin. Perhaps this was not surprising given his immersion in all things American, even while in China, but still Cho wondered why this most intimate of things, so interwoven with his life, always manifested itself in another language. He thought about it in English, he pictured it in English—even in his nightmarish dreams that first announced its monthly arrival; the nightmarish dialogue, when there was dialogue, was also in English.

Cho pumped his arms harder, walking even faster, willing himself to somehow drive the burning lust from his mind.

After storming around the park five times, Cho dropped to a park bench to rest and watched a flock of twenty or thirty geese swimming on the small pond in front of him. They moved in unison as though controlled by some unseen force. The grey patterned birds swam away from him, almost as soon as he sat, then honking, took flight—an undulating wave up and into the cloudless blue sky.

"What have I become?" he thought almost tearfully to himself as he tapped out a cigarette. The answer came hard and fast and demanding satisfaction. It pushed him up out from the bench, towards a pair of women walking the track for exercise.

Now, it demanded. Now. In the daylight. Now. With people to watch. Now. Now. Now. Now. Now. Now now now nownownownownownow.

He wrenched himself free, moaning and staggering away from the pair of women, towards a wooded area at the end of the paved trail. He slumped down on a fallen log, panting in shallow breaths, holding his hands to his chest. Slowly his mind cleared, like the pain of a groin kick ebbing away, "the need" moved back to the darker animal recesses of his mind. But he knew, he knew, tonight was his last chance before it would take over completely. Tonight, he would have to go away for a day. Tonight. And, he realized, somehow tonight he would have to give Xia Zin, the Dragon Team leader, the slip.

The thought of those dead eyes lodged in Xia Zin's expressionless face, frightened him, but not so much as "the need" demanded him. Demanded him absolutely.

FAIRFAX, VIRGINIA--GROUP 929 OPERATIONS CENTER

"Ah, gentlemen, please come back in," said the Group Chairman, as Weir, Sims and Catabin entered the room. The three had said little to each other during the break and they continued the silence as they assembled themselves on three chairs at the far end of the room from the podium. Once they settled the Chairman began speaking in the sort of low pleasant voice one might hear on National Public Radio or the BBC—measured, superior and unemotional.

"We have arrived at a consensus as to how to proceed in this situation," he began, looking at the others around the table, as if to include them in his pronouncements. "And, we concur that a quasi -breakout has occurred. The president is being informed as we speak." He pressed a button on a small remote control, a section of the wall slid sideways to reveal a large flat screen, labeled at the top "EO2 Operation Protocols." Underneath script flowed in bullet-paragraph form.

"Ah, yes, Captain Weir and Mr. Catabin. Colonel Sims will brief you on the meaning of the terms here. Colonel Sims, you will oversee operations and coordinate with Operative Smith. Captain Weir, I believe you have already met Smith in Boulder." He then turned back to the screen and with a blood-red laser pointer highlighted each paragraph as he went over Group 929's plan to deal with the crisis. The red remained fixed on the last paragraph when he absentmindedly set down the pointer and left it on.

Weir noticed that the red dot hovered over the phrase *Free Transport*. In his mind the smeared light beam splashed over the room --bathing them all in blood.

And so it has come to this, Weir thought to himself as he drove west on I-66 in the heavy traffic after the meeting. He gripped the steering wheel mechanically, automatically weaving in and out of lanes, as he thought about the day's events. When the three of them walked back into the room, Weir already had a sick feeling about where all this was heading. Sims' recital of his part in the Woods' elimination shocked Weir. Just to hear it seemed somehow filthy and corrupt. He knew the details even better than Sims. But to actually hear it recited out loud made Weir want to melt away. Even worse, even more chilling, was the clinical way in which Group 929 members received the news. Like they were listening to the frigging damn weather report, he mused.

Weir had shot and killed Ed Wood. Oh yes, he thought, I killed the hell out of him allright. *Killed the hell out of him.* The bruised area in the center of his chest, where Wood's 9mm slug had slammed into his Kevlar vest, reminded him of the encounter every time he moved. Only later did he learn that Wood was not a crazed, American Muslim convert intent on waging jihad in America, as Sims had first described the man to Weir. Yes, he thought, Sims let me get my hands wet before letting me in on the full story. Then Sims ordered him to abduct Pat Wood. And when Weir balked, Sims reminded him that he had no choice. None. *Do you want your children to be orphans?* Sims asked him flatly, face flushed black, eyes reptilian.

Abduction was not killing in Weir's mind. And he had done it. Lying to himself about what would happen afterwards. But, he told himself, I knew what dark treat I had in my hand when I pushed it on her face. I knew. I knew. It was pathetically easy. She whimpered when he first entered the darkened room at the Bed and Breakfast and then froze, like a gazelle sometimes does before the lion has its way. *Don't resist and you won't be hurt*, he had told her. He held the drug-soaked gauze to her face. She tried then to move but he held her tight from behind, lifting her off the ground so her legs only twitched in the air. Then he and Martinez carried her limp body away. Later he realized he had not just knocked her out --he had killed her too. And Sims had known all along what that rich cocktail of drugs would do to her. *Makes it all the easier*, he had explained to Weir afterwards.

While still in shock, Weir gathered the two bodies, dumped them together in a field, took some photos, and shipped them to a special NSA pathology unit for the official autopsy report necessary for civilian paperwork. And, the autopsy was a good backstop for any busybody that popped up in local enforcement. Then they were off to the funeral home in Ohio. Like two sides of beef wrapped up in one neat little package.

Only it wasn't so neat. Weir learned a lot during the meeting. From what was said. And from what was not said. The banality of it all was the most unnerving thing about the whole experience. You would have thought they were discussing stock options, not life and death. Not mothers and fathers and sisters and brothers and sons and daughters. Not living flesh that feels pain and sorrow and love and separation and loneliness. No, none of that was said or alluded to. No, Weir shook his head as he drove reviewing the situation, what was said was much more neat and clean and analytical. Sort of the way the men at Group 929 conducted themselves. Ordered. Civil. Well-dressed. Erudite. There had been nothing around that nasty little table to hint at death or decay. Or deception. Weir grimaced as he automatically wove out of one lane and into another, his orders were explicit. He would harvest. He would harvest expeditiously.

"Harvest," now there's a new euphemism. Harvest the DEA team when they arrive in Culpeper. Harvest the Sheriff. Harvest the Chinese national Wang Lee. Harvest anyone else who it appears has knowledge from this latest data leak. Harvest the hell out of the place. Oh yes, harvest, harvest, harvest. Collateral damage was acceptable to complete the mission.

"I guess Pat Wood was collateral damage," he muttered aloud to the empty car. Weir gripped the steering wheel tighter turning onto the exit ramp for Route 29 at Gainesville. He pulled up to a red light and stopped. *I killed the hell out of that whole family. Ed. Pat. Maybe their kids come next. Maybe they start wondering what happened to mom and pop. Maybe the suits in that room decide the whole damn family has to be cleaned up in a brushfire operation. Brushfire. He didn't know what the hell that was but he was sure it wasn't good for anyone. Not for anyone except the nameless bureaucrats in that merciless room.*

God, what monsters these people were. And God help me for having been their instrument.

It had been relatively late in the game when Weir had learned that "harvest" did not mean kill but simply to abduct and prepare for transport. And transport took place in the lowest level of the Federal Reserve. The level he had been barred from until today. As for transport, well, Sims told him he would see that for himself tonight. Apparently a series of transportees were returning just in time for Weir to be initiated into the elite group in the Federal Reserve basement. Sims had rocked back on his heels and thrust his head upwards when he had told him, *Ha! Yes indeed Weir, you will become one of us!* Then Sims had jammed his hands in his pockets and jiggled his keys and change --- eying Weir with something other than delight.

What have I become? Weir asked himself. The light turned green. He drove back into hell.

CULPEPER VIRGINIA—THE ABANDONED NALLES FARM

Cho had scouted out the old farm house during his motorcycle trips around the Culpeper County. Located just on the outskirts of town, near the Buffalo Wild Wings Sports Bar, it was the perfect place for him to disappear. With grey wood siding that had long ago given up the last vestiges of paint, the old farmhouse stood firm against the ravages of the weather. Its old tin roof was rusted brown-- but it still kept the rain out. Furthermore the second floor was empty and dry and far away from prying eyes.

Practice makes perfect. Cho knew the truth of that. Ritualistically Cho had begun to prepare a week before the need took over. When he was in San Diego and Beijing, Cho had a special safe place to use every month. In Culpeper, he had to work on the fly but he had found the farmhouse almost immediately. He tracked and identified his "subjects" as he called them. Then he captured them. Then he collected his kit. Then he tried to hold off as long as he could.

But yesterday in the park he almost lost it, he had almost surrendered so sweetly to the desire. But, somehow he had fought it, knowing that today he would submit to that which could no longer be denied. In his rush to get to the farmhouse, he forgot to say anything to the villainous Dragon Team leader. Cho just left after dinner giving the leader the slip. Cho had fired up the motorcycle and had driven off into the night. At the abandoned farm, he stashed the bike in a broken-down barn, covering it with an old tarp he had found there. The owners of the safe-house to whom the motorcycle belonged, knew better than to ask questions about its whereabouts. They were just glad to know their relatives in the mainland were still alive. For that matter, Cho thought, they probably were glad just to be alive. The reports of missing Chinese-Americans having spread like wildfire amongst the expat Chinese community around the world. And most knew Dragon Teams were the culprits.

When Cho turned towards the house, the world seemed to shift. The need controlled entirely. Horrified at what he had become he still moved purposefully towards the house. He didn't want to. God knew he wanted to be anywhere else but here. At the doorway he accidentally scraped the threshold and above he heard the sounds of panic begin.

Up the staircase one foot at a time he fought. He knew what would come.

The caged animals in the second story room thrashed seeking escape. Like the geese at the pond, they sensed something was not right in the fabric of the universe, and they wanted to leave. But they could not.

And in tears of remorse Cho satisfied the need with methodical slaughter.

Later, his humanity shredded, his hands bloodied, he collapsed in self-loathing, questioning as he did during every episode how it was that he had become the monster that he was.

CHAPTER 9

TRANSPORTEES FALL INTO TWO CATEGORIES: 1.THOSE PRE-SELECTED BY
THE ALIEN ENTITY (AE) AND 2. THOSE CHOSEN BY NSA OPERATIVES. THE
SELECTION PROCESS USED BY THE AE IS UNKNOWN; HOWEVER, THE NAME
AND IDENTIFYING INFORMATION OF THE SUBJECT IS ALWAYS ACCURATE
WHEN PROVIDED TO GROUP 929 OPERATIVES. THE AE ALSO GIVES OUT
UNSPECIFIED REQUESTS FOR SUBJECTS. NSA OPERATIVES THEN HARVEST
WHOEVER FITS THE PURPOSES OF NATIONAL SECURITY -- OTHERWISE
KNOWN AS A "FREE HARVEST".

AS AN ADDED SECURITY PRECAUTION, GROUP 929 TECHNICIANS HAVE
DEVELOPED PSYCHOLOGICAL IMPLANTATIONS RENDERING TRANSPORTEES
EMOTIONALLY AND PSYCHOLOGICALLY DEFECTIVE. THE PURPOSE OF THE
IMPLANTATIONS IS TO MAKE TRANSPORTEES LESS CREDITABLE SHOULD
THE TRANSPORT-INDUCED AMNESIA WEAR OFF. VARIOUS ODD, BUT HARM-
LESS, HABITS ARE IMPLANTED WHICH IRREPARABLY HARM ANY TRANS-
PORTEE'S UNAUTHORIZED REPORT. NSA OPERATIVES IMMEDIATELY REVEAL
THE KNOWN HABIT WHEN A LEAK OCCURS OR IS IMMINENT -- THUS
DESTROYING THE CREDIBILITY OF THE TRANSPORTED.

**--EXCERPTS FROM THE NSA PRESIDENTIAL BRIEFING PAPERS ON THE
ROSWELL INCIDENT**

CULPEPER, VIRGINIA---FROST CAFÉ

John Howington and Stu Stover had parked the big Dodge
Durango at the extreme east end of Davis Street near the restored
Train Depot, after which each then had taken a different route on
foot to Frost Café, the point being to flush out anyone following
them. However, he noticed nothing unusual as he meandered to the
Café, stopping at various shops to browse and reconnoiter the street
behind him through the reflections in the store windows. He knew
Stover was doing the same on a different street.

With one last look down Davis Street, Howington crossed to
enter the Café by the corner door. The two-story brick building
anchored the busiest corner in downtown Culpeper, giving patrons

a window from which to watch the never ending parade of people and cars streaming past. Howington had noted this feature when he selected the building for lunch. The windows plus the existence of two exits so necessary for a quick retreat made it a perfect place to eat insofar as Howington was concerned.

After entering he saw Ian Steele and Stover already seated at a booth. As he slid in, Stu Stover scooted sideways to give him room.

"You see anything?" Ian Steele asked.

"No, you?" Howington responded.

"No."

"Ok, let's eat," Howington said.

Stover reached in his pocket and pulled out a handful of quarters and, dumping the collection on the table, he started to feed coins into the table juke box.

"Bloody hell," Steele exclaimed, watching Stover's project, "stop fooling about."

"Oh come on Steele," Stover responded as Conway Twitty's voice began to blare over the loud speakers. "Check out the selections here. You can't eat in place like this and not play old country-western songs."

"Damn," Steele shook his head and looked down. Stover kept punching codes.

"Alright let's try to focus right now." Howington responded. "And, for crying out loud, Stu, leave off the quarters for a bit. OK?"

"What did you find out?" Howington turned and asked Steele.

"Ok, Howie. Here is my analysis," Steele paused for dramatic effect, "We're buggered plain and simple."

"No surprise there," Stover said.

"Well, we already knew that when Stu here took the slug to the leg three days ago," Howington said.

"Yeah, Steele, come on, give a little more here. If I'm buggered, I want to know who is doing the buggering," Stover said.

"Right you are, Stover" Steele said with a gallows smile and then more seriously, "I spent the morning on the internet checking up on our friends at the NSA. Nothing obvious but I do know a few hacking tricks. The info I got was a bit dodgy but as best as I can put it together they know who we are and that we're in Culpeper."

"What? How is that even possible?" Howington exclaimed in disbelief.

"I'm telling you this is a sophisticated operation." Steele rubbed his eyes and continued, "You want the bad part?"

"It can't be any worse than the songs Stu picked," Howington replied.

"They *are* looking for us."

"No joke," Stover said.

"I definitely picked up on 'extreme action,'" Steele said. "They mean to take us out."

Stover and Howington sat in stunned silence.

"I understand what happened with Stu could be some sort of royal screw-up," Howington said referring to the shooting and Stover's bandaged thigh. "I've seen it plenty of times in under-cover work."

"This isn't undercover work," Steele assured him grimly. "This has government written all over it."

"I'll just contact DEA and get it straightened out," Howington said.

"Did you not understand the 'extreme action' part I told you?" Steele asked incredulously. "Look, I know how this works. They shoot first and ask questions later. This is not the DEA we are talking about. This is NSA. They don't mess about. They got Patriot Act authority to do whatever the bloody hell strikes them to do. Period. And right now we're on the menu."

"I get the 'extreme action' part," Stover told him. "But what's 'looking for us' mean?"

"It means, my Ho-Ho eating friend, that an NSA team is al-ready tasked to hunt us down."

"And take us out?" Stover asked casually.

"As I said, they don't mess about."

"So, we're buggered," Stover said. "What else?"

"That was the easy part to find out. The harder bit was that we are definitely in the right place. Whatever it is that kicked off the whole empty house sequence with EPIC is centered here."

"Well, that would make the Warrenton Training Center a prime suspect," Howington said.

"Yeah, that, or the monstrosity on the hill just outside of town," Stover said referring to the Federal Reserve.

"So it would seem," Howington replied, giving reign to his own gut instincts regarding the looming building on the hill.

"What exactly are we into, Steele?" Stover asked as a waitress brought them their drinks. "Have we stumbled onto some high-level drug operation, espionage, what?"

Steele took a sip from his glass, then resumed, "The resources all point to a government operation," he reflected. "But I am beginning to wonder if what we have here is something akin to a narco-state in the making. And if it is, well, it's damn big if it uses the NSA to do its dirty work," he added, referring to a nation-state that is funded by drugs and controlled by a drug cartel.

"How so?" Howington asked.

"Let's look at why we're here. You have a lot of dead bodies on a dock in Miami. A lot of money missing. And we have two Chinese nationals with fake identities who take off in a hurry to Culpeper. Hell, last time I checked, you can't leave China without official say-so. Your source of information for all this is a snitch you guys at Miami DEA use for drug operations. Sounds like drugs to me. Then we have the little dust up here when EPIC picks up an empty house. NSA agents swarm like wasps from a kicked nest. NSA: that's government. Big time. Now remember, look at the forest and not the trees, the purpose of EPIC is to pick up drug-supply patterns from random bits of data floating around in cyber space. Now, what if EPIC has been doing its job all along, but because the scale of national drug-running is so large, the pattern it picks up overwhelms the system. An empty house is the best EPIC can do given the search parameters in the program. But it *is* doing its job."

Howington used the interruption created by the arrival of their lunch to think about what Steele had said. In the excitement of it all he had lost track of why they came to Virginia: the two Chinese nationals.

"What about the Chinese subjects Steele, you didn't mention them," he said when the waitress had left. "Did you find out any more on them?"

"Why, as a matter of fact, I was saving the best for last," Steele said with a wink.

"Do, pray tell, enlighten us." Stover suggested, loading up his French fries with salt. "You've brought us so much good news."

"Right. The Chinese." Steele pointedly directed his comments to Howington, "Seems your informant in Miami was spot on. They might be involved in drugs. But, same as with the NSA, they want in on whatever is going on here in Culpeper. And the NSA knows exactly where they are, which is conveniently enough, at a Chinese takeaway called the Golden Tiger. One of them made an appearance in the local court here two days ago."

"What charge?" Howington asked.

"Impeding traffic. Bugger must have been driving like they do in Shanghai."

"So has the NSA picked them up yet?"

"Don't know."

"At this point who cares," Stover said. "I mean, Chinese or no Chinese, the NSA is after us. Maybe we get lucky and they go after the Chinese first. That's the only thing I see good from all this."

"Nothing good in any of it, Stu," Howington said. "But maybe if we get to our Chinese guests first, we might get a better idea of what's what."

"Yeah, well you know I'm not a glass-half-empty sort of guy, but I think Steele has it right this time," Stover said.

"Before you go about quoting me, wipe the bleeding ketchup from your face," Steele said.

"Just saying, for the record," Stover made an ineffectual dab at his face, "it looks like game over, sure enough. But what the hell, doesn't look like we have any choice about it anyway, so let's just enjoy the ride while it lasts."

"Easy for you to say Stu, you don't have a family. I want off as soon as I can," Steele replied.

As they finished their meal, Howington considered the options. Clearly they had stumbled on something much larger than a regular drug operation. He hated where his mind was taking him. He had seen what happened in Columbia during the height of the cocaine trade. This looked similar but with one difference. It was *his* government, not Virginia or Florida or Iowa. This was the *federal government* of the United States of America he was dealing with. And not only that, but the most secretive branch: the NSA. Howington knew how violent and warped things became when drugs and money and power all jumped into bed with each other. Corruption became the least of your worries then. Survival was more the main objective.

He couldn't go to the DEA. They might be compromised. When you got right down to it, there was really no one he could go to without fear of corruption. Money and drugs had a way of sifting into every facet of an organization once it got a foothold. He didn't know who or what was compromised but he did know that not everyone in the country was compromised. *Not everyone*. He held to that fact. Not everyone was involved no matter how big. In a flash of insight he found a way out of the maze in which they found themselves. The key to their survival was to convince enough people that something was very wrong at the NSA. Ed Snowden had tried that although ineffectually. Still, getting the word out about the NSA would save them, he thought. Not even the NSA could touch them if they got the right information to the public. In another flash of insight, he recalled the last scene of *Three Days of the Condor:* Robert Redford in a blue pea-jacket, with a bundle of incriminating information, positioning himself defiantly in front of the *New York Times*, knowing that disclosure was the only thing that would save him from the knives of the CIA.

Snowden had tried something similar and look at him now, Howington thought, he was a stranger in a strange land, an exile with nowhere to go. And then there was Julian Assange who had let the American public know what was going on behind closed doors during the 2016 presidential election. Even though he told the truth to the world he still stayed trapped up in an Ecuadoran Embassy in London. Howington couldn't end like that. Steele and Stu couldn't end like that. They all had families who were vulnerable and who made them vulnerable at the same time. There had to be a better way. He held on to his original thought. Not everyone was involved.

"I know what we need to do," Howington said.

CULPEPER VIRGINIA ----THE FEDERAL RESERVE

At Sims' insistence, Weir rode with him to the Federal Reserve.

"Here we are," Sims said as he wheeled the black government-issue SUV up the hill to the facility, and drew to a stop in front of the entrance bay at the base of the four-story concrete building. A metal door opened its dark maw.

"Now, Weir, understand, you are cleared for this, but until you get familiarized, stick next to me," he said. "You'll be surprised by what you see." Then he swiveled his head to look directly at Weir. The two dark, expressionless orbs in Sims' face encompassed Weir's entire world at that instant. "You'll understand afterwards," Sims said.

The SUV lurched forward, the line between light and dark cutting across the vehicle until they fully entered and the metal door slid behind cutting them off from the outside world.

A large empty room with a raised loading dock at the end greeted the two men. Weir's eyes adjusted to the gloom and he was reminded of a factory warehouse: unpainted concrete walls and square concrete pillars illuminated by florescent lighting.

Another SUV and two large black vans were already parked in the loading bay, and as Sims parked, Weir noted that there was room for more vehicles.

As the two got out, a door on the raised loading platform opened, and the bright artificial light from the other room cut across the concrete floor.

"Follow me," Sims said. The slamming of the car doors echoed in the vastness of the room.

Weir jiggled his keys in his pocket as he trailed behind Sims down a maze of corridors bathed in white florescent light, the effect of which intensified the white walls and floor. At a door marked "3A-11," Sims stopped and placed his palm on an identifier scanner next to the door jam. Inside, they were greeted by a technician in a white clinical lab coat, in a room dominated by a bank of glass windows, all looking upon a large empty room—again painted white. Weir noticed the room beyond the windows appeared covered by a cushioned coating dotted at intervals by dark disks. The man in the coat motioned for them to follow him to an instrument panel.

"Everything looks nominal for transport arrival," their greeter announced.

"Still on schedule?" Sims asked.

"Yes, 23:27 more or less," he said.

"Ah, very good. Very good indeed." Sims rocked back on his heels. "Weir, let me introduce you to Frank Hill. Mr. Hill is the director of transportation."

"Transportation?" Weir asked.

"He hasn't been briefed, I take it," Hill said to Sims.

"Special case here, special case here," Sims said fluttering his hands in the air. "Group thought it best to immerse Weir directly."

"Mr. Weir," Hill said, offering him a cold, weak handshake. "Just stay out of the way when things start hopping."

"Might as well get started with the brief now," Sims said, "Any objections, Hill?"   "No. Things are quiet at present."

"Precisely why we came up a little early," Sims said as they exchanged glances. "Why don't you take us to Room 35, and while we are on our way you can begin to explain what you do here?"

"Yes, that's fine," Hill said after a brief pause. "We've got time. Follow me.   I'm going to give you the Cliff Notes version here, Mr. Weir. Later you can be briefed more in depth. But this should give you a framework to reference what you see tonight."

As they walked down a long hallway, Hill became more expansive, "In 1948 an alien spacecraft crashed in Roswell, New Mexico. The Army, and then the NSA, took control of the craft for scientific research. The craft is now in a secure location unknown to me. At first this was the only contact we had with the alien entity."

"What? Wait a minute. Did you just say what I thought you said?" Weir asked, stopping. Hill stopped ahead of him and turned around.

"Yes. You heard me correctly."

"Have you seen it?" Weir asked. "I mean come on. This has already been in the movies."

"No, I haven't seen it, but I've seen video and schematic drawings. That's enough for me. And those damn movies you mentioned are just plants by Group." Hill visible gathered his thoughts. "But, that is not my area of expertise. Now, we don't have much time. " Hill turned and started lecturing again in a flat monotone.

"Abductions and cattle mutilations started to occur. Crop circles popped up. We had strong suspicions that alien entities were behind the phenomena from the beginning. In 1973, for whatever reason, the alien entity communicated its desire to continue abductions-- but with our help."

"Our help?" Weir asked incredulously. "I assume we told them to go to hell."

"Initially we did. But the choice we were given was that the abductions would continue with or without our help—but those without our help would be more violent." Hill paused, "More public."

"So?"

"Mr. Weir, what would happen to a society if the members of that society knew that anyone could be abducted at any time? That the government was powerless to stop this violation of public order? There would be anarchy, misery, in effect greater subjugation to the alien entity."

"That sounds more like an excuse than a reason," Weir said.

"Well, we all have our opinions, Mr. Weir, don't we," Hill answered icily.

They walked in silence for a second.

"In fact, Mr. Weir," Hill continued, "that is exactly what we do here. We facilitate the harvest of transportees at this facility. And in a few hours you will see how this occurs. Then, perhaps, you will have a different opinion. Ah, here we are, Room 35." Hill placed his palm against the flat identifier plate beside the door. It unlocked and Hill pushed the door open. They filed into the room. Weir heard the door shut and lock behind them.

In the bright artificial light, Weir saw a row of what looked like ten dental chairs along with rolling stools, lining one side of the narrow room. Various banks of computer touch screens interspersed with seemingly antique toggles and switches jammed the other side.

"This is where we process transportees before and after a transit," Hill told them. "They are under sedation at the time and have little to no memory of what occurs here."

"Totally harmless, I assure you," Sims said.

"Umm…quite," Hill continued, "This is also where we implant security measures for transportees."

"Security measures?" Weir asked, latching onto a single concept that might make sense out of the rush of information he was being asked to absorb.

"Yes, security measures. You'll soon be up to speed on all of this. Group decided early on that transportees, for their own good, mind you, should have certain security measures psychologically implanted, to ease the transition back into their old lives."

Hill was animated now, Weir thought, almost frighteningly so.

"It is quite amazing actually," the lanky transport director continued. "One would think that implantation would require psychotherapy or electronic stimulation. In fact, through analyzing debris from the Roswell site, and applying our own developing knowledge, we now know that memories, habits, personality, really everything that makes us functioning beings, is actually a combination of chemical and hormone interactions." Here he held up his hand as if warding off questions, "I know, I know. You've heard about electronic stimulation and electronic brain waves as measures of brain activity. All true. But what we now know is that electronic stimulation is necessary to release the chemical and hormone baths that actually make up memory or, if you will, as in this case, habit."

Hill walked over to bank of instruments. "It is so simple really. We merely insert nanostimulators into the blood stream. They are pre-programmed to lodge in specific areas of the brain."

"Nano stimulators?" Weir asked.

"Nanotechnology is the new frontier, Weir," Hill said. "Basically we develop motors, batteries, even computer functions, at a molecular level. Bundle it all in a package about the size of a cell and inject it."

"Totally harmless," Sims added.

"Yes, quite." Hill said agreeably. "The nano instruments stimulate predetermined areas of the subject's brain: releasing chemicals and hormones of the subject's own making. And that is the beauty of it all. The subject himself creates the transitioning habit -- and the amnesia. We don't implant a habit-- per se-- we merely release what is already there, but perhaps in a different order."

"It's not totally random," Sims said.

"No, not totally random," Hill agreed. "The habits are designed to protect the security of this operation. It is hoped that the transportees merely have a lost a month. Like an alcoholic bender. But should the amnesia wear off, the security habits will do their job."

"I don't know-- this all sounds very abstract. Give me an example of a security habit." Weir asked.

"Sure," Hill responded. "Transportees always become ill when they see Mt. Pony. I don't mean deathly ill. They are programmed to feel nauseous. The point of it is to discourage anyone from coming back and compromising our security."

"Look, we need to move along here," Sims said darting a nod at Hill. "Mr. Hill, would you mind giving Mr. Weir an injection for his security clearance?"

"Injection! What the hell?" Weir said, his voice rising.

"Now, Weir, what do you think we are going to do --give you a new habit? Ha." Sims asked smiling.

"What sort of injection?" Weir asked determinedly.

"Merely a nanoinjection so that you will be able to access all doors in the facility." Hill said.

"We've all had it. How are you to be the security head for the facility if you cannot open our security doors?" Sims asked rhetorically.

"And what if I refuse?" Weir said, knowing the answer.

"Now, now, Weir," Sims said with a cold smile, his eyes darkening a blue black, "we both know you long ago gave up saying no." His smile vanished. "Do it."

Weir allowed himself to be seated in the chair.

"This won't hurt a bit," Hill said as he sat next to Weir on the rolling stool and begin to enter command codes into a data display attached to an instrument tower next to the dentist-like chair. Weir heard mechanical noises out of his vision.

"Sometimes there is a bit of physical reaction, nothing to be concerned about, but just as a precaution let's put some safety straps on so you don't get hurt." Hill said soothingly as straps mechanically wrapped around Weir's arms, legs and torso.

"Wait just a minute. What's going on here?" Weir asked alarmed.

"Not to worry, Weir, this is all standard procedure," Sims said, leering over Weir's now- reclining body in the chair. A long needle-like probe extruded from the end of a metallic instrument mounted on the upright next to the chair. Hill, humming, was typing more commands in the data display attached to the upright stand.

A red laser dot centered on Weir's nose, and then moved to illuminate an area inside the nasal cavity.

"Is that thing going in my nose?" Weir asked, a note of hysteria in his voice. "I thought this was an injection."

"Hold still!" Hill said peevishly.

"You're making this way too complicated, Weir," Sims chimed in. "Now hold still. The best injection site is in the nasal cavity. You won't feel a thing. Either hold still or deal with the consequences later."

"Weir felt the cold needle prick high in his nose and then nothing. He heard crunching noises, felt odd vibrations and then felt a pressure pushing upwards before a final crack. It stopped. A rush of warmth spread across his forehead.

"That's it?" Weir asked after the needle withdrew.

Sims and Hill looked at each other. Hill said, "You might feel a little dislocation for an hour or so. Just rest here and we'll be back. A technician will be monitoring you remotely," he pointed to a black spherical camera housing in the ceiling.

"What? You mean you're just going to leave me?" Weir asked.

"Ha. Not to worry Weir," Sims said. "All standard procedure, I assure you. You'll be fine."

Weir heard Sims, but he didn't recognize the words. He only knew that they were loud and somehow ugly. Repulsive.

"Alright," Hill said, "the probes are positioning themselves."

"Righto. Have your technician bring him up when he recovers. I want him on site when the transports arrive."

"Is this one up to the job?" Hill asked.

"Group thinks so. I'm reserving judgment. Why do you ask?"

"There's just something about him I don't trust. He asks too many questions. Reminds me of that idiot Snowden."

"Maybe. Maybe." Sims said thoughtfully, "But, he is the security director for the program and asking questions is part of the job."

"I just don't want a repeat of that Snowden freak."

"An interesting comparison, Hill. I'll keep it in mind." Sims said.

The two left the room. After they left, Weir began to whimper, like a dog hurt badly.

CULPEPER—BEST BUY MOTEL

They picked The Federal Reserve first because it was the easiest to access. Later, Howington decided, they would reconnoiter the Warrenton Training Center. The trio found an army surplus dealer just on the edge of town and purchased camo gear and backpacks. It had been easy to hack an ATM at a bank branch office. So they could stock up and pay with cash. At the Wal-Mart they purchased ammo, binoculars and a handful of burner phones. Steele accessed Google earth to get some idea of the topography of the area but in the end they decided the GPS systems on their new phones was just as accurate and easier to use in the field.

"This is the craziest black op I've ever seen," Steele said while they were assembling gear in their day packs.

"How so?" Howington asked.

"This place is visible for miles. If you wanted to keep something secret, why not locate it somewhere more remote? At least the Warrenton Training Center is in the middle of the woods."

"Sometimes the best cover is one right in the open for God and everyone to see," Stover observed. "Who in their right mind would set up a drug operation on the side of the mountain next to a busy highway?" he asked rhetorically. "Oh, that's right," he answered himself in a mock surprised tone. "I forgot. We're talking about the friggin United States Government. You ever hear of the 'guv'ment,' " he went on, mispronouncing the word deliberately and slowly, "doing anything right?"

"Doing it right --or just stupid, the location actually makes it harder for us to reconnoiter, don't you think?" Howington said.

Howington had in mind the spaghetti confluence of roads that ran near the Federal Reserve, a confluence which had made it difficult for them to find a location hidden from curious eyes, particularly since three men sitting in one area for hours on end in the middle of a divided roadway was bound to draw attention. The same was true for any surveillance located in a residential area. In the end, it was Howington had who spied the empty hilltop they would use as an observation post.

"All right, gentlemen, let's get loaded up," Howington ordered as he shifted on his small camo daypack and moved to open the motel room door. In the evening darkness, they had little worry of being seen at the motel. Nevertheless, they hustled into the Durango SUV. Stover drove, taking Route 15 into town, snaking south on South East Street before turning east on Chandler Street towards the Federal Reserve. They bumped over a railroad crossing, then passed the national cemetery extension, a collection of ghostly white tombstones on a dark green hillside. Once past the cemetery, the land rose steeply in a cascade of open and wooded hilltops to a summit about a mile from the road. As prearranged, Stover dropped Steele and Howington off at the edge of the open fields and drove off, all the while remaining in radio contact with the ground team. Stover drove in a random pattern over the roads near the drop-off point: his purpose being to remain mobile so that he could pick them up in an instant's notice.

Steele and Howington quickly marched up the hill. At the first stand of trees, they crouched in the dark and oriented themselves to the ground and the mental maps in their heads.

"We need to bear to the left a bit," Steele said pointing with his whole hand, military style, and started off: his boots making quick work of the steep rough terrain. They stopped again at the summit of the hill where, although topped by trees and rocks, there was a clearing with an open view of the Federal Reserve across the valley. Steele did a quick field check of the surroundings, scanning the sloping hillsides, and walking a thirty-yard wide perimeter, while Howington eyeballed the fully lighted facility with his binoculars.

"They aren't making any secret of the place, are they?" he remarked. Just then he noticed three black vans enter the facility, drive past the guard gate, and angle up towards an entrance bay. A metallic door opened upwards and the vans rolled in. The door snapped back down.

"Some vehicular activity," Howington whispered into a mike clipped to his shirt collar.

"Roger that," Stover replied in Howington's earpiece.

Continuing to scan the facility, Howington saw a three story, semi-circular concrete building spreading open towards him. In the center of the arc created by the building was a flat round paved space, clearly meant to be a plaza, the open space nevertheless struck Stover as so odd that he scanned it closely with binoculars and noted there were no plantings or seating areas within it. The building itself resembled open building blocks set one on top of the other. The open side of the block, which was glass set in a concrete frame faced the circular courtyard. The structure itself was covered with what looked like jungle vines giving the impression of a long ago abandoned ruin. The rear of the semi-circular building burrowed into the side of Mt. Pony, the hillside of which bristled with antenna and venting pipes revealing the complex's vast underground structure.

Howington noted, that from time to time, figures paced outside the building, mirrored by others just as methodically pacing behind the glass walls. It all reminded him of an ant hill on high alert.

Steele crouched down beside Howington. "Sweep is clear," he reported. "It looks like cows use this place more than anyone or anything else," he added, pointing to a dry round splat of cow dung in front of them.

"Ok. Let's set up," Howington said, putting down the binoculars and shifted off his pack. Steele did the same. The two retrieved collapsible tripods and Howington mounted his binoculars on one. Steele did the same, after which they arranged seating using logs and tree trunks, but separated by ten yards, where each positioned to scan the facility.

Situated on the empty hilltop, they heard the faint sounds of the town around them. Sirens sometimes wailed in the distance. Cars engines droned and shifted gears. Dogs barked. Crickets chirped, announcing the end of summer. And somewhere in the large field complex, cattle lowed. All of the sounds were loud enough to hear, but distant enough to give the impression of silence. Howington traced air traffic overhead by the blinking lights. Some lights were lower, indicating smaller single-engine planes. Higher up, jets streamed across the carpet of stars in the clear September air.

In the quiet, Howington wondered how Marcie, his wife, was coping. Thank God, he mused to himself, that they had rehearsed in the past what to do in an emergency. They had a plan and he hoped she stuck to it. Part of that plan meant *even he* did not know where she was nor would he know until he was sure the present danger was over. The lack of information was maddening but necessary. The thought of anyone trying to hurt her, or use her, enraged him in a deep and profound way. The anger curled, hot and heavy, in the recesses of his mind: ready to unleash, wanting to lash at the first opportunity.

Steele's whispered voice coming from Howington's earpiece roused him from his musings, "Head's up. Something's making its way through the brush."

"Where?" Howington whispered back.

"Hard to tell. Bugger seems to be coming from behind my position."

"Probably a cow."

"Shall I reconnoiter?" Steele asked.

"Yes."

"Roger that."

Howington was not worried. The likelihood of anyone being up on the hilltop at this time of night was remote. He settled back to scan the facility.

"Couldn't find anything," Steele reported back ten minutes later.

"Set up position further back. Remain within optics scan of the facility," Howington replied.

Howington heard Steele moving through the underbrush off to the left and behind. A few minutes later, Steele reported he was repositioned. It was then that Howington noted the lights at the facility dimming. At the same time he noticed that the few figures that he saw in the windows or on the ground outside moved out of sight. The facility now appeared empty.

"Something's up," Howington said in the mike, "Stu, get in position for pick-up if necessary."

"Howie, look up, ten o'clock from the horizon," Steele said. At first Howington saw nothing. Then a star winked into existence where there had been the black drape of sky. Then another, then another, the stars reappeared as if an edge revealed them as it slid downwards towards the ground. On a hunch, he scanned downwards to locate the other edge. He saw a star disappear, then another lower.

"You catching this, Steele?" Howington asked, referring to a video attachment to Steele's optics.

"Affirmative." Steele replied adding, "Whatever it is, it's huge." At Steele's observation, Howington noticed the black hole's vast scale. The destroyer -sized dark oblong continued to slide silently downwards and to center over the Federal Reserve complex.

"It's going to land," Steele said.

Howington watched the top of Mt. Pony warp and shimmer as the blackness moved like a ghost down and over the face of The Federal Reserve sending a rippling edge rolling down the building's front until it rested on the black semicircular plaza. Howington watched the building shimmer but not disappear and in a flash of insight he knew that the object somehow projected the images around it as a form of camouflage. Visible stealth it was called. He had heard of efforts to produce such a technology but did not know it actually existed.

"This is one hell of a drug operation," Steele observed dryly as they digitally recorded the scene.

"No joke," Howington replied in the same tone.

Stover arrived on position; Howington waived him off to patrol the side road again in readiness for their exit. But, except for a short increase in venting from the side of the hill, marked by puffs of white vapor in the chill September night, nothing else happened. After fifteen minutes, they shut off the recording.

And, as is usually the case, the unusual becomes the normal. Howington leaned back in his seated position to relax and shifted his feet outward. He looked down at his watch, and in doing so almost missed the black shape's exit. As he looked up, a shifting of light at the complex on the side of Mt. Pony caught his attention. The bottom edge moved silently upwards, the oblong shimmering becoming smaller, the oblong black portion larger, as it slowly moved up and away from the building. It stopped and hovered over Mt. Pony, a black hole in the fabric of the universe. Then at an astonishing speed much faster than its approach, the object shot upwards. In seconds it was gone somewhere off into the blackness of the star-strewn sky. Like distant thunder, Howington heard a low rumble march across the heavens, announcing the object's passage through the atmosphere. Frozen, he continued to stare upwards, a sense of awe and dread spreading across his mind. Then, in the corner of his eye, he saw a flash of light much like a shooting star, burst in a white streak far above.

"Damn!" Steele exclaimed.

"Did you record that?" Howington asked.

"No, too quick."

"Same here," Howington responded.

"What the bloody hell *was* that?"

"I thought it might have been a blimp."

"That wasn't any blimp."

"What was that thing?" Howington asked again more to himself than Steele.

"I think we just saw what all the fuss is about," Steele replied tonelessly.

THE FEDERAL RESERVE—CULPEPER

The bright light hurt Weir's eyes.

He squinted. When a shadow passed over, he opened one eye to see a head and upper body silhouetted against the light.

"He's coming to, Mr. Sims," a woman said.

"Very good," Weir heard Sims' voice crackle over an intercom. "Get him up here as soon as possible." The shadow moved and he shut his eye again.

"Where am I?" Weir croaked, his mouth strangely dry.

"You're in the recovery room. You've been out for a little over three hours," the female voice replied. Weir opened his eye to adjust to the light. He saw the woman with her back to him, monitoring a computer screen and occasionally jotting notes on a clipboard.

"What happened," he asked, "was I in a car accident?"

She turned, and Weir saw that she was a young African-American, slight of build, hair pinned up in a bun. "No. No car accident," she said handing him an opened plastic orange juice container. "You're fine. We just performed a procedure to give you access to secure locations in the facility. It should all come back to you in a moment. You're recovering quite well actually."

The tart sweetness of the juice soothed his dry, swollen tongue and shortly afterwards he felt the sugar kick into his bloodstream, jump starting his still sluggish body and electrifying his lethargic mind. Memories flooded his brain, rushing and tumbling into order: the ride to the center, the walk to the room he was in now, the injection. After that he remembered nothing as if he had just awoken from a deep numbing sleep.

"Feeling better?" the woman asked him.

"Still a little groggy, but yes," Weir replied.

"Good, we need to get you moving back upstairs."

"Upstairs?"

"To the transport room," she said as explanation.

"Right. The transport room," he caught her eye, "what goes on there?" She did not look away but silently looked up towards the ceiling, signaling the conversation was not private.

"You'll be briefed shortly," she replied emotionlessly. But her eyes, for one fleeting moment, conveyed fear. Then the connection shut down. The experience unnerved Weir.

Consequently, it was with dread that he followed her through a maze of white hallways to the door marked 3A-11. Then, at her urging, he placed his hand against the authenticator on the wall next to the door. A red light scanned his palm, the door emitted clicks, and he turned the door knob stepping into a bustling room filled with technicians buzzing about. He felt as if he had just joined a club.

"Ah, Weir, feeling ok?" Sims asked turning.

"Yes, but you should have warned me about the injection," Weir complained.

"Well, yes, perhaps --but what's done is done." Sims smiled. Sensing that the rotund man was in a jovial mood, Weir moved over to the bank of windows overlooking the large empty room beyond the glass. He noted it remained empty, which was not true of the control room. People moved in and out of the room, conferring and monitoring computer screens, speaking softly into microphones attached to their heads.

"They will be arriving shortly," Sims said. "It will be good for you to see this. Now just stand here while I join the others at the control board."

The minutes passed. Then a voice said loud enough for the entire room to hear: "We have acquisition of signal."

"Stations, people," Frank Hill said loudly. The room hummed with activity. The murmuring became louder. All heads were bowed before computer screens.

"Nominal approach," someone announced.

"Switching to main power bus B," another technician said.

"Powering down externals."

"Locking down," Weir heard the swish of airtight seals clamping shut.

"Secondary shutdown commence," and the lighting dimmed.

"50. We have visual," a woman's voice announced, "initiating image capture."

"40. 30. Locking on." Electric sparks began to weave in the room beyond the windows and shadows danced about the control room.

"Switching to main ground."

"20"

"Nominal approach. 5 by 5."

"10"

"Ok people let's be alert," Sims said, "I want full lockdown now."

"Initiating," came a response.

"Water Pressure at 100 psi. Manned and ready."

"All systems are nominal," Hill announced.

"ETA three minutes."

"Docking now." Weir felt his hair stand on end from the electric charge in the air and in the other room the arcs intensified. Weir detected a high-pitched whine coming from above.

"Secondary acquisition."

"Locking on our signal."

"On my mark, 5-4-3-2-1. Entry."

The arc of a bright metallic sphere began to peak through the ceiling of the room beyond the windows and Weir was reminded of a balloon slowly descending through the ceiling to the floor. No doors opened. The ceiling, as far as Weir could tell, remained unchanged, but somehow the shining sphere was moving through the ceiling.

"Initiate drains," was the command as it came to rest on the floor. In response the round depressions in the padded floor popped up.

At once, the sphere began to disappear from the top down. It merely melted away, a solid horizontal line moving down the side. As the line met the circumference of the sphere something began to drip down its sides, in a larger and larger volume, until it cascaded out onto the floor. The sphere disappeared, leaving a slowly collapsing mass of what looked like some sort of yellow glutinous substance streaked with red and grey, within which there was movement of what he saw, horrified, was an arm, several legs, torsos, heads all jerking and writhing. He saw one head open its mouth to release a torrent of fluid. Weir could not tell if it was vomit or some of the jelly like mass. A hand pushed through the mass and grasped at the air.

"Ok, initiate clean up," someone ordered.

Sprinklers began spraying water from the ceiling and the walls. The high pressure jets cut through the still collapsing mound of jelly to reveal a nightmarish mass of people: jerking, quivering, moaning, vomiting, grasping, and writhing in a horrifying mess.

Hill cupped his hand over a mouthpiece attached to his headset, "Send in the teams now."

Weir saw a door open and four figures entered the room each dressed in a yellow- hooded hazmat suit. Surrounding the mass of humanity and slime, they turned on high-pressure hoses and washed down the mess making sure all of it went down the drains-- leaving only the bodies on the floor. A high-intensity ultraviolet light now switched on bathing the scene in a fluorescent red as a fine mist fell from the ceiling. During all of this, the figures in the hazmat suits rolled and turned the living so that the light and mist enveloped the whole of their bodies.

"Decontamination complete," Weir heard a computerized voice say calmly. Minutes passed. Horrified, Weir continued to watch the activity in the room below.

"Departure signal," this announcement brought a new energy to the control room which Weir quickly realized focused on the departure of whatever had just arrived.

"Ok, people let's be alert," Hill said.

"Acquisition of image. Target 1298."

"We always try to video and analyze separate areas of the ship," Sims whispered to Weir. "This is the only time we get a chance. The coordinates are predetermined before each arrival. Hopefully we'll be able to map the exterior of the vehicle with enough detail to learn something here."

"Departure lane clear. Civilian aircraft diverted"

"Confirmed. Towers diverting to alternate routes."

"Terrestrial path cleared. Satellite field clear."

"Affirmative. NORAD confirms."

"Powering up."

"Let's move, people," Hill said sternly into his mouth-piece, looking at the outer room where figures were scurrying to drag away the living and the dead.

"Main bus B powering up. Electronic shield up." Weir began to see arcs of static electricity dance across the ceiling of the now empty reception room beyond the glass.

"Picking up prelaunch targeting."

"Ok. Locked on. Prelaunch target confirmed. Nominal 5 by 5."

"Uncoupling. Vehicle movement detected."

Weir felt a slight vibration in the room as if the gravitational field itself were shifting.

"Building clearance."

"Electromagnetic sensors in place and rolling."

"Nominal feed."

"Accelerating."

"Copy that. Acquiring electromagnetic pulse."

"Altitude adjustment now. Switching to satellite feed."

"Leaving earth atmosphere."

"Nominal insertion into Mars transit."

And then, in a flash, it was over. The entire room powered down. Hazmat suited figures went back into the room to clean up what remained. The buzz of activity in the control room dropped as each person silently scanned their respective screens.

"Jeesh. How do they do that?" one man whispered loud enough for Weir to hear.

Sims clapped Weir on the back. "Now we go back to Room 35 to finish the job."

"Finish the job?"

"Implantation. It's got to happen fast while they are still in the initial unconscious stage."

"And then?" Weir asked.

"Ha! Then they are sedated while we launder their clothes, patch them up and send them back to their little lives, none the wiser."

Weir looked out to the red illuminated reception room, the figures in hazmat suits a sickly green in the blood red glow, the others in the control room bent over computer screens, like so many worshippers at an altar, their faces an electronic blue and green, flickering with inhuman intensity in the darkness—disembodied from any human form, eyes shrunken into dark orbs of evil. And he caught a glimpse of his own reflection in the glass wall—a face, unrecognizable in the distorting low light, dominated by glinting darkness where eyes should be.

"Come on, Weir," Sims said, clapping Weir on the back for a second time. "We've got work to do."

GARY CLOSE

CHAPTER 10

ETHICAL CONSIDERATIONS: AFTER THE DECISION TO COOPERATE WITH THE ALIEN ENTITY (AE) AND THE REALIZATION OF WHAT THAT ENTAILED, DEBATE ENSUED WITHIN GROUP 929 AND WITHIN THE NSA IN GENERAL REGARDING THE ETHICAL UNDERPINNING FOR SUCH ACTIONS. THE DEBATE SOON CRYSTALIZED INTO TWO CAMPS LABELED BY THE MAIN PROPONENTS OF EACH. THE PERCY CAMP, LED BY THEN SEN. CHARLES H. PERCY, CONTENDED THAT FULL DISCLOSURE WAS THE ONLY ETHICAL SOLUTION TO THE GROWING PROBLEM OF ABDUCTIONS BECAUSE, IN THE FINAL ANALYSIS, THE ABDUCTEES THEMSELVES SHOULD KNOW BEFOREHAND THAT THEY WERE SELECTED.

SECONDLY, PERCY ARGUED THAT ABDUCTEES, UPON THEIR RETURN, SHOULD BE COMPENSATED BY THE GOVERNMENT MUCH AS WOUNDED COMBATANTS ARE NOW. WHILE FULL DISCLOSURE WOULD BE POLITICALLY PAINFUL GIVEN THE DECADES OF DENIAL SINCE 1948, PERCY AND HIS SUPPORTERS WITHIN THE NSA MAINTAINED THAT, IN THE LONG RUN, THE COUNTRY WOULD BE BETTER ABLE TO RESIST MORE AGGRESSIVE MOVES BY THE ALIEN ENTITY. IN ADDITION PERCY CLAIMED THE UNFORESEEN ETHICAL COMPROMISES NONDISCLOSURE WOULD NECESSARILY CREATE IN THE LONG RUN COULD PERVERT SOCIETY IN WAYS UNKNOWN AT PRESENT BUT NONETHELESS BE AS HARMFUL AS THE ALIEN ABDUCTION PRO-GRAM ITSELF.

SEN. FRANK CHURCH HEADED THE NONDISCLOSURE CAMP. HE AND HIS ALLIES ARGUED THAT NONDISCLOSURE ALLOWED THE GOVERNMENT TO CONTROL THE ALIEN TECHNOLOGY, RETAIN GOVERNMENTAL LEGITIMACY AND SPARE THE POPULATION THE DEMORALIZATION SUCH KNOWLEDGE WOULD CREATE. CHURCH CONTENDED THAT GOVERNMENTAL CONTROL OF INFORMATION AND OF THE ABDUCTEES THEMSELVES WOULD ENSURE MORE HUMANE TREATMENT THAN THE RANDOM AND UNFETTERED ACTIONS OF A POPULATION WHO LEARNED ABDUCTEES LIVED AMONGST THEM.

SEN. CHURCH'S ARGUMENTS PREVAILED AND HE WORKED, THROUGH THE SO-CALLED "CHURCH COMMITTEE," TO DELEGITIMIZE AND RESTRICT THE CENTRAL INTELLIGENCE AGENCY. GROUP 929 RECOMMENDED CIA RESTRICTIONS SO AS TO PREVENT ACCIDENTAL DISCLOSURE OF GROUP 929 ACTIVITIES SUCH AS THE TRANSPORT PROGRAM. (SEE GROUP 929 RECOMMENDATION AND POSITION PAPER 5558-AD-8327).

IN 1975 CHURCH FAMOUSLY SPOKE OUT AGAINST THE POWER OF THE NSA, CALLING IT "AN ABYSS FROM WHICH WE COULD NEVER RETURN." THIS WAS A GROUP 929-SUGGESTED DIVERSION TO COVER CHURCH'S STRONG SUPPORT OF NSA ACTIVITIES. (SEE GROUP 929 RECOMMENDATIONS AT VOL. 20, 1975-MM-5626 AND ALSO IAN MILLER'S DISSENT WRITTEN IN RESPONSE TO THE OFFICIAL RECOMMENDATION AND FILED IN THE APPENDIX TO VOL.20 AT PAGE 1297(B) (3).

----EXCERPTS FROM THE NSA PRESIDENTIAL BRIEFING PAPERS ON THE ROSWELL INCIDENT

HAZEL RIVER TRAIL---SHENANDOAH NATIONAL PARK, VIRGINIA

Weir checked his boots, making sure that the laces were tight in order to provide a good snug fit, since the trail wound its way up through some rocky and steep terrain and the last thing he wanted was a blister.

Satisfied, he rechecked the contents of the LL Bean day pack: water, matches in a water-tight container, a sandwich, and some jerky, a topographic map, plastic whistle for emergencies, tender in the form of dry river birch bark he had collected and bagged for just such an occasion, extra socks and a sweater, wool not cotton, and a small tarp.

"How are you guys doing?" he asked his family after hitching the pack on his shoulders and snugging it down with a waist strap.

"Just about ready," Rebecca answered as she tightened the straps to the day packs for ten-year-old Hunter and eight-year-old Heather, both of whom were eager to start on what they called "the adventure."

"Ok, I think we're all set," Rebecca said snugging her own pack. Weir was struck by how beautiful she looked with her raven hair pulled back in a ponytail, eyes bright, cheeks flushed a healthy rose. She caught his eye and winked, flashing a hint of a smile in the process.

"Right, guys," Weir said turning to address the children, "We need to talk first."

"We know, Dad. We know," the two dutifully responded.

"It never hurts to be prepared," he reminded them. "Remember this is not a park. This is not like cartoons. These are the woods-- and they don't care if you live or die." Though they had heard the lecture many times before, Hunter and Heather's eyes widened, while Rebecca, arms crossed, frowned her disapproval. "You'll scare the fun right out of them," she had said to him in the past. But undeterred, Weir had insisted the lecture might save their lives one day.

"What is the most dangerous thing if you get lost?" he asked.

"Fear," Hunter answered.

"That's right. Fear. Don't ever be afraid. You can always overcome a problem if you don't let fear take over. Your Mom and I will find you. But it might take a couple days. If you get lost what should you do?"

"Blow the whistle," Heather said.

"That's right. Let people know where you are. What happens if you blow the whistle for a long time and nothing happens?"

"Stay together." Hunter replied.

"What else?"

"If it's light we walk downhill." Heather said.

"If it starts to get dark, what do you do?" Weir asked Hunter.

"Don't walk in the dark," the boy said. "Find a place to sleep. Use the tarp. Build a fire. Come on Dad, let's go!"

"What is the other most dangerous thing in the woods?" Weir asked undeterred.

"Wet and cold," Heather said.

"That's right. Always stay dry. Use the fire to stay warm. And where do you walk to?"

"Keep walking downhill till we hit water," Hunter replied. "Then follow the water because it will lead us to people. Can we go now, Dad?"

"Yeah, let's roll," Weir replied and started walking up the trail head. The children followed with Rebecca pulling drag duty to catch stragglers, quickly falling into a rhythm as they climbed up the dirt road ending at the trail head. Empty cabins tucked away in the woods peeked through the late summer foliage. The Hazel River, off to the right and below, thundered its way through the rocky canyon casting spray and haze into the air.

"Can we go swimming in the river?" Hunter asked.

"Yes," his father told him. "Up above."

Weir loved to hike. As a child growing up in Kansas he had ranged the fields and creeks but for the most part the topography was flat. The Blue Ridge Mountains were different and that was what made them so interesting to him. He loved the varied terrain, the clean water, the hemlocks and oaks towering above on the rocky ledges and mossy hillsides. And he loved the physical exertion of punching his way up a hill side, resting at the top to drink water, and contemplating the shifting patterns of light on the leaves and trail.

He hoped to share that exuberance with his children.

And, with Rebecca. She had been a trooper. More at home at the cosmetics counter, she had jumped into his world of woods and hiking with both feet - literally.

They crossed a small seep coming from the mountainside to the left.

"See the deer prints?" Weir pointed to the soft mud for his children to see the parallel grooves left by hooves pressing deep into the wet soil. "He must have stopped here to drink," Weir said.

"How do you know that, Dad?" Hunter asked.

"See how the tracks are close together. When deer run or walk, the hooves spread out. I'm just guessing, Hunter. But in tracking, you try to think like a deer. The water here is clear and clean. It's on the trail where he can see a long way off. The tracks look like he stopped. So, it stands to reason that he stopped to drink."

"Do you think he saw us?" Heather asked.

"Could be," Weir told her. "Let's look at the tracks some more."

They saw where the deer moved off. Then the hooves dug deep in the mud and the parallel grooves spread out wide, in a Y formation, and disappeared up the mountainside.

"Why did he run, Dad?" Heather asked. "We weren't going to hurt him. I'd pet him."

"He didn't know that, Heather. Deer don't know what we are thinking. And sometimes we do things to hurt deer --without even knowing that we are doing it. Sometimes that happens in other things, too."

"Like when they jump in front of cars, right, Dad?"

"Exactly, son, no one wants to hit a deer when they are driving, but the deer doesn't know that and it panics. If the deer stood still and did nothing, he would be fine. But they jump into traffic and get killed," his father replied.

But, some people hunt deer, don't they, Dad?" Hunter asked. "So maybe he knows about that and thinks we're hunting him."

"Could be."

"I'd run if I was a deer," Hunter said.

The sun angled down through the forest cover: flickering, dancing in the undergrowth. They came to the first crossing of the river.

"Take your shoes off and carry them otherwise you'll have wet feet," Weir instructed.

The cold water shocked and Weir's feet ached from the crossing but then felt refreshed after he dried them off and put on his shoes and socks. They walked over a sandy ridge which followed the river, angling between hemlocks and boulders the size of small cars. The second crossing was more difficult because the rocks were slippery and Rebecca fell, only to jump up again, laughing.

The third crossing was done by hopping from one rock to another without even taking off their shoes. Then they took another trail that angled off the Hazel Mountain trail. An old farming road, it was less steep than the trail, and even had a stone horse-trough at a spring for the horses that had labored the abandoned road a century earlier.

"Let's stop at the falls," Rebecca suggested.

"Sounds like a plan to me," Weir said.

The old road, after climbing around the side of the mountain, leveled out onto the remains of a flat grassy field that had been mostly taken over by the advancing forest. At one end a cliff rose vertically and a small stream fell off its face to the grass below.

"Can we swim here?" Heather asked.

"Sure." Weir answered. He choked a little when he said it: looking into his daughter's trusting brown eyes.

"Sure," he repeated, "just you stay close."

"I'll watch her Dad," Hunter said, "Don't worry."

Weir nodded, tears unexpectedly springing to his eyes. Hiding the welling emotion from Hunter, he busied himself with taking off his pack.

"Water?" he asked Rebecca, unclipping the old-style metal canteen from the pack exterior.

"Thanks," she reached up and grasped the canteen, their fingers touched, and he looked deep into her eyes, the canteen lingering between them.

"Hmm…what's that about?" she asked.

"Just glad to be here. Glad you're here. Glad the kids are here."

"It *is* a good day so far," she said. "They haven't even thought to fight yet." They could hear Hunter and Heather laughing amongst the deep forest green, the tinkling waterfall and the splashing of their play, a testament to the Eden-like atmosphere of the moment. "It's nice to hear you say that, John. My rough-and-ready man in uniform doesn't usually say much more than "let's roll" or "that's a plan," she flashed a lopsided grin at him.

"Got a lot on my mind right now," he told her.

"Work?"

"Yes, it's a lot more complicated than I thought when I signed up."

"I've noticed you haven't seemed yourself lately."

Weir sat down, drawing his knees up to his chest and wrapping his arms around them. He looked through the green to make sure he could see the kids. The silence stretched between them.

"Been a lot of silent evenings," Rebecca prompted him.

"I shouldn't even talk about it," Weir said.

"Honey, you're in the Quartermaster Corps. How top secret can it be?" Rebecca said with a hint of jovial sarcasm.

"It is."

"Ok. Well, there's just us and the trees."

"It's complicated."

"You said that already. Look, what is the basic problem? Everything can be broken down to principle. So…what is the bottom-line problem here? You don't have to tell me specifics."

Weir watched Hunter splash in the shallow pool under the falls while Heather, moving with a ballerina's grace, danced in and out of the water, and found his eyes stung with tears again.

"Basic Principles," he told her, looking up at the green canopy above, "How about this? Is it wrong to hurt people for the greater good?"

Surprisingly, her answer came swift and sure, "Baby, isn't that what the army is all about?"

"What if you hurt innocent people?"

"I think a lot of people were innocent in Dresden," Rebecca replied, referring to the horrendous firebombing of the German city during World War II. "It was terrible that civilians died but it was definitely worse that someone like Hitler lived."

"What if you're not in a war?"

"Baby, what is this? Is it something to do with terrorism? That's the same as war as far as I'm concerned."

"It's not the same as terrorism. Not like you would think it….. but, it's bad. Real bad."

"Why not just tell me?"

"The thing is, Rebecca, the less you know, the safer you are. And, after some of the things I've learned, I'm not sure anyone is safe anymore. So, even if I could tell you, I don't think I should."

"It's a little scary to hear you say something like that."

"Just remember this," Weir said with a sudden sense of premonition, "I won't ever let anything happen to you and the kids. Ever." Just then they heard a minor skirmish between Heather and Hunter.

"Break time seems to be up," Weir said relieved, he jumped up and headed towards the pool. Troubled, Rebecca followed him through the underbrush.

They dried quickly, hitched up their packs again, and started off down the trail to turn left onto the Hazel Mountain trail. It wound around the peak and leveled off into a maze of narrow rocky paths surrounded by hemlock and rhododendron bushes. He stopped at the intersection with Sam's Ridge Trail. There they stopped and, leaning against moss-covered boulders ate lunch. Then, refreshed, they started down the steep switchback.

"Stop!" Weir whispered sharply.

Four deer, two being older fawns, walked single file down the trail in front of them, then angled off to the side. The last deer, older and heavier, clearly a buck by the early autumn antler growth, stood back and looked towards Weir. It snorted, pawed the ground and lowered its velvet-covered rack in his direction.

The buck and Weir stood stock still, breath puffing out into the shadowed forest, each warily observing the other. Then abruptly, the buck snorted and leapt backwards to bound into the underbrush, its white tail straight up like a flag in the shadowed green foliage. They stood silently for an interval, waiting to see if more animals would appear. Then satisfied no more were forthcoming, Weir signaled to start moving again.

"Wow! Did you see that," Hunter asked. "He looked like he was ready to fight you, Dad!"

"Maybe he was. That was his family there."

"We weren't going to hurt them," Heather said. "Why would they want to fight us?"

"They don't know, honey. There are plenty of people who would."

Weir looked at his daughter again. Only he didn't see his daughter. Instead he remembered that first night at the transport center. In the mass of jelly and bodies he saw something. At first he wasn't sure what it was. It was so little and hidden by everything else. He looked closer and then he saw a child's hand and then the girl herself, no older than Heather, looking at the window where Weir was standing. In shock, he saw the child silently mouthing "mommy, daddy" over and over again, until the hazmat suits dragged her off.

"Dad," Hunter said, releasing him from the grip of the memory, "I bet if you were a deer, you'd be like that last big one. You wouldn't let anyone hurt the other deer. I bet you would fight, wouldn't you Dad? I bet you'd take on just about anybody."

CULPEPER COUNTY COURTHOUSE---VIRGINIA

The sheriff marched across the courthouse square. Binford had watched his big bulk hop down the stairs from the Sheriff's Office then charge across the grass to the courthouse entrance. Expecting the visit, Binford got up to meet Carter at the office door.

"Just take messages if anyone calls," he said to his secretary. "I'm fixing to meet with the sheriff and it might take a bit."

"What if the Judge calls?"

"Interrupt me if the Judge or God calls but no one else," Binford said with a laugh. As he moved towards the office door, it banged open and Sheriff Carter entered the room.

"Morning," Carter said as he took off his hat. "Got a minute?"

"Been expecting you," Binford responded.

"What did you find out?" Carter asked once they closed the door to Binford's office.

"My contacts with the Feds say there is nothing to this. They say this guy Weir is legit. And quite frankly, they want to know why I care since the matter is under federal jurisdiction."

"That's rich," Carter snorted. "They must think my mama raised an idiot to buy that story."

"I got to admit, I didn't like it much either, Sheriff. I think I just got the runaround. But on the other hand I know my source personally. I don't think he would just lie to me. You? What did you find out?"

"Well, them Chinese are a close-mouthed bunch. But I can tell the two new ones got 'em scared to death. And they don't do much work either. Been a customer there a lot lately and the new ones seem to ride around a lot on motorcycles-- looking at things."

"Well, Sheriff, nothing wrong in that. And it sure doesn't point to them being involved in the Woods' murder-suicide."

"Hells-bells, I know that Mordecai."

"I got to admit, Sheriff, that I don't like this one bit. Those photos were faked. Even I could tell that. And it's no coincidence that Wang Lee was picked up sniffing around where the Woods couple were supposedly killed and found."

"We could put it in front of a grand jury," Carter suggested.

"Put what? We got nothing other than a suspicious-looking *federal*," and here Binford drew out the word federal to add emphasis, "report and photographs. I'm sure the first thing the Judge is going to ask is why a federal case is even in his damn courtroom."

"Well, there's got to be something. You just can't kill someone in my county and walk away never the mind."

"There *is* the special grand jury," Binford said.

"Heard of 'em, obviously, but we aint never done one here that I know of," the sheriff said.

"It's easy enough to start one up. I ask the judge to empanel the jury. Then we bring witnesses before them."

"What, just send the witnesses in alone? That won't get much done."

"No, sheriff, in a special grand jury, the Commonwealth Attorney sits in with the grand jury and questions the witnesses."

"They'd just lawyer up."

"You can't refuse a subpoena from a special grand jury. The lawyer can come in with the client. But they still have to answer the questions."

"Damn, Mordecai, I think you're on to something here. You don't need no probable cause to call the grand jury, do you?"

"No, the point of the special grand jury is to investigate whether or not a crime has been committed—even whether or not probable cause exists. But they can't issue warrants of arrest," Binford explained.

"Then what's the point if they can't arrest?" The sheriff said, slumping back in his chair.

"The special grand jury issues a report to the court. That, now, can be used to get a warrant, or it can be used to further your own investigation."

The sheriff perked back up. "How quick can you get one together?"

"Well, next week is Term Day," Binford said. Term Day is a special day in the docket of every Circuit Court in Virginia. On that day all the indictments go before the grand jury. It is also used as a docket control date for both civil and criminal cases. Usually a Term Day packs the courtroom because almost every case on the court's docket comes before the court then.

"We will already have a grand jury sitting. We can just ask the court to convert it to a special grand jury."

"Well, the first person I'd haul in is that Weir fellow," the sheriff announced. "And I tell you something else. His boss is a man named Sims. I'd haul his ass in, too. We can track down who prepared the reports and get them in to see how those photos got taken. Say, Mordecai, how long can this go on for? I mean, some of this is going to take getting people out of state."

"No problem. It can go on for months. As long as the special grand jury wants."

"And it don't matter if it is federal or not?"

"Nope."

"Damn, Mordecai, ain't you running with the big dogs now!" The sheriff beamed.

"Ok, sheriff, if we do this I need you to keep up your end of the bargain," Binford countered. "I need you to assign an investigator now to track down who we need to subpoena. I want the subpoenas ready to go out as soon as the grand jury is empaneled. And I want good addresses. None of this posted-on-the-door-service stuff. I want personal service when those papers go out," Binford said, referring to the method of notifying and subpoenaing a witness. Personal service, which is the best form of notification, and the one preferred by Virginia law, is where a deputy actually hands the subpoena to the witness. There is little excuse then for not appearing. Posted Service, when the subpoena and notice is taped to the door of the person's residence, is less effective because it's easier to evade. The intended recipient can just claim he or she never saw the subpoena as an explanation for not coming to court.

"I'll get Randy on it," the sheriff responded, referring to his best civil process-server, Randy Collins, who knew every back road in the county and everyone who lived on them. "If Randy can't find 'em it's cause they are either dead or gone or gone dead."

"Well, make sure he knows that he needs to serve them federal folks off federal property."

"No problem."

The two looked at each other, the enormity of what they had just planned beginning to sink in.

"Don't worry, Mordecai. I got your back," the sheriff said, sensing the prosecutor's more cautious mood.

"This isn't some drug dealer were going after here, sheriff. This is the United States Government. This is the FBI. And, to tell you the truth, I don't really want to do it."

"I know it but, damn, someone killed those two people. It's our job to find out who did it and then bring 'em to justice. I know it and so do you."

"You ever heard of the law of unintended consequences?" Binford asked.

"You're the one that went to law school, not me."

"Well, sheriff, it's pretty simple," Binford explained. "Whenever you do something, whatever it is, there are always consequences that neither you, nor I, can predict. But those consequences happen--always. And, usually they're not good."

"Yeah, well, I don't know much about unintended consequences. But I know something else. We got a duty. The people elected us to keep 'em safe. I cuff law breakers. You bring 'em to the court."

"It's a lot more complicated than that, Tucker," Binford responded blandly using the sheriff's first name.

"Not in my book."

"Do you really think it's that simple?" Binford asked, his eyes straying to the century old portrait of Robert E. Lee hanging in the office.

"Damn straight," Tucker Ray Carter answered. "And to hell with the unintended consequences."

CENTREVILLE, VIRGINIA—NEW AGE INTERNET CAFÉ

Cho pulled the motorcycle into a parking space in front of an internet café located in a shopping plaza just off Interstate 66 and Route 29. A low brick sign at the entrance announced that the conglomeration of shops and asphalt parking spaces was the Crestview Shopping Plaza, a shopping center the main attraction of which, as far as Cho was concerned, was not the concentration of Asian shops, although he did like to be among what he thought of as his own people, but because he needed an internet Cafe. Besides, today he was in a "hate" mood when it came to America. The brutal drive from Culpeper to Centreville had almost ended in death more than once as he battled the rush hour traffic on Route 29 and then later on Interstate 66. He looked at the Vietnamese Pho Bistro café with hunger. A bowl of noodle soup seemed just what he needed. Later though, first he had business at the internet café, he decided grimly.

Taking off his helmet and placing it on the gas tank, Cho swung his stiff leg over the seat and, hopping onto the ground, he looked around at the pedestrians. No one looked suspicious to Cho, and he relaxed-- at last free from the murderous and now cocaine-addicted eyes of the Dragon Team leader.

The evening before, Cho had slipped out to monitor the Federal Reserve on the side of Mt. Pony and he found that, from that one spot on top of a hill, he could watch the facility and not be affected by the sight of the mountain itself. Through trial and error Cho found that the unexplained vomiting which occurred each time he looked at the mountain seemed to lessen as he neared the hilltop.

Inexplicable, but there it was--and he took advantage of the knowledge. Last night however, he had run into a surprise in the presence of two other men on the hill. He was unaware they were situated on the hilltop until he almost stumbled upon them. Cho was able to give them the slip. Then, from a distance, he tried to watch the two men and the Federal Reserve at the same time. He learned nothing other than that someone else was as interested in the facility as he was --and it took no great leap of faith to conclude that they were probably there for the same reason as he.

As far as Cho was concerned the mission was now officially a failure. Worse it was compromised. First had come the blood-splattered disaster in Miami. Then there was his arrest and appearance in the Culpeper courthouse, the Dragon Team leader's decline into drug addiction, his increasingly erratic demeanor only adding to the desperation of the situation. Now he faced the presence of others, at what should have been a secluded spot, presumably interested in the same phenomena as was Cho.

It was time to seek further instructions.

Looking around one more time to make sure he was not followed, he entered the darkened internet café where banks of computer screens lined the wall. A scattering of scruffy looking young men and women faced the glowing screens. He walked up to a counter.

"How much for computer time?" he asked the twenty-something young man behind the counter.

"Five bucks an hour."

Cho counted out five one dollar bills.

"Take the second to last booth," the man pointed towards an empty screen and booth.

Cho sat at the screen and logged on. He could have easily contacted his handlers in China from Culpeper, but he did not want anyone tracking his communications from Culpeper and certainly not from the Chinese restaurant where he stayed.

Cho had found the fact that Americans assumed everything on the internet as being private both naive and stupid. Even Edward Snowden's NSA leaks didn't seem to shake that sense of entitled privacy that all Americans assumed as a matter of course. He knew all email, all internet searches, even the documents created separately on a computer was incessantly scanned by the United States government just as it was by his own government. Cho knew this from his own work in China, where he had often read the meanderings of American citizens written on their computers in Iowa, or Nebraska, or wherever, stored in their document files, never intended for distribution but by the graces of Chinese Intelligence downloaded and delivered to his desktop as soon as they logged onto the internet. Most of it was garbage. But whenever topics of interest were flagged, the internet search bots picked it up and sent it up to a human like Cho for review.

So, Cho knew, whatever he wrote would be monitored either in the United States or in China.

When the Google search engine came up, he called up the *Shandong Jinxiang Steel Co. Ltd.*, which popped up in Chinese. To throw off any tracking, he chose English and the site, which originally was in Chinese script, switched to an English version.

This company provided a convenient cover for Chinese espionage activities, such as the one Cho was on, and as a result received special considerations by the government. Pulling up the contact tab, he entered the correct security code for communication with the company, before typing in English: *RE: Project 27803. Your last shipment of steel was insufficient. I will need more products with instructions on installation. The construction project is now halted until delivery of product and installation instructions. It is my opinion that the project is compromised. Please have your product representative contact me through regular channels,*" and pushed "Enter;" sending a message the consequences of which he could not begin to fathom.

FAIRFAX COUNTY—NSA MONITERING STATION

"Gotcha!" Skyler Braeden said.

At 5 foot 6 and 350 pounds Braeden was a mountain of a man albeit a jiggly one. With his thinning hair and thick plastic-rimmed eyeglasses, he looked exactly what he was: an internet guru, a computer genius, an intellectually active, but socially backwards, bureaucrat. Outside of the NSA, Braeden would not have survived long in the commercial world. He was too socially awkward, too inner-directed, too single-minded in his quest of all things in the cyber world to survive a competitive commercial jungle.   But the NSA had swooped him up after monitoring his activities at MIT and online in various gaming sites. He cheated. When he tired of the game, he would reveal his cheat codes on gamer chat rooms. NSA operatives had found a kindred spirit in Braeden and knew it.

"Gotcha!" Braeden said again. While trolling the Chinese interface between western and internal Chinese internet traffic, he had sensed that the cyber connection to Jinxiang Steel was bogus. In fact, it reminded him of a backdoor entrance he had constructed once in Runescape. An internet-based role play game, Runescape functioned with multiple players across cyberspace, a game in which, after becoming bored with being relegated to insignificant roles, he had created a backdoor to the site, hacked it, and became the game's most important character.

And since Jinxiang Steel's programming felt the same to Braeden when he downloaded and analyzed it, he had set up a program to monitor contacts. One set of contacts always used the same entrance code which made no sense to him since such codes should be individualized for the sake of security, suggesting to him, as it did, that the entrance code was used by outside agents using the steel company's site to contact more secretive entities in China. And to Braeden, that meant the government and more specifically those areas of government involved in espionage. More recently, the word had gone within the NSA out to cyber sleuths like Braeden, that any communication between Virginia and Chinese governmental entities should be examined thoroughly and reported up the chain immediately.

"Let's see where this worm goes," he said to himself, unconsciously licking his lower lip as he hunched over the keyboard. Tracking the message was easy. It landed at a computer in the Ministry of State Security in Beijing. And the source, surprisingly, was only about a thirty-minute drive from where Braeden was sitting.

If this were Runescape, Braeden would immediately send a warrior out to take down the interloper. That decided his next action. He first recorded the entirety of the transaction, its tracking and its destination and saved it all on a memory stick. Then he punched a code into the phone.

"Braeden here, switch me through to the director's office," he said. "Look, I don't care if he's in the bathroom downloading a duce, get me to his cell. This is priority one." He listened with increasing agitation. The grandmaster in Runescape would take no guff from an underling like this. Another pause. He drummed his fingers on the desktop.

"Listen, knave, I don't care if you didn't get the memo --there's a priority one directive at play here. You want to explain to the director why you delayed?" Satisfied with the response he waited while electronic beeps and static, much like the noise on a Star Trek Communicator, popped out of the phone ear piece. It stopped.

"Director. Braeden here. I think I have a priority one contact." He paused. "Yes, its destination was the Ministry of State Security." He paused again then in answer to a question he said, "Just down the road at a Centreville internet cafe."

Cho bit down on a particularly grisly piece of pork. Vietnamese soup is a conglomeration of noodles, chicken stock and a variety of chopped meat and vegetables garnished with a generous dose of herbs and cilantro. As he maneuvered the morsel in his mouth to bite down more securely he thought of the other night and nearly gagged. The delicious treat in his mouth reminded him of the piece of grisly meat that had landed on his forearm as he had chopped and slashed in the abandoned farmhouse.

In shock he shot straight up in his seat and spit the morsel out into the bowl. Then furtively he looked around. Good, he thought, no one noticed. Of course, as he observed other customers in the long café dining room, he noticed most of them were slurping noodles and dropping bits of food back into the bowl as they used chop sticks to lift food to their mouths. He blended, he thought. I am a master at that apparently. I blend unnoticed: the secret horror of my life hidden from all.

How was it, he wondered, that he had become this, this thing that stalks the night, that collects small things to mutilate and slash, all the while horrified at what he does but unable to stop? San Diego, yes, he understood that. It had started there. But what had happened? And why this place Culpeper? Why the vomiting? Why the fascination with that mountain, that facility in the side of the hill, the shape of Mt. Pony that haunted his dreams? And this last episode had been the worst, by far the most violent and messy. How could he, who had never hunted, never even baited a hook, how could he need to kill?

Cho bent his head down and stifled a sob. It wasn't fair. His mother could not understand why he stayed away, but Cho did not trust himself enough to put his family in jeopardy, because sometimes, yes sometimes, he wanted to do more than kill animals. Sometimes there was a darker need. One he barely acknowledged. It had almost been his undoing in the park the other day.

And that need was growing. Animals would not service it forever. He knew, in the depths of his heart, that soon he would need more. And he could not control it.

Was it wrong? Cho *did* think about the morality of it all. Sometimes. More so earlier, but less so now. Killing animals was ok, he had decided. We kill them and eat them all the time. The fact that they suffered was bad. But not that bad; after all, they weren't sentient. They didn't know what was happening, not really. He tried to forget the terror in the eyes of the dogs he had sacrificed. Maybe killing dogs was wrong. Maybe. But he had relatives that ate dog meat and thought nothing of it.

The real question, he guessed, was whether or not it was wrong for him to kill when he could not control himself? So, if he had no control, and it wasn't wrong to kill, maybe, just maybe it would be ok to kill something more satisfying than brute animals.

And what, he asked himself, might that be? In the darkest part of his mind he knew. He knew. He certainly had thought of more satisfying elements he could add to the mix of subjects. Oh, yes. He knew.

The mentally ill had been the first to come to mind. Shuffling and jabbering to themselves, living in worlds that did not exist, sleeping under bridges. They were drains on society. They weren't sentient. But they could scream. He had seen that often enough roaming the streets of San Diego. Once he had wondered along the seafront and in a grassy area he saw a deranged woman sobbing and screaming at the sky. She stood in dirty clothes, her gray hair swirling in the wind, grasping with one hand a shopping cart full of her belongings, the other hand clenched and punching at the sky. Other pedestrians had made a wide path around her, avoiding contact, twittering and laughing nervously. Cho on the other hand sat nearby on a bench and watched her. Oh, how he watched her, like a lion watches his prey before running and sprinting to capture and savor hot blood spurting from the jugular. He began to plan how to kill her when, shocked and disgusted at himself, he had leaped to his feet and hurried away.

And then there were nursing homes. Would it be wrong to kill the aged who really did not have a life worth living anymore? Would he not in some way be a deliverer of salvation, of release from a life of urine-soaked sheets and ceiling-gazing. And again, many of them were not sentient. He knew that was true because he had roamed the halls: seeking, always seeking. And there were many lying in their own filth, mouths agape, drool running down their checks. No, they were not sentient in any real meaning of the word. Less so than the cats and dogs he easily snapped up as subjects. No. Not sentient.

Sentient. He loved the word. It was so clinical. It excused so much.

Now, however, it disgusted him to think that he had ever contemplated such things. Leaving the cup of noodle soup unfinished, he left the Café, still so distracted by the grisly meat he did not notice the black GMC SUV with tinted windows idling in the parking lot.

"Mr. Cho?" a trim man with a military hair cut asked moving swiftly from Cho's flank.

Instinctively sensing danger, Cho sprinted towards his motorcycle.

The SUV squealed in front of Cho so that he nearly ran into its side. A rear door opened and two men jumped out, grabbed the now-confused Cho, and pulled him inside.

"I demand diplomatic immunity." Cho sputtered after they cuffed him and shoved him roughly to an upright position. "I demand to speak to the embassy. I am a citizen of the People's Republic of China on a diplomatic mission."

The men in the vehicle remained silent as the SUV sped onto the highway.

"Will someone tell me what is going on here at least?" Cho asked.

In response one man looked to another and asked, "Martinez, you ready?"

The Hispanic man nodded yes.

"Do it."

Martinez produced a hypodermic needle, to Cho's growing horror, popped off the cap, and jammed the needle into the side of

Cho's neck --pushing the plunger down in one brutally quick and smooth action.

Cho slumped.

"He was kinda mouthy, that one," Martinez said.

"One down and three to go," the other man said.

WARRENTON TRAINING CENTER—CULPEPER

"I know one of the subjects Martinez just picked up," Weir said.

"You mean transportees," Sims corrected him.

"Yes sir, transportees," Weir answered lapsing into formal military protocol. "I know one of them."

"So?"

"Sir, I'm not comfortable participating in the preparation for transport. Frankly, I'm not comfortable with any of it. I was there when they brought Steele into the loading area this morning," Weir answered. Seeing the British SRR warrior knocked out cold and being wheeled into a receiving room at the Transport Center had been a shock he would never forget. He knew a man named Steele was one of the three agents on the prowl in Culpeper. He even knew the agent named Steele was British. But in one of those strange slips of the mind, he had not connected the man on the loose in Culpeper as being the same Steele who saved his life in Iraq.

It had been early in the war when Weir, as part of a light recon unit looking for traces of Saddam Hussein's nuclear weapons program, had along with his unit been ambushed in the unstable morass that passed for civil society outside the green zone in Baghdad.

Two of Weir's men had been beheaded in front of him, on the field, while civilians cheered "Allah!" over and over again. Then, while his team members' blood pooled on the dirt alleyway, the Iraqis put a hood over Weir's head, stuffed his mouth with a sock, and jammed him in the trunk of a car. Speeding and weaving around traffic, they had dodged American patrols for hours before stopping for the night. They left him in the trunk. The next day was more of the same before finally the car stopped and he was hustled into a dirty, hot room where he had lain bound, gagged and hooded on the foul dirt floor while one man after another took turns urinating on him.

Weir remembered that time had seemed to stand still as, terrified, he had heard screaming that went on for days: screaming and silence and then screaming again. He'd known that one by one his team members were being killed, their throats slit in front of a video camera for posting on the internet. The copper smell, which large amounts of blood exude, had drifted under the doorway to his room: in waves, crashing against his nasal passages, one set after another of nauseating odor.

Later, after the first orgy of bloodletting, his tormentors would sometimes come in his room just to scream at him in accented English while they kicked and punched him.

He had waited to die.

No, that was not true, he wanted to die. And somehow his captors knew that, and knew that prolonging the agony, prolonging the uncertainty, was in fact, the worst thing they could do to him besides sliding a dull knife slowly across his throat.

More days passed. He was alone, all of his comrades having spilled their lives out in wet waterfalls on the floor in the adjoining room. Weir did not know how long he stayed in that Iraqi dirt-floored hut. He did remember the last day.

It was the best and the worst.

Oh, yes. The last day. His captors dragged him into the next room. He kicked and screamed because he knew what was next. Cursing, they pushed him through the doorway where he had landed on his knees. A sheet hung against one wall. At the other end of the room stood a small video camera on a tripod with a man adjusting the viewfinder. Five men stood next to the sheet. A reception committee. All hooded. One man held a large butcher knife. Oddly, Weir noticed that the blade was clean and well oiled. It gleamed and the light caught his eye, making him squint.

The men began chanting.

Weir had never told anyone what happened next. We all have our secrets, he had often told himself. And, somehow, the lie detector operators who administered the mandatory testing on him, never asked the right questions, never got close enough, to elicit any deception on his part when he retold the story. Weir urinated when the chanting started. Then, babbling, he offered to tell them anything they wanted. Just not the knife. Please, he pleaded, not the knife. No, he never told that part.

Perhaps it was the soiled pants. Perhaps they never meant to kill him. But after some discussion and laughter, his captors kicked and punched him back to his cell.

All pretense at dignity gone, Weir lay on the ground, in his own filth, and prayed without hope. And he vowed to God, that if he did survive, he would dedicate his life to working for good.

That night was the worst night of Weir's life. Spent. Broken. He lay like a dead thing.

And then, much later, it became the best day of his life.

Flash grenades went off in the next room. He could still smell the phosphate odor they left, and it was then that Weir rejoined the world in a cascade of light and concussion. He heard shouting. And amazingly, he heard someone yelling "British Forces! Get down!" Automatic weapons fire pounded the hut. Splinters of wood and clots of mud showered him. Men screamed. One of Weir's captors pushed the door open to his cell, but fell in a hail of lead. A uniformed soldier ran in behind him, looked at Weir prostrate on the floor, and shouted, "You American?" and when Weir nodded yes, had shouted, "In here now!" And just like that, Weir was sprinted out of the hell hole that had been his universe, by a team of crack British SRR commandos. And the man who first saw Weir was Steele.

"Weir, we've talked about this before," Sims said almost gently, snapping Weir back to the present.

"Yes, Sir, I understand, but this is different."

"Hmmm….well, there is different and there is different. You related?"

"No, Sir. He saved my life in the sandbox…in Iraq."

"Ha. A war buddy. That's what this is all about? You've got to be kidding me," Sims voice hardened, "Make no mistake Weir. This is an extreme black project. And you are going to perform your duty. Tomorrow we have a scheduled transport. And in no way, not under my watch, are we going to fail to meet our quota. You got that! Now get out!"

When, woodenly, Weir left the office. Sims slammed the door behind him and went straight to the phone.

"Sargent London," he said. "We've got a problem. Yes, it's Weir. He's getting a case of cold feet. No, no…none of that. We don't have time. Look, we're going to transport tomorrow night. After Weir leaves home tomorrow, you put some men on the Mrs. and the kids. No, no, nothing like that. I want this covert. I want all three of them on live feed. Yes. Just like before. If I need to dial up the feed, I'll use the same channel. You just make sure when I need the feed that I got their sweet little smiling faces on monitor."

Sims slammed the phone down. There was more than one way to ensure compliance, he thought grimly to himself. Then, when this mess is over, he mused, he was going to have to decide what to do with Weir. The new recruit was a good man in some ways, but unpredictable and prone to attacks of Boy Scout ethics-- and Sims learned the hard way, a long time ago, that the Boy Scouts had nothing to do with what went on in the real world where aliens roamed at will and the United States Government spied and manipulated its citizens without remorse. And all of this took place in a twilight war conducted by the NSA in a desperate attempt to hold off the invading species. Sims knew that what he did was horrible in the eyes of many. But then not many had looked into the same abyss as Sims had.

BOOK TWO:
MARS

"MARS IS THERE, WAITING TO BE REACHED."

-- BUZZ ALDRIN, APOLLO 11 ASTRONAUT.

CHAPTER 11

MANNED SPACEFLIGHT ESSENTIALLY BECAME MEANINGLESS ONCE THE ALIEN ENTITY (AE) FORBADE LUNAR MANNED EXPLORATION. WHILE THE UNITED STATES CONTINUED WITH SHUTTLE AND SPACE STATION PROJECTS, NSA ANALYSIS DISCOURAGED CONTINUED EXPENDITURE FOR MANNED OPERATIONS. NASA WAS ABLE TO PRESERVE ITS SHUTTLE AND INTERNATIONAL SPACE STATION PROGRAMS PARTIALLY BECAUSE OF BUREAUCRATIC INERTIA. NSA OPERATIVES WITHIN THE MANNED SPACE PROGRAM WORKED TO DERAIL ANY MOVEMENT TOWARDS NEW MANNED SPACE PROJECTS.

EVENTUALLY, PRESIDENT OBAMA ENDED THE SHUTTLE PROGRAM. THIS WAS SPECIFICALLY AS A RESULT OF NSA RECOMMENDATIONS.

IT SOON BECAME APPARENT THAT, WHILE HUMANS KNEW AND UNDERSTOOD LITTLE OF THE AE, THE SAME IN ODD WAYS WAS TRUE OF THE AE'S UNDERSTANDING OF HUMAN ACTIVITIES. IN 1979 PEYTON VACHEL POSTULATED THAT THE AE DID NOT PERCEIVE ROBOTIC EXPLORATION AS A THREAT. NOT ONLY DID THIS REVEAL SOMETHING ABOUT THE MAKEUP AND PERCEPTIONS OF THE AE BUT THIS PERCEPTION DEFICIT CREATED A LEGITIMATE MEANS FOR THE UNITED STATES TO GATHER OFF-WORLD INFORMATION. WHILE OBVIOUS ONCE POINTED OUT, THIS WAS IN FACT A THEORETICAL BREAKTHROUGH FOR NSA AND GROUP 929 UNDERSTANDING OF THE AE AS WELL AS A GUIDEPOST FOR FUTURE EXPLORATION AND POSSIBLE RESISTANCE. (SEE "ALIEN DEFICITS IN PERCEPTION: A REVERSE ANALYSIS," VACHEL, PEYTON; NSA INTERNAL JOURNAL, PP 129-177, DEC. 1979.) VACHEL'S THEORY RESTED ON THE FACT THAT THE UNITED STATES HAD PLACED THE VIKING LANDER ON MARS IN 1976 WITHOUT INCIDENT. FURTHERMORE HE CONCLUDED IN HIS PAPER THAT THE PROLONGED VOYAGER FLYBYS OF THE INNER AND OUTER PLANETARY SYSTEM ELICITED NO AE ACTION AND POINTED TO A POSSIBLE PATHWAY FOR HUMAN SPACE EXPLORATION.

WITH NSA SUPPORT, NASA LAUNCHED A SERIES OF UNMANNED INTERPLANETARY PROBES. AFTER THE MARS TRANSIT WAS DISCOVERED, NASA FOCUSED MORE INTENTLY ON MARS THROUGH THE USE OF THE HUBBLE TELESCOPE AND ROBOTIC LANDERS. IN 1999 NSA AND GROUP 929 DISCOVERED, THROUGH THE LOSS OF THE MARS POLAR LANDER AND THE MARS CLIMATE ORBITER, THAT THERE WERE LIMITS TO AE

IGNORANCE WHEN IT CAME TO THE USE OF UNMANNED DEVICES. AFTER THE MARS CLIMATE ORBITER DEVIATED FROM ITS INTENDED COURSE AND BURNED UP IN THE MARTIAN ATMOSPHERE, LATER ANALYSIS DETERMINED THAT A GRAVITATIONAL TRACTOR BEAM LOCKED ONTO THE ORBITER FORCING AN INCORRECT ANGLE OF ORBITAL INSERTION. THREE MONTHS LATER, THE MARS POLAR LANDER SUFFERED A SIMILAR FATE. SUSPICIOUS OF THE CIRCUMSTANCES SURROUNDING THE EARLIER LOSS OF THE OR- BITER, NSA OPERATIVES WITHIN NASA CAREFULLY MONITORED THE POLAR LANDER'S APPROACH. WHILE LOSS OF THE LANDER EMBARRASSED NASA, THE NSA AND GROUP 929 IDENTIFIED THE SOURCE OF THE GRAVITATIONAL TRACTOR BEAM AND AS A RESULT HAVE NOW PINPOINTED THE PROBABLE DESTINATION FOR TRANSPORTEES.[1]

NOT TO BE DETERRED NASA AND NSA SENT MORE PROBES BUT USED DIFFERENT COMMUNICATION BANDS ON THE THEORY THAT THE MARS ORBITER AND LANDER HAD USED A NEW DEEP-SPACE COMMUNICATIONS RELAY WHICH MAY HAVE ALERTED THE AE IN SOME FASHION. THE DE- VICES THEMSELVES WERE LARGER THAN ANY SENT TO MARS BEFORE LEADING TO ANOTHER THEORY THAT SIZE ALONE MAY HAVE TRIGGERED A DEFENSE MECHANISM. AFTERWARDS MARS EXPLORATORY CRAFT WERE KEPT TO A WEIGHT LIMIT OF 1000 KILOGRAMS OR LESS, AN EXCEPTION BEING THE 2000 KILOGRAM MARS RECONNAISSANCE ORBITER, THE FIRST HUMAN--MADE SATELLITE USING STEALTH TECHNOLOGY DERIVED FROM THE ROSWELL CRAFT. SO FAR IT HAS REMAINED UNDETECTED, AND, BE- SIDES CONDUCTING AN INTENSIVE PHOTOGRAPHIC SURVEY OF THE PLANET, SERVES AS A RELAY STATION FOR HUMAN COMMUNICATION SYSTEMS IN THE MARTIAN VICINITY.

[1]THE COVER STORY FOR THE MISHAPS CREATED BY NSA OPERATIVES WAS SIMPLE AND INVENTIVE, BOTH CRASHES BEING BLAMED ON A FATAL DISCONNECT BETWEEN FLIGHT CONTROL AND THE CIVILIAN CONTRACTOR WHO CREATED THE CRAFT. ONE OPERATED ON THE METRIC SYSTEM, THE OTHER ON THE STANDARD ENGLISH SYSTEM OF FEET AND INCHES. A DISCONNECT WHICH, ACCORDING TO THE PLANTED STORY, LED TO MISCAL- CULATIONS IN ORBITAL INSERTION FORMULAS.

--EXCERPTS FROM THE NSA PRESIDENTIAL BRIEFING PAPERS ON THE ROSWELL INCIDENT

REMINGTON, VIRGINIA

From the kitchen doorway, Weir watched Rebecca's hands move swiftly over the granite countertop as she made breakfast. Bacon strips sizzled on the stove in a big cast iron skillet. She pivoted to the refrigerator and pulled out a dozen eggs, then cracked an egg on the skillet, sliding the contents into the hot bubbling bacon grease so as not to break the yellow yoke.

"I thought you'd like a big breakfast this morning," she said brightly turning towards him.

"Smells good," he replied absently taking his seat at the table.

She had noticed Weir was troubled and thought the breakfast would lift his spirits. Disappointed in his lackluster response, she turned back to the stove and cracked another egg.

Weir watched the yolk slide out of the half shell then heard the pop and sizzle as it hit the grease. *The yolk at the Federal Reserve was not as sterile as that*, he thought to himself. *No. Not so clean. It had bits and pieces in it as it slid and spread across the floor.*

"Toast?" Rebecca asked him.

"Hmm...Yes."

She looked at him for a moment, "More trouble at work?"

"Just the usual," he replied and relapsed into silence.

She resumed making breakfast, then with the blue-colored plates on the table loaded with bacon and fried eggs and crispy toast she turned towards the open door leading to the rest of the house, "Kids! Time for breakfast!"

Weir heard their feet pound down the stairs.

"Oh boy! Bacon and eggs!" Hunter said as he burst into the room. Heather followed and sat on Weir's lap. It was a morning ritual that she would sit on his lap while he read the paper before eating. He wrapped his arm around her stomach to steady her.

"Daddy, want to see my picture?" Heather asked. She clutched a paper in her hand. "Daddy, want to see my picture?" she asked again pushing the paper to his face.

"Sure, let me see it." Weir took the folded piece of paper, laid it on the table, unfolding the crayon-colored drawing in sections with his free hand. Four figures holding hands and looking straight ahead filled the sketch. A rainbow arched over the four and a green tree filled background.

"That's you," she said pointing to the tallest figure in the middle. "That's Mommy, and that's me and Hunter." Her diminutive fingers flew across the drawing.

"What's this?" he asked.

"That's the woods, and look, Daddy, I drew the deer in the trees."

Weir looked closely, and he saw under the green lollipop trees four stick figures that were the deer. One had antlers.

"He's watching over the other deer so nothing will happen to them," she explained pointing to the buck. "Why does he do that?"

"That's what he does, Heather. It's his job."

"Like you, Daddy?"

WARRENTON TRAINING CENTER—CULPEPER

Sims bounced into his office through a side door, excited, as usual by transport, in part because it meant that he was doing his job, keeping the world safe. But now, he had to take care of this Weir problem promptly and efficiently. People, like any other problem, pivot on a fulcrum. One only needed to find the right fulcrum, the right point of pressure which, for someone like Weir, was simple. Sims had done it before and he would do it again. Apply the right pressure. Find the right pivot. Push the right button. Get results. That's why he had his job. He got things done. And if Group 929 cared about anything, it cared about results.

All in all, Sims relished the upcoming morning meeting with Weir.

Jingling the change in his pants pocket with one hand, he pushed the intercom button on his phone with his other and barked, "Send Weir in."

The secretary ushered Weir into the office then retreated, closing the door behind. She had seen this mood in Sims before and needed no urging. This was, as Sims had called it, "a come to Jesus" meeting.

"Have you thought about our little conversation yesterday?" Sims asked as soon as Weir was seated.

"Sir, I just can't do it. Not Steele."

"You understand that your involvement is minimal. You provide security as each pod is loaded. That's all. Don't look so puzzled. You thought we sent them up in jelly? We're much more sophisticated than that, Weir. You'll be walked through it the first time by Martinez but besides providing security and ensuring the technicians perform their duties correctly, you really have no physical contact with the transportees. Does that make a difference?"

Weir considered what he had just learned. He did not know what to expect given the lack of training necessary in an extreme black op. Need to know at this level meant just that—you didn't know anything until absolutely necessary. And, as he was learning, that applied even to his responsibilities. His fears centered on a scenario in which he would herd a group of people at gunpoint into a sphere. Including Steele. The use of pods was a new twist. He wondered what else was as yet to be revealed during this evening's transport.

"You know, Weir, you are not the first person in charge of security here."

"I assumed as much."

"Sometimes new people have qualms."

"Like me?"

"Exactly."

"Are you telling me there is an alternative if I decide not to--well, transport Steele?"

"No. You have no choice," Sims said flatly. "It's all or nothing."

Picking up a black plastic remote, he pointed it towards a wall which slid up to reveal a black flat screen television monitor.

Darkness fell upon Weir's soul. Whatever was about to happen, it would not be good.

"No. No choice, Weir," Sims repeated. "You knew when you took the assignment there is only one way out for you. But why speak of unpleasant things? There is so much good in the world Weir--so many good things to discuss."

"I don't understand, sir."

"Your predecessors' questions were always answered," Sims said, waving the black remote in a circle. They did their jobs and they did them gladly. Then, after a while, they were promoted to higher responsibilities."

"Sir, I don't see how my standing aside while Steele is transported is any different than if I strapped him into a pod myself," Weir said.

"Ha! You're such a Boy Scout. That's what makes you a good security officer. But, with Steele, remember we are not killing him. We are sending him off. He'll be back none the wiser."

"How long would he be gone?"

Sims face brightened, "Usually two weeks to a month, sometimes longer."

"I heard one of the technicians at the transport reception say some don't ever come back."

"Well. Yes. Sometimes but not often."

Weir sat silent for a second. Torn between what he knew was right, down in his gut, where reason fled and emotion ruled. Reason said this was his job. He could not abdicate his responsibility. He was after all, in the military, sworn to follow the orders of superiors like Sims. But his gut said that this was wrong. Wrong. Wrong. Wrong. And then to even contemplate repaying the bravery of Steele with what? "I was only following orders. Sorry you never came back, and by the way thanks again for saving my life". Wrong. His gut turned. Reason fled and he found himself looking deep into the coal black hell of Sims' eyes.

"Sir, respectfully," Weir said firmly, "I would like some sort of special exemption for Steele."

Sims' mouth turned into a flat line as he pushed the remote control and Heather, Weir's eight-year-old daughter, appeared on the monitor on a swing set at school, her tennis shoes pumping rhythmically to make the swing go back and forth, laughing gleefully at the pure joy of swinging high into the bright blue autumn sky. Sims pointed the remote again and Weir saw Rebecca standing deep in thought in a grocery aisle, contemplating the ingredients in the can she held in her hand. Oblivious to whoever was shooting the picture, she returned the can and continued walking down the aisle. Weir noticed she was wearing a red sweater he had given her for Christmas last year.

"A careful shopper, your wife," Sims said, "This is the second grocery store she's visited so far." He turned to look at Weir. "I think the Good Book says it best about an excellent wife being worth far more than jewels. Wouldn't you say so, Weir?"

"What are you doing?" Weir whispered, horrified.

"Doing? Why nothing, Weir. I'm simply reminding you of all the good that there is in a man's life: his family, duty, honor, his country." Sims turned to the monitor again and aimed the remote. Hunter, Weir's ten-year-old boy, was smiling at the camera and waving. Though there was no sound, Weir could see him mouthing, "Hi Dad."

"Now, now, Weir, there is no need to get upset," Sims said as Weir jack-knifed out of his seat. "A nice man in a uniform told your son to say hello to you in the camera. Remember, you've always held the military in high esteem. You should. You wear the colors yourself."

"Do *not* touch my family, Sims," Weir said quietly but burning with white hot rage, "You hear me, Sims. You leave my family alone."

"Why so sensitive, Weir? No one said anything about hurting them. But it's good to be reminded of the things that matter. Now that I have your attention, let's get a few things straight. You will do your job. In fact, I want you to personally strap Steele into that pod. And how's this? We'll wake him just enough so you can exchange a few pleasantries before you wrap him up tight. It will do my heart good to see you two reunite. Of course, he may not take it so kindly. But that's all part of the initiation into our little brotherhood here."

Weir sat down again. Silent. Simmering.

"You have a nice family; it would be a tragedy if something were to happen to them." Sims repeated. *"To seal the deal."* That is how Sims liked to think of this last part of the conversation, it being just one of many similar talks he had had with others before Weir. In the end it always came down to this, Sims thought, anticipating the pleasure of bending another to his will. He thrilled at the feeling of complete power that came with total domination of a situation.

"You touch them and I swear…"

"You'll do what, Weir? You can't do anything. Now get out. Follow Martinez. But remember, I'll be paying careful attention to how you perform tonight. All the pods are going on time and filled. Oh, and by the way, did I tell you that tonight is a free range night?" Sims paused, enjoying the wary expression that filled Weir's face. "Free range is the term we use when we have total discretion in subject selection. We can send who ever we want, Weir. Anyone. There are no targets to harvest. Our alien friends are happy with whomever we send. And in three days another free range transport is scheduled."

Sims waited to let the implications of what he was saying sink in. Then his voice dripping of venom, "I think your little family might enjoy some new scenery. Don't you?"

CARRICO MILLS ROAD—CULPEPER.

Weir seethed. With his family in danger, he had no choice. He would do exactly what Sims wanted. No way was his little girl going to end up on the floor of the Federal Reserve, vomiting slime, dragged off by men in hazmat suits like so much offal on the floor. And then to think of Rebecca and Hunter going through the same thing was just too much to contemplate.

No choice.

So Steele had to go. Steele had to go to whatever hell existed at the other end of the transport. And I'll have to stand by and let it happen. Anyone else would do the same. He gripped the steering wheel tighter and sped through the fields that bordered the twisting back road. In fact I'm not going to just stand by and let it happen. I'm going to, as Sims put it, actively participate. To save my family I'll do whatever I have to. Willingly. Without protest. Later, however, there would be retribution. But this was not the time. Not the place.

And then, like heat lightning flickering across the dark of night, an idea came to him, an idea so stunning he almost failed to grasp it. His mind raced. Too fast, he thought to himself. Back up and be methodical. He could not stop the transport. But he *could* do something. Steele *deserved* at least that much. And, the more he worked his way through the choice given him by Sims, the more he decided he could do for Steele. And in some small way, the more he could do to right his own moral compass.

Cruising up Route 3, Weir passed Mt. Pony and wheeled his way into the Federal Reserve. After parking, he bounded up the steps to the outside entrance to the building and opened the door by flashing his hand at the security box. Once inside his office, he called Sims.

"Sims, Weir here."

"Ah, Weir, much less formal. Good. What, pray tell, does that portend?"

"I'm not happy about you using my family. Let's get that straight."

"Sometimes we have to shock people to get them to think clearly."

"I still don't like it, but I have reconsidered. You call me a Boy Scout. I am. And I guess I understand that I did take an oath to uphold the Constitution and to follow lawful orders."

"And my orders are lawful. They come from a Presidential directive." Sims said quickly.

"I know that. I will follow them. Steele will just have to live with the choices he made."

Sims was not surprised by Weir's sudden turnaround. They always did. In some small measure, at that very moment, he felt an emotional warmness towards this man who was his creation, his protégé, his contribution to the project. Sims, through a tried and true method, had seasoned the new security officer: so thoroughly that now he could mentor him. Groom him for bigger projects. Group 929 encouraged such personnel development. In fact, the project demanded it. After all, one could not just advertise for positions. Internal promotion was needed to keep security tight and, Sims thought smugly, Weir seemed to be progressing nicely.

"A wise decision. I knew you had it in you," Sims said warmly in response to Weir's declaration. Silence stretched across the phone connection. "Is there something else?" he asked

"Well, yes, actually there is," Weir told him.

"Alright, what is it?"

"I don't like doing things halfway."

"One of the reasons why we picked you."

"If I am going to be in charge of security then I want to be in charge of security. I'd like to do more than just follow Martinez around tonight."

"Hmmm. Ha! Well, we *have* had a change of heart. Alright, Weir. I respect the initiative. I'll authorize Martinez to brief you early and allow you to take the lead. Of course you'll need to follow his instructions when necessary."

"A good NCO is always someone to pay attention to," Weir said, referring to Martinez's rank as a master sergeant.

"Ha. Yes. Just so," Sims said.

After hanging up, Weir busied himself on the computer, clicking on the schematic layout of the Federal Reserve Center, memorizing hallways, elevator shafts and utility tunnels until, after an hour of searching and downloading, he could draw the diagrams from memory. Then he called in Martinez and, assuring himself that Sims had briefed the young Hispanic NCO on Weirs status, asked, "I want to know exactly the ordnance here. I need location, type and amounts."

"You want the full rundown top and bottom?" Martinez asked referring to the two security levels of the facility.

"No. I have a good understanding of the top levels. I am more interested in what we have down here in the transport level."

"It's pretty standard stuff really, Sir," Martinez told him. "We're not expecting to fight a war so it's mainly anti-personnel ordnance. I mean, if the ships ever intended something worse, we're pre-programed to self-destruct. That would pretty much take care of everything in a twenty mile radius."

"You talking a nuclear device?"

"Yes, Sir."

Weir took in the surprising news. Certainly, he had been on facilities with a nuclear self-destruct option. It was always unsettling but on the other hand he usually never really felt the option was realistic. In his gut he knew this operation was different.

"Ok, on the more mundane level, then, what do we have here?" Weir said.

"There are two ordnance rooms in the lower level. Each is stocked the same with Mossberg 590s and Benelli M4 shotguns. Then we've got..."

"All right, let's break it down," Weir interrupted him. "What kind of ammo do we carry for them?"

Martinez counted off the ordnance with his fingers as he answered, "Twelve gauge 00 hardened buckshot, breaking rounds for door penetration, SCMITER. And then..."

Weir was surprised by the mix of ammunition being described. The buckshot was standard, but the breaking rounds, a solid shot meant to take down doors was interesting. It showed a certain amount of uncertainty about security in the lower level. And the SCMITER system was totally unexpected. A SCMITER round was basically a shotgun round with 12 razor-sharp flechettes packed into the olive-drab plastic shell. Each flechette was really a small stamped-metal dart with a fin system. Body armor melted and steel helmets shattered when hit within the ammo's lethal 500 meter range. As far as Weir knew, the only people wearing body armor were the security detail. He wondered why such ammo would be thought necessary.

"I assume both have ghost ring sights," Weir asked referring to a more advanced sighting system used on shotguns.

"Yes sir."

"What else?"

"We have M-4 carbines. Special Op models."

"The full SOPMOD block?" Weir asked referring to the standard array of special op applications that came with the M-4, but asking in military shorthand.

"Yes, Sir, telescoping stock, nine-inch barrels, rail adapter system, vertical forward grip, night vision and laser pointers, and they are all paired with the M320 grenade launcher."

"Grenade launcher?"

"Yes, Sir," Martinez warmed to the subject, "We have a good selection of M14, M33 and MK40 grenades."

Now, Weir was intrigued. The sergeant just described a wide range of specialized explosive ordnance. Weir had not used a M14 grenade but he knew it was unusual and was used underwater like a mini depth charge. Its utility was that it worked in an oxygen-free environment.

"Grenades, huh? Don't tell me you have a supply of C4." Weir asked referring to the play dough-like plastic explosive.

"Absolutely. Regular block packaging. Radio detonators, too."

"Side arms, I assume."

"Standard issue, sir. Beretta M92F with 15 round magazines. Most are fitted with a pitcatinny rail for lights and laser pointers. That's about it, sir."

"Quite a little arsenal, Martinez," Weir mused. "The explosives surprise me. Has there ever been a need to use them?"

"No, Sir. But we train regularly with all weapons. At least as long as I have been here."

"How long has that been?"

"This is my fourth year, Sir."

Weir leaned back and clasping his hands behind his head, regarded Martinez's guileless face. It was hard to believe that this man had watched and participated in the madness of the transports for as long as he had without so much as a scar or a nervous twitch or some outward sign of revulsion at what it was they did.

"Ever have any second thoughts about any of this?" Weir asked.

"No, Sir. None at all," Martinez said, his face expressionless, "We're saving the country from something far worse."

"Ummm…yes. Absolutely." Weir decided to drop the issue. "Ok, take me to the ammo lockers. I want to inspect them myself."

"Yes, Sir. But we'll have to hurry. The technicians will be ready to get to work soon. We have to stand guard just in case."

"In case of what?"

"In case one of the transportees resists, although most of 'em are out cold." Martinez paused, "We have to watch the technicians too. We had one go loco on us once."

"What happened?"

"He freaked out, Sir. One of the transports was an old lady. He started to shake and cry and then just refused to do his job. I was there when it all went down."

"And?"

"Followed standard procedure, sir. I tazed him and took him out. We had an empty pod. Mr. Sims ordered our team to prep him for transport and that's what we did."

Weir's soul shriveled, "What happened when he came back?"

"He didn't."

Weir absorbed the enormity of what he just heard. Sims' threat about his family was real enough. If he had doubted it before, Weir did not doubt now that Sims would transport his wife and children at the hint of resistance on Weir's part.

At Weir's suggestion, the two quick stepped down corridors blinding white in fluorescents, the floor the only color for relief, and it was gray. Martinez followed the path Weir expected given his examination of floor plans earlier. He inspected the first locker wordlessly. Then they moved on to the second. Once inside, and while cataloging in his mind the locations of the ordnance stacked in the room, Weir began questioning the young sergeant again.

"So tell me, Sergeant, why the use of pods. I didn't see any pods the other night."

"Don't know, Sir. It's just how they want them packaged."

"Anything special about how the techs get the subjects into the pods?"

"No, Sir. From what I can tell, the techs just lift them onto a kinda couch --except once they are in and hooked up-- it folds up around them. When the techs shut the lid, it automatically seals."

Weir learned that the pods were delivered at odd times by the aliens and stored in the facility and that they floated on air, using some sort of magnetic field for lift. "It takes some getting used to," Martinez said, after describing how they floated and moved at the touch of a finger. Of particular interest to Weir was the sergeant's revelation that the pods were not closely watched or counted.

"Who'd want to take a ride in one," was all Martinez could say when asked about the laxness.

The preparation room for the transportees was different than Room 35A where Weir had been injected, with white-coated technicians, huddled around a man who lay on a plastic-covered table, obviously unconscious. Next to the huddle was a floating pod, the lid already open, and on the other side of the room, Weir saw four of his men, armed and detailed.

"At ease," he said, watching them relax ever so slightly.

At first, Weir thought that the pod was metallic but a closer examination convinced him that it was a resin material. Eight feet long, grey, black and purple, the surface was pebbled, not smooth, and at each blunt end was a small extrusion. He noted an odd symbol on one end, not a bar code, but a mix of squares and dots in a square about two inches by two inches, black on white.

"Where's Steele?" he asked in general.

Without looking at him, one of the white-coated technicians pointed toward the end of the room.

Weir's eyes followed the man's pointed finger to see a man lying on a table but without the gaggle of technicians. Unlike the other bodies he saw, prostrate on the tables, he noted that Steele was strapped down.

"Why the restraints?" he asked no one in particular. The technician who had pointed turned and gave Weir a curious look.

"He's under very light sedation," the technician answered looking at Weir oddly.

"Why?" Weir asked but knowing the answer.

"Direct orders from Mr. Sims. Very irregular and over my objections, let me assure you."

"Anything else?" Weir asked to break the uneasy silence.

"Just wondering why you want to have him conscious during transport," the technician said, and Weir thought he detected disgust in his voice. "Sims said you wanted to personally strap him in. I'm just wondering. Why would you hate the man so much that you'd do a thing like that? What'd he do, sleep with your wife? Anyway, let us know when you're finished with him. Sims said you and your sergeant were to strap him in. The lid will close automatically."

When the tech rejoined the group, Weir heard him hiss, "Sick bastard."

FEDERAL RESERVE—CULPEPER

Steele heard trickling water dancing over rocks in a small stream and saw, in a strange way, the light playing and sparkling on the tumbling surface of water, light beams flashing and skipping across his mind in multicolored splendor. Then, the sound of wind chimes began tinkling in harmony with the water-- joining in the symphony of light and sound and peace. And peace. He felt peace. He knew nothing but peace.

Then Steele realized he was lying down and that someone was bending over him.

"Steele, wake up!" A disturbance rippled across the landscape in the whispered urgency of the command.

"Steele, wake up!" The voice repeated and the Maxwell Parish landscape mutated into the glare of harsh un-shaded light as someone, bending over him said, "We don't have much time!"

"Where am I? Who are you?" The questions grated out of his throat. He needed a drink of water.

"You rescued me in the sandbox. It's John Weir."

"Weir," Steele suddenly remembered the filth-covered body he had found on the floor after the special ops mission had blasted its way into the mud and cinderblock hut, remembered how he had half dragged, half carried the lone survivor to the waiting helicopter.

Later he had visited Weir in the hospital to debrief him in hopes of learning more about the enemy. In the process they had developed a friendship that lasted the duration of Weir's tour. Then, like most wartime friendships, it had simply become a treasured memory.

"Listen. This is too hard to explain," Weir whispered harshly, "you're being transported in a pod. It *will* open up again. And when it does, you hunt for another pod. I'm going to try to load it up with ordnance."

"Ordnance? What the hell are you talking about?" Steele responded, still groggy.

"I'm sorry, buddy, but - where you're going - you're gonna need all you can get."

"Where's that?"

"I'm not sure. But when you get there you get to the ordnance. Try to make contact. I'll be working on this end for you."

"What the bloody hell are you talking about?"

"No time buddy. Remember the pod will open up again. You be ready to hit the ground running when it does. Get the ordnance. You use it. There will be hostiles there. You hear me?"

"Get weapons," Steele responded.

"Right. Sorry, buddy. Don't forget I'm down here for you. Now listen, you've got to play dead."

"What the bloody hell?"

"Do it or we're both screwed."

Steele's mind shifted into gear. He knew Weir. And he knew Weir wasn't fooling around. Instinctively, he went with his gut and accordingly closed his eyes.

The technicians looked across the room at Weir, clearly they were curious at the time it took for the new security officer to do whatever it was he was doing over at the pod. Noting their inquisitiveness, he called Martinez over to help him unstrap Steele. They lifted his inert body into the floating pod, struggling with the dead weight, grasping at the jeans and sweater in which he was dressed, their fingers slipping on the clothing. Once they wrestled him onto the couch-shaped interior, the gray pod came alive and the couch wrapped around the lifeless body, leaving only the face, neck and forearms uncovered.

When the couch began to encapsulate him, Steele's eyes popped open, something that Martinez was too busy arranging the straps to notice. When Weir shook his head, Steele feigned unconsciousness again.

"Hook him up," Weir ordered the technicians as he marched out of the room with Martinez in tow.   After they left the room, Weir ordered Martinez to show him where the pods were stored. After a quick inspection, he sent the sergeant off to get lunch at the local Thai restaurant in town. It gave him time to think.

He knew how he was going to get the ordnance. The locker closest to the pods was the obvious choice. And he knew where the extra pods waited, floating on air, in a storage room. He even knew how to open them, Martinez having showed him a concealed soft spot on one end which when compressed, slid the pod open. A second push of the soft spot would slide the hatch closed.

But how to get the ordnance in the pod without being seen was problem one. Problem two was how to get the pod into the transport area unnoticed. Problem three was how he knew the alien entity would even transport the extra pod. He did not. But it was a good guess. And, Martinez had said a few things that gave Weir hope. Like any military operation, there was a lot of sloppiness built into the system. It always amazed Weir that the military had so much "give" to it, so many loose ends, so much slack.   It was the nature of the beast, he had concluded, that when an organization as big as the military, or in this case, the NSA, did anything there was bound to be redundancy. The same rule seemed to apply here. Martinez told him that no one kept close tabs on the pods. That was a surprise. The young sergeant told him that sometimes they just picked up subjects without thought or preplanning, again, a surprise. And, once, by accident Martinez confided, they had even sent up an extra pod without repercussions—so there was hope that his poorly thought out plan might work.

Weir decided that now was the time to do it. Better to try at once, before tons of people come in later for the transport. Better to try now before Martinez comes back with lunch or Sims comes over to the transport center. Slipping out of his office, he walked down the corridor to where the pods were stored.

Most people were at lunch. The lower levels were never occupied heavily in any event. He palmed the security code for the door. Entered the storage closet and pushed a pod out into the hallway.

He turned to pull the door shut.

"Sir?" a woman whose voice he did not recognize asked, a young technician whose nameplate told him she was Nora Burke. "What are you doing? We have our allotment of pods already."

"New arrival," Weir said crisply. "Didn't you get the notification?"

"No." She looked at him uncertainly.

"Any other questions? I need to get this down to the transport room."

"You mean the prep room," she hesitantly corrected.

"Whatever," Weir bluffed.

Damn, he thought to himself after she left. He hadn't even started and already there were questions. But, committed as he was, he would just have to see it through. After pushing the coffin-sized pod down a maze of hallways to the ordnance locker without incident, and palming the door, he entered and pulled the pod inside. After pushing the rubber-like entry point the hatch slid open. He quickly loaded the pod compartment with weapons: C-4 plastic explosives, detonators, grenades, grenade launchers, carbines, shotguns and the 9mm handguns along with as many boxes of ammunition that he could load into the open space, shoving the boxes in between the weaponry and packaged plastic explosive. He had been afraid the pod would somehow respond to the munitions but the couch apparently was only activated by living flesh. When he couldn't stuff anymore weaponry into the cavity, he stopped and finding a pad of paper and a pencil on a shelf, wrote: "Steele, I don't know exactly where you are going. Fight back. I will do what I can to help on this end. Eventually, everyone comes back but not always alive. Good luck. W." Tearing off the paper, he placed it in the pod before shutting the hatch.

Weir was perspiring heavily now. His hands shook and his heart pounded like a sledgehammer: his breath came fast and shallow because he knew that not only was his life on the line but so was that of his family. How, he thought, could he do this without being caught? That Burke woman was going to be trouble unless he took care of her. And, he knew, he would never take care of her in the sense that Sims or some of the other goons in the center would think of doing because he wouldn't kill her. At least he didn't think he would. But, somehow he would have to keep her quiet; right now though, he had to act quick, had to think clearly, if not for Steele, then for himself, for his family.

Weir stood hesitantly in the room. *Get a grip,* he said to himself. *Push this thing down to the rest of the pods and act like you know what you're doing.* He squared his shoulders, took a deep breath, palmed the door open and pushed the pod out into the bright hallway where it slammed against the wall opposite of the open door. In his hyped up, adrenaline-fueled state, he had pushed too hard. Awkwardly, he man-handled the pod around and started down the hallway, telling himself so *far, so good.* But then, looking up at the small dark plastic dome in the center of the hallway ceiling, he remembered that the whole place was wired for camera surveillance. How he had forgotten that he did not know, but committed, he kept moving. *I'll just deal with it when I have to,* he concluded.

Weir finally pushed the pod to the room where Steele and the pods of the others were waiting. As he had hoped, no one was there, it being lunch time. He slipped the pod in the midst of the 15 others, making it 16. All the pods looked the same. Even he would not be able to tell one from the other once they were moved. He hoped that would be enough.

Weir took one last look at the floating assemblage before rushing back to his office to complete the remainder of his plan. Twenty minutes had elapsed. It felt like an eternity.

He waited for Martinez to come back. And he thought about the Burke woman.

Then Weir knew what he would do. In fact it was the only thing he could do. When Martinez came back with lunch he sent him out to fetch the Burke woman. "No," he told Martinez, "I don't want you to call her. Go find her and bring her here. And, if it gets down to it, you get her here whether she wants to come or not. This is a security matter."

Ten minutes later he heard a hesitant knock on his door.

"Come!" he said harshly.

The petite woman entered the office meekly. He noticed she was attractive: in her early 30s, brunette, blue eyes and on the slender side. Her eyes followed his pointed finger towards a seat in front of his desk. He waited a moment, to make her as uncomfortable as possible. She sat with her hands clasped on her lap, hunched over ever so slightly. The tension in the room swirled about with its vortex the scared woman in the seat. He almost felt sorry for her. Almost.

"You have a problem," he said authoritatively.

BEFORE THE WARRENTON TRAINING CENTER

Randy Collins had played football for Culpeper High School and he still retained the big lineman look he'd had from 25-years earlier when he could blow through an offensive line with ease --much to the dismay of whoever was unfortunate enough to have a football in his possession. Now, his buzz-cut hair was turning grey early but his arms were as big and strong as they were when he played football. Not only was he built like a workhorse but Collins knew every road, every trail, and every family in the county. And, if he didn't know someone, he sure enough knew someone who did. It was that combination that made Randy the perfect civil service processor for the sheriff's department. He could go anywhere without fear. He was that big. He could find anybody. He was that knowledgeable about who came and went in the county. And finally the last ingredient of the brew that made him so good was his slow and deliberate and polite way of addressing everybody. His tone and demeanor was the same for the vilest drunk or the frailest little old lady from Stevensburg Baptist Church. He never had any resisting arrest warrants to bring to court. Most folks thanked him for the warrants he delivered --usually given after he had inquired into their family's health and suggested a good mechanic for the invariable car troubles most of his targets seemed to have.

The sheriff took Randy aside earlier that day with special instructions. "I want him served personally. And he has to be served off federal property. Don't ask me why. Some legal mumbo jumbo 'ole Binford says we need to follow." So with marching orders in hand and a free reign from his other duties, Collins soon discovered that his target liked to go out to eat lunch. Like clockwork, he would drive out at eleven-forty-five and head into town.

Collins knew the make of the car his target drove, as well as the license plate number. That was easy enough to find out using DMV records. Parked in a little used driveway, he waited for the right car to drive by.

Just as he thought, his target drove past at eleven-fifty, heading in towards town. Collins started up his unmarked Dodge Hemi and pulled out to follow.

The Virginia Constitution guarantees that citizens cannot just be stopped by the police when they are driving. The United States Constitution says the same thing. The government, meaning the police, or in particular a sheriff's deputy, has to have probable cause to stop someone driving a car. This means the deputy has to think that his target is breaking the law and, if questioned about it in court, he has to be able to say what it was that made him think the target was "probably" doing just that: breaking the law. If the reason doesn't suit the common sense of a judge, then the whole case can be thrown out, never to be brought up again.

Collins didn't need probable cause on this mission. He would merely follow the target, wait for him to get out of the car, and then serve the paper on him. Virginia Constitutional law allows sheriff's deputies to talk to anyone on the street. That much he was sure of. But, Collins was not above using probable cause to serve a warrant if the violation was blatant enough, say an expired license plate or speeding or maybe crossing the middle line once too many times—all of which could constitute probable cause. As a consequence, Collins watched the car intently, but he stayed a respectful distance behind, feeling no need to rush things. His job was to hand a piece of paper to his target. His job was not to get an arrest unless necessary.

The two cars wound through the back roads of Culpeper and eventually ended up in the parking lot of a shopping center next to the local IHOP. Collins approved of the selection; he had always been partial to a big stack of pancakes smothered in butter and dripping maple syrup.

He waited for his target to get out of the car and start walking towards the restaurant entrance. Collins grabbed the subpoena and exited the car, positioning his bulk between the retreating subject and the subject's car.

"Mr. Sims?" Collins said loudly enough for Ford Allen Sims to hear. "I have some papers I need to give to you."

"Papers? What kind of papers?" Sims exclaimed as Collins handed them to him.

"This is a subpoena to appear before the Culpeper County Special Grand Jury next week," Collins explained.

"You've got to be kidding me," Sims replied heatedly. "I'm a federal officer. You can't just subpoena me in a state court."

"Yes, sir. You're most likely right," Collins responded neutrally. "I wouldn't know about such things. You'll need to take it up with the Commonwealth's Attorney."

"Damn right, I will."

"Sir, would you mind signing this indicating that you received the subpoena. I can sign for you but it always looks better to the judge if you do that now."

Sims grabbed the proffered clipboard and scribbled his name on the subpoena copy, then practically threw it back at Collins.

"Hope everything works out," Collins said retreating, his mission accomplished.

A simple act handing one piece of paper to another, Collins thought to himself as he drove off, but the law required that once that paper is taken in hand by the person whose name is on it, he must appear in court. To fail to do so meant that the whole weight of the state government would work to make it happen, even if it meant being physically apprehended and put in jail. The mere fact that so many words on a little piece of paper could carry so much power had always amazed Collins, whose mind worked in more concrete ways. But he knew what the raw power of government could be. He'd wrestled enough runaways to the ground to know that part of governmental power. But, Collins suspected the Sims fellow wouldn't run. Collins recognized in Sims a person used to dictating orders, not taking them. And, Collins had a feeling that the Commonwealth's Attorney was going to find that out.

As Collins drove through the Virginia countryside, all he could do was wonder what tom-fool thing it was the sheriff had talked Binford into doing this time.

WARRENTON TRAINING CENTER—CULPEPER.

Sims fumed.

Subpoenaed to appear before a special grand jury. He knew enough to know what that meant. It meant that damn Commonwealth's Attorney was going to be able to ask him all sorts of questions under oath, all to do with the Wood couple. The subpoena said as much: "In RE: The deaths of Edward and Patricia Wood." Storming into his office, he called the Group 929 attorney and asked for Conyer Somerfield.

"Conyer. Conyer. Yes, that's right," he said impatiently. Sims sat down and examined the subpoena again while he waited for Conyer to answer. He noted the document seemed to be personally signed by the Commonwealth Attorney, which, as far as Sims was concerned, made the whole thing personal. He wanted to stop the subpoena and since this Binford idiot wanted to go mano-a-mano, he decided would take out the meddling prosecutor-- just on principle.

"What seems to be the problem," Somerfield asked in a lazy southern drawl when Sims connected to his line.

"Some damn brown shirt handed me a subpoena for next week. The local prosecutor has been nosing around an unfortunate cleanup we had here. So now he wants me to testify in front of a special grand jury."

"Was it EO2 sanctioned?" Somerfield asked, to establish the legality of the cleanup. Legality of course was a relative thing. The attorney, who had been around the block a few times with ugly cleanups, just needed to know which cubby hole to put this particular problem in.

"Of course it was, you idiot." Sims snapped.

"Now, now, Sims. No need to get testy here. Special grand jury. Hmmm. Well, they are getting a little creative down there in Culpeper. Were you served personally?"

"I told you. The deputy handed it to me."

"At the Warrenton Training Center?"

"No, in front of an IHop in town."

"Ok. You're still on active duty, am I right?"

"Of course."

"Ok. I can file a motion to quash the subpoena. We'll claim the Soldiers and Sailors Act. It will buy us some time. But in the end, Sims, you'll have to appear. Virginia is pretty strict when it comes to the powers granted special grand juries."

"What the hell is a motion to squash?" Sims asked.

"*Motion to Quash*," Somerfield corrected. "It's a legal filing that says the subpoena is illegitimate. Basically it challenges the ability of the government to make you come right now under this subpoena. The Soldiers and Sailors Act exempts active duty servicemen from all sorts of state legal actions. And in this case we will claim you are on active duty and therefore not subject to the subpoena at this time."

"Will it fly?"

"No, as I said, ultimately you will have to appear. You don't actually qualify as being on active duty unless you are out of the country or are about to be deployed. But, we can tie them up for a while. Just remember this is only a stall tactic. Virginia is an unusual state. These special grand juries are powerful creatures of law. Once they get started, they can do just about anything except actually indict someone. They can recommend an indictment but they can't actually do it."

"So what are they good for?"

"Collecting information. Under oath. Questioned by the Commonwealth Attorney and any one of the grand jurors." Somerfield replied dryly, knowing that the phrase "collecting information" would send Sims into a paroxysm of rage.

"Hmph. This is some little piss-ant county prosecutor and sheriff," Sims snapped. "Surely we can do better than just stall. We *are not* going to compromise the entire project over this."

"Of course not. The problem, my ill-tempered friend, is that the newspapers will cover this. And any sort of normal cleanup, as you call it, will only fuel the fires of inquisitiveness. Forget the news media for a second. Think about the internet. If we were to just march in and blow up half the courthouse with the grand jury and the prosecutor in it, the special grand jury process would still continue. The conspiracy blogs will be all over this. There will be videos posted online. Sooner or later they might post videos of the Warrenton Training Center and the Federal Reserve. Am I correct in assuming no one wants *that*? And in any event, another special grand jury would be empaneled and then it would start all over. No, we stall while we decide how to end this in a proper legal manner."

"Proper legal manner, my ass," Sims replied. "That just means you figure out how to execute someone without using a bullet," Sims sneered.

"Why, whatever do you mean," Somerfield said in mock indignation, "I do have to abide by a code of legal ethics. It will all be done with foot- high briefs, continuances and memos and whatever else we can devise. All in a legal manner, of course."

"Oh, of course, all nice and neat," Sims replied. "All right. Do it. And get that prosecutor. It's personal, as far as I'm concerned. The bastard actually signed the subpoena. I want to return the favor."

"Ok. Scan and email me a copy of the subpoena and I'll access whatever documents they have filed online. But listen, how bad do you really want to get this prosecutor?"

"Does it make a difference?"

"The more targets I have, the more options I have. Now understand this, I'm not advising you to use the legal process to pursue a personal grudge. That would be improper."

"Of course," Sims said deadpan.

"But if you were to think that somehow his actions were improperly motivated, then it would be appropriate for me to pursue an investigation of his motives."

"Ha! You lawyers are all alike. Say one thing. Mean another. Ha! Yes, Somerfield, I think his motives are personal in nature. I think he has an animus towards me and my security officer, Weir."

"Well, if that were the case, it would be a matter of prosecutorial misconduct," Somerfield said emotionlessly.

"As you say," Sims replied.

"Let me do a little checking, and I'll get back to you."

That prosecutor was going to pay, Sims told himself as he put down the receiver. If nothing else, he'd make sure this Binford fellow took a little free range ride to Mars. Oh yes, he would indeed. Then, he'd personally make sure the prosecutor took a nice long nap on the chair in Room 35B. Oh, yes. We'll give him some extra refinements, Sims thought with glee. We'll shove those needles in extra hard. Shove 'em in until the bones crunch, shove 'em in and leave 'em in till he gets a good dose of that special brew they make up there at the lab in the mountain. Shove 'em in and shove 'em in again.

FEDERAL RESERVE—TRANSPORT ROOM

Steele wanted to scream, but he didn't think it would do any good. He'd already tried that, when the first wave of panic overwhelmed him, and nothing had happened. He'd tried to rock whatever it was he was in –but the effort had been futile. He did not know if that was because the pod was in something solid or because he was so constrained he could not shift his body weight about. He thought it was the latter. He hoped it was. He prayed he wasn't buried in something, buried deep, buried dark.

When he was twelve, growing up in Eastbourne, a quiet tourist and retirement city on the English Channel, he had begun wandering about and looking for adventure. One bright south-of-England sunny day he had taken the train as an adventure. Jumping on at the main station in Eastbourne, he rode a short way in the passenger car before getting off at the little station in Polegate, a suburb on the South Downs, a ridge of treeless hills that run parallel to the coast. He meandered around the town, as twelve-year-old boys are wont to do, until he had come upon a countryside field with a sign that said: "Westfield Close Development." Deep ditches snaked across the green landscape, mapping out the storm drains for the streets that would eventually be graveled and paved. But for the twelve-year-old, it was a foreign environment to explore and in his just-budding adolescent mind, to conquer. Steele had jumped into the ten-foot ditches. It had been a particularly dry summer for England that year and the clay and chalk soil was crumbly. He'd skipped along the white dirt pathways, ignoring the small landslides of dirt and flint nodules that fell behind him disturbed by his passage, ducking into the five-foot-tall concrete tubes. Enjoying the sense of mystery as he threaded his way in the semi-darkness, he moved slowly, feeling the rough concrete with his hands as he moved forward, savoring the sense of fear that welled up as it got darker, the sense of relief when light pointed toward whatever lay at the end of the concrete maze.

Stop it, he said to himself. But like a movie-- he had to see it to the end. There was no switching of channels in this memory. Willing or not, this would not go away. The memory sat there, like rotten meat, its scent drifting on the currents of his mind, always there, sometimes stronger, sometimes weaker, but once sensed, insistent on returning. Especially now. In this place.

The tunnels had gone on and on, twisting and turning. Where they were not joined, the light streamed in and he ran from one tunnel complex to another, imagining he was with the British light dragoons searching the cliff complexes on D-Day in Normandy.

Then, in an instant everything changed, the ditch wall collapsing over a single concrete storm drain section. Dust and dirt filled each end of the tube and the darkness smothered all. In the center of the tube he saw the dirt fall and fill the entrance. He choked on the dust. Then, when the shock subsided he started to dig his way out.

Steele remembered the digging. It went on and on and on, until his fingernails were broken and the dust was choking him, all the time aware that, as he progressed and the dirt slid into the empty space behind him, he was creating his own tomb. It was then that he had collapsed, hopelessly buried deep in the chalk hills of the South Downs.

But, he reminded himself, that was all in the past. The inside of the pod, as he'd heard it called, was not completely dark. Thank God for that. Not like the storm sewer in Polegate. In the pod, at various places, he saw small pin pricks of light that flashed on and off. Some remained steady, green, amber, blue. Others were white, but they gave off just enough illumination so that he could see whatever was in his line of vision.

The inability to move was maddening. Literally. At first, after Weir had talked to him, Steele played along. Really, what other choice did he have? He knew the armed takedown of him and his friends was anything but friendly. Guns and swift blows to the head had proved that. So Weir had to be a friend. Had to be. Or, in his more horrified moments, Steele thought to himself, *or I'm in a coffin*.

Maybe he was already in the ground, buried deep, buried dark. Buried deep. Buried dark. Those two phrases revolved around and around in his head until he would scream and attempt to struggle again, struggle for release, struggle until exhausted, struggle until the panic would ebb away into a catatonic void.

His mind circled back to the storm sewer. He sat in the dark, shivering with the seeping damp cold. Blackness so thick, he passed his hand in front of his face and perceived nothing. Then, he realized he had heard something. Something scratching and moving dirt in the dark. He heard it but did not know what it was. It wasn't a rescue. These were not the sounds of shovels and machinery and men. No this was much smaller and animal-like.   And that terrified the twelve-year-old boy. Even in the pod, Steele shivered internally at the memory of that awful sound: claws grating against flint nodules in the dirt. He remembered scrunching away from the noise, his back against the mound of dirt he had squirmed out of earlier. There was something definitely tunneling its way towards him, he remembered thinking in disbelief. Something with claws and teeth. And, blood-red eyes full of murderous intent.

And then it had broken through. He heard the fall of dirt and stone. And he heard the sound of something scrabbling through the sliding soil towards him.

Stop it. Stop it, he ordered himself. Concentrate.

Weir had to be a friend: had to be. And he said the lid would open. *It would open. It had to open.* And he said there would be hostiles. Now why would someone who was not looking out for Steele say that? It didn't make any sense. But then, Steele thought to himself, none of this made any sense.

At times he felt movement. Steele had always had a very good sense of balance. Even without a horizon he could tell when an airliner was shifting in the sky. And now, he could tell that the pod had moved. Always laterally. Not up or down. But for some time there had been no movement.

The lights, now that was a different story. The flashes were increasing in frequency. And once, he thought, just on the edge of his vision, he saw a red pinprick.

A red pinprick. Just like the eye he'd imagined he had seen in the tunnel. A red eye boring into Steele's innards: ripping apart his bowels. He'd heard it moving in the dark. Screaming he had hurled rocks in its direction. Once he had heard a thump and a grunt in return. The scrabbling in the dirt, the click of nails on the bare concrete floor between he and it, melded into one long horrible nightmare that went on and on and on until the next day when he heard men and equipment above, clearing away the dirt. By that time, Steele was catatonic. He knew that now. Then he had seemed to live in a dream.

"Damn! Look what we got in here! Looks like a bleeding slaughter house," were the first words he heard as the light streamed in to find him, blood covered, lying against the concrete wall, a bloody rock by his side, a bludgeoned hedgehog at his feet, its head a ruined horror of brain and blood. To this day Steele did not remember how that transpired. Only that he had survived. And now, he told himself, he would survive this. Somehow.

Steele held on to the fact that he had saved Weir's life. Literally. It took all he had to believe that Weir was somehow returning the favor.

The lid would open. It had to.

Several hours later, Weir stood in the control room looking down at the transport area. Three times already he had met the eyes of the Burke woman, willing her to stay silent about what she and he had discussed in his office. Below sixteen grey and purple pods hovered. They were lined up in two lines of five and one line of six if anybody looked carefully: he hoped no one did look very carefully. In fact he was banking on it. The whole process had become so mundane, so matter-of-fact, the horror of it long lost on the numbed intellects of everyone in that God-forsaken facility, that Weir calculated, to count pods on that particular night would seem as pointless as it would on any of the other of hundreds of transports. After all, Weir had told himself more than once while executing his poorly thought out scheme, Martinez had put it best, who in their right mind would want to steal a pod and go to whatever horror lay at the other end of that long trip? No one was going to volunteer for that ride to hell. No one.

Weir had, with the help of Martinez, supervised the movement of the pods to the transport room. No one counted the number of pods being transported. The technicians in charge of movement just grabbed the pods like so much luggage at the airport and skidded the objects along corridors to the transport room: bumping them against walls and doors as they glided in the air. Once in the room, Weir and Martinez had suggested and prodded the technicians to arrange the lines perpendicular to the big window. Weir hoped that would somehow help hide the extra pod when viewed from above.

Although he was outwardly calm, his heart was pounding, his mouth so dry his tongue stuck to the roof of his mouth. He moved to stand next to the Burke woman, touched her arm and said in a barely audible whisper, "Remember what I said."

Sims, who had been absent most of the day, and then when he did arrive, clearly somewhat distracted, spotted Weir and joined him by the window.

"Ah, Weir," he said, trailing Weir as he moved away from his vantage point, "I see you are throwing yourself into your work. Good. Good."

"Yes, Sir," he tried desperately to think of something to say to distract Sims and Frank Hill, the transport director, from the sixteen pods floating below.

"Martinez has briefed me on all the procedures," Weir told him. "We supervised the assembly of pods here." Weir said matter of factly.

"And Steele?" Sims asked, his eyes squinting with interest.

"I have to admit, I was none too happy about sending him out without sedating treatment," Weir said.

"No. I would think not. But there is a purpose, Weir. There is a purpose," Sims fluttered his hands in front of his chest to emphasize the point.

Weir noted that Hill started to look more intently at the computer screen in front of him. Quickly he moved over to the transport director and asked, "Mr. Hill, I have a question," he said. In fact he had no idea what he wanted to ask.

"Humph," Hill responded still looking at the screen.

"I have a question regarding security," Weir said.

"Ha! Security. Do you hear that, Hill? Our man is already on the job," Sims said loudly.

Hill pulled his eyes away from the screen to face Sims and Weir. "Yes?" He asked with some irritation.

For the next ten minutes, Weir asked what even he knew were inane questions about the identity of the persons in the control room, the levels of clearance at the facility and the upcoming process of transport.

"Really, can't this wait?" Hill asked, clearly exasperated.

"As security chief I need to know everything." Weir replied, "The slightest gap in knowledge on my part can lead to an opening for someone or something to breach protocol."

"Really, Sims, do I have to put up with this right now?" Hill demanded. "How long ago was it we gave him a ride on the couch-- and now he wants to know everything? Give me a break. We are about to transport."

"You've done this how many times?" Weir asked. "Surely by this time it is so routine that it can happen without you in the room. In fact I'd expect that sort of redundancy. Surely, Mr. Hill, the whole operation does not hinge on your eyes being glued to a computer screen? If that is true, then you do have a problem. Redundancy is paramount in any black op program."

"Of course there are others that can supervise transport," Hill replied heatedly, "but I like to know things are done right."

"Tell me about transport. Is it merely a reverse of what I saw when the transportees were returned?"

"How technical an answer does your security-conscious mind require?" Hill asked.

"Give me a sketch. I can get more detail later."

"Look. In reality we know very little about what is going on here. That is the truth. Imagine an ant hill. Do the ants know why blades of grass fall down every week when the grass is mowed? Do they understand if enough of them get in the sugar bowl certain death for the colony will probably follow?"

"Your point?"

"Obviously, my point is that we don't really understand anything of what is going on here," Hill said. "We merely record and collaborate. And hope that somehow in the process we learn something. And I tell that to you, Mr. Security Chief, so that you won't continue to pepper me with idiot questions to which there are no answers."

"Point taken," Weir replied.

"The simple answer to your question is, no. No, it is not the same as return," Hill said. "We don't know why. The pods are encased in an electro-magnetic singularity just as the transportees were upon return. But, there is no ship, although, clearly there is one upon return. No ship approaches the Federal Reserve. The singularity moves up through the room and, once free of the facility, simply moves up beyond the earth's atmosphere. Its transit is different, though, than the ships themselves. The singularity transports to the moon. It is all so incredibly fast. These pods that you see will be in lunar orbit within three hours of leaving here. On average that is a 250,000 mile trip."

"I thought Mars was the destination." Weir interrupted.

"It is. We don't know why the moon insertion is part of the process. It just is. Following the insertion into lunar orbit, the singularity slingshots to Mars. Again, it is so fast that it defies explanation. Earthly explanation anyway. Whether the distance is 36 million miles or 250 million miles, it seems to make no difference to the singularity. Transit time is usually two days. Do your understand man? Two days! Impossible but for the fact that we see it happening."

"How long should it take?" Weir asked.

"With our best technology? And we're basically talking Apollo-era technology," Hill went on, "nothing has really changed. It would take a year in the best of circumstances. And we would have to wait for the optimum time to slingshot across the planetary orbital plane. But, what the hell does that have to do with security?"

"You never know, Mr. Hill," Weir answered calmly. "What about oxygen, g-forces, how is that handled in the pod?"

"Like I said, we don't really know. But we can guess. The best theory is that the pod is able to create a gravity-free environment that protects the inhabitants from the otherwise fatal g-forces the speeds we are talking about would create. As for oxygen, the pod creates it. From what we don't know. And the singularity, the silver like globe you saw, it apparently uses gravitational repellant and attraction to move. In essence, it taps the energy of the universe itself to operate. There's no fuel in the singularity. There's nothing in it as a matter of fact. And it has the ability to move through matter without disruption."

"How is that even possible?" Weir asked.

"Perhaps you need to take a course in physics," Hill said disdainfully. "Matter is essentially empty space framed by electronically charged particles. Singularities in and of themselves really. Somehow the alien technology allows the larger singularity to slide between the empty spaces in matter."

"One last question Mr. Hill and then I'll let you get back to the transport," Weir said. "What happens when the pods arrive?"

"I'm done here," Hill said dismissively. "Why don't you ask Mr. Sims about that. Transport is about to transpire and I have to get back to *my job!* Now, if you will excuse me!"

But when the now thoroughly flustered Hill turned away, Weir followed.

"Mr. Hill, I need to understand this fully," he said. "If I have to I'll inform Group that you were being less than cooperative in a security matter."

Hill whirled about. "A security matter! What the hell are you talking about? A week ago you weren't even cleared to be in here and now you're talking about a "security matter. Get real."

"What happens when the pods are opened?" Weir asked, using his no-nonsense tone he affected during interrogations. Thankfully, it worked.

Hill looked at Weir, then at Sims. Sims merely twitched his eyebrows.

"Again, Weir, we are not sure about anything," Hill told him. But you saw the returnees. They're not in the best of shape. Obviously they've been through some trauma. At times it appears they've been biopsied. At other times, the bruising and malnutrition would indicate forced labor of some sort. We act to erase any residual memories they may have of our involvement and also anything of what occurred on Mars. Believe me, we have tried to find out what happens up there but we think the ride in the singularity scrambles recent memory. But that is only one theory. You did notice that sometimes transportees do not come back in one piece."

"You mean dead," Weir said.

"Of course. Again, why, we're not sure. And it makes for quite a mess to fix back home. People have a lot of loose ends to tie up. And then there are those that don't return."

"Don't return?"

"No. A few have never returned."

"And the pods," Weir continued, "you transport them in pods but they are not returned in them. Why? And, how are they brought here?"

"Damndest thing," Hill said, once again absorbed in the subject, which, clearly dominated his life. "We don't know. The pods are dumped empty at Area 51 in New Mexico via singularity. They are obviously reused. We do know that. We ship them here by rail usually. But why the separation? Who knows?"

"Singularity detected," a woman at one of the computer terminals announced.

"Now if there is nothing else, I have my job to do," Hill said returning to scan data streams at his station. "Ok people. Heads up!"

"Scanners are up and running."

"Roger that. Nominal approach."

"Pods assembled and prepped." Weir heard what he recognized as Ms. Burke's voice make the announcement. Internally he winced. He'd had no idea she was so involved in the actual transport of the pods. He automatically moved to stand next to her. She did not look at him. But he noticed her hand tremble as she touched the keypad in front of her.

"Lunar transit traverse."

"ETA three minutes."

"Flight recorder on."

The minutes tumbled away. Weir become tenser as each second passed. His main concern was Ms. Burke. He had successfully diverted Hill, who Weir sensed was about to determine an extra pod was in the room. His last concern was that the singularity would reject all of the pods, or one of the extras and then there would be, as Ricky Riccardo used to say, 'some esplaning to do'.

"Entry in thirty seconds."

Again, Weir saw electrical discharges arcing across the room where the pods were.

"Switching to Main Bus B."

"Internal Power on."

"We are off grid."

"Roger that. Off grid."

"On my mark entry in 5, 4, 3, 2, 1."

Weir saw the silver ball begin to slip through the ceiling of the transport room. Electrical arcs snaked across the floor of the room enveloping the pods. The gleaming sphere moved effortless down and through the floor of the room until all of the pods were engulfed.

In one fluid motion the silver ball slid upwards and out of the room. Electrical discharges fired around the padded room.

And then it was over.

Almost.

"We have an anomaly."

"I copy that."

"What the hell!" Hill exclaimed.

"Scanning."

"Transfer data on my mark."

Hill turned from his computer screen. "There was an extra pod in that delivery. We were scheduled to transport fifteen. But there were sixteen, and what I want to know is, why. Got an answer for that, Weir?"

CHAPTER 12

THE NATURE OF THE ALIEN ENTITY (AE) IS DISPUTED.   WE HAVE NEV-
ER SEEN IT.   WE INTERACT WITH IT -- BUT ONLY THROUGH DIGITAL
MESSAGES.

**---EXCERPTS FROM THE NSA PRESIDENTIAL BRIEFING PAPERS ON THE
ROSWELL INCIDENT.**

INTERPLANETARY TRANSIT—DAY TWO

Steele did not think he was in a coffin, mainly because he saw lights sometimes blink within his field of vision. He heard nothing. He felt nothing. He could not move. But he could blink his eyes. He could see flashes of light. He could open his mouth--but only so far. He breathed. This was better than being in a concrete tube buried by tons of dirt. Buried by blackness so black nothing registered. Better than being buried with something that had teeth and a hunger for blood. Better than all that, he told himself.

Steele thought these things when he was lucid--which was infrequent. He replayed over and over what Weir said to him during the clear times, the times when all his synapses fired in a logical sequence. *The lid will open. There are hostiles. Search the pods for weapons.*

There were more times when the darkness and fear sucked him under the way the undertow does on a stormy beach and the sense of confinement became so intense that the claustrophobic press of total physical restriction overwhelmed him and he screamed. He screamed and screamed and screamed. He screamed until he was hoarse. He screamed until he was deaf with the screaming. He screamed until blood and spittle ran down the side of his face.

No water. No food. Sometimes the strain and stress pushed him into a trance-like state akin to what happened when he was a boy in the storm drain buried with the hedgehog. Perhaps that was sleep. He would come to, aware of where he was and of what had happened. That was when he was most lucid.

The lights were blinking with more regularity now. Moaning, Steele tried to focus. He drew on his military training. Concentrate on what you know and extrapolate from that basis. Do that or sink into a chaos of suppositions and instincts--and die. What did he know? He knew what Weir said.

He said the lid would open. He said there would be hostiles. He said there would be weapons.

Later, after another round of claustrophobic insanity, he fell back into lucidity again and saw that the lights were definitely firing off in a sequence now. The regularity gave him something to focus on. Two red. One amber. One white. Two red. One amber. One white. Left side. Left side. Top. Front. Below. And then repeated. A pattern. It was a pattern new to Steele. He hoped it signaled change.

Later, much later, Steele felt movement.

It startled him. He had become so used to the deadening inertia that the sense of movement was strange. He was moving sideways. Then feet first. No jarring. Just smooth movement.

The lid will open. There will be hostiles. Look for weapons.

Not knowing what to expect, Steele readied himself for action.

Later a wisp of air told him the air seal had been breached. Then the lid slid open. Steele looked through barely opened eyes at an illuminated ceiling. Brown. Smooth. Ambient light. He heard clicking noises. He smelled ozone and dry dust. A shadow passed over his face.

Steele did not scream, although he wanted to, the visceral reaction died stillborn in his throat.

What he saw was beyond reaction. Beyond horror. Steele fought to stay in a lucid place. *There will be hostiles. Look for weapons.* Steeled repeated the mantra over and over while the monstrosity above him reached out and touched a control panel inside the pod by his head. A pincer, pointed, jagged, mottled red and gray, scratched the panel next to his face.

The unmistakable odor of carrion-- dead meat, rotting in the sun for days, blown with flies, crawling with maggots --replaced the sour smell of ozone and dust. The strangely humid miasma fell thickly on Steele in waves from the horror moving above him.

CULPEPER—WARRENTON TRAINING CENTER.

"All right. I want answers." Sims sat behind his desk. His reptilian eyes bored into Weir.

"Answers to what?" Weir shot back.

"Don't screw with me, Weir. Do you want me to play the tapes? I will."

"Tapes to what?"

"Again, Weir, don't screw with me. Why did you put an extra pod in the transport. We have it all on tape."

"Did you get my conversation with Ms. Burke?" Weir asked.

"In the hallway—of course. And we've got you moving a pod. We've got you arranging the pods in the transport room. So I ask again, why did you put an extra pod in the room?"

"Simple. I was doing my job."

"Your job is security. It is not adding pods to the transport," Sims said sharply.

"And in doing so I was doing my job."

"Make no mistake, Weir, we are about this close," here Sims held his forefinger and thumb about a quarter inch apart, "from hauling your ass to Group. So either tell me what is going on or tell them. I don't care much either way at this point."

"I am in charge of security, correct?" Weir demanded. "I ran a check on your security measures. Please tell me that this has been done before? Please don't tell me that in a security situation such as what we have here that you never tested security within the facility. Please tell me you've not been that slack."

Sims leaned back in his chair and clasped his hands behind his head. Silence screamed between the two men.

"I decided what better time to see how good security was than seeing what was in place before I actually had a chance to change things," Weir said. "So I decided to see how far I could get before anyone noticed anything. I must say I was surprised to learn that no one kept an active inventory of the number of pods in storage. That gave me the opening I needed—and I took it."

"You want me to believe this was a security check?"

"Of course. What else could it be? And, let me say that your Ms. Burke was the only member of the team that showed any sense of alarm at my activities. It took me giving her a briefing of the exercise to keep her quiet. But quite frankly that, in and of itself, shows a weakness in the system you have in place here. She should never have taken my word for what was going on. There should have been a mechanism for her to check things out. Nevertheless, she should be commended for at least realizing that something was amiss. The same cannot be said for Mr. Hill. He actually transported the wrong number of pods. And no one caught it. Not him. Not his underlings. That, Mr. Sims, is a real failure in security. So take me to Group. I will be happy to tell them about the sloppy management of the facility and about how I discovered how sloppy it really is."

Weir leaned back and glared at Sims, fire in his eye, mouth set straight and tight. And all of it a front. Weir was bluffing. Big time. And he hoped Sims was a bad poker player.

"What was in the pod?" Sims asked in a deadly quiet voice.

"Check your damn cameras if you want to know," Weir replied.

"I'm not kidding, Weir. What was in the pod?"

"I'm done playing games too, Sims. I'm in charge of security. I've found a serious breach in the security system set up under your command. I can fix it. Or we can take all of this to Group. I don't care much either way myself. Your call."

Sims rocked back and forth in his chair, his hands still tucked behind his head, still glaring at Weir. "I don't like this. Not one bit. Now, get out. And, Weir," he added, "we're not done here. Not by a long shot."

"Understood," Weir said firmly.

Once he was in his car, Weir saw that his hands were trembling. The last two days had been the worst of his life, culminating in the moment when Hill had discovered that there was an extra pod. But Nora Burke had remained silent.

Rebecca knew something was up, but since he didn't say a word to her about it, a wall had grown quickly between them. Secrets are deadly in a marriage. He'd learned that once, and he was sure he had more lessons to learn in that subject. Still, there was nothing to be done about it now. Maybe later, he thought to himself, when he had extracted himself from this nightmare, when he could explain everything to her. But right now he was convinced that the less she knew, the safer she and the kids would be.

His strategy at the Federal Reserve was too busy himself with his work and to avoid Sims and Hill for as long as possible while he refined, in his own mind, his plan for explaining what he had done. The story was plausible. And, with a bit of panache, he thought, he could bluff his way through. However, there was one hole in the story. Why had he stuffed the pod with weapons? That made no sense and he knew it. Thankfully, Sims had not reviewed all of the tapes or he would have discovered Weir's little going-away gift to Steele. Perhaps even Sims could not fathom the idea of sending weapons to the aliens and would look no further.

The poker strategy had worked, he told himself. Weir had no other option but to follow it to the end if need be—bluff as if he were holding a royal flush. But Weir knew he was holding a marginal hand at best. And, perhaps, his card play would have to turn, as the professional card players called it, manic, in a desperate attempt to win the round.

Weir started up the black GMC Tahoe, which seemed to be government issue with Group, and drove the winding road back to Route 3, but instead of turning right towards Mt. Pony and the Federal Reserve, he turned left and headed towards Fredericksburg. After a forty-five minute drive, he wheeled into the parking lot of a restaurant that advertised wi-fi connectivity and after ordering a coffee and bagel with cream cheese, he flipped open his newly-acquired laptop and logged into the public internet portal provided by the eatery. Knowing full well the ability of the NSA to track internet usage, there was no way he could attempt what he was doing now with a computer used at his home or at work. Given the recent pod incident, any research he did online would be sure to send up red flags. A clean computer, never used, on a public portal, was about as anonymous as he could get while online.

Weir used Google and began a methodical search of Mars exploration attempts. He knew the transports had gone to Mars. And, armed with the knowledge that the United States had facilitated abduction transports long before it sent the Mars Explorers to land on the surface of the planet, Weir hoped that, in all the data online, there might be some piece of information that would help him locate his onetime rescuer—and perhaps repay a debt long overdue.

Weir feared, given Sims' apparent distaste for Steele, that there might be a plan to leave Steele there. And Weir felt honor-bound to do all he could to pull the Brit out of the hell that Weir's Faustian decision to choose family over friendship had put the hapless Englishman. Even if it meant going there himself, Weir thought grimly, shocked that he had come to that conclusion.

Sipping the steaming hot coffee, he began reading.

FORT MEADE, MD—NSA HEADQUARTERS.

Conyer Somerfield was an old-fashioned lawyer. Not only did he think of himself that way, but anyone who knew him would describe him as such. He had a courtly manner. A southern drawl. Not a deep south drawl from Mississippi or Alabama but rather one from Virginia or the coastlands of North Carolina. It lent a measure of dignity to his speech as he slowly skewered an opponent in court. Thin and long-faced, the fifty-five-year-old favored khaki pants, white shirts and regimental-striped ties with a blue blazer and wingtip, leather-soled shoes.

Somerfield's one eccentric habit to his northern friends, but not to those who had attended the same Virginia prep school as he had, was a predilection for wearing a blue and white pinstriped, seer-sucker suit.

He wore the suit today as much to annoy the gray-suited bureaucrats that infested the boxy glass building as to endear himself to the cadre of attorneys that worked for him. He knew they smirked a little as the boss came in the office in all his blue and white glory, but he also knew they liked the fact that he was different and that they too were different from the technocrats and spooks that floated about because of the suit, and because of the man who dared to wear such an anachronism.

Somerfield was an old-fashioned lawyer in another way; he knew how to slip the knife in so smoothly, so gently, that his prey never knew what hit until too late. The first step of this process was always to do a background check. He had learned a long time ago that there were always two battles in the practice of law: there were facts and then there was the law. That was obvious. The other battle centered on politics and the personal weaknesses of his opponent. They never taught this second skill of lawyering in the credentialed halls of law school-- that was something learned through experience and a certain amount of courtroom bloodletting.

Propping his feet up on the desk, and crossing the brown, leather-soled wingtips, he started to read the background information gathered on his latest prey: Mordecai Binford. Flipping through the blue case-jacket, he learned everything there was to know about the man. Snippets of information floated out of the folder: *born in Culpeper, father a prominent farmer in the county, attended the University of Virginia with a degree in history, graduated from law school at William and Mary. Married. Four children. Third term as prosecutor. A member of several civic organizations and a deacon at Culpeper Baptist Church. Republican. No known vices.*

So, Somerfield thought to himself with some distain, we have a Boy Scout. He'd seen the type before, a type he had little use for, usually the inhabitant of small towns and small law firms. Somerfield's world was an arena of public bloodletting and gore. Not literally, of course, but the equivalent in reputation and financial reward or punishment, the sort of blood sport that had no room for the niceties of community and the traditional values to which Boy Scouts like Binford usually subscribed. And that was a weakness, one he had exploited before.

His long fingers slipped over several tabs and flipped to a summary of Binford's legal career. The report listed those cases that had garnered media attention: robberies, rapes, larcenies, drugs. The litany of man's darker side marched across the news stories copied in the report. No bar complaints. Somerfield's eyebrows twitched. Most lawyers with Binford's history of private and public practice would have had at least one or two disgruntled clients or constituents who would file a complaint. Usually, those who Binford had put in prison would claim some sort of chicanery by the prosecutor. The Commonwealth State Bar, like all state bars, made it easy for anyone to file a complaint against a lawyer, with or without merit, signed or anonymous, it made no difference. If lawyers were sharks, Somerfield had often thought, what did that make the ethics enforcers at the State Bar? What kind of predator eats its own? He realized his mind was wondering and he focused again. No complaints. That could be an opening. He made note of it with a red pencil.

Somerfield continued reading. Binford had tried several murder cases. One, a capital case, was on appeal, which was not unusual. All capital murder cases had an automatic right of appeal. This one had passed muster at the Court of Appeals and the Supreme Court. Predictably the case was now in Federal Court for review under a standard habeas corpus petition.

Somerfield flipped to the petition filed by the defendant. Not surprisingly, the petition alleged poor performance by the court-appointed attorneys, errors of law made during the trial, and malfeasance by the prosecutor, all standard stuff in the world of capital litigation and usually all of it groundless. Not that that mattered to the miscreants who worked in that area of the law, Somerfield thought wryly. No, the general strategy employed by that particular tribe of lawyers was to malign and smear as much as possible in the hope that something might stick.

Looking to see who was handling the appeal, he was surprised to see that The Defender Council was involved, an organization he knew a little bit about. Dedicated to the elimination of the death penalty, the organization was single-minded in its efforts and ruthless in execution. The DC, as they called themselves, was well-funded, well-connected with the national media, and linked with large, influential liberal law firms around the country.

Somerfield also knew something else, which seemed particularly useful in the current situation. The DC did not take on a case unless there was a prosecutor on the menu, apparently taking delight in the destruction of state and federal prosecutors.

He took note of the federal judge hearing the case. Northern District Court Judge William Roger Tulkinghorn. He knew Judge Tulkinghorn. Nearing ninety-years-old, retired but still taking cases, Tulkinghorn had a reputation of going off the rails from time to time. Should a case pique his interest, or if he became convinced that he saw something that no one else did, he was known to write blistering opinions—leaving the losing party in a wasteland of innuendo and assumptions not based on law or fact but nonetheless destructive and deadly.

And, it was rumored, the old man had recently farmed out more and more of his writing to young law clerks who had just gotten out of law school. Perhaps that, too, explained the sometimes extreme and erratic decisions which appeared under his name.

Somerfield began to plan a way to derail Binford. In the first battle of litigation in court, the contest of facts and the law itself, he knew he would lose in his attempt to keep the Culpeper Special Grand Jury from getting its hands on Sims. The second, more subtle battle was Somerfield's best chance. And here, it seemed, was the key to that second battle. The public and the media always seemed to take a lust-driven pleasure in the destruction of anything that hinted of wholesomeness and decency. He never understood that aspect of public life, but there was no denying it. He allowed himself a smile and dug deeper into the allegations made by the defendant in the habeas petition. Failure to disclose exculpatory evidence seemed to be the main complaint. Pretty standard stuff, Somerfield thought to himself. But then what, really, when it got right down to it, what was a lawyer, at least the sort of lawyer he respected, if not an amplifier of every slur and innuendo imaginable. So even if mundane and untrue, the allegation gave a creative attorney something to work with here, he thought with a satisfaction grounded in experience.

Somerfield scanned the habeas petition and noted who signed it. Roland Sprague. That signified who was actually handling the case. The DC had taken the case on as a cause celeb but it was Sprague and his firm that did the work. Somerfield looked Sprague up on the internet. Quickly, Somerfield surmised the man was a rising partner at Scag, Black and Mullen, and had been farmed out by the firm to handle the case pro bono. For the uninitiated, pro bono means for free. It looked good on paper. The firm got to brag about its high-minded ethics in taking on big cases for free. But Somerfield knew nothing was ever for free on the savannah where predators such as himself and that particular law firm stalked. No, nothing was for free, he mused. Besides the fawning publicity, if they were successful there was the potential for a hefty settlement in a civil suit sure to follow.

After making a few more notes, Somerfield flipped the case file closed, then direct-dialed the senior partner of Sprague's firm, Buck Mullen. A more than passing acquaintance. He and Buck had known each other in law school at the University of Virginia and had shared many things through the years. Women. Whiskey. Court cases. In their earlier years, the two had actually tried a few personal injury cases together as co-counsel. It is in the depths of jury trial that one gets to really know another human being. This was a point Buck had often contended during evening conversations fueled by vodka and the camaraderie of fellow attorneys. Somerfield tended to agree.

"Buck? Connie Somerfield here. You have a minute?"

"Connie? I'm kinda tied up at the moment. Is it important?" Buck responded.

"Well, now, I wouldn't be calling if it wasn't important, would I?" Somerfield said. "Look Buck, I've taken a particular interest in a habeas case your firm is handling pro bono. It's the Culpeper habeas in Federal District Court right now."

"Sprague's little case?" Buck asked.

"Sprague signed the petition. Is he up to it?"

"He's a little hyena that one," Buck answered.

"Good. I didn't expect anything less. Is he going after the prosecutor -- or is all that language in the Petition just for show?"

"Now, Connie you know I can't divulge case strategy," Buck responded.

"Well, at the very least I want you to subpoena him."

"Who?"

"Binford. And listen, Buck, I want you to go after him hard. You hear me? Hard," Somerfield said sternly.

Somerfield concluded the call with some small talk and then hung up the phone. Humming to himself, he began an online research of the local media of Culpeper, focusing on the reporter most likely to cover the court system there, and then put in a work order for NSA surveillance. Within a week he would know every keystroke that reporter had ever typed on her computer, at work or at home. And that would be very useful when she needed to be steered in a particular direction. Local press is what the voters read. That was the pressure point here, he surmised.

Soon, Somerfield thought to himself, this Binford fellow would receive a subpoena of his own because if Binford wanted to play ball, well he sure as hell was going to find out that federal court was where this particular game was going to be played. And when necessary, federal court belonged to the NSA, as Somerfield knew and Binford would soon learn.

Having developed a plan and set it in motion, Conyer Somerfield, deciding that a morning round of golf might just be the thing, called his favorite golfing buddy. Tee time for Somerfield was always whenever he wanted it at the country club because, well, he was Conyer Somerfield. Just an old- fashioned southern lawyer.

CULPEPER COUNTY COURTHOUSE

Mordecai Binford watched Circuit Court Judge Franklin Stringfellow's long and almost fleshless fingers, noting that the veins and arteries seemed to jump through the brown age-spotted skin with every curve and flex of his talons. They scrabbled and prodded through the mass of documents and files on his desk.

"Ah, here it is," Stringfellow mumbled as he tugged a yellow manila folder from the bottom of one of the many piles on the desk top. Binford looked on with growing unease as the whole assembly threatened to topple over, spilling paper work everywhere.

"Damn, slippery little thing," Stringfellow said as he jerked it out with one hand while holding the stack together with the other. "Unusual motion you filed, Mr. Binford," Stringfellow said. "Special Grand Jury…Investigative Special Grand Jury," his long-lined faced puckered with distaste. Hearing no reply Stringfellow opened the file and flipped through the paperwork attached inside.

"Never done one of these before. You confident everything is in order?" he asked.

"Yes, sir. The clerk has subpoenaed seven citizens to appear next month for the grand jury. We have our witnesses subpoenaed to start with but obviously the grand jury may wish to hear from more as the investigation continues."

"Humph. Yes. I see that. You say you want to investigate the death of two people in Culpeper. This is with the cooperation of the sheriff?"

"Yes, sir. He can be over here if you would like to question him."

"No. No. That is not necessary."

The sunlight fell through the one-story high window that illuminated the judge's chambers, a shaft of golden yellow angling across his desk and stabbing into the darkness behind him. Binford's attention wandered along the stream of dust motes to focus on the bookcases lining the wall, housing the brown leather case books of the Virginia Supreme Court. Thrumming silence stretched as Judge Stringfellow glanced at the subpoenas. Even in his somewhat distracted state, Binford noticed the tenseness in the atmosphere.

"I see you have subpoenaed a Mr. Sims and a Mr. Weir."

"Yes, sir. Personal service on both."

"Um...so it would seem," Stringfellow's talons drummed the desktop. "Both U.S. military officers, it would seem."

"Yes, sir. But both were served off federal land and neither actively deployed. And one of the issues is whether or not the death of the Wood couple took place on federal land or in Culpeper County itself."

"I take it someone has already investigated this," Stringfellow said. "That not good enough for you?"

"No, sir. Nor, I might add, the sheriff."

Stringfellow nodded and pulled out a bundle of papers. He passed it over to Binford. "You have undoubtedly seen this motion to quash filed on behalf of Sims and Weir," he said, referring to a request to block Binford's subpoena to bring both before the grand jury.

Surprised, Binford took the proffered documents and scanned them. "No, sir. I haven't seen this."

"It's certified to have been mailed to you."

"Perhaps the mail is slower to my office." Binford said.

"Well, yes. This was mailed and faxed to me. I suspect it was only mailed to you."

Stringfellow's eyebrows twitched. He had seen enough to know this was but a harbinger of what was to come. Sly tricks of the trade. Mountains of paperwork. Motion after motion. Allegations of impropriety. Appeals.

Binford was shocked to see the thoroughness and complexity of the objections. The motion even objected to the service itself, claiming the officer had made an unconstitutional stop to hand over the documents, a charge farcical, in Binford's opinion, but nonetheless time-consuming in rebutting.

He continued to scan.

Then the world stopped.

The motion alleged prosecutorial misconduct on his part by subpoenaing the two men. The motion claimed the subpoena was evidence of malicious prosecution on the part of Binford and asked for a full hearing on the issue.

"You see the last paragraph of the motion? We'll need to schedule a day to hear it. Will that stop the need for the grand jury to meet next month?"

Binford struggled to think. The allegation was untrue. He had never had anyone even hint at such a thing and yet here it was. In black and white. The fact that the charge had been made would be enough in the opinion of some to make it a fact. And experience told Binford the local paper would make sure this most malicious allegation would get plenty of exposure.

"No, sir. We can go forward." Binford responded automatically.

The judge pulled out his court calendar, a large black leather-bound book, and began scanning the court days ahead, looking for an opening to add time for argument on the motion, his long fingers tracing an erratic course down the pages.

"All right, Mr. Binford, we will continue on the same schedule," he said finally. "I'll set the hearing on the motions for Tuesday of next week. Let's see…October third. Opposing counsel has already given their avoid dates and of course you will already be here on other matters. The grand jury is scheduled to be impaneled Thursday, November 12. That should give us plenty of time to conclude the hearing on motions. I see you have Mr. Weir and Mr. Sims testifying on the first day the Grand Jury is impaneled. I assume that will remain the same but *it is* dependent on the results of the hearing Tuesday. Let me see, do you have other witnesses lined up?" he asked thumbing through the paperwork in the file. "Ah, yes, I see you do." He scanned the names listed in the witness subpoena request filed in the mass of paperwork and then, apparently satisfied, Stringfellow carefully shut the file.

"You sure you want to continue this course?" the judge asked. "It would seem that the federal government is very interested in not complying with your requests. This could get quite…um… time-consuming."

Binford did not comprehend the huge leap the Judge had taken, no matter how oblique, in offering any advice in a pending cause. "We'll be ready next week," he answered.

"Very good, then, Mr. Binford," Stringfellow shrugged. "Next week. We can schedule a hearing on the motions at that time." His yellowed talons pitched the folder back on the mountain of papers and folders, threatening to topple the whole structure. The prosecutor sat and stared out the window. "Um...is there anything else?" Stringfellow asked.

"No, your honor," Binford stood automatically and left the chamber.

Once the door to the judge's chamber closed, Stringfellow pulled open a drawer from the 19th century oak partners' desk in the office. As old as the courthouse itself, the scarred desktop told of a century of judges and attorneys dispensing justice in the rural county. Withdrawing an already opened pack of Camel cigarettes, he tapped one cylinder out, jammed it into the corner of his mouth, flicked a Zippo lighter open and fired up the tobacco. He sucked in the hard, unfiltered smoke and felt it penetrate his lungs. Regulations be damned. He had smoked all his life and some stupid bureaucrat in Richmond was not going to tell him to stop now. He had decided *that* years ago when the Courthouse had been declared a smoke-free zone. *Smoke-free zone, my ass,* he thought to himself, there was a time when everyone had smoked in court. He remembered the haze drifting above the proceedings below him during many a trial. It hadn't seemed to hurt anyone then. But a lot had changed in the legal profession since he had first started practicing law. He had, over the years, perceived a disturbing trend in the law as it became even more filled with rules and regulations which really had nothing to do with the nitty-gritty of justice-- but rather to fulfill the political fads in Richmond and at the Commonwealth State Bar. He'd probably violated an ethical rule of some sort or another by just talking about the case with Binford. He remembered when judges and attorneys would settle a case behind closed doors--cutting through all the technicalities and dispensing real justice. Now, they followed all the rules and regulations and dispensed something else. Not justice really. No, now everyone seemed interested in filling in the correct boxes set up by the Bar-- the client's interests being lost in an artificial search for fairness.

For example, Judge Stringfellow mused, what about the quandary Binford now found himself in--not so much legal, but political--and all of it a result of political correctness? Stringfellow saw nothing fair in that melodrama getting ready to play out in his court. Through the years liberal law professors and judges had chipped away at the immunity prosecutors enjoyed in the legal system. To do the job correctly, a prosecutor needed to be able to act without fear of attack. Stringfellow knew that all too well, having been a prosecutor himself before taking the bench. However, that immunity had disappeared like an eroding beach, slowly, imperceptibly, but relentlessly. Now, shortly, Binford would face that reality. *Prosecutorial Misconduct--what a crock.* Stringfellow grunted with disgust. Subpoenaing someone was hardly the basis for such a charge, but this Conyer Somerfield knew his stuff. He knew just enough to make an argument given the slippage in the protections prosecutors had traditionally enjoyed.

Well, Stringfellow thought to himself, I tried to warn Binford, which was the least I could do. But in the end Binford would have to deal with it himself. It was true that in the end each lawyer stood alone on the plain of battle, living or dying by his own hand. There was no merry-band-of-brothers in that bleak landscape --only lonely souls seeking survival. He had come to terms with that awful reality and Binford would have to do the same.

Later that evening, after Binford and his wife, Kate, put the kids to bed, Binford sat with her on the front porch swing. She finally broke the silence by saying, "So explain this to me again."

Binford sighed, "The attorney is alleging that I'm subpoenaing two witnesses for improper reasons."

"So, why is that bad," she asked, tugging back a stray strand of hair to curl behind her ear, "it's not true."

Binford rarely discussed work at home. His wife understood little of the world he lived in, defined as it was by the law on one hand and by local politics on the other. And at the center of local politics, Binford knew, was the local media.

"They are asking for a hearing so everything they say will be in open court."

"Yeah, but usually there is no one in court, so what does it matter?" she asked.

"I already had a call from the *Culpeper Dispatch*. Somehow they know about the motion before I even have a copy of it."

"How can that be?"

"I think this lawyer, Conyer Somerfield, tipped them off."

"OK. Well, you'll just answer and that will take care of it."

Binford thought about the *Culpeper Dispatch*, a local daily newspaper that underpaid its staff, and as a result, the good reporters moved on quickly while the not-so-good remained. Dorcas Snider, who covered the court system, was one of those that stayed. He realized she had taken a dislike to him almost from the first time they met. That had been six years ago. Like a lump of clay she continued to stick to her job. And for years, her distaste for Binford only seemed to grow. He had developed a theory about her, deciding that he probably represented everything she hated. He attended church. He was conservative politically. He was a southerner and proud of it. She was New York City-bred and born, with all that stereotypically came with that.

"Kate, Dorcas will be covering the case."

"Oh, no. Not her."

"Yeah. She left a message for me to call her back. I didn't. But you know when they allege anything negative about me in court it will be headline news in the *Dispatch* if Dorcas has anything to do with it."

"Even if it's not true?" Kate asked.

"Doesn't matter. Just saying it will make it true when Dorcas writes her story. And then, of course, there are the online comments which I'm sure Dorcas will quote in a follow-up story. Then they'll drum up some sort of totally bogus online poll and that will give her a story and an editorial."

The cool of the early autumn evening fell evenly across the front yard and onto the porch. The shadows deepened and crickets added a symphony to the flashes of light in the air from fireflies darting on currents of air. Mordecai and Kate rocked the swing back and forth in unison.

"There's something wrong with that woman," Kate remarked.

"Even so," Binford replied, "she gets to write the story."

REMINGTON, VIRGINIA

While Mordecai and Kate sat in the cool of the evening, John and Rebecca Weir walked underneath the trees in the gathering gloom of their backyard.

"You're holding something back from me again," Rebecca said bitterly.

"You know I can't tell you everything I do," her husband replied.

"Something is up. I can tell it. John, I can't stand much more of this. You're absent when you are here. You leave at all hours of the night. Then that cell phone. Who are you talking to on that thing? Why is it so secret?" she demanded.

"It's my job. I can't talk about it. We've been over this all before."

"John, I woke up and saw you get up and go outside to talk on that damn phone last night. Now who is it that you don't want me to know about?"

"That was nothing. Just work."

"Work? Work? You expect me to believe that?" Rebecca exclaimed. "You work in the Quartermaster Corps. You deal with toilet paper and machine oil and all the other crap the army needs to keep itself going. What's so important about toilet paper, so top secret, you can't even give your wife an explanation about what you do? Give me a break!"

"Come on Rebecca. You know it's always been like this."

She wheeled on him, and jabbing a finger into his chest, "No it has not," she declared. "Don't you even try that with me. This is on a whole other level and I'm telling you I won't stand for it. Not for what I think is going on!"

John reached out to encompass his wife in a hug, alarmed when she pushed him away.

"Don't you dare!" she cried. "Don't you dare! If there is someone else be man enough to tell me. But don't you dare try to cover up with a hug and a kiss. We are way beyond all of that."

"Someone else? What are you talking about, Rebecca?"

"Look, John. I'm no idiot," she said eyes flashing. "I've been through this before as you well know. You're acting just like you did before. Like there's another woman out there. Who is she? Someone at work I'll bet."

"Rebecca, there is no one else, I promise you."

"We'll talk about this later," she said clearly disgusted. "But I swear, John, you'd better change. And whatever or whoever it is that you're seeing had better get it straight that I won't stand by while they wreck my family. There'll be hell to pay you better believe that! And by the way, you'll be sleeping in the spare bedroom," she said on the way to the back door. "I already have your stuff moved down there."

Stunned, Weir sat down by the swing and slide set he had put up for the kids and pushed a plastic seated swing back and forth absently.

This was not a good time to tell Rebecca he might be gone for a few days, he thought with gallows humor. As he looked up at the sky locating the reddish blur that was Mars, Weir remembered that a transport was scheduled for the following week. A "free range transport" Sims had said to him with a barely hidden sense of glee.

And, Weir thought, Steele lived in whatever nightmare was out there even as he looked up at the night sky. *Just like me in Iraq.*

HESPERIA PLANUM: MARS

Click. Click. Click.

After the nightmarish monster which hovered over his face had moved away, after Steele was able to stifle the panic and the fear, his training from the military snapped into place. He would observe, evade, survive. He could do two of the three things right now, and so he did them as best he could. And he shoved what he saw above his face into the corner of his mind where all horrors and evil things lurk to be dealt with later. But not now. Not now. He needed to concentrate on what he could comprehend. The sounds he could comprehend. Something was moving about. Stopping. Moving for lengths of time. All measured by the sound of something hard and hollow tapping on a hard surface.

The stench of carrion grew stronger the closer the clicks came towards him, and it lessened when the sounds receded. Ok, so now he knew how to associate the one with the other. Otherwise the air had a dusty smell. Once the ozone odor had dissipated, he detected a slight smell of sulphur underneath it all. Great place, he thought to himself. Smells like a roadside kill and rotten eggs. It would be a bloody shame not to get to the ordnance and take that monster out just to be rid of the smell.

Steele tensed his muscles and noticed a loosening of the material that had held him in absolute bondage since he had been put in the pod.

Now, this is encouraging, he thought as the material began to flow away from his arms and legs. Soon he was completely free of restraint. Steele knew he was weak and needed time to flex his muscles before getting out of the pod. As motionlessly as possible, he tensed and flexed his limbs all the while thinking about what he was about to do.

Weir had said the lid would open, and it had. So it followed that the other two parts of his mantra were also true: there are hostiles and there are weapons. Steele had a good idea of who the hostile was in this case. The bloody thing scratched about like a crab on a concrete floor. And the smell. Well, he'd smelled that once before in Iraq on the day he had discovered fifteen hostages who had been shot and left to cook in the sun for two days. He had rounded the corner of a hooch, and there they were, lined up like bloated laundry, the buttons popping from the swollen flesh. Roadside kill really had nothing on what had oozed from that beastie scuffling about. Now all he needed to do was find the weapons, which meant that he needed to find the pods--well not the pods, just one special pod. *The pod with the goods.*

Once satisfied he would not fall prostrate on the floor, he lifted his head over the edge of the pod to see where he was.

To his left, a line of unopened pods floated and to his right there were three examining tables surrounded by computer equipment and various instruments. The room itself seemed to be large. Equipment and partitions blocked his view to the end wall, but the ceiling evidenced a much more expansive space than what he could see. That and the echoes. The clicking and scraping of the monstrosity that had earlier hovered over him echoed and bounced around the room.

Then Steele noticed the lighting. It seemed to diffuse throughout the space, almost as if it emanated from the ceiling, floors and walls in one uninterrupted stream of photons.

No shadows, he concluded, trying to size up how he could go about concealing himself.

With that he sat up, surprised at the stiffness of his back, and tried to vault over the edge of the pod to the floor five feet below. Instead he fell with an echoing clatter. Surprised that he was not hurt, Steele regrouped and crouched low to the ground.

And then, because of the lighter gravitational pull on Mars, he was aware of feeling that it was easier to move about. He moved from one pod to another, looking for a way to open them, and finally, noticing a small rubberlike extrusion on the end of each, pushed one and heard a rush of air as the lid slid underneath the floating container.

Locating the weapons came next, and he was nearly exhausted by hoisting himself up to look first in one pod and then another, gazing upon comatose strangers, when, just as the scratching sound began again, he found it.

Nearly spent, the Englishman launched himself up to look over the edge. Inside weapons and boxes of ammo gleamed in the light. Instantly Steele was reassured for two reasons. First, the weapons were there. Secondly, they were not encased in the immobilizing material. One sector of his brain concluded that the material was triggered by organic material. Luckily, stocks and webbing were made of plastic rather than wood or cotton. Otherwise the restraining material might have covered it all.

Relieved that something had finally gone right, Steele levered himself up and into the pod, landing on top of loose ordnance and immediately he went for the Mossberg 590 Shotgun positioned on top. Equipped with a matte-black stock and barrel, the gun oozed crude killing power. The pistol grip paired with a ghost ring sight system enhanced its effective range to a hundred meters. He grabbed a box of 12 gauge slugs and a mil spec box of hardened 00 buckshot.

Click, click, click. The sound announced the imminent return of the monstrosity. Steele began to pick up the faint whiff of road kill.

Grabbing the Mossberg and the two boxes of ammo, he stuffed the ammo in his pants pocket before clambering over the pod edge to land awkwardly on the floor. Then he sprinted to a stack of what looked like white boxes, where he could hide and fish out the ammo, then he alternated loading buckshot and slugs into the shotgun, making it one of the most effective killing tools he had seen while in

Iraq. The pistol grip made the gun easy to move in close quarters: perfect for house-to-house urban fighting and close combat. More than once he had used the gun to blast open locked doors. At close range it was that powerful. And to be truthful, more than once, he had pressed the barrel up against a hostile and pulled the trigger --finding little left when the haze of blood droplets cleared the air.

Right now, he knew he needed every ounce of killing power he could get. In all the horror and disorientation earlier, Steele was able to determine that the alien enjoyed a thick, hard exoskeleton. He hoped a twelve-gauge slug would penetrate. It was all he had.

Click, click, click. Scrabbling behind Steele amongst the labyrinth of tank like casements and partitions, whatever it was moved closer, bringing with it a thick stench. Hunching close against the box like structure to his back, Steele nestled the Mossberg against his side with one hand on the pistol grip, the left hand wrapped around the front grip.

Then to his left, about ten yards away, Steele detected movement.

Willing himself to sit still, he watched two mottled grey and black pincer-like appendages stretch out. A rectangular body, encased in a horny exoskeleton of the same coloration, lurched above, bringing with it a full frontal assault on his nostrils.

The thing clicked on the sharp pincer legs towards the three pods hovering in front of Steele. He watched to learn what he could. First it moved to Steele's now empty pod. Then, realizing the pod was empty, it scurried over to the next pod, where Steele had seen a comatose figure. The creature's pincer like arms moved over the now moaning body in the pod.

A second pincer moved up and began manipulating a key pad at one end, when, apparently satisfied, the alien clicked to the third pod filled with ordinance.

That was enough for Steele. As far as he was concerned, this thing was definitely a hostile, and now it was going to mess with his only means of protection.

Time to take it out. Slowly he raised the weapon and centered the body in the ghost ring sight, tracking it as it moved across the floor.

"Put the damn gun down, you frigging cowboy!" a man's voice echoed across the chamber.

Steele almost pulled the trigger in shock

"Put it down, you idiot! You want to bring a whole swarm of 'em on us?" the voice demanded.

"My weapons are in the pod!" Steele stage whispered back.

"Speak up man! That thing is deaf as a doornail. Can't hear a thing."

"I said my weapons are in the pod!" Steele shouted.

"Too bad. You shoot and it will alert the others. *Then there will be trouble.*"

"Who are you?" Steele's voice echoed in the cavernous room.

"I might ask the same of you, my British friend."

All the while Steele continued to monitor the creature. Crunch time: shoot or don't shoot. Trust an unseen voice or trust his last instructions. The creature stopped at the pod. Mottled appendages began to snake out.

The lid will open. There will be weapons. There will be hostiles. So far everything Weir told him was true, although he had not said anything about allies, or for that matter, anything about friends shouting out from an empty room.

Steele squeezed the trigger.

The great gouting burst of noise echoed around and around the chamber as the twelve gauge solid slug of lead, hardened to military specs, punched through the exoskeleton with a crack. The thing stopped and swiveled towards Steele. What passed for a face, stalks with eyes, a jointed slimy orifice that gapped and closed, fixated upon Steele's hunched figure.

"Now you've done it, you fool!" Whoever it was who had warned him cried.

"If you're real, there's a pod full of ordnance!" Steele shouted. "Help me get it out!"

He stood and ran towards the creature, racking a double ought buckshot load into the chamber and fired another round into the creature's face which, less armored, exploded in a mass of fluid and membrane, combined oddly enough with what looked like fiber optic wiring. Now, almost upon the tottering hostile, Steele pumped another round into the chamber, and less than five feet away, he let the full killing power of the load slam into the creature's face a second time where it exploded like a watermelon being hit with a sledge hammer. Legs bucked and the creature fell to the floor, electronic arcs spewing from the wound and slithering across the floor.

"Come on!" Steele yelled as, jumping up to the pod he clambered inside and began pitching ammo and ordnance over the side, having figured that with the lessened gravity, and the fact that the weapons were battlefield grade, this type of transfer would hardly stress the pod's cargo.

But just as he picked up what he hoped was a box of C4 plastic explosives, he saw a pair of grimy bone thin fingers reach up over the pod edge and grab the box.

"Hurry! They won't be long," a man, dirty and long haired, but with deeply intelligent eyes burrowed in a dark, bearded face, told him.

The two quickly emptied the pod and at the last moment Steele saw a hand written note which without reading he jammed into his pocket.

"Right. That's the lot." Steele said jumping out of the pod. "Where to now?"

"Seems like you ought to have thought about that before you started blasting," the man replied, surveying the boxes of ammo piled high, multiple weapons, and C-4. "There's no way we can carry all of this." And then, as they heard the sound of a large object slamming against something hard, "That's the airlock. We gotta get out of here."

"Not without my weapons," Steele told him. "I'd just as soon make a stand here and kill all the bleeding things."

"Not yet," the bearded many said. "Too many. We can cache your stuff here, and they won't find it. Probably. But we've got to be light and nimble very shortly. Here! Bring the stuff here!"

Steele grabbed what he could and found the man crouched over a grate that opened from the floor. He peered down and saw what looked like a vent that angled off after a vertical drop of ten feet or so.

"Dump what you have here," the man told him. "We can come back for it." The man pointed downward. Reluctantly, Steele dropped boxes of C4 down the hole. The two then ran back and forth carrying ammo and weapons.

"Mind if I use this?" The man asked with a Beretta M92F pistol in his hand.

"Take it. Get some ammo too," Steele grunted as he heaved a box of grenades into the chamber.

They continued to move the contents of the pod to the chamber. When they finished, the man dropped the grate. Just then the sound of clicking echoed across the vastness of the chamber. More and more clicks added to the cacophony until it sounded like rain on a tin roof.

"Damn. It's the whole clan," the man said worriedly. "We've got to get out of here now. Follow me!"

Dodging back and forth, they wound their way through a maze of smooth boxlike containers, partitions, tubes, columns and multi-storied enclosed vats. The sound of clicking exploded everywhere around them. Once the man stopped and dropped to the ground, and scrambling under a box-like protrusion from a larger wall, he motioned for Steele to follow. The odor of stinking meat filled the air. Steele saw a pincer step in front of his face. Then another. Thankfully, the creature moved on, and the two scrambled out -- and Steele, exhausted, willed himself to keep moving.

When they ended their desperate, dodging run at the wall of the chamber, Steele was sure they were in serious trouble because he saw no way out. Then the man pulled open a grate and motioned him inside, shutting it behind them before leading the way on hands and knees, in what should have been utter darkness. Light seemed to originate from the very material they were traversing.

Finally, the two came to a stopping point. While Steele sat, the man manipulated a keypad mounted in the side of the wall. The seams of a door appeared, he pushed inward, and the two entered a room about 20 feet square. It was clearly the man's living quarters. Clothing was neatly piled in one corner. Assorted computer instruments lay neatly in another area.

"Me casa, su casa," The man said expansively with his arms stretched wide.

Steele sank in a jumble of exhaustion: physical and emotional. "I have one question before I decide to pass out," he gasped. "Where the hell are we?"

"Nice to meet you, too," the man said with a wry grin peeking out from behind his dirty, matted beard. "Where are we? Well, some people would call this hell. In fact, my friend, this is *hell*. But, it is hell on Mars. You're on Mars. Now, before you pass out, which actually is understandable, I have a question."

"OK," Steele said closing his eyes.

"Are you the rescue effort? Please tell me you're not it."

"Don't worry, I'm not the bleeding cavalry," Steele replied. "Now sod off, and let me sleep."

Hours later, Steele awoke with two needs, not only was he thirsty, but he needed very badly to urinate. He looked about, disorientated, and then it all came rushing back to him: the pod opening, the cache of weapons, the desperate run to the wall of the chamber, the awful creatures, and his curious companion. Reflexively he reached around and grabbed the Mossberg just where he had dropped it when they had arrived.

"Feeling better?" his companion, who was sitting on the floor beside him, asked. And when Steele told him what he needed, the man grubbed about a pile of plastic boxes and tubes. Then he handed Steele a container of water.

"As to the other, well, the bad news is I have to recycle to keep up supplies," he added handing him another container.

After using both, Steele eyed his host with undisguised curiosity.

"Ok, first, thanks for the help," he said. "Secondly, who the bloody hell are you? How did you get here? And what were those god-awful things?"

"All in good time," the man told him. "How about I just sit and talk for a little bit, and then you ask some questions. I have a few myself, but I can understand the shock of all this so let me start off. It's better if you know the situation in case we have to book it out of here. I wasn't kidding when I said don't shoot. We just saw the first contingent. There'll be others, and they are harder to fend off. My name is Alex Reznik. Before I came here, I was an engineer with the Jet Propulsion Laboratory, JPL for short, in Pasadena. Specifically I worked in the Surface Mission Support Area for the Martian rovers *Opportunity* and *Spirit* -- before I actually ended up on this friggin planet."

Noticing the blank look in Steele's eyes, Reznick went on to explain that *Opportunity* and *Spirit* were two remotely-controlled rovers sent by NASA in 2003 to explore the surface of Mars. He described how they landed on two different sites on Mars, *Spirit* near

Gusev Crater and *Opportunity* on the vast plains of the Meridian Planum. He meticulously told Steele about the two rovers' search for water through geology and photography. Like any engineer, he recounted in exacting detail his job and the science surrounding its execution. He told Steele he analyzed the photographs sent back by the rover *Opportunity* and, conjoined with images sent by the orbiting satellite *Odyssey,* Reznik would help plot the course for each Mars day, called a "sol" by JPL technicians. He understood the rover's engineering limitations and could match that with the terrain challenges presented in each photo session.

After laying the informational groundwork of *Spirit* and *Opportunity*, Reznik continued, "As to how I got here, well, the same way you did. I woke up in a pod with one of those monstrosities hovering over me like death. Luckily, something distracted it, and I was able to give it the slip. Been up here for seems like forever, but I suspect it's been a little over a year."

"A year? " Steele said disbelieving.

"I've seen a lot," Reznik replied.

Breaking the uneasy silence that fell between the two, Reznik began again, "But, like I said, I analyzed data for the rovers. They were both way beyond mission parameters a year ago. In fact *Spirit* died while I was still at JPL so I was concentrated on *Opportunity* when they took me. Abducted me."

"Abducted is probably a pretty good term for what happened to me, I guess," Steele said.

"You were abducted. I was abducted and fourteen others were abducted with your group alone," Reznik continued. "Hard as it is to believe, this is routine. And harder for me to believe, but I do now, is that our government is involved. And I mean all the way. They organize. They ship. They return and cover-up. It makes me sick. What really makes me sick is that the government has been do-ing this thing for years. I guess I got too close to it, so they decided to stuff me in a pod just like you."

"Those things we fought. You want to know what they are? Think about it. What do they look like? What do they *really* look like?" The intelligent eyes of the man bored into Steele. Steele tried to erase the horror and the shock and think about what it was he saw. He remembered a large hard body on pincer like legs. It had protrusions that ended in sharp points all about. Yet there were soft parts. The front with stalks and what he assumed were eyes. He remembered looking into the gaping mouth that drooled slime. Then there were the mechanical parts that spewed out of the body --and the electrical arcs.

"I don't know what you're getting at," Steele said. "It looked like something that needed killing to me."

Reznik sighed. "Well, I have been here longer and had time to think about it more. Think about it. They look organic but not entirely. The exoskeleton is like that of a crustacean or insect. And, while we're on the subject, let me tell you something else. They're dumb in an odd kind of way. You just have to watch to see what I mean. And for the most part, they don't pick up aerial vibrations. But they do communicate, I think electronically, but I'm not sure. The electrical arcs, though, are very interesting. First time I've seen the innards of one of those things. And the bits of gadgetry that flew out of the one we killed is also intersting. But before you start hammering me with questions, let me finish my summary of life on this lovely little planet. There are other people here. Don't expect much from them. They are hardly alive as we know it. They use them. Then they return them. Why? I don't know. One of the little mysteries we will have time to ponder. If they don't get us first."

It was an eventuality which Steele found he could not consider.

"I have friends in that group of pods, I think." Steele said.

"Too bad," Reznik replied without emotion.

"No. Not too bad. I'm getting them out, and you're going to help me. Then we're going to take this place apart."

"Good luck with all that cowboy."

CHAPTER 13

APPENDIX B   PAGE 348

MEMO
EYES ONLY
THIS DOCUMENT IS PROTECTED UNDER THE EMERGENCY FEDERAL CODE OF
1951, SECTION 1338B(C)(I). IT IS A CRIMINAL VIOLATION TO COPY OR REPRO-
DUCE THIS DOCUMENT IN ANY FORM. ONLY LEVEL III SECURITY CLEARANCE
PERSONNEL ARE AUTHORIZED TO READ THIS DOCUMENT. CONTACT YOUR
DUTY OFFICER IMMEDIATELY IF: 1. YOU COME INTO POSSESSION OF THIS
DOCUMENT AND 2. YOU ARE NOT AUTHORIZED FOR EXPOSURE TO THE IN-
FORMATION CONTAINED HEREIN. -- SEE EXECUTIVE ORDER NSA 330-1957.
DATE: JANUARY 21, 2000.
TO: TRAVIS DIAZ, CHIEF EXCUTIVE OFFICER, GROUP 929
FROM: NINA PETROV
RE: NASA LONG-RANGE STUDY GROUP MEETING

BACKGROUND:
AFTER THE FAILURES OF THE MARS CLIMATE ORBITER AND MARS POLAR
LANDER THE AGENCY HAS BEEN IN CHAOS IN TERMS OF THE FUTURE OF
MARS EXPLORATION. AS ORDERED, I ASSISTED NASA PLANETARY GEOL-
OGIST JIM GARVIN IN THE LOGISTICAL DETAILS OF CREATING THE UNDIS-
CLOSED LONG-RANGE PLANNING GROUP CHAIRED BY MR. GARVIN. DURING
THIS TIME, MR. GARVIN RECEIVED ENCOURAGEMENT FROM COLLEAGUES TO
ACT AS THE SCIENTIST IN CHARGE OF PLOTTING THE FUTURE OF MARS
EXPLORATION AND, AS A CONSEQUENCE, IS PLANNING A SUMMER CONFER-
ENCE TO CREATE A LONG-RANGE PLAN FOR EXPLORATION.

    IN MY INFORMAL POSITION AS A PLANNER AND EXPEDITOR FOR MR.
GARVIN'S OFFICE, I AM ABLE TO READ AND DOWNLOAD ALL COMMUNI-
CATION, ELECTRONIC OR OTHERWISE. I AM THEREFORE PRIVY TO THE
CENTRAL CORE OF MARS EXPLORATION, BOTH IN NASA AND OUTSIDE OF
THE AGENCY.

    MR. GARVIN IS UNAWARE OF MY CLANDESTINE ACTIVITIES FOR
GROUP 929.

ISSUE:
THE SUMMER CONFERENCE WILL, IN ALL LIKELIHOOD, GUIDE EXPLORATION ON MARS FOR THE IMMEDIATE FUTURE. SHOULD GROUP 929 WORK TO STEER THE CONFERENCE CONCLUSIONS IN ANY ONE DIRECTION AND IF SO WHAT DIRECTION? THE DEBATE SEEMS TO BE BETWEEN THOSE THAT WANT TO SEND ANOTHER LARGE ORBITER OR LANDER AND A SECOND GROUP THAT IS LEANING TOWARDS SMALLER AND LESS COMPLICATED INSTRUMENTS. THERE ALSO IS AN ENGINEER AT JPL PUSHING FOR INSTRUMENT PACKAGES TO BE MOUNTED ON MOVING PLATFORMS. HIS PROPOSAL FALLS WITHIN THE SMALLER-IS-BETTER GROUP. THIS IS BEGINNING TO GAIN TRACTION WITH MR. GARVIN ALTHOUGH IT IS FAR FROM CERTAIN WHICH DIRECTION THE PROGRAM WILL MOVE.

RECOMMENDATIONS:
MY DIRECTIVE FROM GROUP 929 IS TO GATHER INFORMATION AND MAKE RECOMMENDATIONS THAT WILL EXPEDITE EXPLORATION ON MARS WITHIN THE PRESENT POLITICAL AND FISCAL PARAMETERS. IT IS MY RECOMMENDATION THAT GROUP 929 SUPPORT THE CREATION OF A SMALLER-IS-BETTER PHILOSOPHY. NOT ONLY DOES THIS DEAL WITH THE DETECTION OF LARGER EXPLORATION VEHICLES BY THE ALIEN ENTITY BUT IT ALSO PROVIDES NASA THE BOOST NECESSARY TO CONTINUE EXPLORATION WITHOUT MORE OBVIOUS AND DIRECT INTERVENTION BY THE NSA AND OR GROUP 929.

FURTHER, AFTER THE INITIAL MOVING PLATFORMS ARE SENT (THEY ARE INFORMALLY REFERRED TO AS ROVERS AT THIS POINT), IT IS MY RECOMMENDATION THAT NSA AND GROUP PUSH FOR A MUCH LARGER AND MORE COMPLEX MOVING PLATFORM TO BE LANDED NEAR THE SUSPECTED ALIEN BASE. BY THIS TIME, STEALTH TECHNOLOGY SHOULD BE PERFECTED TO EVADE ALIEN RESPONSE TO THE LARGER VEHICLE.

ROUTE CODE:
0790000001000000110011000000715000000007722666666666666
0000030400000020000000029400000110000198700000335261784711

----EXCERPTS FROM THE NSA PRESIDENTIAL BRIEFING PAPERS ON THE ROSWELL INCIDENT

RICHMOND, VIRGINIA: THE POWHATAN TOWERS

Roland Sprague stood an even six feet tall and weighed 165 pounds. He ran every day like a machine. He counted every calorie eaten and every calorie expended. His dark eyes and dark hair framed a large nose that accentuated the gauntness of his face, while his angular body belied the dead-fish handshake for which he was known. He did not endear himself to others but he was smart and he did good work as a litigator.

His approach to life was as measured and calculated as his approach to body weight. While his colleagues at the law firm of Scag, Black and Mullen popped blood pressure pills, and then diabetes pills, Sprague looked on with a sense of self-righteous superiority because he would not allow himself the weakness of overeating and under-exercising. In the same vein, he had set a goal to become a partner in the firm before a single grey hair popped from his head. And through relentless hard work and a ruthless approach to his adversaries, he had clawed his way to partner earlier in the year.

Now Sprague had a new goal, which was to *win* the habeas petition previously assigned to him by the firm, a very different proposition than merely going through the motions, which, if unspoken, was exactly what he had done so far. Habeas corpus petitions from convicted inmates seeking a new trial are routine in federal court, just as the habeas case Sprague was working on was routine, worthy of just enough effort to look competent, but not anything approaching the full throttle methodology he used in cases that counted. Less routine in habeas proceedings is when a federal judge grants the petition, the effect of which wipes a conviction off the books and gives the petitioning inmate a new trial, with all the advantages time confers in lost memories, lost evidence, and missing witnesses. It was, Sprague knew, a veritable playground for the creative lawyer.

Of course, he had planned to do a creditable job as soon as the assignment came across his desk but now the bloodlust ran rampant in his soul. The case was no longer about fulfilling an artificially pious goal of helping the downtrodden. No. Now it had become personal. *He had a prey.* And he wanted to crush it. Winning a case wasn't enough for Sprague when his mindset shifted as it had here. Destruction of his foe, whether it is the opposing attorney or his opponent's client or both, was always Sprague's most fulfilling measure of success. Even more so, now that he knew Buck Mullen was interested in the outcome.

Scag, Black and Mullen prided itself on the pro bono, or free, work the firm did. In fact, all attorneys at the firm, except of course for senior partners, were required to do pro bono work. As a result, the firm got recognition. The attorney got recognition. And usually, the firm and the attorney got clients through the publicity. Less obvious but also just as true, the firm and the attorney also received assignments to choice spots in the structure of the Commonwealth State Bar because it encouraged such public service. The unspoken truth of the matter, though, was that the pro bono work was done not out of any sense of public duty but rather to further the interests of the firm and of its attorneys, something Sprague understood, and directed his efforts accordingly

But, when Buck Mullen told him to go after the prosecutor, when he told Sprague that he had it on good authority that the prosecutor was underhanded, Sprague needed no further encouragement. He had a target and a motivation beyond merely being competent. Now he really wanted to win and win in a way that satisfied him. Winning as Sprague liked to win was a trait he'd discovered in himself while in law school, when he first thrilled at humiliating a classmate during a moot court competition. It had a sublime beauty all its own, hard to describe to the uninitiated who did not travel in the legal circles Sprague travelled. Winning the argument wasn't his goal at that point, destroying his opponent personally was the real endomorphine rush and the real goal. Now, he felt the pleasure points pulse again at the thought of taking out another attorney. That was the best rush, the best game, to see the agony as another's professional reputation crashed and burned in the gore-spattered arena of a courtroom.

It wasn't as if allegations of impropriety by the prosecutor had not already been alleged during the appeals in the state courts. It was just that the allegations were dismissed for lack of evidence. With a growing sense of anticipation, Sprague re-examined the file before him. He could fix the problem of evidence. In the earlier appeals, the courts were constrained to the evidence developed during the trial. Now in the habeas proceeding, which was civil and not criminal, Sprague could subpoena whomever he wanted and question them about any aspect of the case.

He had originally decided to punt on the prosecutorial aspect of the appeal. The defense attorneys in the original trial had actually done rather badly. But with this new directive, he focused his attention on how to resurrect the issue of prosecutorial misconduct in such a way as to win.

Ten years of life tended to erase and shift memories of any witness and Sprague had learned that was his playground. That was where he could manufacture the evidence he needed to argue whatever it was he needed to argue. The questioning session, called a deposition, was something Sprague found particularly attractive. He was in charge. He asked the questions. The subject had no choice but to answer whether or not the question was fair or relevant. Regardless of the presence of an attorney for the subject, the subject still had to answer every question despite any objection by the subject's attorney. "The subject," which was what Sprague termed the poor soul who had to answer his questions, was just that, an object to squeeze out the right phrases for use later in a written brief and argument before a federal judge. Sprague really could not care less about what the intent of the subject's answers might have been during the deposition. Over time, he had learned to merely care about the right words to extract for use later when he fashioned an argument. It was a technique the legal community condemned in theory but in practice rewarded through court cases won. So effective was he at the technique that he found himself a partner at one of the most prestigious firms in the state as a result of that skill.

He stood up from his desk and turned to look out upon the James River. Situated on the twentieth floor and facing towards the river, his office bespoke the power and prestige of partnership in the law firm. Below him, the light flashed and bounced from the turbulent waters that splashed amongst the rocks.

As he watched the water swirl and twist, a plan formed in his mind. He would create a swirling maelstrom the likes of which Binford had probably never seen before. Small-town lawyers were always like that. In the camaraderie and relationships that tended to develop among rural bar associations, trust and fair play were often the hallmarks of good lawyering. A model, Sprague knew, aspired to by most attorneys in the little hamlets of Virginia. Sprague's form of lawyering on the other hand was more direct and honest, in his opinion. Perhaps the legal midgets in Culpeper, Madison or Orange County aspired to something that sounded nobler, but in the end he knew, it was this form of legal butchery that pulled in the good fees and brought the accolades from the Commonwealth Bar Association. And, even more importantly, he knew, brought the desired results.

The dark waters below flashed white then subsumed to black before rushing to the next rapid.

Smirking, he called his secretary and told her to prepare a subpoena for Mordecai Binford.

CULPEPER COUNTY, VIRGINIA: BABY JIM'S SNACK BAR

Sheriff Carter heaved his bulk around on the picnic table set up on the asphalt parking lot, having just heard something that pricked his mind like a blackberry thorn, sharp and insistent, from Elmer Parker, who was talking to a group of tree cutters standing in line at the entrance to Baby Jim's.

Baby Jim's was a landmark and a legend in Culpeper. To the unknowing motorist driving down Main Street, Baby Jim's looked like a dive. Built into the side of a house, surrounded by pavement and an assortment of pickup trucks, its appearance told the world what it was: a mom-and-pop roadside hamburger stand. But it was more than that to those that knew. Named for the founder who started it in 1948, the incongruous combination of side basement and added on serving window dished out home cooking at its southern best. The specialty at breakfast was an egg sandwich. Baby Jims had been serving the two fried eggs on white bread with bacon and cheese long before McDonalds had even thought up the idea of a breakfast sandwich. At lunch, the counter served hamburgers and hot dogs with fresh French fries in a never-ending succession until closing at two in the afternoon. Milk shakes were made with milk and ice cream. The coffee was always fresh and strong. Workers who had to be down in the city, as the locals called Washington DC, would come to Baby Jim's as early as four in the morning for breakfast.

Sheriff Carter liked to eat breakfast at Baby Jim's because he had grown up eating there, and because it was a good place to find out what was going on in the county.

"Elmer, boy, whatcha doing over there?" Carter waved the tree cutter over to his table. Elmer smiled and sauntered over to the seated Sheriff.

"What you been up to, Elmer?" Carter asked him, motioning him to sit down at the table.

The lanky tree cutter sat down, swinging his boot clad legs around in front. Pulling a pipe from his back pocket he laid it in front of him on the carved and grease spattered top.

"Same ole, same ole, Sheriff," he said. "Mainly just tree work down in the city. Been doing a little commercial grass cutting on the side though." Here, Parker's hard and battered hands pulled a fuzzy pipe cleaner from his top shirt pocket. He inspected it and then began to pull it through his teeth like dental floss. Carter had seen a lot of strange habits in his day but even he was taken aback by this.

Noting the Sheriff's shocked expression; Parker sheepishly stopped and began cleaning his pipe. "No use wasting a new pipe cleaner when you can get two uses," he explained.

Carter sipped his coffee. "I hear you say something about working at the Weir place?" He asked nonchalantly.

"Yep. Just talking about a tree job I had over in Remington." Parker fished out a tobacco pouch and pushed a thimble full into the pipe bowl.

"Was it a big job?"

"Naw. Nothing that's gonna pay the rent. But it was on the way down to the city so I took it on the side. Why you ask?"

"Well, hells bells, Elmer, I'm just passing the time," Carter assured him. "It's just that I've run into a fellow named Weir and thought it might be the same person."

"He works for the army or some damn thing like that," Parker said taking a long draw on his pipe. "Didn't really have much to say to me, but he had plenty to say to the Mrs. Them two fight like cats and dogs. Heard 'em going at it while we was there."

"What about?" Carter asked.

"Something about his job," Parker said. "She thinks he's slipping around on her. He just giving the same ole excuse. You know. He gonna be gone for a couple weeks but it wasn't what it seemed like."

"I take it she didn't buy it?"

"Hell no, she didn't buy it."

"He say when he might be leaving?" Carter asked.

"Not exactly, but I got the impression it was gonna be soon. And seemed like he wanted her to take off when he left."

"How'd she take that?" Carter asked.

"Like I said Sheriff, she was as hot as a goat's hind end in a pepper patch," Parker said.

Twenty minutes later, Carter was back in his office, putting in a call to Binford.

"But, Weir's under subpoena," the county prosecutor responded. "He can't just leave."

"I got a feeling about this and so do you," Carter told him. "Them feds always think they can do whatever they want. Would not surprise me at all if'n he were to skedaddle out of here."

"Are you suggesting I try to get a bond on him," Binford asked, referring to a process rarely used to ensure the presence of witnesses in court. The prosecutor, if he can convince a judge, has the ability to require the posting of a bond by a witness for his or her appearance in court.

"You're the commonwealth's attorney. I'm just a country sheriff, so I don't know, but it sure seems to me Weir and Sims don't want to appear before that grand jury. And, I mean, in the worst way."

"They're already alleging prosecutorial misconduct on my part by subpoenaing them," Binford complained. "There is no way I'm going to add gasoline to the fire."

"Have it your way then and hope he shows up," Carter told him. "Oh, and by the way, I hear a Defender Council puke was nosing around. And, I hate to give you more to worry about, but I hear it was *you* he was checking up on. Thought, what with everything that's going on around here, you'd appreciate hearing about that."

"Great. Any other tidbits to make my day? " Binford asked.

WARRENTON TRAINING CENTER--CULPEPER, VIRGINIA

Sims got right to the point. "You transported weapons in the pods," he said flatly.

Weir was surprised at how quickly Sims had discovered his ordnance package for Steele.

"Took you long enough to come to that conclusion," Weir shot back, deciding that attack was his best defense.

Sims eyed the new security chief, wondering how big a mistake it had been to hire the young military officer only to blink his eyes in disbelief as Weir launched into a tirade against the entire operation.

"Honestly, Mr. Sims, I remain shocked at the laxity shown by the facility," Weir said. "True, I did in fact ship a load of weapons. How long did it take you to figure that out? A week! You've got to be kidding me if you think this is a high security operation. It's a joke. Yeah, I took some ordnance and stuck it in a pod. Let's see, how long did it take you to figure out an extra pod had been shipped. Hmmm, that's right, three days and now, a full seven days later, you figure out you are missing ordnance and not only that it is missing, but it's been shipped to aliens! What a mess. Good thing I ran my little test operation now before something nasty really happened."

"You forget yourself, Weir," Sims replied trying to hide the fact that the full frontal attack had taken him by surprise. "I ask the questions and I make the conclusions. Now sit down and shut up," he ordered coldly.

"What?" Weir asked rhetorically, "Are you going to report the weapons shipment to Group? Get real. I'm the one who should be reporting to Group. You ought to be glad I'm not wasting you and the whole operation in a memo on security standards right now."

"Shut UP! SHUT UP!" Sims shouted, consumed with a rage he could no longer control. He knew Weir had him. Knew Weir could ruin his career with that one memo. And now he knew that Weir knew it, and even worse Sims believed the little pipsqueak would carry through with the threat if he could. Slamming his fist down on the table, he knocked his coffee cup to the floor. The black liquid splattered in a fluid arc shimmering through the morning light.

The two stared at one another in the white hot silence.

"Now you listen to me, Weir," Sims said finally. "You want to take me on. Try it. I'll win. And you want to know why? I'll win because Group always protects its own. Always. There's too much to lose if they don't. You've seen enough to know that now. The future of humanity is at stake. The future of Group is at stake. What we do is vital to the national security. Of course the public would be revolted by the transport program if it were known, but then the public has the luxury of not knowing that aliens are demanding our cooperation. They have the luxury of living in ignorance. You did --but not anymore. Group makes the hard decisions and you and I are their instruments. So go ahead and try to rattle the cage. See what happens. Edward Snowden found out. Didn't seem to work out too well for him. Your squeamishness is not going to make one bit of difference in the scheme of things except that you won't be around to participate. Comprende? Now that we've established what I already knew, that you shipped weapons to the transport destination, tell me why."

"I already told you," Weir responded defiantly. "I tested the security measures in place."

Sims crossed his legs, ankle on knee, and inspected his sock before tugging it up. "Get out," he ordered, his voice laced with venom.

Weir was shaking when he left Sims' office. He had to get Rebecca and the kids away. He knew Sims was planning something terrible for him and perhaps for his family, and all this happening while Rebecca remained convinced that he was having an affair. He had strayed once, but never again. His wife and children were the most important people in the world to him. He had to protect her and the children. But how? He drove to the Federal Reserve in a daze. His bluff could last only so long. He knew that now. He could tell Sims was not going to let him get by with the pod shipment-- and he believed Sims when he had threatened that Group always took care of its own. They were like the damn mafia, he thought to himself, a brotherhood of blood. The work they did was so terrible it could not stand the scrutiny of light and therefore they did anything-- anything-- to keep what they did hidden. A dark jewel in the slime of the night, the Federal Reserve's apparent purpose seemed in Weir's mind to pulsate with evil and horror and pain and secrecy.

Though the day was bright, the head of security drove into the midnight of his soul.

Sims waited until Weir left the building. Then with grim satisfaction he called his operative for select harvesting. Weir had a surprise coming. A dark treat indeed.

HESPERIA PLANUM: MARS

"Do you at least have a plan?" Reznik asked his fellow castaway.

Steele shrugged, then grinning, "Not yet. But we'll come up with one."

"We? Who said anything about we?" Reznik asked. "There's a lot about this place you don't know anything about. How about we take a little tour and then let's see if you still want to play charge-of-the-light-brigade."

"Fair enough. But what about those things out there?" Steele asked.

"I've got another route. They shouldn't be a problem." Reznik grinned through his tangled beard, "Never go to ground with just one exit, I always say."

"Right," Steele leaned back and clasped his hands behind his head, "So tell me more about this place."

"No." Reznik replied eying the Mossberg 590 at Steele's feet. "I'll show you. I think that what I tell you then will make better sense. Just follow me and do exactly what I say. And that includes don't shoot unless I say so. We got that clear."

"You're a right enough drill sergeant, that you are," Steele responded. "I got it, no shooting unless you give the order."

"Ok, then. Let's gear up and go." Reznik rummaged in a pile unnoticed by Steele until then. The castaway turned back to Steele with a visored helmet and a gray suit. Separate boots appeared from the pile. Then Reznik took another suit and shook it out. Steele noticed that it too was gray, like nylon, but scuffed and dirty. The suit opened in the middle and had a hood device attached to the neck area. Where the red dirt and stains allowed, the one-piece suit glistened.

"Put it on," Reznik ordered as he put one leg in and then the other.

"What is this?" Steele asked skeptically.

"Just put it on," Reznik said, pulling the hood over his head. "I'll explain later. Don't be concerned about the suit tightening up."

Steele watched in disbelief as the suit began to take form and mold itself to Reznik, the hood extending and wrapping around his head leaving the face exposed. Reznik then stepped into the boots which seemed to meld with the bottom of the suit leaving no sign of a seam.

"Put it on!" Reznik ordered in a muffled voice through the helmet he had secured to the top of his suit. "We're going to need the suit where we're going."

Turning his back to Steele, he pushed a green glowing button on the wall-mounted keypad next to the door.

When Steele put the suit on, he was surprised to find that the sensation of breathing was unaffected by the helmet. The middle opening closed of its own accord, the fabric molding itself so closely to his body that he felt as if he were wrapped in a tight blanket, although, as he bent to pick up the Mossberg 590, he noted that his mobility was not affected.

Reznik turned around and looked at him. "Good. Now, put the gun down --we won't need it." He scooted out the doorway. After a slight hesitation, Steele left the dull black shotgun and scrambled after him. Then the two continued down the corridor on hands and knees.

"Where are we going?" Steele asked.

"Soon enough you'll see," Reznik answered cryptically as he crawled through the passageway ahead, a shaft that wound up and down, twisted and curved, split and intersected. Steele had no idea where they were, but his guide was unerring as he followed the path marked with orange and brown stains, much like those on the suits until, finally, they came to a larger chamber where they could stand. Steele took note of a grate-like apparatus about twenty feet above him. He also saw the seams to what looked like a door in the chamber wall, five feet tall and two or three feet wide, on the right side of which were three glowing circles--green, yellow and red--flush with the walls.

When Reznik pushed the green button it faded and the yellow pulsed. The two tunnel entrances closed with an ominous click as a sliding door from the top of each latched in place. The red light pulsed and the yellow faded. When Reznik pushed the red button the seams of the door became more pronounced and Steele felt a rush of air as it slid open. Reznik stepped through the blinding bright glare now flooding the chamber. Following Reznik's silhouetted form, he found himself standing on a platform, built into the side of a hill. Before them stretching to the horizon were rust-colored hummocks, eroded craters, and endless rows of sand dunes. The sun seemed oddly small and weak in a salmon-colored sky and a low, pinkish haze, hanging like smog in the Los Angeles basin on a hot day, obscured the details in the distance.

"Welcome to Mars," Reznik announced, his voice tinny in Steele's suit.

Steele stared uncomprehendingly at the enormity of the utterly alien vista spread out before him. Overwhelmed, he staggered and slumped down on the metallic grated platform, convinced now, beyond all doubt, that he was on another world. The reddish sky and cratered plain spread before Steele silently screamed in no uncertain terms that he stood on alien soil. Martian soil: a landscape 140 million miles away from home, from family, from everything and everyone that he ever cared about.

Apparently unaware of Steele's collapse, Reznik continued, "Mars," he repeated. "Or more precisely, the Hesperia Planum. It took me a while to figure it out. But then I realized there really was only one place on Mars like this. See how rounded everything is. And then look off to the right. See those lines, those depressions in the surface, there is only one place that has that. Tyrrhena Mons. And once I identified this mountain, or really, inactive volcano, the rest was easy," he said with pride. "Tyrrhena is the only mountain in Hesperia Planum of this magnitude. And by that, I mean this thing is 1.5 kilometers high."

Hearing no response from Steele, Reznik turned. "Hey! What's wrong? You ok?" Reznik moved quickly to Steele's side and bent down on one knee to look closely at the sitting, but slumped, form.

"Yeah," Steele muttered. "Yeah," he said a little louder, "I'm ok. It's just a lot to take in at once. Go on."

Reznik, remembering his own shock when he first woke in the pod, and then later when he discovered where he was, felt a surge of sympathy for the Englishman. "I understand. You sit. I'll talk." Reznik turned and sat next to Steele facing out towards the receding cratered plain.

"It really makes sense once you think about it, why they would pick this place to set up a base," Reznik continued. "This is one of the most geologically stable places on Mars. The volcano is extinct and there are lava tubes to build within. But more than that, there's a lot of water under here. In fact, this whole landscape was made by water. Look at those rills." Reznik gestured towards a series of sinuous dunes that ran in intersecting lines. "They really are nothing but the sediment deposits from shorelines. Now that brings us to the base. Look closely over there. Do you see the transport moving?"

Steele followed Reznik's gesture and focused on a softly-mounded hummock of red and brown. Then he detected movement. A lone craft, cigar-shaped and reddish in color, moved smoothly across the landscape. It glided in the thin atmosphere of the planet, giving no indication of exhaust or chemical burn for thrust. As he watched, incredulous, it slid into a canyon and disappeared from sight.

"Look over there," Reznik pointed further down the canyon opening. Silhouetted, Steele saw an insect like creature stepping lightly along the rim of the canyon. It appeared to be similar to that which he had killed earlier and he tensed, drawing his arms inward, ready to jump up.

"Don't worry. It won't see us." Reznik assured him. "Which brings me to those things. They are almost like ants. I don't know how else to explain it. They move with purpose. And in an odd sort of way, with intelligence. But I swear, Steele, this is the worst-run place I have ever seen. I can't imagine these things having the ability to invent the technology we see here. Much less build the base to the scale that we see. I mean, why would something that big build a chamber and exit like the one we just used? It's almost as if the base were built for humans --but used by those things."

"You'll note the hard exoskeletons," Reznik added. "It seems to offer protection from Mars' UV radiation . And somehow they're able to store oxygen because they go outside without preparation or protection."

Steele looked at his enclosed fingers, "These suits, how safe are they?" he asked.

"Wondered when you would get around to that subject," Reznik said. "I call them 'pressure suits'. Don't worry about the suit. Damn near indestructible as far as I can tell -- and hard as a rock where it counts. Like around your chest and shoulders. But you haven't asked me the two most obvious questions. First, where does the oxygen come from? There are no tanks. And secondly, where did I get these things?"

Steele realized for the first time that there were no obvious tanks on Reznik's suit nor were there any on his when he put his own suit on.

"It took me a long time to figure this one out. The suits are really genius. There is no way those things crawling around out there could come up with something like this." Reznik pulled on the stiff material on his arm to emphasize the point. "The suits pull the oxygen from the atmosphere--as far as I can tell. Nanotechnology at its best. They filter the carbon and leave the oxygen storing it in the fabric itself."

"You've lost me," Steele said. "Oxygen? There's very little of any atmosphere on Mars and even less oxygen from what I know about the planet."

"No. You're not thinking about where the oxygen is. That's the problem," Reznik explained. "Mar's atmosphere is 95 percent carbon dioxide. Carbon Dioxide. Co2. One atom carbon. Two atoms oxygen. The suit merely filters the oxygen and leaves the carbon. After a while you'll notice a black dust on the suit. That's the residue carbon. But they do have to recharge. There's not much atmosphere to speak of so the suits don't have much to work with. Obviously the base is oxygen rich so I assume the suits recharge inside."

Steele took the explanation at face value. He was breathing. There was no question about that. And his companion sounded like he knew what he was talking about. Who was Steele to argue? He shrugged. "Where did you get the suit?" he asked.

"Ah, yes. I *did* bring that up, didn't I? Well, we need to take a little walk. This is something you'll need to see to understand. You up to it now?"

In answer, Steele stood.

The two men walked to the end of the platform, and jumped three feet to the sandy surface of Mars. Then Reznik started walking towards the canyon. Steele followed, keeping his eyes peeled for another alien.

"How are these things powered?" Steele asked referring to the pressure suits.

"Again, I'm only guessing," Reznik replied. "But on earth I know there were experiments with fabric that created electricity from the molecular alignment of metallic strands within a flexible membrane. Perhaps this is the same thing."

They walked in silence. Steele was too enmeshed in the experience of actually walking on another planet to notice Reznik's mute trudging before him. The sensation of less weight became more apparent with each step. At 38 percent of Earth's gravity, Mar's relatively light grip on Steele made walking much less arduous. That and the oddness of the sky consumed Steele, but when he asked questions, Reznik's answers became shorter and terser until, after about an hour of walking, Reznik stopped and pointed towards a low hill.

"We're going through a hatch at the top of that hill. Follow me and keep radio silence. We'll talk more once we go inside and are off radio. They're deaf. But I don't know about radio transmissions at close range."

At the top of the low hill, a four-foot metallic tube protruded about five feet into the air. At the top was a grate. Reznik jumped up and motioned Steele to follow. The two of them stood on the edge of the tube and shifted the grate aside. Reznik motioned for Steele to go into the tube which, like the tunnels they had left, was illuminated by the material of the tube itself. He followed the reddish stains left by, he assumed Reznik, and climbed down, holding onto a cable attached to the side of the passageway. Ten feet down he found himself in another chamber much like the one they had left. Reznik pulled the grate shut behind him and slid down the cable to the chamber floor where the tunnel was large enough to walk upright. Steele noticed dusty footprints on the floor and pointed at them. Reznik nodded his head up and down and pointed at himself. He motioned for Steele to follow him, then he turned and walked away.

The tunnel, exuding light as had the other, moved in straight lines, turning at 90-degree or 45-degree angles. Another outlined door. More keypad lights. A hatch slid up, which opened to reveal a vaulted cavernous chamber filled with tanks and piping and what looked like bundles of wires snaking about the room. Reznik gripped both sides of his helmet and pulled gently upwards, a slit appeared at the base of his throat and the helmet slid up and off. The remainder of the suit gripped the JPL engineer's body. Steele imitated Reznik with the same results.

"Ok. We're in," Reznik whispered. You can talk but keep it quiet. Sometimes those praying mantis things are in here. Follow me."

"What is all of this stuff?" Steele whispered as they traversed through the maze of machinery.

"I think it has to do with the tissue collection." Reznik answered cryptically.

Steele heard something faint at first, and then louder, as they moved towards the noise.

Something.

Louder. Then loud enough for Steele to know it was not good. It was not anything he wanted to see, or hear, but Reznik moved forward resolutely.

The sound cried of agony and loss. Low and somehow, bloody, the sound gurgled across the air to him speaking of things unspeakable, things of horror and loneliness, things that come in the middle of the night during our worst nightmares.

And then they rounded a corner and he saw them.

He saw men and women and children all pointed inward, clustered in groups of twenty or more. Heads bent. Weeping. Moaning. Shaking. Dirty. Trembling in hives of horror. Leaning inward, shoulder to shoulder, unaware of anything but the inner world of terror each inhabited.

Then he noticed they wore skin suits--dirty like the one he wore--hoods back.

"What the hell?" Steele said.

"Quiet. I told you-- you had to see this to understand."

"What the hell is going on here?" Steele demanded angrily.

"I told you. If Dante ever had a vision of Hell, this was it."

"I mean there are kids here," Steele observed hotly. "What does that to kids?"

"You've got to see this to understand the absolute evil that happens here," Reznik replied.

"I've seen enough," Steele said enraged. "Let's get 'em out of there."

"Don't think I haven't tried," Reznik told him, "but they're unresponsive to anything except the aliens."

"You've tried to get them out of here?"

"I did manage to release two," Reznik told him. "I did it one at a time. I got each back to the chamber and took off the suit. But as soon as I fell asleep or wasn't paying attention, they left. I found the first one in the chamber where we exited. He died from exposure to the Martian atmosphere. He was just a kid."

For the first time, Steele saw the bearded survivor's eyes well up with emotion.

"I did it one more time," Reznik continued. "I got an adult the second time. I don't know, I guess I thought maybe the kid was too immature to understand what was going on. But I couldn't watch the second guy all the time. They're passive. They moan and cry a little, but they don't fight. They do what you physically move them to do. They even understand simple verbal commands. But, there is no real understanding. No real ability to communicate. At the first opportunity, they just walk away. The second guy made it to the platform before he died. You know, exposure to low atmospheric pressure is an ugly thing. The eyes protrude out of the head. All the exposed water in your body boils off -- and that includes the lining of your lungs."

"What do they use them for? Why do they want people?" Steele asked baffled.

"I've followed them," Reznik told him. "I've followed them. It's crazy. They use them to dig. They use them to handle material. I can't understand the point of it all. Sometimes they put them in what looks like labs to me. The aliens manipulate it all. They seem to control everyone through some sort of mind direction. I don't know. I just know it didn't happen to me. And it didn't happen to you because that freaking monster was never able to inject you. They do that when someone is pulled from the pod. They seem to inject something into you that keeps you in the state those people are in now. And then there are the animals."

"Animals?"

"They bring in animals and dissect them," Reznik said. "They dump the animals in these vats. The people after a while disappear. I've never found them, so I don't know what happens to them. I've looked, but I don't know. I'm hoping if the NSA is involved in all of this that they get returned. I mean I've heard about people being abducted, but I always thought it was just urban folklore. Now I'm hoping there's more to it. I'm hoping the abductions are real, and that these people get to go home."

Looking at the mass of humanity before him, Steele wondered whether survival was even an option for them.

"This whole place is crazy," Reznik said. "Obviously the technology is light years ahead of anything we have but then other parts are so crude. And stupid. It's offensive actually. Maybe not to you but to an engineer there are parts of the operation here that defy explanation because the methods are so crude. I don't understand any of it." Reznik stopped talking abruptly, as if he realized he was beginning to lose control. The two stood silent and looked at the sea of misery.

Then Steele asked in a whisper, "So this is where the people in the pods are going to end up? I mean the ones who came with me?"

It was a question that he hoped Reznik would not answer.

But he did.

On the way back to Reznik's hideout, Steele thought about Reznik's story and what the JPL engineer had shown him. After the human storage area, Reznik took Steele to the alien feeding area. The horrid smell of the aliens made more sense after he saw them feed. The monstrosities submerged themselves into vast tanks of what Reznik described as a fibrous "protein" bath.

"Are you telling me they grow meat?" Steele had asked interrupting Reznik as he began to explain the process while they watched from a hiding spot nearby.

"Despite its seeming similarities I wouldn't call it meat."

"Well, whatever. What is the stuff made from?" Steele demanded.

"I suppose from the animals they gather. But the volume consumed is much larger than the few animals they bring up so obviously it is an organic replicating process at work in the tank."

"Obviously," Steele replied dubiously.

"How often do the aliens put people in the vats?" Steele had asked later, shocked that the idea had even entered his mind.

Reznik looked away from Steele but did not answer.

"People go in the vats?" Steele asked insistently.

"I only saw it once," Reznik admitted. "Only once."

The two had walked slowly to another observation post that Reznik used. An alien emerged from the liquid, and Steele noticed that Reznik eyed it closely. When it passed by, gleaming wetly red, Reznik seemed to relax.

"I don't know what happens to the people here," Reznik volunteered. "I think they are returned to earth. I really do. I think the abduction stories are true. They have to be for there to be so many abduction claims out in the public domain."

The gurgle and gush of blood and gore from the large vat-like pool announced the emergence of another alien which lumbered past the two men, dropping something that hit the ground with a wet slap. Then, to Steele's horror, Reznik had darted out to gather the remnants that had fallen to the floor.

"Dinner," Reznik had told him, gleefully, holding up the grisly prize while, to Steele's amazement, the stains of gore melted into the floor leaving it as clean as when first made.

"See what I mean," Reznik had pointed to the disappearing smear, "See what I mean: absorbed, probably by some sort of nanotechnology in the structure itself. A highly technical civilization built this facility. But then to feed like that? It's outrageous. Why not use feeding tubes for crying out loud. And submerging themselves in a vat of blood and fiber? It's out of a bad horror show. "

Steele could not shake from his mind the odd gleam in Reznik's eye when he held up the fibrous morsel. That was when he decided no matter what, no matter how, he was not going to settle for survival and turn into what the JPL engineer had become, a lonely figure living on the edge of horror and starvation. He was not going to end up eating the remains of what the aliens dripped onto the floor.

"Do you know where the pod group is that I arrived in is now?" Steele asked as Reznik trudged ahead of him, "dinner" strapped to his back now frozen dried in the cold dry Martian atmosphere.

"I've got a good idea," Reznik answered reluctantly.

"Have they been opened?" Steele asked.

"Some have. But most have not."

"I'm going to get them." Steele said resolutely.

"And, like I said before we went on our little excursion, do you have a plan?" Reznik asked, skipping sideways to avoid a low outcrop of rock in the Martian sand.

"I'm thinking the two of us can come up with one," Steele said lurching to the right to avoid the same outcrop. "I have a few ideas. I've got plenty of weapons. And I think there are people in those pods who know how to use them. The plan is to get to the pods, get those that are not injected or whatever it is the aliens do, and arm them. I've got C-4 explosive. I've got grenades. I've got surprise. I think we can take them on. The only problem I have is once we kill off the aliens, then what? Is there a ship and if there is one how do we fly it?"

"Don't think I haven't tried to puzzle a way out of here," Reznik told him. "But I never thought about how weapons could change the equation."

"And?" Steele asked.

"There might be a way."

"Go on, then, give it to me," Steele said with enthusiasm.

Reznik pointed to another cigar-shaped craft moving in the distance, "The key is to get one of those things."

"You mean you can actually fly one?"

"I think so. Every single one of those craft is flown by humans. I've even been on a couple and watched how to operate the things. The aliens never even knew I was there."

"The craft are really made for humans if you ask me," Reznik volunteered after a time.

They stumbled on across the rock and sand in silence. Steele satisfied himself with observing the alien landscape. To his surprise, he saw a dust devil in the distance and pointed it out to Reznik. It moved silently across the cratered floor of a valley leaving a light-colored trail behind. A few wispy bluish-white cirrus clouds scurried through the upper atmosphere in contrast with the overall salmon-colored sky. At one point, Steele stopped Reznik and pointed out two moons zipping across the sky at the same time.

"Sometimes you see them both at the same time like now," Reznik explained. "Usually not. They circle the planet once a Martian day, more or less. That's why you actually see them moving as opposed to our moon. Those things are whipping around the planet. We had a hell of time calculating the two rovers' orbital insertion because of those things."

When the two got close to the entrance from where they had started their journey that morning, Reznik turned away from the path they had taken earlier and scrambled up the edge of a jagged ridge of reddish rock. Steele followed up and over the crag, rocks scattered from under his feet until stumbling and sliding down the other side of the outcrop, he found himself in a cleft that opened to a larger crater.

"Check this out," Reznik said proudly and Steele saw that a box-like contraption just below the rock floor was shimmering and glinting in the harsh Martian sun. Through its transparent top he saw thin brown wrinkled strips hanging on horizontal bars. Then it dawned on Steele, he was looking at jerky.

"I found this cleft after I'd been here a month or so." Reznik said. He pulled the "meat" around and unstrapped it from the rope that held it to his back. Then he deftly cut the now solid fiber into strips, explaining, "The sun heats up the box and dries it even more than just laying it out on the rocks."

Pulling some strips out of the box, he hung the newly-cut strips in their stead and shut the transparent lid.

"Let's go. I'm hungry." Reznik said.

Once inside and unsuited the two settled back in Reznik's refuge.

"We can't kill all the aliens," Reznik said flatly as he handed Steele a slab of dried "meat". "There's too many of them. But there is something we can do."

Steele looked across the cramped cubicle at Reznik. His dirty, ragged clothes hung limp on his darkened frame. The survivor bit into the dried strip and pulled a jagged piece of dried fiber off with a snap of his neck. Then he chewed methodically. Suddenly, to his surprise, instead of finding himself repulsed, Steele found himself ravenous. Mouth watering, he put the substance in his mouth and gnawed a chunk off of the main strip. He was surprised at the salty, meaty taste. It was classic jerky and it tasted good.

Reznik continued, "We can get out of here and try to make contact with earth," Reznik continued. Then afterwards we can hole up at the power plant and greenhouse."

"As long as that means we get my friends out of those pods," Steele said.

"Of course we might just get killed."

"No problem. Been there before," Steele replied. "I'd rather give it a shot than live like this. No offense."

"What? You don't like my accommodations? I'm shocked. No, seriously, you know before I was abducted I trained to drive *Curiosity*."

Steele had no idea what Reznik was referring to and it showed on his face.

"Damn. Don't you know anything about Mars?" Reznik asked. "*Curiosity* is the last rover we sent to Mars. It should be on the surface right now. It's the largest rover yet. *Spirit* and *Opportunity* were a lot smaller and dependent on sunlight for power. *Curiosity* is about the size of a car and it runs on nuclear power-- so it will last for years-- and, unless the mission has changed, it's in Gale Crater right now."

"So the plan is what? Get to this rover and then what?"

"Well, let's talk about getting to the rover first." Reznik warmed to the conversation, laying out his plan.

When Reznik finished, Steele laughed, "You *are* one for understatement, aren't you? '*We might just get killed*'," the Englishman shook his head, "you ought to have said '*we might just live*'." Steele reached over and stretched out his hand to clasp Reznik's thin and bony claw of a hand, forming a bond shared only by those going into battle.

"*We just might get killed*, bloody optimist you are," Steele said chuckling.

Later, after they had hashed out how to implement Reznik's scheme and he had lain down to sleep, Steele felt the cold hollow wind of fear whisper through his soul as he listened to Reznik's steady breathing. Nothing was ever easy, he thought. *And nothing goes right.*

CHAPTER 14

MEMO

EYES ONLY

THIS DOCUMENT IS PROTECTED UNDER THE EMERGENCY FEDERAL CODE OF 1951, SECTION 1338B(C)(I). IT IS A CRIMINAL VIOLATION TO COPY OR REPRODUCE THIS DOCUMENT IN ANY FORM. ONLY LEVEL III SECURITY CLEARANCE PERSONNEL ARE AUTHORIZED TO READ THIS DOCUMENT. CONTACT YOUR DUTY OFFICER IMMEDIATELY IF: 1. YOU COME INTO POSSESSION OF THIS DOCUMENT AND 2. YOU ARE NOT AUTHORIZED FOR EXPOSURE TO THE INFORMATION CONTAINED HEREIN.   -- SEE EXECUTIVE ORDER NSA 330-1957.

DATE: FEBRUARY 8, 2004.

TO: TRAVIS DIAZ, CHIEF EXCUTIVE OFFICER, GROUP 929

FROM: NINA PETROV

RE: NASA REQUEST FOR PROPOSALS: SCIENTIFIC INSTRUMENT PACKAGE: MARS LANDER

BACKGROUND:

NASA WILL ASK FOR BIDS AND PROPOSALS IN APRIL OF THIS YEAR TO FORMULATE THE SCIENTIFIC INSTRUMENTATION OF THE PLANNED MARS LANDER. IT IS EXPECTED THAT THE DECISION AS TO WHAT INSTRUMENT PACKAGES TO SEND WILL BE ANNOUNCED LATER IN THE YEAR. CONVERSATIONS WITHIN THE CHIEF INVESTIGATOR'S OFFICE INDICATE TO ME THAT NASA IS LEANING AGAINST SENDING THE PACKAGE OF MOST INTEREST TO GROUP 929: SPECIFICALLY THE RAD INSTRUMENT PACKAGE.

ANALYSIS: RAD (RADIATION ASSESMENT DETECTOR) IS AN IMPORTANT AREA OF INQUIRY GIVEN THE PARAMETERS OF INVESTIGATION TASKED TO THIS INFORMANT. THE PACKAGE WILL MEASURE RADIATION DURING INTERORBITAL TRANSIT. THIS HAS NEVER BEEN DONE AND WILL PROVIDE INVALUABLE DATA FOR PROJECT ARES. SECONDLY THE PACKAGE WILL CONDUCT SURFACE AND SUBSURFACE RADIATION/ THERMAL IMAGING. THIS ON-SURFACE CAPABILITY WILL HELP GROUP 929 IDENTIFY THE SPECIFIC SITE OF THE ALIEN ENTITY'S POWER SOURCE AND ACTIVITY LEVEL. THE OBSTACLE IS THE CHIEF INVESTIGATOR'S INSISTENCE ON DEDICATING ALL

RESOURCES TOWARDS THE DETECTION OF WATER AND OR CLUES TO THE PRESENCE OF WATER IN THE PAST.

RECOMMENDATION: GERMANY'S SPACE AGENCY, DLR, IS FUNDING RAD. AS GROUP 929 KNOWS, THE CHRISTIAN-ALBRECHTS UNIVERSITAT-ZU KEIL IS THE ORIGINATOR AND DEVELOPER OF RAD IN CONJUNCTION WITH THE SOUTHWEST RESEARCH INSTITUTE. IT IS SUGGESTED THAT GROUP 929 PRESS FOR AN EXECUTIVE ORDER DIRECTED TO NASA FOR THE INCLUSION OF RAD ON THE LANDER. HARMONIOUS ALLIED RELATIONS ARE OF UTMOST IMPORTANCE TO THE BUSH ADMINSTRATION DURING THE PRESENT HOSTILITIES IN IRAQ. THIS WILL GIVE COVER FOR SUCH A DIRECT INTERVENTION BY THE PRESIDENT'S OFFICE. ADDING THE SCIENCE PACKAGE WILL ENHANCE GERMAN STANDING AND REWARD GERMAN COOPERATION WITHIN NATO.

ROUTE CODE:

88852222006702222288885550000000303000006
00000333011104050607059482990000000000000

--EXCERPTS FROM THE PRESIDENTIAL BRIEFING PAPERS ON THE ROSWELL INCIDENT

CULPEPER--CHICK-FIL-A

Rebecca settled into a corner table and waited for her husband to arrive. The text he had sent her that morning --**Lunch?**--had been cryptic and he had not responded to her return text or phone message, all of which infuriated her. She had seen this behavior once before and she had sworn she would not endure it again. Although she had no proof of an affair, the clues were everywhere, even down to this meeting, since the last time she had met him at a fast-food joint under similar directions and circumstances he had broken down and confessed his indiscretion. Pregnant with their youngest, she had decided to stay in the marriage, and until recently had not regretted the decision. Deep in her heart she knew he was the love of her life. But the late nights and the unpredictable schedule he kept now all pointed to another foray into the realm of unfaithfulness. And that was something she would not forgive a second time even though it would, she knew, destroy her soul.

That, and the silence that had grown between them. Clearly something was bothering him just as it had before, probably because of his high sense of personal honor and integrity, which was, she thought, ironic given the affair. But then men often thought with body parts other than their brain, hard as it was for her to accept it.

Rebecca began to tear up at the thought of it all.

"Stop it," she whispered to herself and angrily jabbed a napkin at the corner of her eyes. She would not cry. She would not let him hurt her again.

When she saw John pull up in his government-issued black SUV and stride purposefully into the restaurant, she noticed the jut of his jaw, the clinched teeth and realized everything about his body language meant something serious was about to happen. Her stomach rolled with anxiety.

"So, what's this all about, John?" she asked. "And don't try to put me off. We've done this before, remember?"

Inside she was crumbling but she was not going to let him know it. Not at this point.

"I don't know what you're talking about," he replied frowning. "Listen we don't have much time. You've got to get out of here. I want you to leave. Visit your parents. Visit Carol out in Colorado for a while. You just need to leave and take the kids for a little bit. I can't tell you why, but you and the kids need to be kept safe. It--It's work related. That's all I can say."

"That's not enough, John. You're scaring me. I deserve to know what's going on," she replied.

"I can't tell you. You know that."

"I'm not buying it, John," she told him. "You work for the Quartermaster Corps. There is nothing top secret or dangerous in that. I know it. You know it. So don't pull that crap with me again. I'm not going anywhere until you tell me the truth."

"So what are you saying?" he said hotly. "I've got to admit to an affair then you'll agree to leave?"

"You tell me you're seeing someone else and I'll be out of there so quick you won't believe it. And I won't come back, not this time."

***

Later, Rebecca peeled out of the parking lot. Eventually, when he saw she would not do what he wanted, he finally admitted to an affair.

She knew he would.

"Let me just get it out of my system. I just need some space."
He had said to her. That was when she slapped him.

"Don't you dare pretend to be a victim!" she had hissed at him
while the red mark of her hand glowed red on his face.

As she stood to leave, he said, "Don't trust anyone. Be careful.
Don't call me. I'll get in touch with you."

She had laughed, "Don't trust? That's some advice, John-- coming from you. Don't worry, my lawyer will get in touch with you.
When you get home tonight I won't be there. That I promise!"

Thirty minutes later, she regretted her words. As she pulled up
to her house she saw a black SUV parked in her driveway with the
side door open. Inside she saw Heather and Hunter seated in the
middle passenger seat next to a man in uniform.

"*Safe*," she remembered John telling her while she walked over
to the open vehicle door. "*I want you and the kids to be safe.*"

CULPEPER--WARRENTON TRAINING CENTER

Sims loved M&Ms. Especially the red ones. He didn't know
why. He just did. And seeing a red one almost within reach, he
wiggled his finger to maneuver it around so that he could squeeze
it between his forefinger and index finger. It was a manipulation he
had done many times before. His mouth began to water in anticipation of the prize he was about to snatch.

It slipped and the pile of greens and blues and yellows and
browns slid over the red M&M as it skidded from between his fingers.

He sighed. No matter. They all tasted the same in the end. It
was just that he wanted the red one. He popped three or four in his
mouth and crunched down on the hard shell to relish the soft chocolate flavor of the interior. There was something innately satisfying
in crushing the little round candy in his mouth. He loved the initial
crack of the shell before it caved into a mass of hard bits and softness.
Like people, he thought absently. They always had a hard outer shell
and a soft interior.

Always.

Then he picked up the phone in response to the electronic buzz
announcing a call.

"Yes," he mumbled through the candy sliding around in
his mouth.

"Smith here. The package has been collected."

"Very good," Sims sat up straight in his chair and swallowed the chocolate mass in one gulp. Bring it for transport."

"What is the ETA for transport?"

"Tonight," Sims answered. "At twenty-two hundred."

"Normal preparation?" Smith asked.

"I want transfer to be recorded," Sims answered. "I want the data file at my office immediately afterwards."

"All three subjects?"

"Yes."

"Anything else, sir?"

"Just make sure that data file is in my office."

After the phone call, Sims leaned back in his chair and continued to fish for the red M&M. He would get it, just like he would get Weir, whose so-called qualms about the program and "in your face attitude" were getting on his nerves. Sims had little fear that the recipients on Mars would be all that concerned. Shoot, he thought to himself, if you can fly spaceships the way these guys did, if you could go to Mars and back in a matter of days, a few rifles and grenades would hardly qualify as a threat. But, it was the principle of the thing. Weir had acted without clearing it with him. And then he had the gall to threaten him with Group. That was his big mistake. He would show Weir once and for all who was boss. And what could happen if you crossed the boss.

The wife and kids would go on a little trip. Thousands had already taken that trip and been none the worse for wear except to have been implanted with those strange little habits. He snickered inwardly at that. Strange little habits indeed. Weir would have to worry about whatever crazy little things his family would do-- rather than try his boss' patience or threaten his job with Group.

Weir would learn. He would learn the hard way. And it would be fun to crush the hard shell of that particular red M&M.

NSA GROUP 929 OPERATIONS CENTER--FAIRFAX, VIRGINIA

The Group 929 Chairman stood at the podium in the conference room and looked down the half- empty table. This was the executive committee. In time, the full committee would be informed but for the present he had thought it best to brief these men first.

"This meeting will not last long," he said bringing the gathering to order. "Traffic is bad enough at four so we don't want to get stuck in it at five or six," he said referring to the clogged mass that Washington area traffic became starting at four in the afternoon.

"We've had a breakthrough," the Group Chairman continued. "I wanted to inform you first before we decide what if anything to do next. Let me introduce to you Nina Petrov. Ms. Petrov, as many of you know, has operated within NASA for us. I'm sure you've read the dispatches from her over the years regarding various aspects of the Mars project. Ms. Petrov, would you inform us of your findings?"

"Thank you, sir." The petite woman with long dark hair and dark features stood and took the podium. She had practiced the briefing beforehand, at the insistence of the Group 929 Chair, so she easily found the remote to operate the flat screen behind her.

"As you know, it was my recommendation that Group push for the inclusion of the RAD package on Curiosity," she began. "The manufacturer of the package created a separate search function in the programing and hardware in addition to the scientific mission outlined by NASA. NASA's main concern was payload weight and power usage. We were able to meet both concerns easily using the nanotechnology provided by NSA research."

The Chairman interrupted her, "What import is that to us?" he asked.

"It means that NASA believes RAD is there for one purpose only. In fact, it serves the role outlined by NASA but it serves an entirely separate function for NSA," here she spoke with emphasis, "and NASA is unaware of this separate functionality."

"Ok, go on," the Chairman waived her on.

Petrov punched up a high resolution photo of Gale Crater. Then she zoomed the image to that of Curiosity on the surface. It was not detailed but it showed the rover on the slopes of Sharp Mountain, the large mass of rock, rubble and alluvial debris rising from the center of the crater. Behind Curiosity was a trail of tracks left by the lander's six wheels.

"Here is Curiosity at about 10,000 feet on the face of Mount Sharp. The Mount itself rises 18,000 feet from the crater floor and is elevated above the rim of the crater itself. This is important because it gives us an elevated position from which to observe the surface using RAD."

Petrov then pulled up another schematic photo of Curiosity itself.

"The RAD package is located here." She used a laser pointer to highlight the scientific package situated on the right front top of the rover.

"Excuse me," a man with round, wire-rim glasses interrupted her, "I don't understand why we ever needed RAD. We have an orbiting vehicle. Why go to the trouble of putting something on the surface?"

"An excellent question," Petrov replied. "And the answer is simple. When the Mars Reconnaissance Orbiter, or MRO, was built in the early 2000s, and it was launched in 2005, the stealth technology just was not there to do the type of surveillance that RAD can do covertly without the AE knowing. This was our earliest opportunity to get the hardware to Mars. We took it. Plain and simple. But your point is well taken. The RAD package works anywhere but is best situated above the horizon. And since we are now above the horizon, RAD is able to look over the crater rim and out to the surrounding surface."

Here she shifted the photo on the screen to a view showing the edge of Gale Crater and the Badlands beyond, taken by Curiosity's Mastcam, a camera mounted on a thick pole jutting above the rover platform.

"The RAD is capable of several functionalities," she explained. "The first thing we checked for were radiation thermal signatures like this. We used the over the horizon imaging functionality here."

The normally staid group moved towards the screen in unison when the image flashed upon the screen.

"This is Tyrrhena Mons. It is over the horizon but RAD bounces imagining using the atmosphere boundary itself."

The x-ray like graphic showed larger empty spaces underground, connected by thin ghostly lines-- all indicative of an extensive structure in the mountain.

"This," she said, circling the entire photo with the laser pointer, "we believe is the AE center."

She pushed the remote again and a white plume showed on the screen underneath of which spread a web of the same ghostly lines. "This corresponds with the up-to-now mysterious methane plumes that have been observed for the past thirty years," she explained. "We believe this is evidence of some sort of power plant or manufacturing plant used by the AE."

"For what purpose?" someone asked.

"Well, obviously, it has something to do with DNA extraction and the tissue samples taken from abductees," Petrov responded.

"Now, now," the Chairman interrupted, "we know you have a theory, Ms. Petrov, but it is, you must admit, not supported by hard evidence."

"I want to hear it," the man who earlier asked the first question announced.

"Go ahead," the Chairman nodded his assent to the request. "You've got five minutes."

"We know that the AE began human abduction as early as the 1960s, perhaps earlier," Petrov began, clearly gathering her thoughts. "But let us use that as a bench mark. The number was so small and in most cases unreported that as a result the whole phenomena slipped under NSA radar, so to speak. I will however confine my remarks to the livestock mutilation phenomena, the first of which were reported in Pennsylvania in the early 1960s, but did not receive national attention, or NSA attention for that matter, until the 1967 event in Alamosa, Colorado, when a saddle horse was found mutilated, drained of blood, and surrounded by a strong chemical odor. The owner of the horse was able to publicize the bizarre nature of her pet's death through contacts in the media-- which in turn led to NSA interest. Investigators sent to the scene found fifteen circular burn marks incised in the ground and a Forest Ranger dispatched with a Geiger counter recorded elevated radiation levels in a two block radius around the horse carcass. After the reports made the press, a Colorado Superior Court Judge from Denver came forward and reported seeing three reddish-orange rings in a triangular formation flying in the area where the horse carcass was found."

"You can look at my memo for the statistics," she continued. "But they show specific areas of interest." Petrov ticked off the points with her fingers, the forefinger moving from one finger to the other to emphasize the facts. "Blood, brain and spinal matter, reproductive organs, the tongue, eyes, and small particles of flesh."

She gripped the podium, leaning forward, "And in every case there are either reports of lights in the sky, odd marks on the ground or heightened levels of radiation. That is the cattle and animal mutilations. But that is not all. At the same time, humans were being abducted, which I believe is related to the cattle and livestock mutilations."

Petrov moved away from the podium, lost in the moment, then began pacing back and forth as she spoke.

"The most fascinating event and the one that prompted me to construct my theory is the little known, but first, human abduction, that of Antonio Villas Boas, who was captured, examined and then introduced to a female-like humanoid. A meeting that led to what he described as almost automated or externally controlled, sexual intercourse, after which he was released. Now one might put this off as the delusions of a Brazilian farm boy-- but he never wavered from his story, became a respected lawyer, and died in 1992 without ever recanting. In addition, after the abduction, he was examined by physicians and found to be suffering from radiation poisoning. There was no possible source of radiation to explain this radiation sickness."

"I might add, we are all aware of the examinations made by Group after transportees return. Malnourished, injured, sometimes they show signs of sampling, and then of course sometimes they come back in pieces."

Silence. Each thought of the actual consequences of the technical things they discussed in the clean, well-lit, civilized space called the executive board room. Group did not like specifics. Petrov did not know that, but she understood that, in that moment, the room became defensive and therefore less open to her message. She plowed on, knowing her time was almost up.

"I propose that the AE abductions and mutilations point to some sort of DNA, organic harvesting process on Mars," Petrov continued. "In addition, for whatever reason, the evidence supports the idea that humans are being used for hard labor, since the physical condition of some transportees is little different from that of survivors lost in the wilderness or survivors from prisoner-of-war camps."

"The mental condition of the abductees is also evidence of something else. They have amnesia, which would appear to have been induced. But the bits and pieces of what we are able to obtain from abductee memories revolve around sampling procedures and directed movements by the AE. By that I mean that they are controlled by outside forces and are forced to perform tasks outside their control. Clearly there is some sort of mental manipulation going on. Our own use of implanted habits is based on technology gleaned from the AE crash site. It is easy to assume the AE expertise in this field must be light-years ahead of our own and therefore it is reasonable to conclude they are using humans for some sort of physical task while on Mars."

"I understand it makes no sense. But the evidence, taken as a whole, leads me to these conclusions. Given what we have just discovered with RAD, I propose that the evidence I've just outlined, plus the methane plumes and the large complex on Tyrrhena Mons, all point to the existence of a large industrial processing facility. Clearly, human and other mammalian DNA is necessary for this process. In addition humans are used for physical labor of some sort and I would suggest the existence of this complex indicates a human presence is needed there. Primarily though, I propose, gentlemen, that we are being harvested for our DNA."

"Ahhmmm," the Chairman cleared his throat and moved towards the podium. "Yes. Well. Thank you very much, Ms. Petrov," he said hurriedly, ushering her aside. "I am sure the committee will consider your remarks with all due deference. Your work at NASA has been instrumental in guiding the rover program and has been duly noted. Thank you for your presentation."

"Now, gentlemen," the Chairman said, dismissing Petrov, "let us get to the issue at hand."

HESPERIA PLANUM: MARS

Steele slowly followed Reznik, crouching, down a long narrow tube; infused with blue-white light, the tunnel's length was hard to gauge, narrowing, as it did, in the far distance to a pinprick. Reznik from time to time would hold his hand up to stop-- before moving on.

After they had awakened from their exhausted sleep, Steele had insisted they begin the plan outlined by Reznik after the dinner of jerky and water the night beforehand. Reznik had grudgingly complied when Steele insisted he would go alone that day if necessary. Both were well armed, Steele with the Mossberg SP590 as well as a package of C-4 and detonators, while Reznik had opted for the M-4 Special Op Carbine with a M203 grenade launcher. The two carried plenty of ammo in satchels Reznik had cobbled together from his collection of trash.

"This could get hairy," Reznik had warned. "We go slow and hope to get them out without fuss. But if we kill one of the alien buggers, we've got to be ready for a fight."

"No problems here, "Steele assured him.

"No. I mean it, Steele," Reznik had said, "there is a reason I've not tried this before. They are everywhere in that room. I've watched, hoping to catch someone not sedated-- like you. But those things are in that room 24/7. And-- don't trust any humans you see. Just ignore them. They could be forced to do anything, given the condition they're in. I've never had to confront them, but it could be the controlled humans might be more dangerous than the aliens themselves."

"I thought you'd brought people here without a problem."

"I culled them from the huddle," Reznik explained. "Never from direct alien control. I don't know what they might do," Reznik added ominously.

The two continued to inch down the five-foot high tube until Reznik stopped and pointed at a grate. "Through here," he said in a normal voice. The sound jarred Steele until he remembered that the aliens were deaf. Reznik manipulated the lattice-like circular cover. It popped off with a jerk and Reznik set it aside. Then they ducked into a large vaulted cavern-like room filled with sealed boxes the size of cars connected by tubes and bundles of coated wire-like material.

"The unopened pods will be this way," Reznik said as they ducked through the maze of mysterious equipment, their footsteps echoing against the plastic-like material of machinery and tanks. At one point, as they passed the old weapon cache, Steele realized the vaulted room with its long table and lab-like equipment next to a raised couch was the same he had first seen when he exited the pod. Finally, Steele and Reznik rounded a corner in the maze -- and there were the pods, although, to Steele's dismay, only six hovered in the air, which was ripe with the odor of flyblown meat.

"Keep an eye out." Reznik said.

In response, Steele slipped the safety off the shotgun. As they inched to the first hovering pod both looked apprehensively about the room.

"Ok, here goes," Steele said, circling around the floating encasement until he found the end with a small flexible protrusion. When he pressed it, the sound of air seals breaking filled the room, as the lid slid under the pod exposing an Asian man apparently unconscious, covered with the now-retreating nanosealant.

It was not until they opened the fifth pod that Steele, to his considerable relief, saw Stu Stover and in the next, and last, his friend Howington. It was at that exact moment that they heard the pincer click, click, click, on the hard floor as an alien pranced over to the pods.

"They must have detected the pods opening. I was afraid of this," Reznik said.

"Well, I'll blow them to kingdom come if they start to mess with anyone," Steele replied.

"Hold on, cowboy." Reznik's eyes held the same crazed gleam that had startled Steele before. "We'll shoot if we have to. But not until I say so."

The two watched the alien halt and absorb the sight of six open pods. Then it moved towards the nearest pod.

"We're gonna have to do something," Steele said.

"I know. Wait. Maybe it won't do anything. Like I said, these things are dumb as a box of rocks."

They watched the alien scuttle about the room. It did not directly manipulate any pod so Reznik and Steele waited. The alien then stood stock still: every appendage, everything thing about it, screamed rock solid statue-like stillness.

"Oh, crap," Reznik said with foreboding. "I've seen this before. When they don't know what to do, they do this. It's some sort of signaling. There's going to be a boatload of the bastards shortly. We gotta move. You ready?"

Steele flashed a grin, "Born ready. You mean we get to start shooting?"

"Oh, hell yeah," Reznik responded, racking a grenade on the grenade launcher, taking aim and firing the weapon. The missile slammed into the center of the creature, buried itself deep inside, then exploded spraying the area with organic waste, shell and bundles of fibrous wire and machinery.

"Let's roll," Steele shouted.

The two ran back to the pods slipping and sliding through the alien's slimy remains. It still stood, but the frontal region had exploded outward. Green and yellow matter slithered out of the shell in ropy coils slopping onto the floor in wet slaps. Electronic arcs shot throughout the interior, lighting up a horror show of multi-colored gore left by the grenade's explosion.

When the two got to the pods and checked on the occupants, they found, as they had hoped, that the confining nanosealant had retreated from the majority of the transportees-- leaving them free to move. Steele looked at the Asian in the pod they had first opened. His eyes were twitching and he was mumbling. "This one's waking up!" Steele yelled.

"So is this one!" Reznik responded looking at Stover. "We've got to hurry and get them out of here." Reznik slapped Stover. "Do what you've got to do to get them up and out. Once we start running, we can't have stragglers."

Steele shrugged, then jumped up into the pod with the Asian. Mars' reduced gravity made the maneuver easy. He leveraged the Asian over the edge of the pod and dumped him out, letting the man fall five feet. He landed like a bag of potatoes---hard and soft at the same time. The man groaned and began moving.

"Right," Steele said to himself. He went to the next pod and dumped the young woman. Soon they had all six awakening bodies on the ground. Reznik continued to shake and slap the abductees. Steele went to Howington and checked him for injuries.

"Come on Howie, bloody well time to get up." Steele shouted in Howington's face.

Both Reznik and Steele stopped and stood when they smelled the odor of approaching aliens. The clicking on the floor grew closer.

"We've got to get them out of here fast," Reznik said.

"We can hold 'em off for a while," Steele replied. "You stay here and keep working on these poor sods. I'll set up a flanking position and lay some C4. That ought to occupy those bastards for a bit."

"We can't fight them all, Steele. We may have to leave some of these people here if things get too hot."

Two nightmarish creatures moved around a corner.

Steele locked eyes with Reznik. "I'm not bloody leaving one person here. You got that. Not one." Then he sprinted across an open space to a two-story box-like protrusion from the floor and darted around the corner. Reznik looked at the creatures with mounting terror. Behind them he saw something else : a hoard of humans in pressure suits. They moved in lockstep. And Reznik's worst fear in hatching the escape plan unfolded before him.

BINFORD RESIDENCE--CULPEPER

"Prosecutorial Misconduct Claimed," the headline screamed in the silence of the early predawn darkness. The reporter byline was predictable to Binford. Dorcas Snider. Outside his house, the little town of Culpeper looked idyllic in its early morning slumber, but inside, in the circle of light around his chair, the local newspaper seethed evil.

He had known, of course, known that the story would be in the paper, having had a brief and hostile discussion with the reporter for the *Culpeper Dispatch* the day before. He knew she had to have been tipped off by someone. The fact that a motion was filed in the complex legal world of a Virginia Circuit Court could not have made it to the desk of a reporter barely able to spell names correctly, much less understand the true meaning of any legal filing-- unless that legal document was directed to her desk.

It had been planted. He knew that. But why?

He suspected that Conyer Somerfield had faxed the motion to the *Culpeper Dispatch* just days after he had faxed a copy of the motion to Circuit Court Judge Stringfellow. And it was clear to him that he had spun the story to suit the federal narrative. The questions posed by Dorcas for the *Dispatch* were too slanted and sophisticated not to have been formulated and planted by someone with a lot more knowledge of the legal system than Snider possessed, and that someone had to be the attorney from Maryland, Conyer Somerfield.

The questions from the local reporter were only the beginning of the onslaught he'd experienced; besides Dorcas Snider's phone call he'd received a threatening voicemail from the editorial board of the *Washington Post* and then another call from CNN within minutes of each other. Somehow, this story was beginning to go viral, but why or how was still the mystery. Yes, he had subpoenaed a federal employee, in fact two of them, but that was not something to file the sort of scorched-earth motion Somerfield had filed. Nor was it the basis for prosecutorial misconduct. Not in the world Binford knew and understood.

Binford slipped on a sweater to guard against the brisk autumn air. The annual preparation for winter was well on its way in Culpeper with leaves turning a brilliant red and yellow throughout the county, including the dogwood in front of Binford's house, which sported red berries and the dull red leaves of the season. As he stepped outside, little puffs of white exploded in front of him as he exhaled into the crisp darkness. Pausing for a moment on the front porch of his Victorian home, he then bounded down the wooden steps and across the sidewalk, hoping a short walk would help him clear his mind. Turing down S. East Street, he strode towards the center of town.

As he walked, Binford began to understand why he was so devastated by the headlines. Not only was he being accused of doing something underhanded, but he was being unjustly accused. He also knew that the mere fact of the allegations being printed would give the hyenas always in the shadows a reason to dart out into the light to nip at him. Culpeper was a small, southern town, but its politics were personal and sometimes vicious. You weren't the prosecutor for very long before you created enemies

And then there were the jackals, the malcontents who seemed to infest the online blogs and letters-to-the-editor section of the paper. The worst den of malfeasance was the *Culpeper Dispatch's* website where its policy of allowing unsigned blogs underneath online stories allowed character assassination full reign. And shockingly, the reporter, Snider, quoted from these blogs in her stories, as if they were legitimate sources.

Well, two people were dead, Binford focused on that fact. And the sheriff was convinced that something was not right about the federal report. Not only that, but Binford was convinced that something was not right about it either. The haunted look in Mrs. Wood's eyes still burned in his memory. She and her husband were looking for something, they had said. He'd helped them as much he could. And then, they were dead. A murder-suicide, so the feds said. So the report signed by Weir said. But Binford knew that report was false. The photos which the feds had included in the report were fake. And so duty required he look into it.

The frustrating thing was he could not talk publically about his and the sheriff's motivations in issuing the subpoenas. He could only take the public abuse and hope to survive both politically and personally. Because he understood, more than the sheriff, that the allegations were toxic for the two of them. The allegations could cost them their careers. Even worse, their reputations, their friends, even, God forbid, their families. He'd seen it happen in other counties.

After returning from his walk and while driving to the courthouse, he thought he would talk with the sheriff. Get his take on how things stood in the county regarding Snider's story. But, as soon as he walked through the door, his secretary told him the Attorney General's office had called twice already.

Minutes later he had the AG's office on the line.

"This is Susie Dade," a woman replied when they were connected. "I'm an assistant attorney general handling the habeas proceeding now in federal court. The Ellis case?"

Binford recalled the case immediately. He had tried it ten years earlier during his first year as prosecutor. A nasty holdup at a convenience store. The clerk, a young mother and new bride, had been shot needlessly when Roland Ellis decided he didn't want any witnesses to his grabbing $27.53 from the cash register. She was pregnant when he shot her. Ellis got life without parole in a jury trial.

Now on appeal, the Attorney General's Office was handling the case. As is normal procedure in Virginia, after the trial phase, the Attorney General's Office handled all appeals. Binford knew little of that process.

"Yes," he said, "I recall the case."

"Ellis's attorney has made some additional filings in the habeas action."

"Ok. And that means?" Binford asked.

"It means Mr. Binford, they have requested an emergency hearing in front of Judge Tulkinghorn on Friday."

"And?" Binford asked with foreboding.

"They have subpoenaed you for depositions to take place in two weeks."

"For what?" Binford asked incredulously. Given the almost glacial nature of habeas actions, a hearing scheduled so quickly augured something seriously wrong was afoot.

"I have to inform you that they claim you committed several Brady violations during the trial," the expressionless voice continued. "They want to question you about that."

"Brady violation," as Binford knew, was legal shorthand for conduct prohibited by the Supreme Court case, <u>Brady versus Maryland</u>. In <u>Brady</u> the Supreme Court ruled that prosecutors had the duty to give defendants any evidence that would help the defense, which, in effect, forced prosecutors to second-guess defense counsel as to what would be helpful in the defendant's case. Binford, unlike many prosecutors, had decided to give defense counsel every shred of evidence he had rather than try to guess what might be helpful to a defense attorney, a process called an open file policy because, in effect, he opened his files to the defense to inspect.

"And the Judge is going to allow that?" Binford asked. "You've got to be kidding."

"The motion they filed for the emergency hearing is very detailed," she concluded. "I'll fax it to you. Read it, and then get back to me."

Less than five minutes after he had received this arbitrary directive, Binford's secretary announced that Dorcas Snider from the *Dispatch* was on the line.

"Mr. Binford, I'm working on a story for tomorrow's paper," Snider declared after he picked up the phone. "It is about the Ellis Case, which you prosecuted ten years ago."

"Yes?"

"The motion filed by Ellis's attorney alleges that you hid evidence of innocence during the trial. What do you have to say about that? Do you think you should apologize to Mr. Ellis for acting unlawfully by hiding that evidence?" she asked.

"What?" he replied shocked at the naked bias inherent in the question. "Are you kidding me?"

"Is that your answer?"

"Do you have a copy of the motion?" he asked on a hunch that they had tipped her off before even sending him a copy. It was a breach of legal ethics, but organizations like the Defense Council and their minions got a pass on such violations, a double standard prosecutors had learned to deal with.

"Yes, a copy was faxed to my office yesterday. What about my questions?" she asked, this time with a hint of self-righteousness.

Binford knew that he could not trust her to speak off the record. He would love to tell her that he knew nothing about the motion, that he had not even seen it and besides any of that, he was sure he had done nothing inappropriate during the trial. But he could not be sure that whatever he said would not end up in print or if it did would be twisted by the reporter's malevolence. And, at this point he was not even sure that, under the ethical rules governing attorney actions, he could even discuss the case, something Dorcas Snider would refuse to understand.

"I really have no comment at this time."

"That's it?" she asked sarcasm dripping from her voice. "Don't you want to tell your side of the story?"

"Goodbye, Dorcas," Binford hung up the phone.

He sat stunned. Two bad stories in two days--and Dorcas Snider would not let the opportunity go to waste. He knew that. Her style of journalism was to unquestioningly repeat every allegation of wrongdoing over days-- even weeks. It made for headlines and allowed her to cut and paste old stories to make new ones--adding one new piece of information as the hook to hang the paragraphs of old stories upon.

Binford leaned back in his chair and looked out the office window to the courtyard, sprinkled with the first red and yellow leaves of fall.

Binford wanted justice. Not this. The cut and thrust of legal argument in court was to be expected.   This, on the other hand, reeked of politics, politics of the worst kind, the kind that destroyed and left survivors wandering lost on a darkling plain.

And so now he found himself in a fight he never asked for, against two opponents unknown, but who seemed bent to destroy his reputation, not to mention a reporter who would sell her soul to take him down. It was almost as if orchestrated. He put that thought aside. It sounded too conspiratorial, too paranoid.

The autumn sunlight fell bleakly across Binford's face.

NSA HEADQUATERS--FORT MEADE, MD

Conyer Somerfield tucked his blue pin-stripe shirt in tight and adjusted the bright yellow bowtie before leaving the restroom. His wingtips clicked on the marble floor of the office building. He smiled at one particularly pretty secretary. He'd had his eye on her for some time now and thought perhaps it would be a good opportunity to lay the groundwork for a romantic fling. He stopped.

"Ah Miss…" he paused to show he did not know her name, although he did very well know it: Anna Krider.

The pert, 27-year-old blonde looked up at him with surprise.

"Yes. Sir. Krider. Anna Krider." The words tumbled out.

Somerfield, the conqueror of many young women, sensed this would be an easy hunt, an easy capture. Washington, DC, and its environs were full of eager women looking for advancement. The smart ones learned early that the older men in power could give them the career boost they needed--if they played along. Of course, such exchanges of help in return for companionship were never openly spoken and, in fact, on occasion, the younger women actually believed a relationship had developed. He sometimes thought they were intentionally blind to what was really going on. Inwardly he shrugged. He could not care less.

"Would you do me a favor and bring these files to my office," Somerfield asked. "Also, before you do that, would you print off any news stories in the *Culpeper Dispatch* relating to the same named individual on this note?" He walked on before she could answer.

Later, Somerfield leaned forward to open up the folders Ms. Krider had breathlessly brought to him. The news stories were just as he had thought they would be, all assailing Binford's integrity. That was how to hit a Boy Scout. Some men would laugh at the allegations and reply, *"Hell, yeah, I fought hard in court. I'm keeping my county safe. You got a problem-- bring it on!"* Those were the type of men you could get to with promises of power, or money, or perhaps with some sort of blackmail. But Binford's type usually collapsed when you went for the heart of who they thought they were. He was a Boy Scout. He thought he was a good person. And he thought everyone else should think so too. Laughable, really.

Somerfield loved it when a plan came together so well. Not one point of attack but two; his little motion to quash the subpoenas, which he was bound to lose, being one; and then the habeas motion, being the second. Surprisingly, the reporter he talked to at the newspaper had needed little prodding to cast the motions as negatively as possible. Better still, she had asked no probing questions, accepting whatever he told her. *Off the record, of course.* He'd suggested the same tactic with Buck Mullen, the senior partner at the firm in Richmond handling the Ellis habeas motion. Obviously the reporter was as inquisitive with them as she had been with Somerfield, given the superficial and biased story she wrote. Most reporters were lazy. This one was not only lazy, but she had a bit of an axe to grind. That was obvious. Good.

The stories were helpful. They would put a lot of pressure on a man like Binford. Now he needed to take the next step and offer him a way out. An honorable escape, of course; a Boy Scout would have it no other way.

But first, he thought, he needed to confide something to Miss Krider. He'd thank her for her help, tell her that he had noticed her exemplary work, and then he'd go on about how important this particular project was and how he was grateful to her for her help--that it was so hard to find discrete help in this business. Oh, yes, that would be the first of many such confidences that should eventually lead her to the bedroom. He dialed her extension.

"Miss Krider? Could you come to my office please?" Somerfield asked, straightening his bowtie for the second time that day.

CHAPTER 15

THE AE BASE IS LOCATED ON MARS. CENTERED IN AN AREA CALLED HESPERIA PLANUM, IT APPEARS TO BE PRIMARILY UNDERGROUND. THE MARS ORBITAL OBSERVER HAS USED PASSIVE SURVEILLANCE METHODS TO MONITOR THE AE FACILITY, BUT THE ORBITAL PLATFORM, WHEN DESIGNED AND LAUNCHED, LACKED THE STEALTH-PENETRATING TECHNOLOGY RECENTLY DEVELOPED TO UNMASK AE CLOAKING DEVICES USED ON THEIR SPACECRAFT. NONE-THE-LESS, THE ORBITER HAS TRANSMITTED IMAGES FROM THE SURFACE WHICH APPEAR TO SHOW VEHICLES AND OTHER OBJECTS. ORBITAL IMAGING OF THE AREA HAS BEEN KEPT TO A MINIMUM TO MAINTAIN SECRECY, NOT ONLY FROM EARTH OBSERVATION BUT FROM THE AE INSTALLATION ITSELF. GROUP 929 DETERMINED STREAMING DATA FROM THE ORBITAL VEHICLE WAS MONITORED CLOSELY BY OTHER COUNTRIES AND THEREFORE ENCRYPTION WOULD ONLY RAISE QUESTIONS NOT EASILY ANSWERED.

THERE IS CONTROVERSY WITHIN THE NSA REGARDING THE "OTHER OBJECTS" SEEN ON THE SURFACE. RESOLUTION ON THE MARS ORBITER HIRISE CAMERA IS RELIABLE AT ONE METER. ALTHOUGH IMAGES ARE CAPTURED AT LESS THAN THAT, THE QUALITY DEGRADES QUICKLY, AND THUS THE IMAGES OBTAINED BELOW THE ONE METER THRESHOLD ARE QUESTIONABLE. (SEE FOLDER 15 FOR A SAMPLE OF IMAGES TAKEN BY THE MARS ORBITAL OBSERVER). ANALYSTS ARE DIVIDED OVER WHETHER SOME OF THE OBJECTS DEPICTED ARE LIVING OR ROBOTIC. THE IMAGES ARE DIVIDED INTO TWO CLASSES. A CLASSIC CIGAR-SHAPED, SURFACE-SKIMMING CRAFT, AND SMALLER, BUT INDISTINCT IMAGES OF OTHER MOVING OBJECTS, LESS THAN ONE METER IN WIDTH. INDEED SOME PHOTO ANALYSTS QUESTION WHETHER THIS CATEGORY EXISTS AS ANYTHING OTHER THAN A GEOGRAPHIC ANOMALY UNIQUE TO THE MARTIAN SURFACE BUT AS YET NOT UNDERSTOOD. THIS ARGUMENT IS BASED ON THE FACT THAT THE SECOND CLASS OF OBJECT, IF IN FACT AN OBJECT, IS TRANSIENT IN NATURE AND NEVER IN THE SAME PLACE DURING DIFFERENT ORBITAL PASSES. OFTEN, THE PHENOMENON IS NOT RECOVERED IN ANY IMAGES TAKEN AT ALL. IT IS HOPED THAT THE GROUP 929 PACKAGE ON THE ROVER CURIOSITY WILL HELP RESOLVE THIS ISSUE.

--EXCERPTS FROM THE PRESIDENTIAL BRIEFING PAPERS ON THE ROSWELL INCIDENT

MARS--HESPERIA PLANUM

Cho felt cold. And he hurt. Someone was shouting at him. Then he felt his body falling but he could do nothing but wait for the final impact. Was this a dream? Would he wake? He fell and fell and fell. And then nothing.

Someone shouted at him again. His head jerked sideways and the slap of hand on skin reverberated. He felt someone straddle him and shake his shoulders. Another slap.

English. The shouting was in English.

Then with a snap, like a rubber band, Cho woke, blinking his eyes in the harsh light. Above him a man with a thick dirty beard bent down close.

"Get up if you want to live," the wild-eyed man shouted inches from his face. "Hurry up!" Cho turned his head and watched the man straddle another prostrate body slapping and shaking it as he did Cho.

The man turned and yelled at him again, "Get up!"

I must be in a dream, he thought, but oddly, if it was a dream it was a dream he'd had before, but only now remembered. He turned his head again towards what made no sense. And upon seeing the unspeakable, foul darkness embodied before him, searing terror blossomed in his heart and when it did, the things from his nightmares seemed to sense his presence and began to tick, tick, tick toward him. Oh yes, he knew this place, he knew this terror. Intimately. He had been here before.

Cho crabbed backward and then, standing, staggered toward the man who was now dragging a body across the floor to disappear behind a box mounted to the floor. Following him, Cho saw others in various states of consciousness. All were prostrate but one woman, who was struggling to sit up.

The man grabbed a hand gun and slapped it into Cho's hand. "Use it if they get here," he said wildly. Then he yelled out, "Hurry up, Steele!" With that the man darted out into the room towards the walking nightmares and behind them, a horde of silvery suits mounted with visored helmets.

Then the world exploded and Cho fell hard against the floor from the concussion. Crawling to the corner of the reddish box they sheltered behind, he looked back at where the blast had thrown him to the floor. One monster lay on its side, legs twitching, orifice gasping. From the broken exoskeleton green and yellow fluid oozed. Behind the shattered horror, another stood and, behind it, he saw the suited humans stand up. He knew they were human because he himself had worn such suits.

More terrifying to Cho was the alien that scurried at astonishing speed over the damaged shell and arrowed towards him.

"Steele! No more C-4!" Cho heard the bearded man yell, at which the creature stopped its charge at Cho and turned towards the bearded crazy man who laughing manically began spraying it with the M-4 Carbine. Most rounds missed, but as the creature got closer more hit, making it jerk as chips of the outer shell peeled off and flew into the air, cartwheeling off into the distance. Then, perhaps realizing the fusillade of bullets grew worse the closer it got to the bearded berserker, the creature turned and took cover behind a piece of machinery. A second monster on four pointed insect like legs, as if on cue, moved towards the bearded man.

Cho fumbled with the gun and switched off the safety. At the same time, a man on his hands and knees beside him was shouting, "Stover! Stover!"

Having unlatched the safety and pulled the slide back to chamber a round, Cho steadied himself and squeezed off a shot at the now lumbering creature. He fired another. And another, aiming at the frontal region where optic eye stalks and other appendages seemed to erupt from the hard carapace. And, in the confusion, he became aware of one thing, one overriding thing; it felt damn good to shoot at the nightmare that visited him every night. Oh, hell yeah, damn good. He squeezed the trigger over and over and over again, screaming in rage, a rage pent up over the years and now being released in explosions of pure hatred and revenge. He kept pulling the trigger though the magazine was empty.

Someone darted out from his left but in front of the advancing creature. As he ran, the figure turned and fired, spewing a clip of ammo in murderous fusillade.

Cho's world exploded again, and he found himself again face down on the floor, deafened by the second concussion, bleeding from his nose. He rolled over and looked at the remains of the second destroyed hulk. The creature was blown into two parts with organs and material sliding out from the shattered remains of its shell, with what looked like electric arcs and bits of electronics sliding out with the organs and fluid.

The whole place stank of road kill. Cho turned back to see what was happening behind him just as the man who had shot the monster shouted, "Howington! Stu! Damn glad to see you! Take these carbines. The ammo's in these bags. We gotta get out of here. Shoot anything that doesn't look human. Follow me --or Reznik here," he added, indicating the bearded man. "And you," he said pointing at Cho, "follow us. They're coming. Once you hear that tapping, you know they're close. Let's roll!"

Cho heard the sound which recalled to him cold, lonely hours huddled in the dark, lost without hope. Tick. Tick. Tick. Tickticktickticktick.....like rain pouring down on a tin roof.

The group of eight stood and shuffled off with the Reznik in front. Cho behind him. The two young women said little, their eyes shined with fear and shock, although they seemed to understand the men were less of a threat than the dead creatures on the floor. The rear guard was made up of the other man and his two friends. Directly behind Cho was the Dragon Team leader who, upon waking, merely nodded and followed Cho's direction.

The sound of a gathering storm grew louder behind them, and at Reznik's urging, they moved through the maze of mysterious objects of all shapes and sizes in the room and crossed a larger open space. At that point a group of suited humans angled from the side at a trot, oddly enough in unison.

"I was afraid of this," the man identified as Reznik said. "They don't have weapons but they'll grab us just the same to slow us down."

"What do we do now?" Steele asked. "They're blocking our way."

"Shoot 'em!" was the response.

"Hell no, I'm not shooting them! They're just people in space suits!"

"No, they're not! They're under control. They'll slow us down if we try to skirt 'em."

"I'm not shooting!"

"Fine by me," Reznik shouted as he stopped, dropped to one knee and started firing at the line of figures. "Keep running!" But, without a unified leadership, the group of recovering transportees milled about directionless. The suited figures dropped as they were shot, but the remaining kept coming in lockstep.

Then from another angle, Cho saw another carapace armored monstrosity scurry quickly towards them and, before they could stop it, with two pincers it grabbed the Dragon Team leader by the torso and dragged him away in fusillade of falsetto screams.

Cho, reacting late, aimed his reloaded revolver and let off a few rounds at the car -sized creature but without effect, only to see his fellow countryman become engulfed by the advancing suited humans.

"There's no time!" Reznik shouted, and ran in a new direction. "We've got to run. We can't kill them all!" Cho followed. He could tell the others were behind.

"What the hell is this place?" Cho heard one of the men ask.

"You wouldn't believe me if I told you," Steele replied before shouting to the rest, "Let's go! Howington! Stu! You take rear guard. Ladies! Let's roll!"

They stumbled into a narrow opening between what seemed to be machinery or electrical appliances of some kind, turning and twisting, the smell of dead meat so strong Cho felt he would gag. But again, in an odd way, he knew he'd seen this before. In another life.

The man named Reznik stopped, bent down and pulled up a grate. "In here! Now!" he ordered. Cho jumped and rolled to one side after hitting the floor. The others followed.

Then it was a long hot slog, bent over, in a tube. Half crouched, half running, Cho felt exhausted. Just as he thought he could go no further, they stopped again.

When Reznik pushed a green button on the side of the tube, a curved door slid upwards, and Cho along with the others tumbled into a hexagon-shaped room stretching upward at least one hundred feet, the walls of which were covered with metal grates. Cho noticed a small metal ladder climbing to the far away ceiling.

"We can hole up here for a while." Reznik said. "Steele, you shoot when I tell you. You got that? We lost one because you didn't listen to me.

"Now, listen up the rest of you. We've got some time to talk. I know you've got questions. But don't make the one mistake that will kill you. You do exactly what I tell you when I tell you. You do that and maybe we'll make it out. You don't and you'll die and probably take the rest of us with you." He turned and glared at Steele. "Stay here, I've got some scouting to do. Don't move and sure as hell don't open that door." Then without another word the man turned in what Cho interpreted as disgust and scampered up the ladder --disappearing into the vastness of the ceiling.

WARRENTON TRAINING CENTER--CULPEPER

In the end, Rebecca Weir had fought. Sims watched it on the video his operative had dropped off at the office. Apparently, she'd ridden in the car docilely until she saw the hypodermic come out; then she fought. Smith had turned on the camera by then, so Sims saw her kick and scream in the van before being tazed into submission. Sims was glad. Usually the fighters adjusted poorly upon return. He wanted Weir to have a handful when she came back. He relished the thought of what sorts of bizarre behavior she might exhibit after they give her a ride on the couch. After they injected her pretty little neck with the Nano electrodes, she would learn to do God knows what. The prospect of what sorts of habits they had injected into transportees amused him. He hoped she'd return wanting to eat crickets. That was the most repulsive response to the nano-stimulation treatment in Sims' estimation. He'd seen transportees gorge themselves on the insects. Yes, crickets, they were the worst. That ought to put some spice in their sex life, he thought to himself. He wondered how Weir would react to kissing his wife after she had had one of those dark, squirming little snacks.

He fast-forwarded the video to see her pushed into the pod. He had toyed with leaving her conscious during transit but decided that would be too much. He did not want Weir so distracted by a crazed wife that he could not work. She might not recover from an untreated transit. That had happened in the past. Some came back alive but mentally damaged. He needed Weir broken but serviceable. So he authorized that she be sedated. He watched the lid being closed. Then he fast-forwarded to the next section on the video in which her pod and that of her children were placed with the other pods.

Fast-forward again. He stopped to see the pods move up and out of the transport room at the Federal Reserve on Mt. Pony.

Right now they were in transit. She was on a little trip. And Weir would learn who was in charge around here.

Too bad about the children, he thought randomly. But the lesson had to be taught. And children usually came back in one piece. Being younger, they seemed to adjust better. Usually.

His secretary interrupted to announce that Weir waited in the outer office.

"Ok. Tell him to wait. I'll be ready in a bit." Let the little piss ant wait for a while. It would do him good.

CULPEPER COUNTY COURTHOUSE--CIRCUIT COURT ROOM

"All Rise!" The bailiff said loudly. The courtroom floor creaked as men and women stood for the entrance of Circuit Court Judge Franklin Stringfellow. His tall lanky form draped in a long flowing black robe entered from a side door and he bounded up the stairs to the judge's bench.

"Be seated," the bailiff ordered loudly. Chairs protested as bottoms settled in for a long morning session.

Binford sat at the prosecutor's table, across from him sat Conyer Somerfield and his assistant. Two more young women in sober black dress suits sat directly behind Somerfield in the side gallery. Binford knew the look--young, eager, bloodthirsty. They would be Somerfield's paralegals or interns. Four against one, he thought to himself wryly, fair odds for a prosecutor.

Binford studied his opponent, medium height and thin, dressed in a conservative pin-stripe suit with brown wingtips and wearing a red tie with his button down, white oxford shirt, Somerfield looked every bit the lawyer in the still traditional Virginia legal culture. Binford was surprised that his first meeting with Somerfield was in the courtroom. Usually out -of- town attorneys would meet with the prosecutor beforehand. Not this time. And that usually meant the relationship would be anything but cordial during the proceeding in question. Of course, given what had occurred so far between the suspicious filing and language of the motion itself, Binford had to admit he expected a contentious hearing. And he looked forward to wiping the floor with Somerfield's motion. Prosecutorial misconduct, indeed. He was beyond feeling shocked, now he just wanted to win the argument and grind Somerfield into the dirt.

Binford heard the door to the courtroom open, and he looked to his side. Of course, he thought, Dorcas Snider, the reporter from the *Culpeper Dispatch*, would be here. She looked about the room, and locked eyes with Binford before moving to the gallery. He knew that, whatever happened today, her story would paint it in the worst light possible from his standpoint.

"Gentlemen. I've read your briefs. Mr. Binford is the Commonwealth ready to proceed?"

"Yes, your Honor."

"Is counsel for Mr. Weir and Mr. Sims ready?"

"Yes, your honor," Somerfield's rich southern accent filled the large two-story plastered room.

"Very well. Opening statements?" the judge inquired.

"Yes, your honor," Somerfield said rising from his seat and facing the judge. Inwardly, Binford groaned. Opening statements were usually a waste of time, dealing as they did with motions that had been briefed beforehand, as these had been, so the statements were usually more for the benefit of the client than anything else. In a flash of insight, Binford understood that Somerfield's opening was not for his clients since neither Weir nor Sims was present in the courtroom, but rather for the benefit of the newspaper reporter.

"Very well. Proceed, Mr. Somerfield. It is your motion."

"Thank you, your honor." Somerfield remained standing, clearly at ease in a courtroom. "With all due respect, your honor, my clients, Mr. Weir and Mr. Sims object to the Commonwealth's subpoena of the two for whatever sort of special grand jury proceeding he has planned next month. My clients do not dispute that they were handed a subpoena by a deputy of the Culpeper County Sheriff's Department, which the court will learn more about through the evidence we plan to present in support of the motion. But they object to the manner in which they were served. It was your honor," and here Somerfield turned to look directly at Dorcas Snider, "*an abuse of power* both by the Sheriff's Department and by the Commonwealth Attorney to even attempt such service of process."

Advancing, Somerfield placed his hand on the wooden white rail that separated the judges' bench from the courtroom floor where attorneys stood. "It was an abuse of power so outrageous, your honor, that I personally decided to argue this case. We will show, first, that the stop of Mr. Sims was illegal and unwarranted. Therefore, the service of the subpoena itself is flawed. Secondly, Mr. Sims is a federal employee, in fact your honor, he is an active member of the Armed Forces, as is Mr. Weir, and as such is immune from state service of process while on assignment under the Armed Services Act, which I have already cited in the brief to the motion. In addition, I must tell the court that this outrageous conduct is so disgraceful that I have felt it my duty as a member of the bar and an officer of the court to file a complaint with the Commonwealth State Bar regarding the actions of Mr. Binford."

"That, sir, is not a matter before the court as counsel well knows," Judge Stringfellow interrupted him. "What the Commonwealth State Bar does is their concern not the concern of this court. You will therefore direct your attention to that which *is* before the court."

Stringfellow stared down at Somerfield clearly irritated. Binford knew Judge Stringfellow did not like grandstanding - especially on things that all involved knew were not in the jurisdiction of the court. The only person probably clueless to that distinction in the courtroom was Snider.

"Proceed," Stringfellow said after clearly making his point with silence.

"Yes, your honor, thank you." Somerfield continued smoothly. He didn't really care about the ruling-- he had made his point, he thought to himself, watching the reporter scribble with abandon as he spoke, the point being to put pressure on the Boy Scout. The point was to stop the blasted grand jury proceeding before it got out of hand. And, as an added benefit, the point was to give him the pleasure of slicing open the innards of another opponent, one in a long line of courtroom adversaries to fall under Somerfield's genteel butchery.

FEDERAL RESERVE--CULPEPER

Weir marched out of Sims office and made his way angrily to his car. The video he had just seen made it very clear that Sims had carried out on his threat to transport the new security chief's family. Weir wanted to leap across the desk and throttle the evil little succubus, but he restrained himself.

"They'll be back, Weir." Sims had said menacingly. "In the meantime, you stay on your job. You stop threatening to go to Group. You take whatever I give you and you say 'Yes, sir, how much, sir!' I warned you about messing with me. Now your nice little family is on a trip. They'll be back. The question is, do you want them back?"

Weir had sat tightly clinched, willing himself not to kill Sims, knowing that given his training, it would have been easy to choke the life out of the pompous bastard.

"I asked you a question," Sims said in a voice drenched with threat. "Do you want them back?"

"Yes, sir."

"Well then, you ought to ask, don't you think?"

"Ask?"

"Yes, you ought to ask to have your family returned."

Understanding that Sims meant to belittle him as much as possible at this moment, Weir said, "Yes, I do want them back."

"Then why don't you ask?" Sims demanded, his face dark with rage.

"Would you send my family back?" Weir asked.

"You need to say please." The room grew quiet as Weir plumbed the depths of his self-control while Sims continued to stare at Weir, his eyes black pools of malevolence. Finally Weir was able to control his anger enough to speak.

"Would you please send my family back," Weir asked, as mentally he envisioned gutting his superior like a fish.

Sims flashed a smile, and then said without emotion, "Why of course, Weir," he said in a pleasant a voice as though they had been discussing a car rental. "Happy to oblige. You understand, of course, that we don't have total control over the situation. But I expect they will be back in two weeks. Maybe a month." Weir had been shocked at the change in Sims. "Just think of it as a bachelor's weekend." Sims added with what seemed to Weir to be a manic enthusiasm. "You can watch football. You can eat pizza every night. And you won't have the kids around fighting. Oh, I grant you, it will seem a bit lonely but not for long, Weir. Not for long. They'll be back good as new. You'll see-- good as new."

When Weir got back to his office he stared blankly at a photograph of Rebecca, Heather and Hunter remembering the hike they had taken on the Hazel River. He heard Hunter again, innocently saying, "*I bet you'd protect us like that deer. Wouldn't you Daddy? I bet you wouldn't let anybody hurt us.*"

So much for that! He had seen what happened to returnees, dumped like so much garbage on the floor when the aliens were done with them. It was clear the abductees had not been treated well while on their "little trip" and he was sure Rebecca and the kids would be no different.

Weir and his family would become part of the little fraternity up on the hill. He suspected more than one technician at the Federal Reserve had a family member who had taken a ride on the couch. Perhaps Sims himself was in that group.

Well, Weir was sure as hell not going to let that happen to his family. He could do something to prevent it. He knew it. He had contemplated drastic action to help his former rescuer, Steele. Now, he was going to do it. He was going to go up there after them. But he would be armed. And he would know what to expect. And when he got back, all hell was going to break loose, because he was going to tell that Grand Jury exactly what was going on around here. He had had enough. And if he couldn't get back, well, at least he would have tried. At least he would be with his family.

At least his little girl would not be deposited on the transport floor like so much waste.

No. He would change it all. Weir would go to Mars.

FORT MEADE MARYLAND--NSA HQ

Conyer Somerfield reviewed the Culpeper judge's order the day after the hearing. The judge had retired to review the case file before rendering a final opinion.

Somerfield had been surprised that the judge actually kept his word and sent out the opinion via fax this early in the day as he had promised. He had come into the office early, before seven am, and the faxed order had just come over the wire as he entered.

Not surprisingly, the judge had denied Somerfield's motion. Sims and Weir would have to appear next month before the grand jury or face contempt charges from the court.

The very idea amused him. A show cause from the Culpeper Circuit Court was like a tick bite on a hound dog, since all it meant was that the recipient had to "Show Cause Why the Defendant should not be held in contempt." Hell, he thought to himself, it would be fun to just let the judge issue the show cause, and then appeal the whole mess to the Virginia Court of Appeals. That would slow things down quite a bit. But Somerfield had another plan in mind, a plan approved by Group 929, a plan less dramatic.

He turned from the computer monitor and picked up the phone. He punched in the number for Sims' direct secure line.

"The court denied our motion," he told Sims when he had him on the line. "He's ordered you and Weir to appear before the Grand Jury next month."

"Well, screw that!" Sims shouted. "I'm not going. You can tell that little piss-ant prosecutor to pound sand!"

"Whoa there, partner!" Somerfield said. "Remember we talked about this. I never expected the motion to be successful. I just wanted to put some public pressure on him. Did you see that article in the paper today?"

"That reporter sure hates Binford," Sims responded.

"That she does," Somerfield chuckled. After reading her file, including a summary of her emails and social media posts gathered by the NSA, he knew exactly which buttons to push when it came to Dorcas Snider. All he had to do was to mention what a conservative religious fanatic the prosecutor was and you could almost hear her salivate like Pavlov's dog. Pathetic, really, when one thought about it.

He could not have written the story better himself. "*Prosecutorial misconduct.*" That was the ticket. And he had ginned up the DC operatives to post online. Surprisingly, the *Culpeper Dispatch* allowed anonymous online posting in reaction to stories, a detail Somerfield had passed on to Buck Mullen in Richmond. He was sure some of the negative posts came from his firm.

"Ok, so you got the idiot reporter to do a hatchet job on Binford. What does that do for me?" Sims asked.

"As I said, this is just the beginning," Somerfield told him. "I'll wait until next week and then file a motion for a rehearing. That should tie us up for another week or so. By then the second prong of our strategy will start to unfold. After Binford goes through the depositions, we'll offer him a way out. So patience, Mr. Sims. Patience."

BINFORD RESIDENCE

Binford turned and looked out onto his backyard as his tea steeped in his mug. The homes on South East Street were built on lots that stretched to the railroad tracks in the rear. He watched the sun flash over a smattering of October clouds above the tree line behind his house. He loved this time of day when the pure morning light streamed through the kitchen window to bath the room with energy and warmth.

Binford cradled the steaming brew in both hands and walked onto the back porch. He thought again about the court appearance yesterday. He knew the judge's order would be waiting for him when he got into the office. Unless the sky was falling, the order should uphold the subpoenas issued for the special grand jury. He could not imagine a no-nonsense judge like Franklin Stringfellow doing anything other than deny the spurious motions to dismiss the subpoenas. He had not looked at the paper yet this morning, but he could predict Dorcas Snider's angle since Somerfield had emphasized his own spin on the subpoenas: that they were illegal and tantamount to prosecutorial misconduct by Binford.

Yes, he thought, Snider will have a field day with that. In a small community like Culpeper, the charges loomed large. Never mind that they were not true nor based on law or fact. Snider had neither the knowledge nor the inclination to question the slurs. And Binford knew that Culpeper citizens liked to think of their county as something akin to Mayberry in the Andy Griffith show. They could put up with a lot from public officials. He had seen that in the apparent forgiveness of a sitting mayor's drunk driving conviction, despite which he had been resoundingly re-elected after serving the mandatory ten-day jail sentence. The electorate looked more sternly upon questions of integrity. And, knowingly or not, Snider was pushing the one destruct button that local politics had in Culpeper. How much he could stand politically Binford did not know. But he was certain he was on a short leash. Already the blogs in the paper online were calling for a recall election. And, in Virginia, it only took one percent of the electorate that had voted in the previous election to petition for a recall, which, in Binford's case, meant 500 signatures on a petition. Binford knew how easy that would be to get. Anyone will sign a petition. It was a very short leash once the political storm hammered long enough. He'd seen it before. He hoped he wouldn't be the next victim of that sort of political witch hunt.

He heard a rustle behind him as Kate prepared a cup of tea for herself. She walked out onto the porch with him. Her cup sent white wispy streamers into the air.

"So explain to me again how they were able to get an emergency hearing so fast?" Kate asked joining him.

"The attorney general's office did not really contest it as best I can tell."

"Well, that just smells." Kate responded. "Aren't they supposed to represent you in this thing?"

"Not really. They represent the state's interest in retaining the conviction. But no Kate, they don't technically represent me."

"So you've got to go to depositions in two weeks?"

"Looks that way."

"What are depositions anyway?"

"A habeas corpus is a case in federal court," Binford explained. "It's not criminal. So I am a witness. The petitioner, in this case the guy I convicted, gets to ask me questions about the case."

"I thought you were immune from all of that."

"Not in a civil case."

A gaggle of geese crossed the orange and blue sky. In the distance, they heard the birds honking-- a sure sign of coming winter storms.

"Is this open to the public?" Kate asked. "Will that Dorcas woman be there?"

"No. This will just be me, along with the assistant attorney general and the Defense Council attorney."

"Are they after you? Is that what this is all about?"

"I don't know, Kate. They're pulling a lot of stunts. I mean, there should be no way that this would make it into the newspaper unless the Defense Council was pushing it. But that's politics."

"What do you mean politics? I thought you were arguing law. Not politics."

"There's politics all over this, Kate. Why does the AG's office just roll over and allow the deposition on such short notice? And the way the newspapers have latched onto this so quickly? There's something driving all of it. Then look at this article." Binford handed a torn-out article from a legal journal to her.

"This says the attorney general is hosting a fund-raiser in Richmond for the Defense Council," Kate said. "What is that all about? I mean I thought they were on opposite sides. Why would he do that?"

"I'm thinking about it, Kate. But I think what is going on is that he's going to run for governor, and he wants to soften his right-wing image."

"By hanging around with sleaze-ball, left-wing organizations like this Defense Council?" she asked incredulously.

"So it would seem."

"I never really trusted him. He says all the right things but there is something about him…"

"Women's intuition?"

"Whatever. I think he stabbed the Lt. Governor in the back just to line up his nomination for governor next year. He's too ambitious by half. Anyone who wants power as much as he seems to can't be trusted."

Just then, Binford thought he saw movement in the trees near the rear of his lot on a path often used by trespassers. He handed the mug of tea to Kate.

"I'll be right back," he said over his shoulder as he bounded down the back stairs.

Binford moved quickly through his backyard, dodging around bushes and a picket fence, catching a flash of movement amongst the white pines that bordered the railroad tracks. As he crossed an open field nearing the trees, he heard the sound of feet crashing across the gravel on the elevated railroad bed.

"Hey!" Binford yelled, running through the branches, the pine needles whipping across his face to emerge just in time to see the back of a man wearing camouflage running up and over the tracks. He heard the slide of gravel on the other side and then the crash of a body moving down through underbrush. Binford followed.

"Hey! You!" he yelled again but to no avail.

He returned to the pine trees and, after carefully examining the brown needle covered ground, Binford saw scuff marks in the soft soil which corresponded with the location where he first saw movement. It was clear the man had been there for some time judging by the grass which still retained an impression in its bent leaves.

"What were you after?" Kate asked when he returned.

Binford took the mug from her hand as stepped back up on the porch.

"I thought I saw a deer," he said.

Later Binford called Sheriff Carter, "Someone was spying on me," he reported.

"Hells, bells," Carter scoffed. "Don't get all spooky on me. No one's spying on you. Just some damn drunk looking for a place to sleep it off."

"He was wearing camouflage. Drunks don't do that."

"Says you," Carter laughed. "Alright, I'll do a little checking." The sheriff paused, then with concern in his voice he asked, "How you doing, Mordecai? You holding up ok?"

"You mean the newspapers?"

"Hell yeah I mean the newspapers. That woman Snider has it in for you, I tell you what. The only good thing is that most people forget this stuff in a couple months."

"You see the blogs?" Binford asked.

"Yeah. You shouldn't read 'em. For the most part, it's nothing but a damn cockroach party. I mean how much weight can a comment have if there ain't a name to it?"

"Easy to say don't read it, but I'll bet you can't stop reading them when it's you they're after."

"You got a point," Carter responded.

"What I can't get over is that this is all hitting at the same time."

"Yeah, well, you just got to keep on trucking. Know what I'm saying?"

"Listen," Binford responded, "You check on who was spying on my house. The feds fake a homicide report and then, when I subpoena the two main culprits, all hell breaks loose. It's starting to look connected to me. I just don't know how, but I don't like it."

"It was just some damn drunk."

"Check anyway."

WASHINGTON DC--K STREET

After reading the Culpeper Circuit Court Judge's order, Somerfield ordered a car and driver to take him to the District. For fun, he used Ms. Krider, his newest project, and bypassed his personal secretary to order the car and make the reservations at McCormick and Schmick's. He enjoyed seeing the young secretary's eyes widen at the opportunity to work directly with him on a project.

McCormick and Schmick's was one of a gaggle of similar eateries that lined K Street just blocks away from the White House, where, in the toxic stew consisting of lobbyists and legislators power players met and trade secrets. The food was good and the service excellent, so it was often the locus of activity when Congress was in session.

When Somerfield's car pulled up to the front of the restaurant, he jumped out and slipped into the dark interior crowded with men and women smartly dressed and for the most part engaged in the loud buzz generated at a bar in Washington at midday.

"Eduardo. How are you my friend," Somerfield asked the maître d' Eduardo Ruiz, a swarthy Ecuadorian who flashed a bright white smile at Somerfield.

"Mr. Somerfield. I've been expecting you. We have your usual booth ready. Please, let me take your jacket." Ruiz leaned forward and held his hand out to coax Somerfield from the garment.

"No. Thank you, Eduardo. I am just a bit chilled."

The two men negotiated through the crowd at the reception area, and walked to a rear booth.

"Here you are. I have a fine white wine just in. Would you like a glass while you wait?"

"Certainly. How are things, Eduardo?"

"It is as it is," Eduardo replied.

"Yes. That is a good way to put it."

Eduardo grabbed a passing a waiter and ordered the wine for Somerfield, then he turned back to the now-seated lawyer, "I will direct your guest to the booth?"

"Yes. Please let me know first before you bring him," here Somerfield handed the maître d' a hundred dollar bill.

"As you wish," Eduardo took the proffered money without re-action, just as he had many times before. Theirs was a relationship built on simple rules. Somerfield paid well, and, in return, Eduardo delivered service with discretion and perfect timing. Both men understood the rules and each tacitly let the other know that they liked the relationship as it was. Simple and built on mutual respect. It was a common enough relationship in Washington.

Somerfield arranged himself at the cloistered table and took the proffered glass of wine when it arrived. Eduardo had excellent taste in wine, and it showed in the selection he sent to Somerfield: a dry Muscadet-Sevre et Maine. Somerfield would never like a cheap jug wine like a California Chablis, but the Muscadet was excellent. Somerfield swirled the clear liquid in the glass and took another sniff of the dry aroma. He absently took a sip and thought again about his discussion with Ford Allen Sims, the head of the Warrenton Training Center.

The man was becoming erratic. That much was clear.

Somerfield had dealt with Sims for several years and had noted his increasing tendency to fly off the handle. Of course, Sims was where the rubber met the road, so to speak. It was all well and good to talk about the Group 929 program in Culpeper in the abstract, but then Sims had to deal with it up close and personal. So, Somerfield was willing to cut the man some slack; however the program could not afford loose cannons. Somerfield was not ready to label Sims a loose cannon, but he was concerned: concerned enough to think about it. And that in and of itself is a little worrying.

We'll see how he reacts to this little crisis, Somerfield decided. Somerfield did not have the power to hire or fire anyone outside of his department, but a word from the agency's top attorney was often enough to end anyone's career. Somerfield knew that, and he used it to his advantage when necessary. He would spread the tidbits and opinions judiciously about the agency and, before one knew it, he or she was toast. There was nothing like a little hatchet job every once in a while to put the fear of God into his department. Yes, he liked being feared. It is better to be feared rather than to be loved. It may be time for another hatchet job down in Culpeper.

Eduardo interrupted Somerfield's musings to announce the arrival of his guest.

Somerfield stood and waited.

"Buck, how good of you to come," he said.

"How can I refuse an invitation from you?" Buck responded.

The two sat down on opposite sides of the white linen draped table.

"Wine?" Somerfield asked. "Eduardo has an excellent Muscadet uncorked."

"That would be fine," Buck responded. "So, Connie, what's this all about?"

"Let's order first."

"As you wish."

"The fish is very good here." Somerfield said.

"You order for the two of us--it will save time."

Eduardo entered, took the order for grilled Chesapeake Rockfish and, after leaving, sent another glass of Muscadet for Buck Mullen.

"How's the practice going?" Somerfield asked.

"Hell, Connie, I hardly even see a courtroom anymore," Mullen confided. "But things are going splendidly. After we merged with Sampson-Brass Associates, things seemed to just pop. We picked up a good nuclear waste poisoning case out of Georgia with that acquisition -- it ought to pay off well. The best part is that one of our plaintiffs was pregnant. She didn't know it at the time. She had a damn flipper baby." Here Buck guffawed before continuing, "You can bet the utility company wanted to pay off big time once she showed up to depositions with the baby. Those flippers were just- a- flapping."

Somerfield slightly smiled. "I'm sure your attorney showed proper sorrow at the tragedy of it all."

"Of course, of course, tragedy it was," Buck deadpanned.

The two looked at each other blankly, then when the silence had stretched long enough, they could no longer contain the mirth and broke into laughter. "Flipper baby," Somerfield gasped out, "who came up with that one?"

"Roland Sprague."

"*The Roland Sprague*?" Somerfield asked meaningfully.

"The one and only. You should have seen the video he had filmed and produced for discovery. He had that little baby just- a-rolling around on the floor."

"Tragic."

"What was tragic was how much the utility paid out. They didn't want that video getting loose, I can tell you. Imagine what would happen if someone leaked it onto the internet."

The Rockfish was served, and the two men tucked into the tender flaky white flesh. Somerfield picked at his, dabbing small morsels into his mouth between bits of salad and wine. Buck tore into the side of fish like a bird of prey, pulling long strips of flesh with his fork.

"I'm ravenous," Buck said between mouthfuls.

"So it would seem," Somerfield responded, the light glinting out from under his darkened eyes.

Finished, the two dabbed the napkins to their mouths almost simultaneously.

"Now, Connie, can you tell me what's up?" Buck asked.

"It's this case in Culpeper."

"The one you called me about? I told you I'd take care of it."

"Well, yes, I know you did. And I have no doubt about it. But there are some things we need to talk about that aren't -- well, suitable for phone conversations or email."

Buck leaned back in the booth and eyed his friend speculatively. "This is spook business, isn't it?"

"Spook business, as you call it, is my business, as you well know."

"Anyone going to die in this? I just need to know so I can figure out how to handle the ethics probe if it gets to that."

"No, Buck, no one is planned to die," Somerfield assured him, "at least that I know of."

"What a business you are in," Buck said. "I love it."

Somerfield swirled the wine in his glass before broaching the reason for the lunch. "I might need you to back off the prosecutor at some point. There are national security issues here. But I won't know until after the depositions."

"Hmm, 'back off.' Now that is an unusual request. First you want me to go after the prosecutor because he's dirty. Now you tell me you may want me to back off. You know, Connie, I don't have complete control. Once we added Binford to the suit it's not as if the client doesn't have a say in how we handle the case-- not to mention the judge," Buck said flatly. Both men knew that a client could refuse to drop a defendant, an allegation about the defendant or to offer the defendant a deal. The judge also had to approve any such move by the plaintiff or the defendant in a criminal or a civil case.

"Judge Tulkinghorn?" Somerfield snorted. "That old fool? Don't you worry about him. And your client? Come on, Buck, you can steer a plaintiff as well as the best of 'em. In the old days I've seen you wheedle more plea agreements in a day than a hound dog has ticks."

"You forget, Connie, I'm not trying this case," Buck reminded him. "Sprague is."

"Well, you need to teach him--you were good at settling a case, Buck--show this Sprague a thing or two. But remember," Somerfield's voice took on an edge, "if we need you to back off, back off."

"It's kinda hard to claim a prosecutor is a lying piece of shit and then to 'back off' as you say," his companion replied. "Let's just forget the client and the judge. We've already ginned up the media on this. You know how they like their prosecutors--roasted extra crispy ---I can't just back off. I do have to think about the reputation of the firm. The reason why you came to me was because we have the connections. But connections have their limits. Journalists think they're morally superior. I can't *make* them face the fact that I manipulated them into putting pressure on this Binford guy, then turn and go switching up the story. Just can't do it, Connie."

"I came to you because you already had this habeas suit going on Binford, that and the fact that we go back a long way," Somerfield replied. "So, yes, the connections are helpful. But they aren't why I came to you. I came to you because you had Binford on the line, and right now I need the little dumbass tied up. Later it may not be necessary."

Somerfield leaned inward to look directly into his compatriot's eyes.

"Buck, this is a case of national security. If I ask you to back off, you need to do it. Do you understand there really isn't a choice here. No choice at all."

The two men stared at each other. Buck picked up his spoon and stirred the cream-tinted coffee, and then said, "Alright, I take your meaning, Connie. No choice means more than you are saying here. I understand that."

"It's a tough old world sometimes."

"Not for us, Connie. Not for us. Maybe for Binford."

"And maybe for Sprague, too?" Somerfield replied, his eyes narrowing.

"Maybe so."

Eduardo appeared at the table interrupting the conversation, "Dessert gentlemen? We have a fresh cheese cake." The two declined.

"If you would please put this on my tab," Somerfield directed. "Add your usual tip."

Perhaps it was the interruption. Perhaps it was the inherent power displayed by Somerfield's obvious mastery over the obsequious Eduardo. Perhaps, it was the acknowledgement of Somerfield's slightly veiled threat. Buck did not allow himself to delve too deeply into his motivations. It never turned out well when he searched the dark corners. More and more of his life had dark corners. Dusty and drab, they lurked behind his every move these days. Best not to probe, he had unconsciously decided a long time ago. For whatever reason, Buck shifted to comfortable territory and asked, "If I back off as you put it, what do I get out of the deal?"

Buck poured himself another cup of coffee from the silver service on the table.

Somerfield saw the opening proffered by his colleague's acceding to his request. He knew to pitch something to Buck that would assuage his ego and allow the partner to go back to the firm with a nice little package. With the aplomb of the best of the diplomatic corps, he turned the situation into a joke between two lawyers, between two friends, between two men of the world.

"Why, Buck, you will get the good will of a grateful nation." Somerfield said, his eye brows twitching in mirth.

"And?"

"Let's just say I can arrange for a very good retainer from a company in Dubai."

"I am, as always a loyal citizen of the United States." Buck said.

"Indeed."

After the two bade farewell, Somerfield decided to take a walk. He crossed Farragut Square to 17th Street NW. The afternoon had warmed while he and Buck lunched, so he told his driver to wait while he took in a stroll down 17th to the Mall, that green strip of monuments and museums at the heart of the national government.

Upon reaching the World War II memorial, Somerfield ambled down a stone walkway to the middle oblong pool and sat on a stone bench under the Pacific Theatre section.   It was here that he would sometimes come to center himself--to center his soul. It was a place that the Chairman of Group 929 had recommended to him early in their working relationship. He, too, had needed to come here, he confided, and ponder his role in Group's projects.

As Somerfield looked at the pool before him and the twin fountains, he considered the irony in the memorial that few understood. The granite itself came from Culpeper, Virginia. The very county where the United States was involved in a war that dwarfed World War II--something he could never say aloud or explain to his family or his friends. But, like the Group Chairman, it was something that he sometimes had to tell himself when he had qualms about what it was that he did. War required hard decisions. Hard decisions like the decimation of Binford.

Somerfield told himself that war erased the normal bounds of morality, but sometimes he had to remind himself of that fact. What was moral about sending men to die on those cliffs on D-Day? What was moral about dropping a nuclear weapon on a civilian city in Japan? The answer the monument thrummed out in the grey granite and splashing water was that the conflict had to be handled, and that men had to suffer and die in order for that evil to be handled. They had to be handled. The war had to be handled. And, Binford *had* to be handled.

He knew it was devastating for the prosecutor. How could it not be devastating, destroying a man's reputation? But Binford had brought it upon himself by planning to empanel the special grand jury. Unknowingly, the county prosecutor had crossed a line never before crossed. Never had an organ of government delved into the workings of Group 929 nor of its main project in Culpeper.

And now Binford had to be stopped. He had to be handled. In this twilight war there were casualties. Oh yes, there had been plenty of casualties over the decades. Not in the millions dead as represented by the monument: but bloody nonetheless--and just as necessary.

CHAPTER 16

FOOTNOTE 49, VOL. 3, CHAPTER 10, PAGE 174.

MEMO
TOP SECRET/EXTREME SANCTION
DATE: JULY 10, 1947
FROM: COMMANDING GENERAL ROGER M. RAMEY, 509 BOMBARDMENT WING, ROSWELL AAF
TO: ROBERT P. PATTERSON, SEC. OF WAR
RE: ROSWELL INCIDENT PRELIMINARY CONCLUSIONS

PLEASE BE ADVISED THAT THE INITIAL ANALYSIS REGARDING THE CRASHED SAUCER INDICATES A HUGE LEAP IN AERONAUTICAL AND ELECTRICAL TECHNOLOGY BY A COUNTRY OTHER THAN THE UNITED STATES. IT IS NO COINCIDENCE, IN MY OPINION, THAT THE CRASH OCCURRED NEAR ROSWELL. THE 509 IS THE ONLY WING PRESENTLY ABLE TO DELIVER ATOMIC BOMBS TO THE SOVIET UNION.

CLEARLY, WE CANNOT ALLOW THE SOVIET UNION TO KNOW THAT WE HAVE THE CRAFT AT ROSWELL NOR THAT WE ARE AWARE OF THE APPARENT ADVANCES IN MECHANICAL AND ELECTRICAL TECHNOLOGY FOUND THEREIN.

IT IS MY RECOMMENDATION THAT WE ACT AS QUICKLY AS POSSIBLE TO MOVE THE OBJECT AND ITS CONTENTS TO A MORE SECURE LOCATION, AND SECONDLY, THAT WE CONTAIN KNOWLEDGE OF THE CRAFT TO AS FEW PERSONS AS POSSIBLE.

WHILE WE CANNOT IDENTIFY THE SOURCE OF THE CRAFT THERE CAN BE NO DOUBT THAT THE ONLY COUNTRY CAPABLE OF MANUFACTURING SUCH A VEHICLE IS THE SOVIET UNION.

ONE PUZZLING ASPECT OF THE CRAFT IS THE STORAGE AREA. TWO POD-LIKE CAPSULES WERE FOUND IN THE DEBRIS FIELD. WHILE EMPTY, THEY APPEARED TO BE THE RIGHT SIZE TO CONTAIN A BODY. SECONDLY, THERE WERE OTHER CONTAINERS FILLED WITH WHAT COULD BE CALLED BOTANICAL SPECIMENS. THE INTACT STORAGE AREA IN THE CRAFT CONTAINED MORE EMPTY SPECIMEN CONTAINERS.

NO OPERATIONAL MANUALS OR NAVAGATIONAL MAPS WERE FOUND. SYMBOLS ON CONTROL MECHANISMS ARE UNDECIPHERABLE.

THE PROPULSION SYSTEM IS ALMOST NON-EXISTENT. IT WOULD APPEAR THE BOTTOM OF THE CRAFT IN SOME MEASURE GENERATES AN ELECTRO-MAGNETIC FIELD WHICH WOULD MOVE THE CRAFT; BUT THAT IS MERE SPECULATION AT THIS POINT.

TWICE NOW A LARGE CYLINDER-SHAPED OBJECT HAS TRAVERSED THE AREA. IT CAN HOVER OR ACCELERATE AT HIGH SPEED. OUR AIR FIGHTERS HAVE SCRAMBLED ON BOTH OCCASIONS BUT ARE NOT CAPABLE OF CATCHING THE UNIDENTIFIED FLYING OBJECT (UFO). I WILL ATTACH AS A SEPARATE REPORT THE OBSERVATIONS MADE BY THE FIGHTER PILOTS UPON DEBRIEFING.

--EXCERPTS FROM THE PRESIDENTIAL BRIEFING PAPERS ON THE ROSWELL INCIDENT

MARS: HESPERIA PLANUM

After the wild run through the Martian facility, Howington and the remainder of the transportees were suffering from the shock of the transport and the mad dash for refuge. It wasn't until they had refreshed themselves with the water and jerky Reznik brought back from his scouting trip, and had time to reorient themselves, that the group began to perk up.

The two women huddled together in silence while Cho sat by himself on an opposite wall of the hexagon room. As for Reznik, he acted the part of the ungracious host, doling out the water a sip at a time from a larger container.

"Ok, Reznik," Steele said while chewing the dried meat, "they've got questions. Now's as good as any time to get them briefed. Tell them who you are."

With obvious reluctance, Reznik introduced himself.

"I drove the Rovers *Spirit* and *Opportunity* for JPL," he explained. "I've been here…well I don't know how long. At least a year. I woke up in a pod and got the hell out of there as fast as I could. I've been alone since then and had a lot of time to observe the place. I never thought I'd speak with another human being until Steele showed up. I'd almost given up hope." His voice trailed off and, his eyes glistening with emotion, he looked away.

"I'm sorry but what do you mean you drove for JPL?" Howington asked, obvious in his attempt to fill the uncomfortable silence left by Reznik's raw admissions. "That phrase, drove for JPL, doesn't mean anything to me."

"Jeez! I can't believe the ignorance of people when it comes to the space program," Reznik exclaimed, clearly exasperated, his countenance shifting from sorrow to irritation in an instant. "The two rovers on Mars? Do you at least remember that?"

"Yeah, I remember something about that," Howington answered, refusing to be insulted by the survivor's abrupt shift in attitude.

"Ok. Well, someone has to tell the rovers where to go. The Jet Propulsion Laboratory, JPL for short, was in charge of the program for NASA. I was one of the guys who programmed the drive for a Martian sol. That is what we called a Martian day: a sol. Anyway, one morning I saw something that I wasn't supposed to see, and some boys in black SUVs picked me up. Next thing I know I'm on vacation here. It's been a blast, let me tell you."

"How'd you get here, Steele?" Howington asked.

"Same as you lot," he said. "It's just that I knew someone at the… at the…the…well, I don't know what to call it. I knew someone who told me about this place before they shut the lid on the pod. I didn't get knocked out like you. So when the lid opened, I knew to get out and to get weapons."

"Yeah. Weapons," Stover interrupted. "How did we get the ordnance?"

"Wait, Stu, I've got more to ask," Howington declared. "You said that we're on Mars. How do you know that? All I see are a lot of warehouse interiors and…Well, I've got to admit those things weren't human but…"

"Just the gravity alone ought to tell you where we are," Reznik said matter-of-factly. "It's just one third of earth's gravitational pull. Didn't take me two minutes to figure that one out."

Howington sat back digesting the information. "Ok. So let's say this is Mars," Howington said, although it was clear that he still had his doubts. "What *are* those things? And, why in the hell are *we* here?"

"And add to that," Stover interjected, "what sort of place is this anyway? What's its purpose, besides being a horror show on steroids?"

"I don't know the answer to any of your questions," Reznik admitted holding his palms up. "I have theories. But I don't really understand this place."

"Tell us what you think you know," Howington said, exasperated.

"Fine. I got nothing else to do than sit around and tell stories," Reznik replied. "First, the facts that we have. Then the conclusions I've drawn. *We are on Mars, make no mistake about that.* And, I know that from personal observation and my professional training. Secondly, the technology that brought us here and that built this place is far beyond anything we have. By 'we,' I mean humans. And I know because I've been on the cutting edge of Mars exploration for the United States for the past twelve years. We can't even begin to duplicate this. Not the transport. Not the facility. Not the nanotechnology that keeps it running. Not the robotics evident in the creatures. Not the mind control exhibited in the transportees. Finally, although those creatures are clearly not earth-based, they bear a strong resemblance to crabs and praying mantis-like insects. I think they are artificially modified versions of the real thing."

"Yeah, I understand what you mean," Stover interrupted. "They do resemble insects…sort of."

"They *are* mechanized," Reznik said, clearly irritated at the interruption. "When we killed one, it manifested indications of electrical and mechanical components. The movement itself is not organic. That is the first time I have seen the interior of one of those things but it complies with the theories that I created based on observation. Fourth fact, this place is badly operated. There is inefficiency everywhere and a combination of crudity with sophistication in the engineering. I guess you need to be an engineer to understand. But some of the engineering here is so advanced and… well…elegant. Then there is the presence of these organisms and the way in which they are maintained. Repulsive in its crudeness."

"You mean the way they feed?" Steele asked. "Howington, you gotta see that freak show," he added.

"Yeah. It makes no sense." Reznik replied. "And, fifth. There are humans here. You saw them in the pressure suits."

"It's true," Steele said in response to a chorus of protests. "I've seen them. Pretty horrifying."

"Alright," Reznik raised his voice over the general hum of comments. "Either I brief you on the situation or not, but - if I do - it's without all these interruptions. Jeez, I forgot how annoying people can be sometimes." Howington, Stover and Steele gave each other meaningful looks. Steele shrugged his shoulders as if to say Reznik was in charge at the moment and to follow his instructions.

Apparently satisfied with the response to his demand for silence, Reznik continued, "I suspect that people are rotated through here in two to four week intervals…and then returned to earth. I call them transportees. Just my own jargon. And they are clearly under some sort of external mind control while they are here."

"Now my conclusions," Reznik continued. "Although in possession of this facility, the aliens that we see are not its designers. I think of them more as some sort of intergalactic squatters. In fact, the facility seems to be constructed for human occupation and use. Look at the size of the doorways and of the cigar craft. Well, you haven't seen them yet, but it is a means of transport for humans and alien on Mars. Humans are used for labor and testing. All of them are sampled for tissue. But while humans are here, they *are* under some sort of mind control."

"Who is doing the controlling, if that's the case," Howington asked.

Reznik shot Howington a withering glare as he replied, "My guess is that there is an artificial intelligence running everything. Clearly the things we see are not capable of higher thought. At the same time, the compound exhibits extremely advanced technology. Ergo, an outside element controls the organics. There are no other life forms here, so simple logic dictates the existence of an Artificial Intelligence as the controlling force. We think of computers as the basis for artificial intelligence, but our limited knowledge in this field probably is useless and perhaps misleading in determining where the AI physically resides. Believe me, I've looked and seen nothing that resembles a mainframe computer. For all I know, the platform for an advanced created intelligence could be in the molecular structure of the planet itself. Who knows? It just is. And, I know I'm repeating myself, but for good reason. Don't be tempted by the fact that you see people--humans. They are not their own masters. You saw that in the marching formation earlier. But I have seen them working and performing all sorts of tasks individually. And before you interrupt, yes, I've tried to communicate with them but with no result. All of this begs the question, what are the aliens doing here?" Reznik continued. "First, I take it as a given that the United States Government is somehow involved in this since the cooperation of some human entity is clearly exhibited in the transport of humans. But when I think about how I was brought here, I'm sure there is NSA involvement."

"Now, as to why our government is involved, I don't know," Reznik admitted. "But they are building something here. This facility is mainly a reception and processing area from what I have seen. Don't think that humans are the only thing being processed. I've seen animals and plants moved through here. There's another facility-- that's where we were planning to go before you guys showed up-- which is an actual green house, completely automated. It explains the methane plumes we detected in the Martian atmosphere before I was taken. But I digress."

Reznik licked his lips and took a sip from his water container.

"I got a little off track, but here is what I think," he continued. "We're in some sort of processing center. I believe an alien entity is collecting samples of Earth flora and fauna for unknown purposes and, based on Mr. Steele's experience, I would say the United States Government is involved. The occupants of the facility should really be seen as part of the overall project and not the originators or creators of the operation here. Finally, there is no way off this planet unless we submit to their ministrations--which I think would be none-too-gentle --or we figure out a way to get a rescue here. It's either that or we stay here and die."

"Quite a summation, if I must say so myself," Howington commented. "So what's the plan?"

"It's very simple. First we get pressure suits for everyone."

"Whoa, there. Pressure suits? What the hell is that?" Stover asked.

"Don't worry, mate. Think space suit." Steele explained.

"As I was saying," Reznik continued. "We get suits for everyone. We hijack a cigar skimmer which should not be too hard, given the weapons we now possess. Then we head towards Gale Crater. It's about two thousand clicks from here, so I estimate it will take a week. At Gale Crater, we locate the rover *Curiosity*. I can hijack the electronics on the rover to broadcast the truth about what is going on here and tell the world that we are here. Then we can hole up at a power facility northwest of Gale."

"And do what?" Howington asked.

"Wait to be rescued," Reznik said flatly.

"And what makes you think there is anybody to rescue us?" Howington asked.

"I told you I worked at JPL. I heard enough scuttlebutt to suspect there is some sort of big project to send a manned mission to Mars," adding, "engineers, we talk."

"I never heard of it," Stover said. "What I read in the news is that NASA scrapped all manned spaceflight outside of earth orbit."

"They never scrapped Ares really. I know that because I had to download data on the rover images to the Ares Team. And that was after NASA had announced its cancellation. At least what I heard sounded like it was funded --but not through NASA." Reznik replied.

"You'd think we would have heard about it." Stover was clearly skeptical.

"Yeah, well, you'd think we would have heard about all of this, too," Howington said.

The group grew quiet contemplating the idea of a rescue. Then the older of the two women, Abbey Wentworth, quietly answered Howington's observation, "We have. We have heard about it-- but we just weren't listening." She looked about the room as if to see some flash of understanding from one of the other occupants.

It was the first time either woman had spoken at any length. All eyes turned to the two of them. The woman who spoke continued to look at the others in expectation of affirmation to her observation. Her hair, though undergoing the effects of pod encasement during transit, and the mad dash to the hexagon refuge, bespoke of someone who had known the attention of countless hairdressers. The blond mane hung thickly in a straight line about her jawline. Her eyes were a startling green, and they twinkled above finely-shaped lips and a small jutting chin. She was petite and well-proportioned, and wore clothes that sprang from an L.L. Bean Catalogue: conservative but classic in a fashionable way. A wedding ring flashed in the glow of the walls.

"We do know about this. Think about it." She said.

"Explain," Howington commanded.

"Roswell, the saucer crash, Area 51, cattle mutilations, crop circles, abductions--it was all there for us to see. It's been going on for a long time. We just ignored it."

"It's true," Stover said. "I'd have figured you for a nut case a month ago if you had told me about this."

"We just didn't listen. I just didn't listen." Wentworth said again quietly. She looked around the room, almost pleading for absolution as if they understood her inner turmoil.

Wentworth's last conversation with her mother had been two years earlier. In the bright light of a Hartford, Connecticut winter day, sun streams had raced through the wavy 19th century glass to splatter against the Oriental rug and wood parquet floor that comprised the lobby of the mental health facility. She had sat in one wingback chair while her mother sat opposite. They stared at each other across a gulf as deep as the cosmos itself.

"Mother, you have to stop doing these things; saying these things." Abby had said then with exasperation.

"Abby, I can't. I can't stop telling the truth," The regal looking lady replied archly.

"Can't stop telling the truth? Mother! Really I've heard all I can take of this. You were not abducted. There are no aliens roaming about Connecticut."

"So you say."

"Mother, how can I listen to someone who dumpster dives every chance she can get? Who has filled our house with... with....your house is filled with the refuse of God knows what. How can I bring my children to a house that stinks of the garbage truck? Your grandchildren. Mother this has got to stop."

"Abby. They're out there. And if you aren't careful, they will come for you."

"Stop it! You know this is not real, Mother. You know it!"

"I can't stop it as you put it. I remember now. I didn't for a long time. For a long time, I tried to forget that I had gone missing for a month. Your father, he just put it down to some sort of feminine fluke, but I knew there was more to it than that. The dreams came at night

and showed me. Then the dreams stopped, and I remembered," her mother said with certainty.

"I know mother. We've been through this."

"Then why don't you believe me?" The elder woman had asked, the dust motes dancing through the sunbeams in front of her lined face.

"If you don't stop it Mother, we have no choice but to keep you here. No choice. I came her hoping I could talk some sense into you."

"And I hoped you would believe your mother before it is too late," she said with a hint of sadness. "They're out there, and one day they'll come for you."

Abby Wentworth jerked back to the present.

"We all knew this had been going on," she said quietly, "But, we've been blind to it until now. My mother tried to warn me about this, but I wouldn't listen. I had her committed."

"What's your name, ma'am?" Howington asked.

"Abby. Abby Wentworth."

"You?" he asked of the younger woman who had reached over to hug Wentworth.

"Leotie Thunder."

Howington turned and honed in on Cho. "You?" he asked almost accusingly.

"Cho Tsing," he replied. He looked about the room; then he added, "Ms. Wentworth is right. We have all been blinded by, by... whatever. The truth about this has been in front of us all along."

Silence. Finally, Reznik broke the spell.

"Well, since we are all doing show and tell, why don't you tell us who you all are?" Reznik said nodding to Howington and Stover. "I already know our British friend, but no one else does. And, while you're at it, explain how you know each other."

Howington, Stover and Steele each explained that they were DEA agents. Howington revealed that he had come to Washington while investigating a drug-based, gang-land style multiple murder, but that his regular assignment was in Miami, as was Stover's. Leotie described her life at the reservation and adjustment to Tampa while Wentworth's recitation revolved around prep school, Swarthmore College and her family.

Eyes began to droop as the adrenaline high of arrival and escape wore off. Then there was nothing but the mind numbing, bone chilling deadness survivors often experience after a harrowing rescue.

Stover yawned, "I don't know about the rest of you, but I've got to get some shut eye." He stretched out on the floor.

"Reznik, are we safe here? Can we take a rest?" Howington asked.

"You'll be ok." Reznik replied. "Take a break. Steele knows what to do if something comes up. I've got an alternate hiding place big enough for all of you."

"Steele, you stay here and keep watch while they rest," Reznik ordered. "I've got some checking to do before we get moving again. I'll be back in a couple hours." The Robinson Crusoe-like figure jumped up and opened the side door.

"Don't move or open this door," Reznik warned. "Steele, you do like I told you." Then he slipped through the door and shut it behind him.

"Is this guy reliable?" Howington asked Steele.

"Who else do we have to rely on?" Steele replied. "So far he hasn't steered me wrong."

The men and women arranged themselves on the floor and quickly fell into a deep sleep. Steele stood guard but - eventually - he, too, dozed off.

He woke to the door opening. Reflexively, he reached for his hand gun, but relaxed when the wild hair announcing Reznik popped through the opening.

"We've got problems," Reznik said.

"What now?" Steele asked stifling a yawn.

"More transports," Reznik said shutting the door behind him. "The activity level will be up around here now. I can slip around without being seen, but I don't know about a whole group like this. So we either get out now or wait until they process whoever arrives. And honestly, we aren't ready to leave yet. I don't have enough pressure suits lined up, and we 'll need to bring some provisions."

"How many pods will arrive?" Steele asked.

"It's hard to know. Sometimes groups as large as twenty or more arrive. Sometimes just one or two show up."

"I'm not sitting around and letting one more person get taken by these things," Howington announced grimly while sitting up.

"Easy to say when you've got guns." Reznik said evenly.

"Look. I'm not criticizing you," Howington explained. "I'm amazed you have been able to exist here as long as you have. *But we do have guns.* Let's use them. If those things abuse people as much as you and Steele say, then if I've got a means to stop it, I will."

"What do you think Reznik?" Steele asked. "Could we do it?"

The wild-haired man thought back to the shivering, moaning hives of people he had seen and tried to contact through the past year. The first time he saw one of the controlled transportees, he almost fainted with shock. First there was the astonishment that another person was on Mars. But then a growing horror almost overwhelmed him when he saw the dead look in the woman's eyes because, for just a moment, he had a flashback to The Walking Dead. An older woman, he had seen her walking in a jerky but determined way through the maze of piping and machines in the large hanger-sized cavern he had first found himself in and the same cavern where he found Steele. Her jeans, sneakers and the pull-over sweat shirt that sparkled with Christmas decorations jarred his sensibilities. Once, to his relief, he determined she was not a zombie, he tried to talk with her. She did not resist him, but she did not respond to his presence--except for one thing. Yes, one thing. He still remembered in icy clear detail the drool that erupted from her mouth in a long silver string streaming down her chin. And then he heard again the low painful moan that followed as he had restrained her. He'd stood in front of her and put out his hand. She didn't resist. But the terrible sound that emanated from the depths of her soul made it clear she didn't want to comply. He let her go and followed her as far as he had dared in those first few days after escaping from the pod. With that image before him, Reznik realized with a jolt that he had become numb to the dreadful things happening in the facility. He had become numb to the idea that people were stumbling about the complex. He had classified them as something other than people. They had become transportees. Not grandmothers or grandfathers. Not fathers and mothers and sons and daughters--no, he had relegated them to the realm of things. Dead things. Horrible things. He realized there was only one right answer.

"Damn right we can do something." Reznik said, his eyes gleamed madly in the ambient light.

MADISON COUNTY VIRGINIA: ROCHELLE

Two days are an eternity.

John Weir stumbled about in a world of grays punctuated by the deepest shadows of despair. At times he was numb. Then the reality of what had happened would cascade down on him in an unending torrent of worry and desolation.

Today his family was probably on Mars. Or at least very near to it. Today, because he had tried to help Steele, his family was being punished. He had no reference to what they would endure on Mars. But he knew how they might look when they came back.

If they came back.

There was nothing for it, he knew, but to go to Mars himself. He would not sit idly by while they endured whatever it was that made people into what they became when deposited on the floor of the transport center. He would not let that happen.

But how? It was easy to say, to think, that he would rescue Rebecca, Heather and Hunter, but not so easy to do. In the two days since Sims had shown him the video, Weir had tortured his mind trying to think of a way to get in a pod and to bring weapons with him, particularly since he knew so little about the process that he did not even know how or when pods were designated for transport. There were scheduled pickups he knew that, but little else.

Clearly he needed someone to help him. But who? He knew so little about the workers at the facility that it was impossible to know who to trust. In the end, it came down to one person with whom he'd had the most contact besides Sims. Nora Burke had helped him before. Perhaps under duress --but he had sensed there was more to her willingness to help than just his pulling security rank on her. He sensed an inner well of humanity inside the diminutive brunette. An innate decency, it could be called. He hoped he could tap into that now.

Acting on impulse, Weir jumped into his Ford F-150 green pickup truck at the crack of dawn. Driving down Route 29, he passed Culpeper, crossed the county line into Madison County and eventually turned east onto Jacks Shop Road. And a few miles later, he saw Nora Burke's house sitting in an amber broom sage field.

Weir's visit was unannounced, and he hoped she would listen to him. He knocked on the door of the white clapboard farmhouse.

"Mr. Weir?" Nora's surprised face poked around the opening door.

"I know this is a surprise, but I wonder if I could speak with you for a few minutes?"

"Why? What's this all about?" she asked with a touch of alarm in her voice.

"This won't take long and it is awful cold out here." He smiled.

She hesitated, then stepped back and opened the door, "Of course. Come in. I was just fixing myself some coffee."

Weir followed her through the house which was decorated in a primitive country style. Antiques and faux antiques filled the front foyer and side rooms. She led him to the rear of the house, around a staircase, and into a country kitchen with a round oak pedestal table in the center. The morning light filled the room with warmth and cheeriness.

"I know this is irregular," Weir explained. "But I needed to speak to you today."

She gave him a quizzical look then motioned for him to sit. "How do you like your coffee?"

"Black."

She poured the steaming black liquid into two heavy ceramic mugs, set one in front of Weir, while she kept the other. Then she sat down across from him.

"I know I leaned on you pretty heavy there at the center," Weir opened. "I just want to tell you I am sorry for that, and perhaps when we finish this morning you'll understand."

"This sounds like it will take more than a few minutes."

"Well," he replied, "I might have been a little optimistic in that."

"It's not like I have a lot going on this morning." Her eyes travelled up and down his face, as if she were trying to fathom Weir's purpose.

"When you saw me with the pods I was doing more than a security check," he told her earnestly. "I was sending weapons in another pod for someone who was being transported. His name is Ian Steele. He saved my life in Iraq. I owed him. But I needed you to stay quiet or Frank Hill would have stopped the whole transport. As it is, Sims deduced what I did and he..." Weir choked up with emotion, "…he transported my wife and two kids in retaliation. They're gone."

"That was the special transport?" she asked tonelessly.

"Yeah. It was Thursday."

"I wasn't involved in that one."

Unsure as to how to proceed given her lack of emotion at the mention of his family and of Sims' cruelty, Weir had no choice but to plunge ahead.

"So, they have my family," he repeated. "I don't want to happen to them what I've seen in the transport room. I'm going after them, and I need your help."

Burke peered at him over the coffee, deliberately took a sip and put the mug down. "Get out, Mr. Weir," she said, stony-faced. "Get out right now. I am not going to be a party to breaking the law. In case you didn't notice, when you signed on to this project, you took an oath to follow the lawful orders of your superiors. You shouldn't have done what you did with the pods-- but don't think I'm going to risk my reputation, my job, for your mistake. You'll be lucky if I don't report this conversation. Now leave." The chair scraped the wood floor as she pushed it back to stand up.

Weir sat motionless shocked at the quick turn in the conversation. Surely he hadn't misjudged her that badly.

"I understand your reluctance," he said. "I really do. But haven't you ever thought about the people who we do this to?"

"Look, I do my job," she told him and Weir noticed that, apparently, she could not meet his eyes. "I do it for the science. I don't ask questions."

"Is it your job to forget that these are people? Like my wife and kids? Like you?" Weir said.

She shook her head to show disagreement. "It's not my concern. I'm a scientist. I have no control over what goes on there. I only know that this project is doing things I never thought possible. You have no idea how exciting that is. Eventually the world is going to be a much better place because of what we're discovering. And the transportees? They come back; it's not like we are killing them or anything. A little worse for wear, but fundamentally they're fine. It's a small price to pay."

"We're talking about people, not transportees," Weir reminded her grimly. "You don't get a pass on that. You can't look the other way. That argument failed at the Nazi war crimes trials, and it won't pass now. You must know it's wrong. And all of the people don't come back. You know that. Did they deserve to just disappear? Did their families deserve the uncertainty of not knowing? Did that little girl the other day in the reception room deserve to be dumped on the floor like so much garbage? I know you saw that. Don't tell me you think that's ok. Don't tell me you're as ruthless as Sims."

At the mention of Sims, Weir saw a change in Nora's face.

"That nasty little weasel," she snapped. "I'm nothing like him."

"How Nora? How? Tell me the difference."

"He's there for power. He likes to tell people what to do. I'm there for the science. If a few people are hurt, I've decided it's for the greater good. And I don't actually do anything that hurts anyone. On the other hand, I think he enjoys causing a little pain every once in a while. But I know this: the number of people we potentially could help based on these new technologies will far outweigh whatever happens to a few individuals."

"What kind of world are you talking about?" Weir demanded. "I'll tell you. It's a world where people like Sims thrive. It's a world where the weak and powerless are seen as impediments to the greater good and are disposed of without thought. It's a world where worth is measured in utility, not because humans are innately valuable. It's always easy to justify evil when you rationalize the sacrifice is for the greater good. Always. That excuses the whole transport program; I'll grant you that. But is that how you want to live? Don't you see, Nora? You're no different from Sims or Frank Hill. If you want to see what their kind creates, read the history books. I'd suggest you start with Nazi Germany, then work your way to the Soviet Union. It's not pretty, especially if your existence doesn't add to the greater good; however that is defined at the moment. And who gets to decide? The rich and powerful, that's who. It's always been like that when humans start down the road justifying wrong. I imagine the rest of us had better watch out, because people like you and Sims will be deciding who contributes the most for the greater good, and I don't think we'll pass the test. The thing I would worry about, if I were you, Nora, is whether or not you'll always pass the test."

Weir kicked up and out of his chair before striding towards the front door.

"I guess I misjudged you, Nora," he said over his shoulder as he turned the front door knob. "You and Sims are going to do just fine in this new world you're creating. God help you."

As he started to walk out Nora said, "Wait...Just...Wait."

"I know you're right," she said quietly as he reentered the kitchen. She turned and looked outside through a window above the kitchen sink and shuddered. "I saw the little girl. I can't get her off my mind." She breathed in deeply before continuing, "Once I saw a woman dragged out of the room screaming her husband's name. He was there--but in two pieces." She stifled a sob, "I can't stand it anymore."

"You're not the only person who has been warped by the place," Weir said flatly, remembering the part he had played in the death of Ed Wood and his wife. "It sneaks up on you. Very few people intend to do evil. But it is so insidious, so hideous in its camouflage, that evil takes hold before most realize it. I wish evil looked as ugly on the outside as it is inside. But it's never that simple, is it? The lucky ones recognize the ugly part, recognize it for the darkness evil always reveals. Most, though, are too blind to see the difference between the darkness and the light until it's too late and they are consumed. I'm ashamed it took what happened to my family to make me do something, but I'm going to do something about it now. I can't live with myself without trying."

"I don't want to hurt anybody ever again," Nora said.

Weir put his arm around her and hugged her to his shoulder. "I'm sorry, Nora. I'm glad to hear it and I wish I could tell you that no one else will get hurt, but I can't. We've already hurt people. We both knew what we were doing was wrong, but we tried to pretend otherwise. So we have to make it right, even if we get hurt. We have to fight --we have to act so the evil doesn't grow any stronger--or we are just as guilty as the monsters that created this mess. I don't want to hurt anyone else either, but I'm afraid we are beyond all of that now. Restoring the good always comes with a price. It's never free. So we are going to have to fight: and there will likely be casualties - and that will be on us. We helped create this. Now we have to fix it."

Nora nodded her head slightly, "Let's go for a walk."

The two stepped out the rear of the house after she wordlessly donned a tan barn jacket. He followed. She took a well-worn path that wove between woods and fields. As they breathed in the cool fall morning, Weir savored the dry oak leaf smell drifting in the autumn air.

"I wanted us out of the house," Burke explained as they walked. "I don't know but sometimes I get the impression that creep Sims is watching me." They stopped at a wood fence which bordered a horse paddock. "What do you want me to do," Nora asked, leaning back against the fence.

"I need to get into a pod, and I need another pod to go with me filled with weapons. My problem is that I don't know exactly how pods are timed for transport, and I need someone to get my pods into the transport room. I know Sims and Hill will be watching my every move so someone else has to do it."

"And that's why you need me?"

"Exactly. And there's more. I'm going to document what I know about the program. Then I'm going to give it to you to keep. If I don't get back, I want you to take what I give you and get it out on the internet."

"Why not just take it to the police?"

"Because I don't know who to trust," he told her. "This thing is so big it touches everything. The internet is the only thing that still is free. I mean I know the NSA monitors it, but that's the important thing to remember. They monitor. They try to control, but the internet is just too big to control anymore. We can get it out and then let those that care, that are still able to see evil for what it is, join the fight. I know this, Nora. *Knowledge is like water, it finds a way. It finds a way to break out.*"

"Well, you don't mess around, I'll give you that," she told him thoughtfully. "Not that I am backing out, but why not wait a little while and see if your family comes back. The chances are that they will. I mean, you don't even know what's up there or how to get back. Couldn't you fight better from earth than take the chance you won't get back?"

Weir looked up at the sky, "No. They're up there. I don't know what is happening to them, but I know it can't be good; and I know I've got to go and try to protect them."

Nora digested this then asked, "Do you read much, John?"

"No, why?"

"Something I'm reading by W.H. Auden just came to me. He writes about the world being in darkness but dotted by flashes of light."

"Right now I think the world is filled with little flashes of light," Nora said. "Each being a spark of goodness against the night. And it gives me hope."

"We have a chance to stop all of this," Weir replied.

"I know," Nora said. "I hope people will see the light and ignore the darkness."

MARS: HESPERIA PLANUM

"Do no harm."

"What?" Reznik asked, his filthy hair swinging in the air as he swiveled towards Leotie Thunder.

She gazed steadily at Reznik and Howington. They had been discussing how to blow up the reception area. "I said: do no harm. I think you forgot something."

"What would you know about it?" Reznik snarled. "You haven't even been outside."

"I've been listening. You said there are people here, right?" Hearing no response she continued, "Dude, if I understand correctly, I would have been one of those zombies you talk about," she said hotly. "One of those things in pressure suits, *and I'm people.*"

"Point well taken," Howington said. Steele moved over to take part in the conversation. Reznik looked angry, his eyes flashing, his hands clenching.

"You want to stop all of this, but based on what I am hearing, it sounds like a lot of things are going to get blown up. And not only that, but a lot of the machinery that runs this place is going to get destroyed. Right?"

"You got that right," Reznik replied.

"The sooner this place is put out of commission the better," Steele affirmed.

"How are all the people here going to get home if we blow everything up and then leave?" Thunder asked.

"You know, she's got a point," Cho Tsing broke the silence.

"You're kidding me, right?" Reznik said heatedly. "You come up here as little more than a lab rat to these monsters, you haven't even seen what they do, and now you're questioning whether we should wipe the slate clean?"

"I mean no offense, Mr. Reznik. But Ms. Thunder has a valid point," Cho continued. "Are you willing to kill all of those people to, how do you put it, wipe the slate clean? I don't think it's the right way to go. We should do what we can to stop this, but not at the risk of hurting more people." He glanced at Leotie Thunder, who looked at him quizzically. "I think there's been enough of that around here from what you've told us."

Leotie mouthed "Thank you" in Cho's direction. The small act of communication electrified Cho -- startling him in its power.

"You know, boss, I've got to agree." Stover said oblivious to the exchange between Cho and Leotie. "If we destroy this place, how will anyone get back? And, do we really want to cut off a possible route of escape if we need it?"

"Un-freaking-believe-able!" Reznik said with disgust.

Finally, Howington shook his head and said, "I hate to admit it, Reznik, but I think she might be right."

The JPL engineer slumped back against the wall, the wild light slipping from his eyes, the certainty that action confers seeping away and leaving a void in its place.

"Ok. I guess you're right," he admitted. "This place does that to you after a while. It's not easy to know how to fight back. It's not easy to know what the right thing to do is. In fact, I haven't been able to think that there's anything that's right for a long time."

In the end the group decided it would be better to liberate who they could from the new transport, then leave. Reznik then led the group to his more permanent lodging where Steele had first bedded down after being rescued. Then he, Steele, and Howington scouted out the "pod reception area"--Reznik's label for the large room he led them to and leaving Cho and Leotie behind with Wentworth.

"How do you know when a transport is coming?" Steele asked as they crouched behind a boxlike protrusion from the floor.

"The noise," Reznik responded. "I think it must be a power surge of some sort. The reception area just seems to wind up with activity. That and the fact that some of the instrument panels light up which are normally dark. It took me a long time to figure it out."

"So…is something about to happen?" Howington asked, nodding towards the empty space in front of them.

"I think so. It's hard to tell but the power surge is definitely ramping up," Reznik said referring to the high pitched hum that had begun to permeate the room.

Howington shifted a satchel from his back and laid it on the floor. "Ok. Let's review the plan one more time. The pods arrive in a thing you call a quantum bubble. Once it dissipates, we move in on the pods. Steele and I will neutralize any threats. You will open the pods and expedite personnel to the rally point here."

Reznik suppressed a grin. "If that means you kill any aliens that get in the way and that I get the people out and here --then, yes, that's the plan."

"Right, after that, you take point. Steele and I will take the rear. We'll keep non-combatants between us. Keep the Beretta in your leg holster until we leave. Once you're on point-- you're on point. That means you keep the gun up in front of you--safety off. We're gonna be hot, and I don't want you missing a shot because you forget to flick off the safety."

Howington looked at Steele. "You ready?"

"Ready," Steele said. "Remember to shoot those bastards in the face. That's their only weak spot." The two men rechecked the Mossberg 590 shotguns they each carried along with a satchel of C-4. M33 grenades were attached to their web belts, grenades that were intended for the M203 launchers mounted to the M-4 Carbines slung across their backs. Then the little rescue group settled in a protected niche and waited. They could smell the presence of aliens and from time to time hear the clicking of pincers on the hard floor. Each scrunched close to the wall when one of the monsters came close. Reznik seemed less concerned, having seen the process before. He merely motioned with his hands to remain still when the odor of road kill drifted strong in the air.

Howington leaned against the wall and closed his eyes, still disoriented, worried about Marcie and hoping that she had gotten away from whatever was happening in Miami. And, now, he was on Mars. On Mars and preparing to fight monster aliens. It was as though he were living in a bad science fiction movie, not only living it but now a main character since he and Steele, who both had military training, were in charge of the rescue operation.

Howington shifted his posture to ease the pressure of the carbine against his back and considered the presence of Cho. He had not said much but Howington was becoming more convinced, with each passing hour, that Cho had been involved in the gang-style shooting on the Miami docks. It could not be coincidence that the trail from Miami led to Culpeper, and that here he was with a Chinese national, transported with the help of the federal government. Cho acted like he was hiding something, and Howington's well-honed skills as a detective thrummed with alert signals every time he looked or interacted with the quiet man.

Howington started forward as Reznik shouted, "Get ready! The quantum bubble is breaking through!"

Getting on his knees, Howington leaned forward to look about the empty room and, raising his eyes, saw a silver sphere, shimmering in the light, move slowly through the roof of the cavernous space. Electrical arcs snaked across the curved ceiling and ozone filled the air. He stared, transfixed by the impossibility sliding out of the ceiling and down to the floor. Had it not been for the reels of science fiction he had watched through the years, Howington would have had no point of reference to absorb what was taking place before him.

The sphere looked as solid as metal. Its surface gleamed in the ambient light--flashing reflective bursts of white and blue as the accompanying electrical arcs blazed in crooked jagged streams of energy into the cavern. He watched it clear the ceiling and glide in a straight path down to the floor where the top disappeared as a straight line of nothingness moved mechanically down the face of the sphere. As the line slid to the bottom third, three pods revealed themselves hovering within.

Then the sphere erased itself.

Electrical arcs slithered across the floor. The high-pitched hum filled the chamber.

And then silence slammed into the cavern, just as Reznik had described it to Howington and Steele. In one instance, the room thrummed with electrical discharges and power consumption, the next an unnerving silence.

"Wait for it." Reznik cautioned. "Wait for it."

Slipping safeties off on their shotguns, Howington and Steele stood in a crouched position, and swung the deadly weapons forward as three truck-sized aliens marched out to the pods and began to manipulate them out of the room. The pods floated on air like dust motes in an oddly graceful motion.

"Now!" Reznik shouted.

Howington and Reznik and Steele ran toward the aliens which were moving away from the rescue party. Howington motioned to the right for Steele while he veered left. They ran on either side of the rear alien. As they passed it, both paused and fired slugs at point-blank range into the front of the hard-shelled organism. One slug skittered across the top of the alien, scattering shell and tissue across the floor. The second slug entered the front. The alien stopped and, spying Steele, moved quickly towards him pincers outstretched and open leaving the pod hovering alone. Steele racked another shell into the shotgun and took aim as he moved backwards. He pulled the trigger, and the blast reverberated about the cavern. The alien stopped, apparently unhurt.

"Watch your backs!" Reznik yelled.

Howington twisted around to see the other two aliens turning about to address the threat.

"Grenades!" Steele shouted in response to the sight.

The two men swung around the stubby M-4 Carbines which hung by a strap behind them. The Mossbergs clattered to the floor as they brought the M-4s up to load with high explosive grenades stored on a belt each had strapped at the waist. Howington slid the grenade launcher forward, slipped in the deceptively small grenade with its attached explosive launching unit, and then pulled the slide back with a reassuring click before pivoting and launching a grenade straight toward the creature.

"Hit the ground!" Howington ordered.

The grenade Howington shot and a second launched by Steele exploded almost simultaneously inside the same alien, whose front carapace lifted up and flipped end over end in the air, spatting onto the floor in slow motion. Yellow and green viscous material spouted up and splattered about. Electric arcs shot out of the blown-off top region as the creature tottered and crashed to the floor. The second alien came alive and moved purposefully towards Steele who back-pedaled while Howington fired another round towards it. The grenade bounced off the carapace and fell to the floor where it exploded behind the monstrosity, lifting it upward and over onto its back. With an arch of its pincers, it flipped over and gathered itself up on its spindly legs to arrow towards Steele.

Steele slid and fell from the blast, then watched as the creature righted itself.

The other alien moved towards both men, jagged pincers out.

"Move!" Steele yelled as he crawled to his feet, his head ringing from the concussion, blood streaming from burst vessels in his ears.

The two men split, attempting to separate the remaining aliens. The strategy worked. The two beasts separated following Howington and Steele individually.

Breath raging in his lungs, ears ringing from the multiple concussion of two grenades exploding, Howington sprinted across the open space, the alien clacking behind him. And gaining.

Howington was not thinking so much as he was working on instinct. Instinct to get away from something that wanted to hurt him, kill him, eat him. He fought to push down the primal panic welling up with each frenzied step and impose the reason and logic of his frontal cortex, smashing down the terror-induced flight-or-fight response, and harnessing the adrenaline rush into a controlled and effective burst of focused energy. Reaching behind, he pulled a grenade from his belt and slid it into the grenade launcher, then pulled the slide back, locking in the grenade.

"Shoot! Shoot!" Steele ordered.

Howington turned to aim, only to be lifted off the floor by a mottled pincer which clutched him so tight that he nearly passed out from the pain. Lifting the M4 and poking the barrel almost against the slime covered frontal region of the creature, he pulled the trigger and held it down until the clip emptied.

Thirty rounds of .45 caliber lead slammed into the frontal carapace, the slugs tumbling through flesh and vessels, creating maximum damage to living tissue. In the process, electrical enhancements shorted and exploded. Droplets of green and yellow slime splattered Howington with gobbets of gore before the pincer, losing its grip, released the DEA agent, who rolled away and joined Steele in further distracting the aliens. Reznik, meanwhile, according to plan, ducked and ran as unobtrusively as possible to the now-unattended pods floating on air, pushing the rubber-like extrusion on the end of each and running to the next. Lids popped, breaking an air seal with a sigh after sigh as lids slid down and under each tube like pod. Reznik moved from one to the other anxiously, watching for the confining material to melt away, the occupant to wake, and hoping that the aliens would stay far away.

MARS: HESPERIA PLANUM

Rebecca Weir felt so cold. So very cold.

Dread came pitter-pattering next. Somewhere on the edge of darkness, somewhere at the frontier of her mind, there was something large and dark stalking her. Something as cold as evil itself.

Rebecca was looking for it now. Alone. In the illogical way that the unconscious works, she was drawn to the thing in the woods. Dark and foreboding, the trees whipped above her head as she took each hesitant step toward the blackness she now knew called her.

And then she floated deeper into the woods, deeper into the place that held the horror, which held the thing that above all else, she did not want to see. Because something in that cold darkness had taken her children, and there was nothing she could do.

"Wake up!" Someone called.

But she didn't want to wake up. Her children were there.

"Wake up!" She felt her face jerk as someone slapped her, and she opened her eyes only to be assaulted by a riot of sounds, smells and light.

"Get up, woman, or you're gonna die!" a bearded man with crazed eyes shouted.

More gunfire. Then a muffled explosion. The smell of death.

She gagged. Then rough hands grabbed her and physically dragged her from where she lay. Dumped on the floor, Rebecca could only watch as men shot at things beyond description, beyond belief, but real.

And then she noticed other capsules floating on air similar to the one she had just been hauled out of: grey, coffin like, lids open. The wild man leapt to another and lifted a small child, only to drop the limp form to the floor.

Heather!

CHAPTER 17

EVERY PRESIDENT HAS LEFT A MESSAGE TO HIS SUCCESSORS TO BE INCLUDED IN THE PRESIDENTIAL BRIEFING PAPERS. THE FOLLOWING ARE THE MESSAGES LEFT IN CHRONOLOGICAL ORDER:

JANUARY 19, 1989
THE WHITE HOUSE
1600 PENNSYLVANIA AVE. NW
WASHINGTON, DC

TO WHOM IT MAY CONCERN:

I SOMETIMES WONDER HOW FAR IS TOO FAR, HOW MUCH IS TOO MUCH, HOW SECRET IS TOO SECRET. EVEN KNOWING THAT THE UNITED STATES WAS THE MOST POWERFUL NATION ON EARTH, I NEVER COULD HAVE IMAGINED THAT THIS COUNTRY WOULD BE THE CUSTODIAN OF SUCH IMPORT AS THAT OUTLINED IN THIS BRIEF.

MY PREDECESSOR, HARRY TRUMAN, WAS SHOCKED WHEN HE LEARNED OF THE MANHATTAN PROJECT. RIGHTLY, HE DECIDED TO SAVE AMERICAN LIVES AND USE THE BOMB. THIS IS SOMETHING THAT ONLY THOSE WHO LIVED THROUGH THE DARK DAYS OF PEARL HARBOR OR THE BATTLE OF THE BULGE CAN TRULY UNDERSTAND. I AND MY PREDECESSORS HAVE FOUND OURSELVES IN THE SAME QUANDARY WITH THE POSSESSION AND KNOWLEDGE OF ROSWELL. WE WILL BE JUDGED FOR WHAT WE DO-- AS PRESIDENT TRUMAN IS JUDGED. I PRAY THAT I HAVE MADE THE RIGHT DECISIONS AND FOR THE SAME REASONS THAT HARRY TRUMAN DID WITH THE ATOMIC BOMB.

I CAUTION MY SUCCESSORS IN OFFICE TO USE THE POWER CON-FERRED BY THE PRESENCE OF THE ROSWELL TECHNOLOGY SPARINGLY AND EVEN MORE SO TO REIN IN THE POWER OF THE STATE WHERE POSSIBLE. SECRECY BREEDS MORE GOVERNMENTAL POWER.

I AGREE WITH THE ACTIONS OF MY PREDECESSORS IN KEEPING THE TECHNOLOGY SECRET, AND EVEN MORE DISTURBINGLY TO MY DEEPLY HELD BELIEFS, I AGREE WITH THE TRANSPORT PROGRAM OVERSEEN BY GROUP 929.

UPON THE FALL OF COMMUNISM, WHICH I FULLY EXPECT, I RECOM-MEND FULL DISCLOSURE OF THE ROSWELL PROJECT TO THE AMERICAN

PEOPLE. THAT IS MY MAIN RECOMMENDATION TO THOSE THAT FOLLOW IN THIS OFFICE.

AMERICANS WILL EVENTUALLY LEARN OF ROSWELL, AND I TRUST THE PEOPLE WILL KNOW THE RIGHT THING TO DO WITH THIS KNOWLEDGE.

THE LONGER A DEMOCRACY ACTS TO COVER UP ITS ACTIONS, THE LESS OF A DEMOCRACY IT BECOMES. THE WAR WITH THE SOVIET UNION REQUIRED SECRECY. WHEN THAT WAR IS OVER, THERE WILL BE NO NEED TO HIDE THE TRUTH ANY LONGER. TO DO SO WILL ONLY LEAD TO PER-VERSIONS OF THE LAW AND OF SOCIETY.

GOD SAVE US.
SINCERELY,
RONALD REAGAN

---EXCERPTS FROM THE PRESIDENTIAL BRIEFING PAPERS ON THE ROSWELL INCIDENT.

MARS--HESPERIA PLANUM

"There are two kids here!" Reznik cried to Howington and Steele. They had just dispatched the last alien, its twisted body oozed green and yellow ropy streams across the floor. Thirty rounds of .45 caliber lead, twisting and tumbling through the soft tissue of any organism, will create destruction unimaginable to any but those used to combat.

"You hurt?" Steele asked Howington who had been in the grips of one alien.

"No. Let's move."

The two men ran to the rally point where Reznik had dragged the three transportees. One of them, a woman, sat obviously in shock, cradling the two small children leaning unresponsive against her.

"Are they Ok?" Steele asked.

"Yeah," Reznik told him. "The lady seems to be the mother. The two kids are taking longer to wake up than I expected. We're gonna have to carry them."

"Listen to me," Howington said to Rebecca, "We have to get moving. Your children will be fine, but we need to go now. Can you walk?"

She nodded affirmatively.

"We've got to move now." Reznik told them. "I don't know what will happen but, after this friggin mess, whatever happens won't be good."

"Change of plans, guys," Howington announced. "Reznik, you take point. Miss, you follow him. We'll take the rear and carry your children."

"I'm not leaving my children," Rebecca Weir said, the shock apparently wearing off.

"Look, lady," Reznik said. "We'll explain everything later. No one is leaving your children. But if you want them to live, we have got to move now."

Steele and Howington shifted the two small forms onto their shoulders, heads hanging loosely down each man's back, the M4s slung in front, a shotgun in one hand. Reznik drew his pistol and led, Rebecca Weir in the middle, Steele and Howington at the rear, all moving at a steady jog, the men constantly scanning the surrounding jumble of box-like protrusions, piping and machinery.

"Here!" Reznik darted to the left between vertical columns that joined in a square two stories above their heads, and opened into a small vestibule with no discernible exit. In the distance, they heard clicking on the floor indicating more aliens were in pursuit.

"What is this?" Howington demanded. "Shouldn't we be moving?"

"We can't outrun all of them." Reznik explained. "I told you if we created a stir we might have to take a different route, and believe me, killing three of those things will create one hell of a stir."

Squatting down, he lifted up a square floor covering, using a recessed handle. "Down here, now," he ordered.

Howington jumped first, followed by Steele, and Rebecca, leaving Reznik to let the door slam shut behind him. The one-third-Earth gravity made the ten-foot drop easy to manage for the four adults, although Howington and Steele stumbled because of the ungainly extra mass created by the children.

"Follow me," Reznik told them. The group began trotting down a twisting round illuminated tunnel.

After an interval of a few minutes, Howington slowed.

"Stop! Stop. Reznik, I think these kids are waking up," Howington said as the boy began to moan.

"Good. We need them on their feet," Reznik replied savagely as Rebecca darted forward to embrace them. He watched her stoke their heads for a moment then, "This is all very nice, but we've got a boatload of aliens on the hunt. Get those kids on their feet, and let's roll!"

"Just who exactly are you?" Rebecca said looking up.

Reznik laughed, "Why...I'm your knight in shining armor. Couldn't you tell?" The JPL engineer turned and started trudging off.

"He kinda grows on you," Steele said apologetically.

The group started out again with Reznik in the lead. Rebecca carried Heather. Hunter trailed behind his mother with Steele ready to grab the boy if need be. Howington took the rear. They could hear commotion reverberating down the shaft as aliens stalked the floor above

"What is this thing used for?" Steele asked Reznik about the tube they were jogging within.

"Who knows? Sometimes I think it's a ventilation shaft. Sometimes I think magnetic energy flows through it. Once I saw a beam of light blasting through it. When I say beam, don't think flash-light, think water shooting out of a fire hose." Reznik trudged on a few steps, then added with a snicker, "Let's just hope it's not a sewer."

Rebecca looked back at Steele and Howington quizzically.

"Don't worry, Miss," Howington assured her. "Steele's right, he does kinda grow on you."

The trek took about an hour before Reznik called a halt at what looked like a door with what appeared to be an identifying symbol above.

"Ok. When we get in, do exactly as I say. Steele, you've been outside before, so you know what to do."

"Outside?" Rebecca asked.

Reznik glared at her, then turned and punched the dot upon which the seams of an oblong door darkened and separated. Opening the door, the group entered a larger room containing a jumbled pile of pressure suits and helmets.

"Put them on," Reznik ordered slipping into one. "Don't worry about the kids --the suits adjust to any size."

"Suits! What do we need suits for? Where are we?" Rebecca asked with desperation.

"Jeez!" Reznik exclaimed. "Do I have to explain this every time? What does the gravity mean to you, lady? What?"

"Come on, Reznik," Steele said. "Give her a break. It's a lot to take in all at once. What's your name?" he asked.

"Rebecca. Rebecca Weir. This is Hunter and Heather--my children."

"Rebecca Weir?" Steele asked with surprise. "You're not related to John Weir, are you?"

"He's my husband." She replied, recognition dawning on her face. She had never met Ian Steele, but she had seen him in her husbands' collection of photos taken in Iraq. And, of course, he had described more than once the British friend who had rescued him from captivity.

"I can't believe it." Steele said.

"You're...You're Ian Steele?" She asked doubtfully. "The Ian Steele who rescued John?"

"That's me," Steele replied with a chuckle.

"Listen, you two, we don't have time for this. Suit up and let's go," Reznik snapped.

"He's right," Steele told her. "We can talk later. Just put your suits on, and when we get outside, you'll understand better where we are. But we're safe. That's the important thing to remember; you and the kids are safe right now."

"You have suits for my kids?" Rebecca asked doubtfully.

"Hell of a thing lady," Reznik replied, "but they adjust to any size. Even the helmets. Now that *all* your questions are answered can we continue?"

Steele and Howington helped the new arrivals slip into the suits and mount the hard helmets while Reznik waited with arms crossed. The two were amazed to watch the oversized helmets shrink in proportion to the heads of the children. The suits did the same.

"What *are* these suits made of?" Stover asked Reznik.

"Let's go," Reznik said ignoring Stover's question. "That's the only way we get around the freak show back there. Just stay together. Steele, we're going to use the same route in as we did before. You take the rear so that, if something happens and we split, at least someone will know how to get back besides me."

With those minimal instructions, Reznik turned to the other door, pressed the red button and waited for it to turn green. When it did, he said, "Here we go," and pushed the button a second time and the sound of air escaping filled the room as the door slid upwards. Reznik stepped through and onto a sloping tunneled walkway. A harsh unfiltered light filled the room.

The group followed Reznik upward.

At the opening they stepped out onto a grated platform. Above them arched a salmon-colored sky dotted with scudding cirrus clouds. Below, the reddish cratered landscape stretched to an impossibly close horizon.

"Where are we?" Rebecca asked, holding Heather and Hunter close. "Ian, tell me. What is this place?"

"This is hell, Mrs. Weir," Reznik told her, his voice tinny in every helmet, "Get used to it."

POWHATTAN TOWERS--RICHMOND VIRGINIA

Mordecai Binford pulled into the underground parking lot of the twin skyscraper that housed Roland Sprague's law firm, Scag, Black and Mullen. Binford parked near the entrance to Tower Two, where he knew the law firm was located.

Binford knew of Scag, Black and Mullen, as did anyone else who practiced law in Virginia. A big, high profile firm, it existed because its partners had been adept at merging law and politics in such a way so as to create business without seeming to do so. Politicians left public office to ensconce themselves in the towers, where retainers and consultancy fees poured in, in an unending current of wealth and power. Draft legislation flowed from the towers to organizations like the Commonwealth State Bar or any other number of non-profits, who in turn lobbied for the suggested draft changes in the law. Often the firm lobbied legislators directly for the legal fine-tuning it had created and distributed, reminding the reluctant of how much money had been donated to their reelection campaigns or by slipping a dossier of his or her moral failings under the legislator's office door at night. And since the changed legislation needed a law firm with expertise in the modifications to the Virginia Code, Scag, Black and Mullen always seemed to be at the forefront ready to scarf up the legal work involved in implementing the different regulations, in an unending conveyor belt of influence and wealth for its partners. Fittingly, the two buildings literally did tower over the James River and even more symbolically, over the stately capitol building itself.

Binford's car door echoed in the dark basement. Adjusting his suit, he pulled his tie tight to his throat, and walked towards an elevator for the second tower. His mind wondered back to the events that led to this march across the oil-stained cement. The subpoena had arrived to much fanfare in the press, and when he talked to the Attorney General's Office, there had not been much guidance. "*Read what you can*" had been the assistant attorney general's disinterested advice in regard to preparation which was not as helpful as Binford had hoped, but then, what did he know about habeas proceedings? It was the attorney general's job to protect the integrity of the conviction he had secured in front of a jury a decade earlier. He knew the truth was what was expected of him and was, in fact, his best protector in the unknown savanna he stepped onto when he entered the building.

Truth. That was his protection. Of that Binford was sure. Truth.

After a swift and silent rise, the elevator doors slid open, and Binford walked into a lobby that made him feel shabby and small. Thick, dark carpet flowed to a desk illuminated by a green shade light. Wood-paneled walls stretched up a story or more to a paneled ceiling. Binford's eyes were drawn to the illuminated desk. Like an island in the dark wood and carpet, it lured the occupants of the elevator naturally, without fanfare, speaking of power and authority.

"Mr. Binford?" The businesslike secretary asked when the prosecutor stood at the desk. "You will take depositions in the corner conference room. You can go on in." She pointed across the room to a heavy wood door that hung darkly on large ornate brass hinges gleaming dully in the amber light that fell from chandeliers.

I believe Mr. Scrum is already waiting," she added.

"Mr. Scrum? I don't believe I know him."

"He knows you." She turned dismissing Binford with a sniff.

Binford walked to the door and opened it. Light blazed out into the reception area, blinding Binford and silhouetting a figure standing next to the glass wall. The short thin figure turned as Binford shut the door.

Scrum was, Binford realized after entering the conference room, a vaguely familiar looking man with heavy-lidded eyes that were as flat and emotionless as his acne-scarred face.

Sprague, when he arrived, looked at Binford in a way that told him that he was being weighed and measured according to whatever standard Sprague used--and he sensed Sprague found him lacking. Dark pants held by suspenders hung from Sprague's lank frame. A bright red tie and French cuffs framed by gold cufflinks completed the uniform of a successful partner. He took his seat opposite from Binford.

"We need to wait for Ms. Dade," he announced, referring to the Assistant Attorney General handling the Ellis habeas suit, as he began ruffling through a folder on the polished table top. "Have you met Mr. Scrum, our investigator?"

Binford had been surprised that an investigator of any sort was involved. He knew from the sheriff's comments that someone had been around town looking into Binford and the Ellis case. But Binford had assumed that Carter was referring to a law student working for the Defense Council out of the University of Virginia.

"Ah, here is Ms. Dade," Sprague looked up at the opening door. "Susan, this is Mr. Binford."

It was Binford's first time meeting Dade in person. Pulled back greying hair, gathered in a tight bun, emaciated thin, hawk-faced, mid-50s; she looked the stereotypical career government lawyer.

Sprague flipped his folder to the first tab and nodded to the court reporter before turning to Binford. "Are you ready to begin?" He asked smiling, his eyes dark pools in the shadow of thick black eyebrows. He stretched his arms forward, clenching his hands in what was clearly a nervous habit, before delving into the questions.

"For the record," he continued, "my name is Roland Sprague, Mordecai Binford is here as well as Susan Dade representing the Attorney General. First order of business. Would you swear in the witness please?" he said looking at the reporter. She looked at Binford, "Raise your right hand." Binford did, immediately struck by the oddness of being the person questioned and under oath rather than being the person asking the questions. "Under penalty of perjury, do you swear to tell the truth and nothing but the truth during these depositions?"

"I do." Truth. Binford held onto that one word, so small but so fundamental and powerful that a whole system of justice was built upon it. Truth. He sensed that Baal Scrum was hostile, but believed that Sprague, being an officer of the court like Binford, would seek the truth and recognize his forthright answers as just that.

Sprague began working his way through Binford's experience, before getting to the guts of the Ellis case itself, at one point asking if lie detector tests were given to all of the witnesses. Binford thought the question odd as he knew, and expected Sprague to know, that lie detector tests were so unreliable that they were not allowed as evidence in a trial. In fact, just to mention the existence of such tests during a trial could almost certainly lead to the judge kicking the case out and starting all over again. Laymen think lie detector tests are science. Law enforcement and criminal attorneys know the opposite to be true.

"I think most were given tests," Binford replied surprised when the assistant attorney general did not raise an objection to the meaningless question. He was not sure how aggressive she should be during a deposition, but he felt more than breathing was required of her. Her inaction puzzled him.

An hour later, still working through the details of a case that Binford barely remembered, Sprague asked about his discovery policy.

In any criminal case, Virginia law requires the prosecutor to reveal certain elements of the case to defense counsel. The Virginia rule is rather restrictive but includes any statements made by the defendant, any scientific tests made, and any evidence that would tend to show the innocence of the defendant. Binford's rule had been to give defense counsel everything he had--often referred to as an open file policy.

"So you are telling me that you had an open file policy, is that correct?" Sprague asked.

"Yes. I give defense counsel everything that I have."

"Does that include the results of lie detector tests?"

"Everything that I have in the file is open for review but often lie detector tests are not forwarded by law enforcement because they cannot be used," Binford replied.

"If a lie detector test showed a witness was lying, would you consider that exculpatory?" Sprague demanded.

"In what sense," Binford answered. "Lie detector tests cannot be evidence so, no, they can't be exculpatory. But if I had them, I would give them to the defense."

"How do you explain that no lie detector tests were given to the defense?"

"I don't know. I gave them everything that was in the file," Binford answered not thinking that the issue of lie detector tests was that important.

"But you would agree that they could be exculpatory."

"I'd want to know about them if I were defense counsel," Binford answered.

An hour later, the legal inquisition came to an end and, dismissed by Sprague, Binford left the building. Driving away he glimpsed the James River tumbling over the rocks below, the dark water roiled around the deadly rocks. His experience, he found, had left him uneasy, in part because the Assistant Attorney General had been too quiet. But, he told himself, he had the truth on his side, and that would protect him from whatever was out there.

As soon as he arrived home, Binford called the sheriff, who had scouted out a description of the trespasser in Binford's back yard. A description which convinced Binford it had been Scrum in his backyard.

MARS--HESPERIA PLANUM

Leotie Thunder knew it was crazy. She knew it was impossible. But there was something about him that spoke to her heart. Spoke to her soul. Immediately. She had dated and even thought she had been in love. But this was different. How could the curve of his lips impart so much to her? The way he looked into her eyes melted her mind, melted her very essence hidden somewhere deep inside: hidden even from herself. Hidden, until he looked at her, until he smiled at her, and then she unfolded, expanded, felt her universe explode into color and possibilities. It was as if he knew everything there was to know about her without speaking.

How could that happen so fast? And in this place?

But the human heart knows no logic, no calculation but the calculus measured by passion and understanding. That was the key in Leotie's mind: passion and understanding. It was that intangible mixture of the two that created love. And in the end, wasn't that what every woman, really, deep down in the inner recesses of her soul, wanted? She had often pondered the essence of love and attraction. But the definition escaped her. But, she knew, she had found love here.

His dark brown eyes said that to her every time their eyes met across the space between the two in the awful confines of the chamber in which they sheltered.

Once, his hand brushed hers as they both reached for water. Was it an accident? She hoped not. Because his touch had opened the world to her and made this madness she found herself in on Mars not only bearable but joyous.

Joyous. How could that happen here? She had not felt that for over a year while she studied music at the University of Tampa. Although the ornate campus exuded beauty and color --she walked a world cast in grey. Cast in shadows and loneliness. Cast in meaninglessness.

Until now.

Leotie knew, despite the irrationality of it all, that her soul's counterpart sat across from her --in a cramped room that stank of unwashed bodies--on the surface of Mars no less. Love swelled and burst through the confines of reason and calculation and filled her with happiness unknown until this day, this place, this world. It was as if the universe had sought out two sparks of humanity and placed them here, on Mars, because that was the only place the two could unite.

She glanced up and saw him looking at her. He did not look away. And hot fire kindled in her breast.

She loved him. She loved him like no other. And yet she was sure he hated her.

MOUNT PONY--THE FEDERAL RESERVE

Despite the chill of the late October evening, Weir found that he was perspiring. He could not afford to let himself be caught because, if he were, then his plan would come crashing down, and his family would be lost to him forever - his family as he had known and loved them. And, he had vowed, he would die if need be, to stop that from happening.

Weir stood outside the center and looked out upon the town of Culpeper. Little did the people who lived there below know what transpired here, he thought. The quiet little town seemed the last place a national conspiracy of the sort Weir was enmeshed within would transpire. And perhaps that *was* why it was in Culpeper. No one would ever suspect that anything of that magnitude could happen here. But, if his plan came to fruition, then everyone would know. Everyone.

He watched a car drive up the side of the mountain, and park at the far end of the asphalt lot dug out of the side of Mount Pony. Nora Burke walked down the lot and past him, not making eye contact. Weir lingered. Taking the air, he had explained to some of the technicians as he made his way out of the building. They hadn't questioned him. Why should they? He was, after all, the security chief. But he needed to be outside at the appropriate time to let Burke know that "the plan" was on schedule and ready to be put into action.

"The Plan." The two had actually laughed about it as they discussed how to get Weir and weapons on Mars. But now that they were about to act, nothing about what was about to happen seemed amusing.

Weir turned and walked into the rough cement-walled center. As he and Burke had arranged, Weir took the elevator back down to his office. She knew he was there and ready to launch.

Burke's specialty was quantum physics. But she knew computers, and she knew the facility's intranet like the back of her hand. Weir needed her to do two things: implant a program that made the security cameras record a loop to show that there was no activity in the areas where he and Burked needed to work and, secondly actually push his pod and the pod full of ordnance into the transport room. Finally, she needed to encode the correct number of pods for transport in the flight data paradigm to ward off any inquiries by Flight Director Fields.

The plan was simple; but its execution was fraught with danger for the both of them. They had no illusions about what would happen should Sims or Group 929 discover the transport. Weir would already be on Mars. Burke would follow. Not voluntarily, of course, but at that point it would not matter. And it could be that neither would catch a ride back. Burke told Weir there had been transports with no return. There were always free transports. She suspected these special deliveries had two purposes but, up until that morning at her house, she had never allowed herself to consider how necessary those special transports were to Group's purpose. When someone needed to "disappear," Group had the perfect dumping ground. And for that matter, so did Sims.

They had learned about the unscheduled free transport earlier that day, nearly a week after Weir had enlisted Burke's help. Weir knew where the pods were and where the ordnance was. He would just have to make do with whatever he found in storage, which, he had given her to understand, was enough.

Weir waited for the signal.

It came in a text from Burke. A single letter: M.

Weir started out the door, but not in time.

Sims.

"I was just coming to see you," he told Sims who stood at the door as he opened it. "I wanted to check with you about some security measures. You see...."

"So, you were coming to see me," Sims interrupted sardonically.

"I understood a transport is planned in two hours," Weir explained. "I wanted to check with you about security measures since I hadn't been informed."

"Yes. Well. I wanted someone else to get some practice at handling these things," Sims said, giving him a knowing look. "I thought you might have other things on your mind right now."

"I do my job, Mr. Sims. You know that. I don't like what you did, but I have a job to do, and I am going to do it."

"Really? I'm surprised. I thought you might take the night off as scheduled. You wouldn't be planning any more arms shipments, would you?"

"Why are you here, Mr. Sims?"

"I would think that is obvious. I don't trust you. When I heard you were on campus, I decided to look in on my freewheeling chief of security."

"Look. I thought we'd taken care of this earlier. I wanted to talk with you about security for the transport. Who do you have overseeing preparation?"

"Martinez."

"Good man."

The two stood eye to eye inches apart.

"Don't forget what's at stake here," Sims said, tapping a photograph of Weir's family on the security officer's desk.

"I never do," Weir replied tightly, his eyes blazing.

When Sims left, Weir sat down, weak with anxiety. It had been a close thing. Martinez complicated the plan, but he would just have to deal with it. *Embrace the suck*, as they termed it back in Iraq. After gathering his wits about him, Weir jumped up and rushed down the hall way to the elevator.

Nora Burke trembled as she slipped the thumb drive into her computer. Ensconced in her cubicle at the transport observation deck--sometimes called the flight deck--she watched the download bar zip across the screen. The program enabling her to control the security cameras downloaded in less than a minute. That was the first order of business. She recorded a thirty-second loop of empty hallway for each of the ten cameras affected by the plan, before programing the cameras to replay the loop over and over until countermanded by her entry of a disable code. Next she accessed the flight director paradigm and coded two more pods into the system, praying that the program covered the cyber trail left by her intrusion, even though she knew that such events were never really untraceable. But the plan called for no one to look very hard for evidence of tampering-- because nothing would appear out of the ordinary--and because transport was so commonplace, so very, horribly, commonplace.

Having downloaded the data and entered the necessary alterations Burke left her station and headed for the pod area, only to find Martinez standing by the pod storage chamber, his hand resting on the sidearm holster at his waist. He wasn't supposed to be there and, even more troubling, she didn't see Weir.

Making his way to the bowels of the center without seeming to rush, Weir heard voices ahead where there should be no voices. As he got closer he recognized Burke and Martinez arguing over access to the pod room.

"Just tell me this, Sergeant Martinez," Nora was saying. "Have the transports been taken to the room?"

"I don't know if you're authorized for that information," he replied, his voice rising.

"Come on, Sergeant. I help on the flight deck. Of course I'm authorized to know this. Otherwise, how am I to do my job?"

"Sargent Martinez, stand down!" Weir ordered as he rounded the corner to the hallway where the two stood.

"Sir! I was told you weren't on duty tonight." Martinez did not take his hand from the holster.

"I said to stand down!" Weir ordered with steel in his voice.

Martinez faltered and slowly lowered his hand.

"What the hell is going on around here?" Weir asked.

The sergeant explained that Sims had put him on strict orders to prohibit access to the pod area and, that with Weir being off duty, Martinez was in charge.

"I should report this whole incident to Mr. Sims," he added sheepishly.

"Martinez. Let Ms. Burke in." Weir ordered after the sergeant's explanation.

"With all due respect Captain Weir, I can't do that without first clearing it with Mr. Sims," he replied. The radio on Martinez's shoulder beeped. "Martinez here," he said into the mike clipped on his left shoulder.

"Have you had contact with Weir?" the Sims' tinny voice said from the device.

Martinez looked at Weir and Burke. Weir shook his head no. Burke also shook her head in the negative.

His loyalty was to Weir. He liked Nora Burke. In fact, she was kind of cute, and he had considered asking her out. Sims was someone in a suit. And not someone to return loyalty if given. That much had

been clear to Martinez from the first time he met the head of the project.
On the other hand, Martinez liked Weir and respected his abilities as an
officer and as a leader. He knew where his loyalty would lie in a foxhole.

He pushed the mike button.

"Negative." Martinez said. Then, releasing the transmit button, "Tell me Captain Weir --what is going on?"

Weir and Burke told the sergeant everything. His eyes saddened when Weir told him about his own family being transported by Sims.

"They did that to me," he said, his voice cracking. "They do it to everyone sooner or later."

"What do you mean they did it to you?" Burke asked reaching out and touching the young security guard's shoulder.

"My cousin Tomas. They sent him off. Sims did it to instill loyalty, he told me. He said he wanted me to know that no one is hurt. But I knew he also meant I could be sent. Anyone could be sent. And, when Tomas, come back he not the same. Not the same at all."

"We want to stop all of that," Weir said. "Will you help?"

After that, it was easy. Nora and Martinez loaded the weapons into one pod and Weir into another. No sedatives, he insisted. Then Martinez pushed the two pods out into the transport room. Three pods hovered. Sitting on the flight deck, Nora looked out to the room below as the two joined to make five. The exact number the altered flight paradigm called for.

Frank Hill and Sims hovered about but did not question the flight since it matched the paradigm in the computer system. Transport had become so commonplace she thought again, that even when things change before our very eyes, we take it as normative. How easily evil could become normal. Standard procedure. Unthinking.

Looking down at the room as the countdown droned on in the background and arcs of electric blue shot across the room, she performed her duties at her instrument panel mechanically, haunted by the fact that Weir lay inside one of those pods. Alone. Awake. On a quest with no end in sight and no plan but to save his family --in a place as removed from earth as heaven is from hell.

And then Weir was gone. The room powered down, but Nora remained at her counsel. "God speed," she whispered to Weir as he left earth's atmosphere.

MARS--HESPERIA PLANUM

Reznik, Steele, Rebecca, and the children tumbled into the sanctuary along with the remainder of the refugees. It was a tight fit. The children stayed close to their mother.

"We can't stay here any longer," Reznik said when Rebecca balked at the plan to expose themselves to the rigors of the Martian surface by going to Gale Crater. "Not with all the commotion Steele and the rest of you have brought. Not that I'm complaining, but these buggers are going to start hunting us down. I don't care how poorly run this place is, I doubt you can just destroy those things and get away with it. We need to get while the getting is good."

"When do we go?" she asked anxiously.

"Tomorrow wouldn't be soon enough," Reznik replied.

And so it was that, early the next "day," the group gathered up what it could of Reznik's cache of food and water along with extra pressure suits he had stashed for all of them.

"I just stripped the suits off transportees in the hive," Reznik explained as he handed them out. No one but Steele understood the import of Reznik's explanation. So only he was burdened by the image of Reznik stripping off suits, or the results of going into the thin Martian atmosphere without them. Better to save someone you knew rather than someone you did not, he told himself. No wonder the bugger was irritable after having made that sort of moral calculation, Steele thought. A new respect for Reznik grew in Steele when he saw the pressure suits and understood where they came from.

Once equipped, the group donned the suits, screwed on their helmets, packed the gear with makeshift straps and containers, and followed Reznik through a maze of tunnels and warehouse-sized rooms, stepping over pipes and mysterious fibrous bundles. Every ounce of weaponry and explosives that came with Steele in the pod found a home on some member of the expedition.

They filed out onto the Martian surface from the same exit Reznik and Steele had used earlier. During the ensuing trek across the orange and brown craters and rock-strewn sand, Reznik took point followed by Steele. Stover took rear guard. The remainder milled in the middle.

At one point, Reznik pointed in the distance to a hanger like rounded structure near the deep chasm that bisected the area, its jagged cliffs in stark contrast to the smoother features of the sloping cratered plain, a structure that, from above, would not even rate a second look by photo analysts at JPL or NASA.

"That's where they keep the skimmers," Reznik told them. "I've only seen a total of three; so, let's hope we get lucky."

Steele marveled inwardly at the incongruity of it all. Clearly the complex was large and sophisticated but, like Reznik, he too was surprised at the aliens' obtuseness. Had this been a human base, the area would be on lockdown after the destruction the group had created in the transport room. Surely, somehow, a controlling entity knew there were hostiles amongst the personnel. Surely there would be a response. He gripped his black matte M-4 Carbine tighter.

Down through the dust and stones they walked, dust devils skittering in the distance, giving Steele, in particular, a better understanding of the size and complexity of the compound, including as it did, nine other structures like the one they had just left, structures that looked so organic that they might have been formed from the ground itself. But structure, he realized, was not really the right term for what was on the sloping surface.

Steele had heard of advances in three-dimensional manufacturing. He liked to read the science pages of the *New York Times* online, and he had seen a story about the new manufacturing process. Reznik's explanation made perfect sense to Steele. Reznik postulated that, in fact, the whole complex was probably the result of nano-driven three-dimensional manufacture. Obviously, a process way beyond that of humans, but using the same technological concepts. Certainly, it would explain how the area did not show the scars of construction a similar human-created base would exhibit. The buildings themselves grew from the ground around them. And Reznik had hypothesized that this also explained why most of the structures were underground--to get closer to the raw material necessary. Including water. Water. That had surprised Steele as it had Reznik. Mars was abundantly blessed with water, but it was all underground. The small amounts that made it to the surface froze or boiled off quickly giving the illusion of a desert world. Not so, Reznik assured Steele--even as he drank his own recycled urine supplemented by some other source known only to Reznik. That had not given Steele a lot of confidence until Reznik pointed out how crucial water had to be to manufacture the structures themselves. The fact that Reznik had a hard time accessing water did not make it rare--only hard to get when one lived on the edge as Reznik had for almost a year.

No matter, Steele thought to himself. I'm daydreaming. *Got to stay focused.* He turned around to see who was following. The group stayed bunched up and silent, except for Stover who hung farther back, his feet kicking up reddish dust, scanning for threats. Just as Steele was doing himself.

After several hours of trudging through the dry, alien landscape, Reznik called a halt where they sheltered under a rocky outcrop. Below them stretched the sloping side of Tyrrhena Mons, the mountain that dominated the cratered site. It was then that Steele realized what Reznik had warned them of before the trek began. There was no way to drink water while inside a suit and so while he did sweat, and the suit vented the moisture in the same mysterious manner in which it absorbed oxygen, he could not ingest water, leaving his mouth as dry as the Martian dust swirling around him. Steele looked up to see the Martian moons zipping across the sky. It unnerved him to see celestial bodies act so out of character from his earth-based point of reference. The moon moved but not visibly, and the difference hammered home again how far away and alien Mars was from his suburban home in Fairfax, Virginia.

"Up! We need to move!" Reznik said, calling a halt to the too-short break. The other nine shambled into the proper order and marched off towards the hanger. Feet moved up and down unused to the lighter gravity and, as a result, stumbled more in the loose rock and dust. Steele thought the lighter gravity would be a help in the trek but, in fact, the oddness of weight combined with the added mass of what they carried made for sometimes treacherous footing. This was made all too apparent when Rebecca's foot slipped on the side of a crater. The loose scree slid out from under her weight, taking her down the side of the depression in an uncontrolled tumble. Lighter gravity and same mass meant the same inertia and the same capacity to hurt. She banged her head roughly against a boulder at the bottom.

"I'm alright. I'm alright," she had said waving her hands. The group had to form a human chain, linking hand to hand, to reach her and help her ascent over the loose material.

After that incident, all were more alert to their footing.

And, it was because of that, that Steele didn't see the aliens leaping across the landscape towards him and the others until they were almost upon the weary band.

"Two o'clock! Form skirmish line!" Steele yelled running forward, his M-4 raised, hoping against hope that the ammo would fire in the oxygen-free Martian atmosphere. As Steele shouted the warning, the men spread out in a ragged line to catch the oncoming threat. Stover ranged to the left in a forward flanking position. Leotie, Rebecca, the two children, and Abbey Wentworth formed a second reserve to protect their rear, the three women armed ready to jump in as needed.

"How many?" Steele asked of Stover.

Stover, moving to higher ground, had the advantage provided by the elevated view scape. "I see five," he cried. "They're travelling fast, but they're in line."

"Right, you don't fire until we do."

"Roger that," Stover replied.

"Alright, everyone, just like we planned, pick your target and fire," Steele instructed. "When it goes down -- move to the next target. Fire in front of you before moving to another--remember--zones of fire. You guys in the rear be ready to back us up."

"They're almost here," Stover announced. "Get ready."

"Safety off!" Steele shouted. "Check 'em."

"Coming over the hill!"

At the first sight of the hideous beings swarming over the rise, Steele, like the rest, opened fire on the monster coming closest to him. Slugs pounded out of the short carbine barrel and slammed into hard shell and soft interior. Stover opened fire from the left flank, his M-4 Carbine spewing slugs of death down onto the advancing aliens. Behind, Steele was aware that Wentworth had fired off a grenade, and he saw the corresponding explosion of ground in front of the advancing line.

Field Marshal Helmuth von Moltke, the elder, famously wrote of military strategy that "no battle plan survives first contact with the enemy".

Steele and the band of humans on Mars were about to learn that lesson again.

GARY CLOSE

CHAPTER 18

"THE UNITED STATES CANNOT BE SEEN AS UNABLE TO LAUNCH MANNED CRAFT TO THE MOON OR ANYWHERE ELSE. AT THE SAME TIME WE CANNOT RELY EXCLUSIVELY ON ROBOTIC CRAFT TO MONITOR MARS. THE AE BAN ON MANNED EXPLORATION -- AND ITS ABILITY TO DESTROY CRAFT THAT IT PERCEIVES AS A VIOLATION OF THAT BAN -- PREVENTS A COMPREHENSIVE ELIMINATION OF THE AE THREAT WHICH WE KNOW IS BASED ON MARS. COVERT SUPPORT OF PRIVATE EFFORTS TO LAUNCH MANNED SPACECRAFT MAY ALLOW FOR FAILURE WITHOUT NEGATIVE PUBLICITY TO THE ADMINISTRATION. IT IS RECOMMENDED THAT PRESIDENT OBAMA END THE SHUTTLE PROGRAM AND TURN OVER MANNED EFFORTS TO PRIVATE INDUSTRY. PRIVATE INDUSTRY CAN SUSTAIN FAILURE SO LONG AS THE UNITED STATES COVERTLY FUNDS ITS EFFORTS. FOR THE ADMINISTRATION THIS GIVES SUFFICIENT COVERAGE ON THE ISSUE REGARDING THE FAILURE OF NASA TO ADVANCE MANNED MISSIONS TO MARS." -- CONFIDENTIAL MEMO FROM SUSAN RICE, NATIONAL SECURITY ADVISOR TO PRESIDENT OBAMA, 2013.

--EXCERPTS FROM THE PRESIDENTIAL BRIEFING PAPERS ON THE ROSWELL INCIDENT

FORT MEADE--NSA HQ

"Ah, yes. Very good. I'll get back to you."

Conyer Somerfield put the cell phone in his pocket and continued strolling around the manicured park surrounding the boxy glass building which comprised the NSA campus. The period of late October and early November was always his favorite time of the year, bringing with it sunny, usually mild temperatures, brilliant leaf colors, and the anticipation of winter.

He contemplated the ramifications of the phone call from Buck Mullen at Scag, Black and Mullen. Binford's performance at the depositions with Sprague reportedly had been spectacularly bad. Bad for Binford. Good for Sprague and therefore, good for Conyer's plan. Perhaps the best news was that the idiot prosecutor had said that false lie detector results were exculpatory. Well, that wasn't exactly what he'd said, but Sprague knew how to turn what Binford did say into the absolute affirmation that they *were* exculpatory and, therefore *should* be turned over to defense counsel.

Of course, lie detector tests were never admissible in court and, if they were even mentioned, it could be grounds for a mistrial. In fact, lie detector results were not evidence at all and therefore not something the rules required prosecutors to give to defense counsel.

Somerfield weighed his options. He could spring the trap now. Or allow the pressure to build. The newspaper headlines had to create political pressure on Binford. The key was to know when there was enough to give Binford an out. With honor of course. All Boy Scouts needed to convince themselves that they did what they did because it was the right thing to do. The fact was that he had doubts about how this Binford fellow would react, but he reminded himself, Binford was a creature of politics, and Somerfield knew the pressure points in that cesspool of human endeavor.

Pulling out his cell phone, he speed-dialed Dorcas Snider at the *Culpeper Dispatch*.

"What do you have for me today?" she asked, her New York accent thickening with anticipation.

"First of all," Somerfield said, "this is all off the record. Let us establish that."

"Of course. Off the record."

"Well, then, I think I should direct you to the depositions taken by your prosecutor."

"What about them?"

"He admits that false lie detector results are exculpatory, and yet none were provided to the defense in the Ellis case."

"I thought the Ellis case had been already upheld by the Virginia Supreme Court."

"Yes. Quite so. Very astute, Ms. Snider. But the Supreme Court did not have at its disposal the fact that this very important evidence was withheld from the defense."

"How do I get a copy of that deposition?" she demanded.

"It won't be filed in the court just yet. However, I can provide for you the brief prepared by Mr. Ellis's attorney which outlines this very fact and describes the impact such a flagrant withholding of information could have had on his defense. He's going to file it tomorrow."

"I'd like to run the story tomorrow."

"No. Ms. Snider. You cannot use this until it is actually filed with the court. I am merely giving you advance notice. If you write something and publish it before the brief is filed, I believe Mr. Binford would have very good grounds to sue you if, in the end, the brief is not filed."

"I'll hold until you tell me it's been filed," she said with obvious reluctance.

"I'll do you one better, Ms. Snider," Somerfield told her. "I'll direct you to the court website so you can see the brief itself. There is electronic filing now in the Northern Federal District. And, if you want, I'll have the Defense Council attorney call you for background information."

"Thank you. I'll start the story as soon as you email me the brief."

"But you will hold it? You will hold the story?" Somerfield's voice took a steely edge.

"Of course."

"I must say it *is* refreshing to speak with someone in your profession who understands it as well as you," Somerfield assured her. "I assume it won't be long before I see your byline at the *Washington Post*."

"I just want to do what's right for the community," Snider said self-importantly. "From what Baal Scrum tells me, Binford is a cancer on the legal profession. My gut always told me he was two-faced, but with what I've learned from you and Scrum, a story like this is a public duty to publish. Hopefully, it will expose Binford for what he really is."

Somerfield's next call was back to Buck to tell the senior partner to get a copy of the brief to the Dorcas woman.

"Don't worry, Buck. That cow wouldn't burp without my say so. I've got her primed to run a story on Binford. But she'll hold it until I tell her otherwise. What's that? Damn legal ethics, Buck. Since when did you care about that? We're talking national security here. Don't forget, the federal government has the right to hit you with a drone missile while you sit in one those big defenseless towers on the James River. So legal ethics are whatever we say they are in this case. Don't worry, I've got this under control. You just hold up your end."

Conyer pushed the end call icon on his smart phone. He hated it when someone got wet feet. Buck had known the score when he'd first hooked up at the gravy train that emanated from the NSA, and he damn well better remember the deal he'd made with *that* devil. That's for damn sure.

Somerfield's next call, one he made with considerable pleasure, was to Binford.

INTERPLANETARY TRANSIT—DAY ONE

Weir was not ready for the complete immobilization that the nano-engineered-resin enforced on his body. He could not move. Period. He could breath. That much was clear. Somehow the resin allowed the movement of ribs and diaphragm, but nothing else.

Weir was not claustrophobic, but he panicked by not being able to move anything except his eyes and his mouth. Furthermore, he did not know how long the trip had been so far. It felt like weeks, but he knew in total it could only last two days.

God help Steele, he thought. How had he done it?

He had no idea what he would do when he got out of the pod. That was the problem. The first order of business was to get to the weapons as fast as he could and, after that, find his family. But how to do that, he had no idea. And once he found his family, then what? Again, he didn't know. *Embrace the suck. That's the best I got for a plan right now.*

His family. Rebecca's face floated across his mind. He thought again of how they met in Washington, he a young 2nd Lieutenant anxious about his first assignment to Iraq and she a freshman student at George Mason University. She caught his eye on the metro ride into DC. Although he had been supposed to get off at the Pentagon, he decided then and there to follow her into Farragut Square where the young brunette skipped off the train with three other girls.

Using his new uniform to best effect, he had bumped into them, excusing himself profusely and then addressing himself directly at Rebecca, he had asked if they knew the way to the Vietnam Wall.

That was all it had taken. Military men, even those with little confidence, had had no problem meeting girls in the patriotic days after the invasion, especially in Washington, then a capital at war, and very aware of the need for unity and good will amongst citizens still reeling from that awful day in September when the World Trade Center crashed into dust.

And so they had visited the Vietnam memorial together. With knowing looks, Rebecca's friends had made up an excuse to take off on their own, leaving Weir alone with the young student. They'd walked along the mall and taken lunch underneath the Hirshhorn Museum next to the inner court fountain, laughing when the wind picked up flecks of water and spray from the towering stream and flung it onto their table. He wandered through the art exhibit not looking at the paintings at all--instead he watched her as she scrutinized each brush stroke and shaped stone. All of it a mystery to Weir--but one thing he became increasingly sure of as the afternoon wore on--that he wanted to see her again.

And he had.

It all seemed so foreign now. Normal no longer existed. Weir's world collapsed to the dark coffin in which he was riding to Mars.

Weir lapsed into unconsciousness. When he woke, he panicked. The constraint became too much. Raging and screaming, rationality skittered out and into the void beyond the streaking pod between planets.

Later, Weir returned to sanity. He remembered the stupid affair he had in Boulder. Stupid. Stupid.

But he would find his wife. He would save her. He would not let Sims do to her and to his children what he had seen done to so many others.

Weir held onto hope and to hate. Hope that he would live so to see his family home. Hate for what Sims and the whole program at the Federal Reserve on Mount Pony did to him, to his family, and to humanity.

GAINESVILLE-- VIRGINIA

Twenty years earlier, Gainesville had consisted of an octagonal 19th century barn in the middle of a three-hundred acre field, bordered by Route 29 and the Norfolk Western Rail Spur to the Atlas Steel works. Binford remembered when the Prince William County hamlet had been nothing more than a cross roads intersected by railroad tracks. Now the barn had given way to the spreading commercial development coming out of Washington, DC. The increased traffic coming off of I-66 had created a need for more car lanes, more traffic lights and more overpasses on what used to be the flat, isolated cattle field.

The prosecutor turned into the Gateway Commercial Center and parked next to Starbucks where he had agreed to meet Conyer Somerfield. Binford normally did not meet defense counsel anywhere but in his office, but he was intrigued by the federal attorney, even though he would only hint at what he wanted to discuss. Clearly the tall, southern lawyer possessed a mind like a steel trap, and there was something else about him that drew Binford. It was the same sort of attraction a deadly snake creates. You know it's deadly, but somehow you cannot help but be drawn to the creature.

Not that he had come here totally unprepared. Binford did his own research on Somerfield as well. While at one time a person could remain anonymous, the internet made that feat as obsolete as the long-gone octagonal barn in the flat Prince William County field. And that was doubly true for someone practicing law. There are, after all, the bar associations and their lists of members, committees and the like. Furthermore, the continuing-legal-education credits every attorney is required to complete each year to retain his or her license are available for public scrutiny. As a result, Binford knew Somerfield had enjoyed a Virginia private education: prep school at Woodberry Forest in Orange County, College at Hampton-Sydney, law school at the University of Richmond. His education spoke of connections throughout the moneyed elite in the Old Dominion as well as up and down the East Coast. So, Binford understood his adversary in court had not only been a good attorney, but he had connections far beyond Binford's more middle-class upbringing, all of which was enough, in itself, to make him curious to meet the man outside the courtroom.

The federal attorney, when he arrived, wore an expensive blue blazer with gold crested buttons, a button- down blue oxford, shirt and a red bow tie complimented by what appeared to be personally tailored, tan khakis, argyle socks and a pair of tan leather-soled Italian wing tips with the result that it made Binford feel particularly shabby in his poor-fitting off the rack grey suit.

Somerfield made a show of looking about for listening ears. Then, satisfied that no one was close enough to hear their conversation, he looked at Binford and nodded again.

"Good to see you, Mr. Binford."

"Same here." Binford sipped his coffee. Neither made an effort to shake hands.

"I imagine you're curious about my purpose in talking with you here," Somerfield said briskly.

"Would this have anything to do with the motions that got faxed to the *Culpeper Dispatch*?" Binford asked, not bothering to hide his irritation at the grandstanding the federal attorney had used to get headlines on the motion the two had argued in Circuit Court.

"Ha. That," Somerfield said with a grin. "Well, the press is the bastion of freedom and the informer of the public. Wouldn't you say?" Somerfield's eyebrows shot up to emphasize his levity over the ill-concealed accusation.

"It's not how we practice law in Culpeper," Binford replied sullenly.

"Look, I don't want any unpleasantness," Somerfield assured him. "You won the argument. The judge denied my motion, and Mr. Sims and Mr. Weir are scheduled to appear in November before your special grand jury. Allow me a little room to grandstand. After all, my client has to think I did something on his behalf. We both knew you would win, but clients, well, they are a little less realistic. Throw 'em a little twist and giggle I always say."

"So what's this meeting about if not about the hearing?" Binford asked determined to get straight to the point.

"Direct. Yes, I like that. Let us do be direct." Somerfield sipped his coffee, then resumed: "You won the motion. That was a given. But the federal government, whom ultimately I represent, does not want these two men subpoenaed. Even more so, the federal government wants this whole matter dropped. How is that for direct?" Somerfield's tone was light, even jovial. His eyebrows twitched with mirth.

"Why would I drop the grand jury investigation?" Binford demanded. "Two people died. Your Mr. Weir signed an investigative report that relies on what are clearly doctored documents. Mr. Sims is his superior. We want to know how Mr. and Mrs. Wood died, and we don't want to hear that the crime scene photos prove a murder-suicide. They do nothing of the sort. In fact, the photos look to be staged. So again, why would I drop the grand jury investigation?"

"Ah. Yes. Well, that's a good question, and one I would expect you to ask. But I want to be sure you understand the position of my clients, and more specifically, the United States Government, which is that there was a murder- suicide on federal property at the Warrenton Training Center. Furthermore, it is a federal matter and therefore, outside the jurisdiction of a state court. So, even if your grand jury were to recommend indictments, they would be challenged-- most strenuously I might add. And then I must protest the use of the term 'doctored.' Mr. Weir and Mr. Sims are well respected professionals. What you allege is a slur and a slander, and there is also the matter of your career to consider."

"My career? What are you talking about?" Binford fumed.

Smiling, Somerfield pulled a document from a leather satchel and handed it to Binford. "Take a look at this, and then let's talk," he said. "I'll give you some time to digest it all while I check my email."

Mystified, Binford took the proffered documents. Shock registered quickly as he scanned the brief and the attached copy of his deposition. The brief, authored by Roland Sprague, alleged prosecutorial misconduct in the withholding of exculpatory evidence in the Ellis trial--specifically, the lie detector tests-- and requested that the conviction be thrown out by the federal judge.

"This is meaningless." Binford exclaimed. "You know as well as I do that lie detector tests are inadmissible."

"Well, yes. But you did say that you thought they were exculpatory."

"No. I said I would want to see them."

"Same thing."

"No, it is not."

"I think Judge Tulkinghorn will rule they were exculpatory, and that you should have given them over."

"I doubt that. It's not the law."

"Ha." Somerfield allowed a worldly snort to express his appreciation for Judge Tulkinghorn's erratic decisions in the past. "You *do* realize you are speaking of retired Judge Tulkinghorn? Retired, ninety-year-old Tulkinghorn whose cats wonder about the courtroom defecating at will? Retired Judge Tulkinghorn with a compliment of inexperienced interns who love to write opinions? You *do* realize that?"

There was no denying the insinuations, and Somerfield knew it.

"And then, Mr. Binford, we have to consider how the *Culpeper Dispatch* will handle this."

Again, Binford did not reply.

"So, do you think this-this Dorcas Snider is capable of understanding the nuances of legal reasoning?"

"What does she have to do with anything?"

"Hmm…well let me be direct again. Shall I? Ms. Snider believes she has a good grasp of the law. Laughable really, but then there you have it. She will write a story, or should I say stories that, given her style of reporting, will, in all probability, sink your career."

Somerfield pulled out another document and handed it to Binford.

"I'll save you the trouble of reading this," he said. "It's a bar complaint based on the brief. I suspect that probably Ms. Snider will find out about this as well."

Somerfield leaned back in the leather chair and allowed Binford time to stew before he reeled him in.

"Now again to be very clear," Somerfield said, "your Ms. Snider will write what I can only assume will be negative articles. This follows on the articles she wrote regarding my motion and the motions filed in the Ellis case earlier. It's a really unfortunate chain of events, I must say. But it is what it is. And I should also point out that your little newspaper has the most unfortunate habit of allowing unsigned blogs after the stories online. I suspect that could get very nasty very quickly."

"You seem to know a lot about Culpeper," Binford retorted.

"I learned a long time ago it is always wise to be prepared. I'm sure you've learned the same lesson once or twice. But the point is that this will get ugly very quickly. Very ugly. I suppose I should tell you that the Defense Council is well connected, and by that I mean connected to the press. I suspect Ms. Snider's stories will be pushed by the Defender Council to all of their fellow travelers in the news media. And here, let me be direct, I mean the *Washington Post*, *Chicago Tribune*, *New York Times*, *Huffington Post*, *MSNBC*. So I repeat again, this can get ugly especially if it goes viral. Just think of the story line: corrupt small town southern prosecutor frames innocent man. This will, with a little help, become a national scandal."

"And?" Binford asked sensing there was more.

"There is a way out of this," Somerfield said, pushing his coffee to one side and leaning in. "This is a matter of the utmost national security. There are no rules here. Do you understand that? No rules but those that will ensure the survival of the country. I can tell you that, within those parameters, that all of this can go away, if, that is, you call off the grand jury. It's that simple."

"Are you saying that you can control a federal judge?" Binford asked, stunned by the implications of what Somerfield proposed.

"I think you used the operative term, Mr. Binford. *Federal.* This is a federal matter. It impacts the national security of the United States --and, let me assure you, the United States government is determined to protect itself. You would be well advised to cooperate."

"That sounds like a threat."

"Call it professional courtesy," Somerfield said, rising. "Do let me know what you decide. But decide quickly. The brief will be filed tomorrow. Think carefully about this, Mr. Binford. If this gets out, you won't just be dealing with bad press, or a bar complaint, or even some sort of recall effort. Your reputation will disappear down the same rat hole as that of the people you've prosecuted. I doubt you'll find any sympathy as you go down. And remember, if you cooperate, you will be doing your country a service." He allowed a small smile to flit across his long thin face. "Good day to you, Mr. Binford." He turned and sauntered out.

After he left, Binford remained seated, trying to process what he had just been told. At the age of forty-three, he was in the midst of what looked like a promising and long career in law and politics. He'd already been approached about running for the House of Delegates. All of that would disappear if the documents he had in his hand were filed and publicized, and Dorcas Snider's stories, he knew, would take on a new level of animosity. Everything Somerfield said, Binford knew to be true. It would be the end of all things for him.

With a jerk, he stood and walked outside. Near the Starbucks, a small park surrounded a mounted granite globe, its otherwise glass smooth surface floating free on a water cushion in the platform on which it turned. He could with effort make the globe spin, its tons of mass sliding on a watery film, amazingly moved by the concerted effort of just one man. He pushed the globe making it spin.

What did the world care whether he instituted the grand jury or not? No one but Sheriff Carter cared about whatever it was that happened in that sad little field-- captured on those photographs attached to the doctored crime incident report. He really didn't know the Wood couple. He remembered the haunted look in their eyes as they quizzed him about Culpeper. A nice enough couple, but were they worth the loss of his reputation? Were they worth the loss of all the good he could accomplish as Commonwealth's Attorney or in Richmond as a Delegate? Wasn't that something he ought to consider?

The globe continued to move of its own momentum unaffected by Weir's internal questioning. He had always thought of himself as a patriotic American who would do the right thing when the crunch came. Wasn't it the right thing to cooperate with the United States government when you'd been told that national security was at stake? How could that be wrong?

Then why, he asked himself, did he not feel right about it? Why the nagging whisper tugging from deep inside telling him this was wrong? Everything about the situation was wrong. The deception, the threats, blackmail, and death: all of it spoke of something else, something unholy and profane.

Binford tried to close his mind to that small still voice. He knew one thing. If he continued to proceed with the grand jury, Conyer Somerfield was right, his life would be ruined, his career path cut short, his reputation destroyed. And what would it mean for his family? Would they look at him the same after the storm came? And his friends, would they whisper behind his back or just melt away?

Dorcas Snider hunched over her computer screen grinding out another installment in the series of stories on Mordecai Binford's misconduct. "Alleged misconduct" she thought to herself but decided not to include that particular adjective.

Snider had never liked Mordecai Binford. In fact, she had never really liked Culpeper. Overweight, she hated the heat that made her uncomfortable in the south, as well as the attention paid to the ballooning tattoos on her arms and legs. She hated the conservatism.

She hated the religiosity. For God's sake, she often thought as she sat at a Board of Supervisor's meeting, do we really have to listen to some religious nut with a degree or a pastorate offer a prayer before a meeting? She wanted to protest it but knew that would sink her job. So, despite all of that, she stayed because the *Culpeper Dispatch* was the only place that would hire her. She took no umbrage from the lack of job offers or the poor prospects of moving on. Sadly, newspapers were folding at an alarming rate and anyone who could get a job at a daily paper felt lucky--and stayed. The salary was a pittance but she had convinced herself that money did not matter. Making a difference in the world is what mattered.

And she wanted, in the worst way, to change this world. Binford was a problem she thought, a powerful man in a powerful position with a small town mentality. During Christmas, the Binford family often participated in a Christmas open house to benefit charity. She'd nearly choked when, touring his house, she'd seen a portrait of Robert E. Lee in the dining room. The fact that he commissioned a portrait of Ronald Reagan to hang in the Commonwealth Attorney's office only made him that much worse in her estimation. Every slur she heard about the man over the years she had stored up, mixing the innuendo in a toxic stew of envy and enmity that festered deep in her soul. The portraits, in her opinion, were only the outward expressions of the man's racism and conservative mindset. And those things she hated.

And now she had proof of the man's hypocrisy. Not just hypocrisy but according to the Defense Council's attorney, actual malice. Snider wanted to believe more than anything that the defendant Roland Ellis, all those years ago, had been unjustly jailed because that would mean Binford, the author of the injustice, would finally pay for his duplicity, rattling, in the process, the very foundations of the smug little world she found herself trapped within. Yes. Rattle it to the ground.

"Long time prosecutor, Mordecai Binford, has been accused of prosecutorial misconduct, according to a Defense Council brief filed in U.S. District Court," she wrote. "Binford failed to give defense counsel exculpatory evidence, that is, evidence that would help the defendant, despite a legal obligation to do so. The failure casts a long shadow of doubt on the beleaguered prosecutor, who admitted the failure in a sworn deposition taken last week."

That was the tone she needed to call attention to what was going on. She just might win a press award if she pursued the story long enough, repeating the specifics of a story every time a new piece of the puzzle fell into place.

Binford would have a hard time surviving this, she thought. All the better. The world needed changing, and the first thing to change was the prosecutor of this little God-forsaken town.

She would wait for the go-ahead to print. But she wanted to get it out as soon as her source told her the paperwork had been filed.

Binford and his wife, Kate, sat in front of the fireplace. Binford's handiwork burned merrily away casting shadows about the room.

"So that's it," he concluded, reviewing Conyer Somerfield's deal.

"You know what you have to do, Mordecai," Kate said evenly.

Binford knew the answer as well but he wanted to hear his wife say it. "What?" he asked.

"You have to do the right thing," she said. "You need to follow through with the grand jury."

"I know."

The fire flickered and subsided, casting the two in a pale yellow light, while darkness loomed around them.

MARS: HESPERIA PLANUM

Emptying his magazine, Stover reached around and slammed another into place as he continued to fire the M-4 into the advancing alien line which took no notice of either him, or of the fire coming from Steele and the group hunkered down behind boulders with Wentworth in the center firing off grenades.

Stover saw chips fly off the alien bodies as a slug would strike home. But still they advanced at a run.

"I'm losing the flank!" Stover yelled into his helmet. And again, he wondered how it was that the suits even had radio communication and to what purpose? The random thought winked in and out of existence as quickly as a firefly blinks.

"Switch to grenades!" Steele ordered.

Everyone in the group had grenade launchers mounted to the underside of their carbines. It was an easy switch. After a pause, and before the aliens were upon them, a volley arrowed out and hit two aliens directly destroying them in a gout of gore, the missed shots landing behind and detonating to little effect. Stover looked around the terrain and saw no remaining threats but now was hampered from firing towards the aliens because he would in effect be firing back into his own group. The battle plan called for him to remain on post unless circumstances dictated something different. With two casualties, Stover felt the aliens would be no match for his comrades.

Stover was dead wrong.

The remaining three anthropoid creatures bounded up and over the line landing behind Wentworth and the second group. In a lightning fast move, one grasped Wentworth about the waist while the remaining two feinted towards the group only retreating when Wentworth was dragged away screaming.

When Steele yelled, "Regroup!" the front line ran to protect the smaller support group by getting between them and the aliens. All the while every com device echoed with Wentworth's incoherent screams mixed with the cries of the others.

"Quiet!" Steele ordered. "Quiet down everyone! Stover, do you see them?"

"They're about half a click away and booking it. They still have her."

"Wentworth? Wentworth? Can you hear me?" Steele shouted over the screams.

"Yes, but barely," she moaned.

"How badly are you hurt?" Steele asked, only to be answered by silence.

"Wentworth? Wentworth?" Steele's transmission reached out to emptiness.

The group stood stunned at the quickness of it all.

"I don't see them anymore. Too far." Stover said.

"Forget her, we've got to move!" Reznik said. "Get your gear and let's go!"

Needing no other urging, the group formed a line as before, picking up and distributing Wentworth's ammo and gear amongst the remaining nine.

"Stover, you take right flank. I'm taking left flank," Steele ordered. "Keep an eye out. Reznik, you're point. If they come back, we do it the same again."

As he jogged off to the left and ahead, Reznik and Stover moved to their respective positions ahead while Howington covered the rear.

"Move!" Steele yelled. The survivors jogged off, stepping around the jumbled remains of the two aliens that died.

Now it was a stumbling exhausted race to the hanger.

Reznik knew the general direction. He had no path but the way before was relatively clear. The hanger, their objective, was ahead. Reznik had a hard time judging distance, but he estimated it about three miles in the distance. Three miles. On earth that can be the same as thirty miles in effort--terrain dictated all. Three miles on a flat plain would be nothing. But the group had to traverse rolling hills, steep sided craters, boulders the size of small buildings and gripping sand. The march ahead, Reznik knew from past experience, would take more out of the group than any of them could imagine.

Scanning the horizon, always keeping the semi-round dark opening ahead, he saw nothing. But he was aware that any number of dangers could lurk in the shadows or behind a rise in the land.

"Keep your eyes peeled," Steele ordered.

"Safeties off?" Howington asked.

"Good idea," Steele replied. "Safety off. Just keep your fingers away from the triggers. Make sure a round is chambered. We need to go hot."

Each member of the group checked and modified their weapons to fit the command, and then, in the same arrowhead configuration, they wound through the hills and craters. Those who had not been on the surface before marveled at the strangeness of it all, even though each realized that danger was all about them. Rebecca and her children comprised the core of the formation. She had taken Wentworth's duties with the grenades since they all understood that those were the weapons that worked to great effect and should be protected. Unspoken was the fact that the children were with her, and at some primal level it was understood by everyone that they should be protected at all costs.

"No weapons," Howington observed as they started off. "I just realized they didn't use any weapons."

"I've never seen any weapons," Reznik replied. "It's just a very strange place. You'd think if they were hunting us that they would be armed. Even after knowing that we are armed, they persist in acting as if we aren't."

"It makes no sense." Howington said.

"Like I said, operational control here sucks. And don't they remind you of insects? I don't mean their appearance, but the way they mass and attack."

"Think they will be armed now?" Howington asked.

"Who knows?" Reznik said. "But my guess is not."

After an hour of slogging Reznik saw a glint ahead. "I've got something."

"Where?"

"Ahead to the left. In a crater. I saw something move, I think."

"Right," Steele told him. "We'll angle away but still move towards the hanger. I'm coming over to Stover's flank. Howington, that means you watch the rear and the right flank." Steele said.

"We're close enough to the hanger. Can we run to it and set up there?" Howington asked.

"I think, if we hole up out here, more and more will come." Reznik said. "Yeah, we've got to run and gun it."

"Reznik is spot on," Steele told them. "Run and gun. Everyone at a jog. When the bastards get closer, we'll stop long enough to launch off a volley of grenades."

As the group picked up its pace, they saw the creatures rise and fall across the cratered Martian terrain.

"They're angling towards the hanger," Howington gasped.

It was a deadly race as the creatures moved closer until, when they were only 600 feet distant, well within the range of their M203 grenades, Steele called a halt.

"Right lads, let's hit 'em on my mark!" Steele yelled. He watched the ragged bunch of civilians get on one knee and aim the carbine mounted launchers towards the oncoming threat.

"They're bunched up. So, pick a target and lead but at this range this HE ordnance should make a difference."

Eight of the appendaged beings were running and jumping across the reddish rocks and craters now. There seemed to be no leader, and they had not as of yet reacted to his own group's stationary position. Perhaps they were unaware of the hidden humans, but Steele doubted that explained the oddly nonreactive alien behavior. Had they been armed or more --and here Steele could think of no better word than "cognizant"-- he and the rest of the survivors, hiding amongst the rocks, would stand no chance.

"Everyone get ready!" he cried. "Pick your target and lead it. Remember it takes a wee bit for the grenade to get to its target. Aim low. I don't want you over-shooting. I'd rather hit low and get some rock shrapnel. On my mark. Four. Three. Two. One. Fire!"

Steele pulled the double trigger on his own launcher as did the others. Seven carbine mounted launchers coughed out arcing projectiles of destruction towards the dun -colored monsters scampering across the sand.

Before the grenades had landed, the group reloaded and fired a second volley, sending sand, rocks and gore flying.

"Reload!" Steele yelled and a third ragged volley angled towards the six remaining aliens. "Now, up to the hanger!"

"Move your arse, you idiot!" Steele ordered Stover who stood transfixed by the raw destruction. He turned, and they took off at a stumbling run, Steele taking the rearguard, firing off grenade after grenade as the others scrambled up to the hanger opening.

"Ok, Reznik," Steele called out once he got to the hanger wall. "I got us this far. How do we get in? And make it damn quick because they're still coming. We don't have an unlimited supply of grenades, and I figure that, once we hijack one of these skimmer contraptions, they aren't going to just let us go off on a joy-ride. We need to conserve ammo."

"Quit worrying. I know exactly what I'm doing," Reznik replied. "Listen everyone. This will be easy if you do exactly what I say. Walk in a line. Do not do anything quickly. We want to look and act like the herd of mind controls just in case one of those things is inside. I know you haven't seen the other humans, but just act stupid, and you can't be too wrong. Just don't run. That seems to trigger something in the aliens. Now follow me."

Leadership of the group shifted, as planned, to Reznik. Steele, being the one with the most military experience, was in charge of combat, but Reznik controlled everything else.

"I'm staying out here until I know you're inside," Steele said.

"No. We stay together." Howington said.

"No time to argue," Steele replied. "We've got four hostiles out there right now. I'll hold them back until you give me the word that the skimmer is secure and ready to roll. And I'm going to lay a little C-4 for them."

"You persuaded me." Reznik said sarcastically, adding, "Cowboy."

Reluctantly the group lined up single-file behind Reznik, shuffling their feet, and keeping radio silence until, rounding the edge of the tunnel opening, they walked inside. The outside reddish illumination shafted into the downward sloped tunnel giving the place an eerie atmosphere. From the sides of the structure, gas vented, leaving a steam-like trail to drift up along the ceiling. Ahead, they saw a single vehicle floating, tethered to a flat loading platform. Reznik noted that the skimmer floated about three feet off the ground. Cigar shaped, it had an observation port at the front and another at the side facing them. The outer skin sprouted angled antenna that streamed backward from the front observation area. There was no extended under-carriage below, just a flat exposed metallic plate. And, since there was nothing even remotely looking like a door, entry was clearly to be made from the loading dock.

Reznik led the group to the loading platform, where, gripping the resin-like edge, he hoisted himself up and motioned the others to follow. The group helped bring up the ammo and supplies they had lugged in the hours-long slog across the surface. Howington and the others positioned themselves to fire should someone enter the tunnel while Reznik manipulated the rear section of the craft. A door slid upward, and he walked in.

"We're in luck," Reznik announced. "No one's home."

"They're advancing! Hurry up in there!" Steele shouted over the com.

Reznik poked his head out of the open door and ordered, "Come on, we don't have all day!" With no more urging, the group hustled into the craft. Reznik manipulated an instrument panel next to the opening, and the door slid down. An indicator light flashed green and, at that, Reznik said, "Ok, I'm going to start this thing up. Don't take off your suits. We still have to open the door for Steele and there is no air lock."

"Steele, we're in," Howington announced.

Reznik went to the front and sat at one of two molded plastic-like seats. The controls were simple. A bank of lights winked green on a panel in front of him when he toggled a switch. He pressed a green flashing icon on the panel, and the skimmer floated free of its tether. The group felt it float upward, almost like a boat on a slight swell as it releases from a dock.

"We're nominal. I'm moving out now." Reznik said anticlimactically.

The craft responded effortlessly to his manipulation of toggles protruding on the right and left seat arm rests. Picking up speed, the craft moved towards the opening where Steele, who had stayed to guard their rear, had just learned to his dismay that the four aliens, who had fanned out, did indeed possess a weapon as evidenced by a pencil thin beam which sliced through a rock near him, splattering vapor and molten material all about.

"They've got some sort of laser set up at the entrance," Steele said before popping off a high explosive grenade in the general direction from which the laser had originated, and moving away from the opening just as the beam sliced into the sheltering rock from which he had just left.

"They're tracking me." Steele announced.

Reznik slowed the craft. "How close to the exit are they?"

"Right on top of it," Steele replied. He dropped most of his ordnance so that he could crawl to another dip in the land. Grunting and scrabbling in the dirt and stone, he crept across fifteen yards to the more defensible position.

"Can we get out?" Reznik asked.

"They're responding to threats now," Steele replied. "I don't know how a skimmer would be classified."

Reznik inched the skimmer closer to the opening so that he could look out onto the new battlefield between Steele and the aliens. As the skimmer lifted higher, a laser beam arrowed out from the ground, barely missing the nose of the craft, melting the tunnel above.

Hitting full reverse, Reznik shouted, "Hang on!" as the craft slammed into the floor and skidded back against the loading dock knocking the group about like so much baggage.

"They're in full-attack mode." Reznik said.

Steele knew the answer to this riddle. He'd made the same decision in Iraq all those years ago. The grit and blood hovered about him again as he remembered the first days after the 3rd Commando Brigade invaded the Al-Faw Peninsula. When they had met unusually stiff resistance taking casualties, he had called in a medevac for three of his men hit by a sniper. The problem was that the helicopter could not come down until they had cleared the sniper and his support. Pinned down and alone, Steele decided to draw the sniper and whoever was with him away from the intended LZ for the medevac. He had moved and shot, pulling the sniper away from the LZ. The helicopter was able to land and evac the wounded Royal Marines without a repeat of Black Hawk Down--an event which everyone was fully aware during those first months of the war. Alone, Steele had maneuvered through the hostile territory for a day before he could rejoin his fellow commandos.

Steele hated what he realized he had to do now but military training kicked in as it always does for those who have been in the blood and gore of actual combat. The mission was all. It had to be. And the mission here was to get those people out of this hell-hole and to Gale Crater where, perhaps, Reznik could let the world know what was going on.

"You can't get out of here unless I draw them off," he told Reznik. "Now put the pedal to the metal on my mark."

"What about you?"

"You just get to that crater."

"No." Howington interjected. "No. We stay together. That's the plan."

"You know I'm right," Steele said. "I'll draw them off. Otherwise that laser will slice you in pieces. I'll hole up here, and later we can join up. But only after you get to that crater."

"The hell you say." Howington responded.

"They're moving. When I say go -- you go. Steele, out."

Seeing the four aliens begin to advance towards the opening to the hanger, Steele switched from the grenade launcher to the carbine and, sighting in on the first alien as it came up on a rise, he unloaded ten or so rounds into the creature. He saw bits fly off as the slugs hit home. It turned towards him. After the second alien popped up,

Steele fired off four HE grenades, two on the rise and two behind, where he assumed the other aliens were bunching. Rock flew into the air, knocking down one of them. Then from the general direction he had hurled the grenades, a high energy laser beam shot out and pulverized the lip of the crater he was in. A boulder the size of a small car exploded, shooting shrapnel into the air. Two bits of rock slammed into Steele's body, but the pressure suit prevented any penetration. His shoulder took a direct hit from a rock. The second skimmed across his back.

Scrambling up, Steele sprinted away, the laser cutting behind him. Leaping forward he tumbled head first into a shallow crater. Recovering from the shrapnel hits, he laid out C-4 explosive in the crevice of several boulders near the crater floor and slaved the detonators to explode simultaneously.

"Get ready!" Steele yelled to the skimmer. Then, like a machine, he fired off every grenade he had with him, one making a direct hit. When he finished, he had fired off at least fifteen rounds. The good news was that he had their attention. The laser began firing back slicing the area around him. With molten bits of rocks shredding in all directions he fired off shots at the three aliens bounding towards him, presenting himself as a target for their laser, knowing that, on the run as they were, it would be difficult to aim.

"Now! Gun it, Reznik!" Steele yelled. He stopped and waited until the alien group was close to his initial rock-protected hide-out. Then, when they disappeared below the crater lip, he pushed the radio detonator and a great spout of rock angled upwards as the high explosive C-4 blew out the side of the boulders, tossing two mangled aliens over the crater lip before smashing lifeless to the ground.

Needing no further instruction, Reznik pushed the throttle to full power. The skimmer started slow but accelerated exponentially so that by the time he exited the hanger the craft was moving lightning fast. He had no way to judge the speed, but the landscape moved in a blur. He saw a great cloud of debris in the air off to his right, but only for a second, then the skimmer was moving up and away from the battlefield.

Steele turned to see the explosion and then the skimmer shooting out from the hanger opening. By his count he had killed or disabled three aliens. One was left. He prayed it did not know how to use the laser.

Reznik settled the skimmer on a flat trajectory north east towards Gale Crater.

"Steele. Do you read? Over? " Reznik repeated again and again as they flew away, but to no reply. After a few minutes he stopped, knowing they were out of range.

After Reznik guided the craft back towards the rust-colored surface he slowed down intending to hug the ground as much as possible. As he had explained earlier, they did not know what the alien reaction might be to taking the skimmer, but he did not want to draw attention to the craft-- so as a result hugging the ground, even to the point of dropping into chasms and craters, made perfect sense, particularly now that he realized that the aliens knew how to use lasers.

After an hour of flying, Reznik turned and said, "Ok, I think it is safe to take off the helmets." Howington noticed that everyone looked hot, tired and shell shocked. He imagined he looked the same. Cho glanced at Leotie and noticed she looked back at him. She gave him a tired smile. Without thinking, he moved across the tube to sit next to her.

"Are you alright," he asked.

"I don't know what to think," she answered, dazed.

Reznik remained silent guiding the craft over the impossibly close and alien landscape. The group settled in the empty tube, their backs against the sides, legs outstretched, silent, stunned by what had happened.

"Alright." Howington said gruffly looking about. "This has been tough on everyone. But we're safe for right now. Stover I want you to gather all the supplies we have and make a count. We may still need weapons. I want to know what we've got. And food--see what we were able to get here. Reznik you said this thing might have water. Where?"

Reznik gave Stover directions to the water locker tucked into the side of the craft near the rear. Luckily, it contained the precious fluid, although Reznik assured the group it would process more water if needed.

Later, Howington sat next to Reznik and looked at the oncoming landscape. Like the rest he was exhausted.

"You plan on stopping anytime soon?" Howington asked Reznik.

"Soon," Reznik replied. "But I want to put as much distance as I can between us and the base." He sat ramrod straight, never taking his eyes off the unfolding landscape, dipping below the horizon whenever possible.

"What do you think happened to Steele?" Howington asked.

"Who knows?" Reznik replied. "He seems one tough hombre. The fact those things figured out they needed a weapon is disturbing. I've never seen that. But, on the other hand Steele obviously knows how to use explosives. I give him an even chance."

Howington considered the answer. "I'll take fifty-fifty odds anytime in a place like this." He watched the disheveled JPL engineer as he reacted to a rising crater rim. "It's sort of like playing a video game isn't it?"

Reznik nodded.

They glided over the rim of the crater then dipped down the other side in a long gradual decline.

"You ever wondered why the base, this thing, seems more fitted for humans than those things back there?" Reznik asked Howington. "I've been struck by it before. But piloting this skimmer just seems so right for a human. The chair is proportioned correctly. Green means go. Red means stop. Logically, it all points to a human creator. Now, doesn't that strike you as odd?"

"It's all odd."

"Yes, but, the trail seems to end at that conclusion. It is an incomplete equation, if you will."

"I thought you said earlier that you thought this was some sort of alien research station. Have you changed your mind about that?"

"This skimmer speaks volumes once you've spent any time in it," Reznik told him. Before you came I'd hitched a ride and watched-- but now that I'm operating the thing there are elements that indicate strongly to me that this was made for humans--by humans. The question is: Why? And you know what? I think neither we nor anyone else on earth has a clue as to what is really going on here."

"And that, my friend, is dangerous." Howington replied.

"Indeed. For us obviously, but perhaps doubly so for those on earth who have been playing along."

Howington thought back to those frantic days after he had left the Miami docks and travelled to DEA headquarters in Washington. When the computer program fell into the "empty room" or whatever it was that Steele had called the phenomena, all hell had broken loose for him, Stover, and Steele. And while Howington had, at first, thought what they had stumbled on was a narco-state drug operation being run by rogue elements of the United States Government, he now knew that drugs had nothing to do with whatever it was they had uncovered during the EPIC search launched from Steele's office. It was this. This God-forsaken place on Mars was somehow connected to the government, as well as to the black SUVs that nearly killed them at the Fairfax Government Center, to the helicopter that followed them, to the abductions in Culpeper, a realization that struck fear into his heart. Something this big, this awful, this covert, would not be a subject that any government would readily reveal to the public. People could easily die over something like this, he thought. People *had* died, he corrected himself. And, with a dreadful certainty, he realized that, in all probability, more people would die before it's all over.

Two thousand kilometers ahead, on Gale Crater, the rover Curiosity maneuvered higher on Sharp Mountain, its metallic body flashing blood red in the Martian sunset. It inched forward, maneuvered around a house sized bolder, then the independent six wheels began churning as it moved up a sand dusted flat rock. The trip ended just as planned and programed earlier from JPL. Having gained another hundred feet in elevation, the mast camera began surveying the horizon, pointed towards Tyrrhena Mons, which was beyond the horizon, on the Hesperia Planum. Unbeknownst to NASA and JPL technicians, the RAD package on the rover's deck concentrated its examination of the far away mountain -- using the above horizon technology with which German engineers had equipped it -- allowing NSA analysts an even clearer thermal radiation signature of the base from which Reznik and the others had escaped.

HESPERIA PLANUM -- THE BASE

Steele stumbled into the hexagon refuge left by the others twenty-four hours earlier. It had been a close thing. Once the skimmer escaped the hanger, Steele became the sole target for the remaining alien on the surface.

And the bugger knew how to use that laser to effect; Steele grimaced as he looked at the charred black streak on his leg. Had the suit not been so tough, decompression would have killed him. After slicing through the edge of a rock the amber pencil thin beam had merely touched his leg lengthwise, not allowing the full power to engage. Involuntarily, he jerked his leg immediately away, but not before the burning pain drilled every nerve in his body.

Then it had been a game of hunt and seek until standing with his back to a rock wall, he saw the last alien move in for the kill. Steele fired his last grenade to such good effect that the monster's guts exploded in a horrific puss-yellow deluge as it collapsed. In a final gesture, Steele emptied his M-4 carbine magazine into what he guessed was its head.

Steele limped back alone and collapsed. He knew the skimmer had made it out of the hanger. He'd watched it zip up and away. Mission accomplished, he had thought as he fell asleep from exhaustion and battle fatigue.

Steele did not know how long he slept, but, when he woke, he heard the sound of electrical machinery ramping up. Curious, he went out into the tunnel where the sound was even louder and, in a flash, he realized another transport was arriving -- or perhaps had already arrived.

Knowing what he had to do, Steele readied himself to get to the transport room before the monsters.

"No damn bloody rest in this sodding place," he muttered as he gathered what ammo he had left after the slog across the desert.

No grenades. But plenty of C-4 left. He grinned. Steele liked blowing things up.

CHAPTER 19

DURING A REEXAMINATION OF THE ROSWELL CRAFT IN 2014, ISRAELI CRYP-
TOLOGIST TOMEK BEN-ZVI FORMULATED AN AS OF YET UNTESTED THEORY
REGARDING THE MARKINGS SEEN ON THE CRAFT AND LATER OBSERVED
ON THE PODS. THE VAST MAJORITY OF MARKINGS ARE ONLY ACCESSIBLE
DURING MICROSCOPIC AND MAGNETIC EXAMINATION. ACCORDING TO BEN-
ZVI THE MARKINGS ARE, IN FACT, NOT LETTERS AS WE UNDERSTAND
THEM BUT RATHER ENRICHED BUNDLES OF INFORMATION MEANT FOR A
SCANNING PROCEDURE. ACCORDING TO THIS THEORY SPACING AND SIZE OF
THE SEEMINGLY RANDOM CONFIGURATION OF MICROSCOPIC AND/OR MAG-
NETIC DOTS, SQUARES AND SPLOTCHES CONVEY COMPLEX INFORMATION
INSTANTANEOUSLY GIVEN THE CORRECT READER. THIS WOULD SEEM
NEARLY IMPOSSIBLE TO PROVE BUT FOR ONE RANDOM CONFIRMING TRANS-
LATION MADE BY BEN-ZVI. THE PROCEDURE HE USED HAS NOT BEEN
DUPLICATED AND THEREFORE IS SUSPECT. NEVERTHELESS, THE SCANNING
CODE AND ALGORITHM DEVELOPED BY BEN-ZVI DID TRANSLATE A SIMPLE
INFORMATION BUNDLE FOUND IN THE CRAFT. ODDLY, THE INFORMATION
BUNDLE IS ONLY DECIPHERABLE IN LATIN. THE FOLLOWING IS THE FRAG-
MENT BEN-ZVI CLAIMS IS DECODED. IT IS TRANSLATED TO ENGLISH FOR
THIS SUMMARY: "MANUFACTURE DATE: 1283 CE, PART CODE: 004197304,
APPROVED FOR TIME TRANSFERENCE, IBT. PRIORITY ONE." THIS WAS
TAKEN FROM A STRUT WITHIN THE CRAFT. WHILE INTERESTING, WITHOUT
DUPLICATION IT IS RECKLESS AT THIS POINT TO GIVE CREDENCE EITHER TO
BEN-ZVI'S THEORY OR TO THE CONTENTS OF THIS SHORT AND OBSCURE
"TRANSLATION"-- IN THE OPINION OF GROUP 929 ANALYSTS. BEN-ZVI
HAS BEEN GIVEN PERMISSION TO FARM THE THEORY AND ALGORITHM TO
GOOGLE FOR FURTHER EXAMINATION."

**--EXCERPTS FROM THE PRESIDENTIAL BRIEFING PAPERS ON THE
ROSWELL INCIDENT**

FORT MEADE MARYLAND--NSA HQ

Conyer Somerfield threw the Styrofoam cup of coffee across the
room. The black liquid steamed as it flew through the air, splattering
against the white wall of his office; droplets blanketed a photograph

of Somerfield and past Virginia Supreme Court Chief Justice Harry Carrico shaking hands.

"Son…of…a…bitch!" he shouted, balling a crumpled fax between his fingers. He didn't like it when a plan fell apart. Especially this plan.

"Nuts!" had been the message, handwritten, from Mordecai Binford's office fax number signed by Binford. There was no doubt it came from the piss ant prosecutor.

When Somerfield calmed down, he dialed the number for Buck at the Powhatan Towers and told him to file the brief. Then, he punched in the number for the *Culpeper Dispatch*. If Binford wanted to play --Somerfield would play. And, when it was over, he would have Binford's head on a platter.

CULPEPER COUNTY COURTHOUSE--CULPEPER

Having sent the fax, Binford walked outside into the crisp autumn air.

The prosecutor scuffed his feet in the fallen leaves. Overhead, the sky arched blue and the sun felt warm through his dark suit jacket. Ambling to the Civil War statue that dominated the space between the courthouse and the sheriff's office, he looked up at the granite figure standing at ease, rifle grounded, sleeping roll wrapped around his back, hat appropriately slouched. The man depicted looked heroic, as intended. But Binford had often wondered how heroic any of those poor bastards had really felt when they faced oncoming hordes of blue coated soldiers who kept coming and kept coming and kept coming until General Grant finally ground Robert E. Lee and the Army of Northern Virginia into the red mud clay at Appomattox

The problem was that Binford didn't feel heroic. He was worried. In fact, worried didn't even begin to describe what was tunneling through his gut. Here he was staking his career, apparently, on a hunch by the sheriff, for a couple not from Culpeper, for a death cleared by a federal investigation. Only, he knew that wasn't really right. He knew the report was faked. And he knew it didn't matter where the Woods came from. What mattered was that they had died--in Culpeper--and it was his duty to find out how. It took the blunt intellect of Sheriff Carter to focus him on that central principle but, once convinced, Binford embraced it for the rightness that it described. Binford knew that he didn't want to live in a place where people could die and the government could lie without consequence about who and what killed them.

It just wasn't the country he believed in. Norman Rockwell's America was Binford's America, and this had no place in that vision.

But, he knew overwhelming forces were coming, just like the man represented in the statue must have known that wave upon wave of blue uniformed havoc would march over a hill until retreat or death ensued.

No. It did not feel wonderful. It felt awful. And the worst part was that he kept trying to convince himself to go along with Somerfield's request. It would be so easy. Too easy in the end, he'd finally decided with his wife Kate's help. It was wrong. The easier the road --the more the likely the evil.

And the counter punch threatened by Somerfield was all based on lies and innuendo. The claims of prosecutorial misconduct, the claim that he had hidden exculpatory evidence, all of it untrue. But how to counter those charges when someone like Dorcas Snider wrote the news articles, wrote the editorials and allowed unsigned blogs online? The *Culpeper Dispatch* controlled public opinion. That was the iron rule of local politics in this town. He knew it. Dorcas Snider knew it. And the Culpeper voting population went along for the ride. For them, he suspected, it was like watching a game show.

The awful certainty of what was about to happen to him and to his family consumed Binford. The newspaper articles would hurt anyone's reputation. For Binford, who cared more for reputation than anything else, the onslaught was all that more terrible.

Turning, he walked towards the iron gate that lead out to Davis Street under what now seemed to be an indifferent sky. Across the street stood the two story brick building where Binford had first started his career in law. Little had he known then that it could come to this--an inglorious end trying to right the world's wrong, in an insignificant hamlet, the consequences of which would mean nothing in the larger scheme of things. Nothing except, probably, Binford's career, because Binford knew that this Somerfield didn't play by the rules. He had however, received some pleasure when he'd sent the fax: "Nuts!" It had felt good to send Somerfield's offer packing. He hoped Somerfield understood the meaning behind the answer.

It was the same answer Gen. McAuliffe had given to the German demand for surrender at Bastogne during the Battle of the Bulge.

CULPEPER DISPATCH--NEWSROOM

Had there been an editor, Dorcas Snider's story on Binford and the Ellis case probably would have been toned down. "Rumor" would not have been allowed as an acceptable source. But since, in Snider's world, "rumor" had as much legitimacy as any other source, she had fallen into using it in her stories. It was easy and though she would not admit it-- sometimes she made up the rumor herself. The rumor was, according to the Defense Council attorney, that Binford would face disciplinary charges based on his conduct during the Ellis trial. That was good enough for Snider. She threw it in like one tosses in a little salt to make the stew better.

No one in the almost abandoned *Dispatch* newsroom knew or cared what it was she did anymore as long as she filled the front page with a story, any story. It had been years since a real editor had actually been at the paper. In a cost cutting move, management had simply eliminated him and his job --loading the responsibilities on the under qualified community editor, Harold Skimpole.

Skimpole, tall and thin with a shock of badly cut red curly hair set over a dash of permanent freckles and an overbite that accentuated his receding chin, smiled as Snider stalked over to his desk.

"I've got the lead story--for a while," she announced, daring the always affable man to object.

"Yeah? What is it?" he asked warily.

"Binford's finally been caught lying. This Ellis case is blowing up in Federal Court-- the Defense Council is claiming Binford hid some exculpatory evidence during the trial."

"Do you even know what exculpatory evidence is?" Skimpole asked, "because I don't."

"Look. I've written one hell of a story," she told him. "If you want to nitpick it, go ahead-- but only after I talk to the publisher."

She didn't really understand the concept of exculpatory evidence, but Somerfield and the attorney with the Defense Council had both assured her, off the record, that lie detector results were clearly something Binford should have submitted. However, she wouldn't admit that to this simpering twenty-six-year-old.

"Hey. Back off!" Skimpole put on his best smile and held up both hands in front, "Just doing my job. Let me look at it."

She nodded and stomped back to her computer where she accessed the final version and sent it to Skimpole's station.

"Got it!" He smiled and held his thumb up. Then he began reading. The smile disappeared.

Skimpole didn't like the story. He liked to write feel good pieces for the paper. He liked to edit contributed articles about community groups that were building ramps for the disabled or going on mission trips out of country, stories with fairly low journalistic standards. But Snider's story was complicated and reeked of Snider's dislike for Binford, something about which she made no secret in-house. But now the vitriol had a place to move and manipulate words printed for the world to see.

It made him nervous.

He looked up to see the rotund Snider standing above him, hands on hips, staring intently down at his computer screen.

"I don't know Dorcas; maybe we should ease back a little on this," he said. "How do you know there is an ethics investigation coming? Who's the source?"

"I'm not revealing my source to you or anyone else. You ought to know better than that, Harold. Now, are you going to print the story or do I go see the publisher?"

The one man who could stop the story for a day contemplated what Snider could do to his job. She *did* produce a lot of copy. It had never occurred to him that those burned by Snider's tactics also had a reason not to trust her or her product. Skimpole was a simple man who didn't want any complications, something Dorcas could provide in spades.

"Hey, no worries," he said. "I'll send it on."

The electronic script instantly went to a printing plant in Charlottesville to be arranged on a page. Headlines were written there by other underpaid disgruntled employees who had never even been to Culpeper and, as a consequence, had fun sensationalizing the headlines as much as possible.

And Binford's world shifted just as Somerfield had predicted.

HESPERIA PLANUM--THE BASE

Steele hustled down the corridor and out into the warehouse-sized room where he and Reznik had seen the quantum bubble slip into the chamber earlier.

All about him electrical devices hummed and, above the ceiling, he saw arcs of electric blue zip randomly.

Clearly having arrived just in time, he readied himself by checking again that his M-4 was loaded, that the C-4 and detonators were in his pouch. That was the extent of his weaponry. The remainder was with Howington and the others in the skimmer or left scattered about the Martian surface. The cache did not inspire confidence, but Steele knew that he would use what he had to effect.

The all-encompassing sound ramped up the octave scale announcing the imminent arrival of something from above. Steele crouched down behind a box -like protrusion and waited. Unlike his last foray into this chamber with Reznik and Howington, he had no desire to engage the aliens. He only wanted to get whoever was coming out of the pods and to safety. That was the mission. His only mission. Evade and survive.

Then, as before, the silver globe slid silently through the ceiling, its shining structure trailing electric currents. But, to Steele's surprise, there were only two pods in the transport. As soon as the shell erased itself Steele ran out to push the rubber like extrusion on each, hearing the satisfying rush of air as the seal broke and the lid slid down and under the floating containers. He knew that it would take some time before the confining material would retreat, but none the less, he wanted to know what was in the pods.

Jumping up easily in the low gravity, he grasped the edge, and pulled himself up to peer in and saw, to his amazement, that the pod was filled with weapons and ammunition.

"Weir!" he said out loud-- thanking the friend so many millions of miles away.

The man must have somehow managed to send up more weapons for him. What was in the other pod? Hoping it might be food, he jumped down and ran to the other floating object and looked inside.

"Are you going to kiss me or what?" Weir said hoarsely. "Get me out of this thing."

Steele stepped backwards, tripped and landed flat on his back, exclaiming, "Bloody Hell!"

Weir freed himself enough to lean over the pod's edge to look down on his astonished friend. "Miss me?" he deadpanned.

"Good God, man!" Steele exclaimed, jumping to his feet. Rebecca and your kids...."

"Are they here? Are they ok?" Weir demanded eagerly.

"Yes, and no. Yes, they're safe, and no they're not here. We've got to get away now. We'll talk later," Steele said, looking anxiously about as he detected the odor of rotten meat.

Clicks on the floor announced an alien's arrival.

"Can't we ever catch a bloody break around here?" Steele said angrily as the advancing alien rounded a corner off in the distance. "This is really starting to piss me off."

Unslinging his M-4, he racked a grenade into the undercarriage mounted launcher and trotted towards the oncoming monstrosity. "Get ready to run and don't forget to gear up," Steele shouted over his shoulder to Weir who stood transfixed by the sight. He fired the grenade point blank into the insect like monster, the projectile penetrated, seconds passed -- and then the front region of the alien spouted out a thick mucus green and yellow stream with the accompanying muffled explosion. The great gory gout sprayed Steele in a yellow and green slime shower.

"Bloody hell!" Steele exclaimed. "I have had it with these things." he wiped the gobbets from his face, then turning back to Weir shouted, "Let's go! We can come back later and get the rest of the gear. Right now we've got to book."

They ran --their ammunition and weapons cached in the same duct Steele and Reznik had used earlier.

Once back in the same hideout the other survivors had used a day earlier, Steele and Weir collapsed, spread eagled on the floor while Steele answered Weir's questions about his family.

"Gale Crater? Why on earth would they go there?" Weir asked.

"This Reznik knows how to hack into the rover's com system. He plans on sending out an SOS as well as get the word out about what is going on here."

"Then what?" Weir asked.

"Then he knows of some sort of greenhouse, powerhouse place that he planned to hole up in until a rescue mission gets here."

"Rescue mission?" Weir exclaimed. "You've got to be kidding me. We can't even send astronauts into space anymore now that the Shuttle Program's been scrapped."

"Reznik thinks there's some sort of black ops program to send a mission to Mars. He called it the Aries Project."

"How long did you say he was up here? That thing got scrapped years ago."

"He says not."

"Hope he's right," Weir said. "When are we linking up with them?"

"I hadn't really thought about that part. I just got here myself. And then there is transport to think about. We can't just hike to Gale Crater."

"I don't care what it takes I'm getting to Rebecca and the kids."

"Roger that," Steele replied. "One problem though, do you have any idea where Gale Crater is 'cause Reznik never did clue me in on that little detail."

MARS: HESPERIA PLANUM--SKIMMER FLIGHT: DAY TWO

The skimmer moved silently across the relatively flat lava field that stretched away from Tyrenas Mons from which Cho and the others had escaped.

Cho looked out the front observation port and marveled at the scene spreading out before him. The reddish landscape and the salmon sky contrasted so strongly with everything Cho had known on earth that it was difficult to orient himself. The twisted trail that took him to this place was just as surprising to the security analyst as the double moons skimming across the sky. From the first transmission report that had crossed his desk, to the strange journey that had ended in a rain of death on the Miami docks to the little Virginia town and now to this alien planet, this odd sensation that he had been here before, this seeming attraction to Leotie Thunder that blossomed and consumed. He marveled at the rightness of it even as the improbability of it whispered to him that this could not be, could not be random, and could not last. As a consequence he had been short with her. But somehow, in the cramped confines of the skimmer the two eventually found seats next to each other and kept those positions throughout the flight.

Could he be happy? Cho wondered. He felt happy when he thought of her. So strange was the feeling that it somehow seemed right that it would happen here, millions of miles away from home, in a place as twisted as this planet.

How was it that a smile could encompass everything, define everything, create everything, he mused. Cho thought he knew love. But this was something else entirely.

"You paying attention, Cho?" Reznik asked irritably. The JPL engineer was teaching everyone how to fly the skimmer, Cho being the last. He had been pointing out the general layout of the cockpit. Reznik's plan was to fly the vehicle nonstop the 2000 kilometers to Gale Crater. Each of them would fly in turn allowing the others to rest. Reznik estimated that, at their speed and given that they were flying without a map or guidance, it would take at least ten days to get to the crater.

"Yes, I'm watching." Cho responded.

"Yeah, I saw you watching alright," Reznik said with a leer.

"I don't know what you mean."

"Look, I don't care who you decide to make time with, just don't do it while you're learning how to fly this thing. I grant you though, she is a cute little thing," Reznik said. He pointed to the grips on both handles of Cho's seat. "It's pretty simple. The left hand controls speed. The right hand acts like a joy stick but remember it controls pitch, angle, everything. And, we don't want to go full speed. I think I understand the propulsion system but I don't want to take the chance of running out of gas --so take it easy and remember too that skimming this close to the surface requires the ability to maneuver. The faster you go, the greater the chance we end up smeared on the side of a rock wall. Now, grab the handles and let's see you fly this thing."

Cho tentatively gripped the upright handles as Reznik released them on his chair, and Cho felt a slight electric current pass through his hands, like a static charge, when the craft responded to his guidance. It jerked as he over compensated, and then leveled off.

"Sensitive thing isn't it?" Reznik said.

"Yes. How again do you know where to go?"

"See the display?" Reznik said, pointing to the flashing green, yellow and blue lights on the instrument panel before them. "This panel flashes information to a receiver the pilot uses. Probably some sort of display in a helmet or goggles. That's my guess. If you look closely, there are slight dots and formations within the lights. So if we had the right reader, for lack of a better term, we could probably navigate using the information being conveyed right before us. But we don't. So the short answer to your question is, you watch the horizon, pick a point and aim towards it and towards a second object behind it. You do that, and we'll stay in a relatively straight line. The thing is there are cratered highlands to the north and south of us so as long as we stay in this lava plain we'll be ok. Later we'll have to traverse some more broken terrain, but by then, I think we will be able to aim towards Gale. It sits on the edge of Hesperia." Reznik glanced towards newly minted pilot. "Relax, Cho. It's not rocket science, and probably we're all going to die before we get to Gale -- so just enjoy the ride, and begin by aiming at that rill up ahead."

Once alone at the controls, Cho carefully maneuvered the craft over the flat landscape. He was no geologist, but it was fairly evident that they were flying over a lava flow or perhaps an alluvial flow. The ground below remained flat with few craters and more sand dunes running in parallel ripples, reminding him of the flats he had seen in the Arizona Painted Desert on a trip he'd taken while a student in San Diego. Suddenly he became aware someone was joining him in the other seat.

"It is beautiful isn't it?" Leotie asked, to which, tongue tied, Cho could only nod.

"Do you think we have any hope? Any hope of getting out of here?" she went on.

"We have an old saying in China," Cho told her. "Dripping water can eat through a stone. I think there is hope as long as we keep working at staying alive."

"I'm glad you're here," she said quietly, and then sat silent until, his shift over, they sat together as far removed from the others as possible in the tubular craft.

"Do you think I'm crazy to feel this way?" she asked, leaning her head against his shoulder.

"What way?" Cho's heart skipped. He could barely contain himself from sweeping her up in his arms, but fear of how she would react prevented him.

"I know you feel the same way I do. There isn't time to play games. We may be dead tomorrow. I don't want to lose what I know we have and I know we'll lose it if we don't say somethingwhile we still live."

Deep down inside Cho a snake uncoiled and announced its first stirring. A month had almost elapsed since his last episode in the abandoned Culpeper house, and in the confusion and fear of transport he had forgotten his old companion. But it had not forgotten him. And, it would be fed.

"I don't know what you are talking about Leotie," he said.

MARS: HESPERIA PLANUM--SKIMMER FLIGHT: DAY THREE

"We need to stop," Reznik announced to the group which had been flying steadily since the escape three days earlier. "The water levels are down to almost nothing. We can't live without water."

The skimmer recycled water from the cabin and from their wastes, but still a certain amount was apparently lost in the process. Reznik, who had studied the craft as only an engineer can, had begun to believe he understood a little about their transport. He was fairly certain the propulsion system worked off of the weak Martian magnetic field--thus the lack of fuel tanks or chemical burn. Electrical power seemed to be generated by the same process. And he had noticed certain changes in the frequency and flashing of instrument lights which coincided with geographic location-- to include interludes of amber. Reznik knew the Martian magnetic field, only half as strong as that on earth, was more volatile, and the instruments seemed to mirror that one known fact, meaning that green meant full power and amber meant perhaps drawing down on stored power. And since green, red and amber worked as indicator lights in the base, he assumed the same meanings for the skimmer.

What concerned Reznik were the indicator lights near the water dispenser which was nothing more than a nozzle that supplied lukewarm water when touched. He had noted that spilled water quickly disappeared from the floor through the same Nano-driven process he'd seen at the base. Even so, the lights had turned amber and did not return to green.

"Mars is full of water," Reznik went on. "It's just underground and frozen solid. I have to assume the skimmer was designed to tap into that supply. Everything else about it is self-sufficient. I'm gambling this is no different. We'll drop down in a likely looking place and see if the craft automatically does anything. Until then, well, we are on water rations for the duration."

Reznik looked for a shaded crater wall and settled the craft down.

"Now what?" Howington asked.

"I'd say we all suit up and, at least, two of us go outside," Reznik told him. "It may be we have to manipulate something outside. I don't know." Reznik said.

The amber light remained amber. All were anxious to get out of the bus sized skimmer after being cramped inside for three days. After suiting up, all but two, Cho and Leotie, exited the vehicle.

"Why in the shade?" Stover asked when they exited.

"I thought perhaps some condensation may have formed on or near the crust," Reznik replied. "Let's walk around the skimmer and see if anything is happening."

"Has it occurred to anyone that no one seems to be following us?" Stover asked as they ambled about the craft, inspecting its undercarriage as it floated two feet above the surface.

"Yes. Stover you have asked that," Reznik replied. "About a million times. I don't have an answer other than what I've said before. This is the worst run place I have ever seen."

"It reminds me of a badly managed fast food joint in Culpeper," Rebecca said. She held Hunter and Heather's hands as she followed Stover and Reznik.

"John and I would get an ice cream and watch the employees as much as the customers -- as entertainment," she said. "The employees could have cared less about the place, but it somehow still functioned. We saw people steal drinks, get free food from employees behind the counter, use the restrooms without buying anything -- it was low level chaos. But it functioned just enough that the management didn't seem to care. I think the alien base is a lot like that from what you say. Those things don't really seem to have much interest. Otherwise, we would all be dead. Reverse roles and you understand what I mean. And anyone can see humans built the base. Haven't you noticed that?" she asked.

Reznik grunted at her observation. "Yes. I think the same thing. Red, Green, Amber are universal colors among humans and convey the same meaning. The construction scales are human sized--all the doors and portals seem made for humans. And the skimmer. There is no doubt about that after you look at the waste disposal."

"You mean the toilet?" Rebecca asked with a chuckle.

"Well, yes," Reznik answered uncomfortably.

"Hey! I think I found something," Howington said from the other side of the skimmer. The group rushed around to see Howington bent over and looking under the craft. He pointed. "Look. There. Am I seeing things or is this something important?"

They looked underneath and observed a pencil thin, almost unnoticeable red laser like particle beam penetrating the Martian surface.

"Cho. Look at the water indicator and tell me if anything is changing," Reznik snapped.

"No," Cho replied from inside the skimmer. "Still amber."

"Ok. We wait. Maybe it takes a while," Howington said. "Reznik, I want to look around a little."

"Suit yourself," Reznik replied.

Howington and Stover walked in silence away from the skimmer. Howington pointed to a landslide that lessened the crater wall's slant. "Let's walk to the top and see what's here," Howington said.

"Boss, I don't want to rain on your party, but we just flew over this. I know what it looks like."

"Humor me, Stu."

They scrambled up the slope, rocks and debris sliding down as their feet purchased altitude one step at a time. When they got to the top Howington motioned for Stover to follow him away from the crater. They had left the skimmer, and the remainder of the party beyond the rim and out of sight. Howington walked about 100 yards to a small dune; then he placed it between the two of them and the skimmer.

"What's up, Boss?" Stover asked. Howington held up his hand.

"Reznik? Cho? You read me?" Howington asked.   Silence. "Stover, try the same thing." Howington ordered.   Stover's attempts to raise the rest of the party received the same result.

"Reznik told me line of sight seemed to be the limit for radio communication with the suits and the ship," Howington explained. "I just wanted to try it out before we talk."

"It's Cho isn't it?" Stover asked.

The two had not had a moment alone to really compare notes about the Chinese national. Howington was not surprised that Stover had questions about Cho. The two DEA agents thought alike and the fact that Stover independently suspected Cho confirmed Howington's own logic.

"Yeah. I think he was mixed up with the shooting." Howington said referring to the massacre at the Miami docks. "Did you see how he reacted when we first mentioned that we were DEA agents?"

"Damn straight," Stover replied. "And, Boss, I'll tell you something else; there is no way it's a coincidence that we go to Culpeper after The Rat tells us two Chinese nationals take off to Virginia leaving their dead buddies spread out on a dock in Miami. Then, we stir up things at the NSA and end up with a bunch of NSA spooks shooting at us. Then, lo and behold, we find out a Chinese national is nosing around Culpeper at the same time we are asking the same kind of questions. Then, guess what? He gets picked up just like us. He's tied in. I can smell it."

"Well we sure don't have anything more than a suspicion --and that's not worth a bucket of spit," Howington said, remembering the way The Rat's dark eyes glinted in the Florida sunlight a million miles away. "We ought to press Cho about that a little," he continued. "Ask him about the other Chinese dude, and see what he says."

"Right. And, did you notice him and Leotie Thunder seem to have a thing going on?" Stover asked.

"Correction. She has a thing going on. I don't think he has a clue."

"We might be able to use one against the other to get some info."

"Yeah, well, that's a volatile combination right now," Howington observed. "We still need to work together to get out of here, and I don't want female histrionics or male pride to hinder our survival."

"I'm just saying…"

"You leave that stuff to me, Stu. Just concentrate on Cho and the other dude he came with."

"Right." Stover paused then asked, "Boss? Got a question before we go back."

"Shoot."

"Why do we care? We're on Mars for crying out loud. I figure we're probably going to die here. I mean, what chance do we have if we get to the crater? The food is running out. And even if we get to *Curiosity* and get away, we don't know what sort of place Reznik has for us to hole up in -- but -- if it was so good, why didn't he stay there rather than that little rat trap we arrived at? And rescue? What chance is there of that? None I'd say. So why do we care if Cho was mixed up in that mess in Miami? It's not like we're going to report our findings to anyone."

"Call it professional curiosity, Stu. I'm a DEA agent. It's what I do."

"As good a reason as any I guess."

The two turned and walked back to the skimmer.

"See anything?" Reznik asked as they scrambled down the crater wall.

"Not a thing worth mentioning. I can't believe I'm saying this but, after a while, Mars is pretty boring," Stover replied laconically.

Mars: Hesperia Planum--The Base

"Gale Crater?" Weir replied in answer to Steele's question. "Everyone knows where Gale Crater is."

"Bloody hell. Everyone?" Steele replied.

Explaining that before he left, he'd read up on Mars exploration as much as possible, Weir said, "Tell me where we are, and I probably have a pretty good idea of where Gale is." When Steele told him Tyrrhena Mons, he smiled and said, "Two thousand clicks away and all downhill from this mountain."

Steele shook his head. "Who would have figured you for a space geek?"

Steele used the last escape as a template for his and Weir's own attempt, taking only the weapons they knew they could carry to the hanger and caching them at the hideout where Steele took a suit from one of the abductees and gave it to Weir. It took the two of them three days to rest, make a plan, and gather what supplies that they could before beginning the final hike to the hanger.

"Until you actually see it, you don't really believe you're on another planet," Weir said as they steeped out onto the grated exit platform.

"I know. You're taking it better than I did the first time I came up here," Steele replied. "Come on. We've got a long walk ahead. I'll take point," he added as the two wove their way among the boulders and crater walls towards the hanger. The plan was simple: get to the hanger, get a skimmer, and get out. Steele admitted that he had no idea how to operate the vehicle, but he claimed that, if a nerd like Reznik could figure it out, they could as well.

"I've flown bloody helicopters for crying out loud," Steele said. "There's nothing harder to fly than one of those contraptions."

"What if there's no skimmer inside?" Weir asked.

"Then we sit and wait."

"I think we're going to be lucky in one respect," Steele said as they walked.

"What's that?"

"I think we killed off more aliens than they can replicate," Steele replied. "There was only one when you arrived. No others followed. And I haven't seen them since. I never knew how many were here, but I know I killed a fair number before you came."

They saw no carcasses at the site of the earlier skirmish between the escaping group and the pursuing aliens just three days earlier. Only scuffed dirt, explosion marks and shattered boulders marked the desperate struggle to escape.

As they got closer to the hanger, the two hugged the ground. Steele leading. He crouched low and peered around the edge of the hanger opening. Then motioned for Weir to follow.

The two moved into the dark slanted room. Below, they saw two skimmers tethered to the loading dock.

And it was that easy. Steele untethered one craft. The two entered, and finding it empty, quickly settled into the chairs. Steele gripped the chair handles, accidentally knocking the craft against the other before understanding the basic navigational functions. Then, they were off.

"Well!" Steele exclaimed as they exited the hanger. "That was too easy."

Easy as the escape had been, Steele and Weir both knew the hard part was ahead, waiting for them in the red hills and craters that spread out before them. Somehow, they had to find the others. Somehow, they had to figure out a way to get off the planet.

Somehow, Weir had to save his family from the grip of this harsh alien world.

ROCHELLE-- MADISON COUNTY

Nora Burke had found her soul again.

For the past few years, the NSA scientist had forgotten she had such a thing. She had forgotten that there was a center to her being, a place that had a universal value, and that she alone was responsible for.

And she heard what her new found soul whispered to her every day when she prayed.

For Nora Burke prayed.

She kept it a secret. She found it awkward. How do you talk to the creator of the universe? But after she had shipped Weir off, she had come home and hunted down the old Bible her parents gave her as a high school graduation gift, a book she promptly had packed away and never read.

Until now.

Because now she knew that she was in a battle for good and evil, and that like King David, she was in the midst of an evil and bloodshed, she, like him had helped create. Every pod she had helped send, had been like David's order to leave Uriah outside the battle lines. Perfidy. Treachery. That was her sin against humanity. Every time a pod had gone up under her watch, she had been guilty of the hurt and sorrow created by the alien's vessels. She was as guilty as anyone else in the program, maybe more so because she knew right from wrong, good from evil, light from darkness.   And now she sought forgiveness.

And, in her halting prayers, she also sought help. Because Nora knew that, what it was she and Weir had planned, would unleash a storm not unlike that unleashed by Edward Snowden when he attempted to shed light on the NSA's web of surveillance throughout the world. Of course she knew Snowden's attempt to unleash the truth had been twisted and diverted to hide the NSA's real mission.

Snowden's leaks had astonished the world. What she and Weir planned was exponentially more shocking. It would probably bring down a government. It would most certainly change forever the way the world looked upward at the stars.

Following Weir's suggestion, she bought a new laptop, and downloaded into it the hundreds of documents Weir had gathered from his own work computer--photographs, memos, documents, diagrams-- all of it detailing the transport program and the reasons for its existence. She also copied files from her own work--including a few technological reviews of that material found in the Roswell craft. The tech savvy Burke was able, with Weir's knowledge of passwords and security protocols, to cover the cyber tracks such downloads would normally create. The center itself had become so smug in its invulnerability that the guards normally did not check Burke when she left or entered the building. And just to be safe, she and Martinez made sure he was on duty when she had a package to take out.

Martinez had become one of the trio working against the program at Mount Pony. She and he on earth. Weir on Mars.

"I swore to uphold the Constitution," Martinez explained, "but what is going on here you can't find in the Constitution. What they did to my family is not in the Constitution."

She sat at the kitchen table and downloaded the last of the documents she needed. Now she needed a signal from Weir.

"I don't want to do this until I get back with the kids," he told her before he left. "You know as soon as I come back, they will be on me. That's when I need you to get this stuff out. But, Nora, if things go wrong up there, or if something happens that makes it seem right to you -- get this stuff out. This may be the only time anyone has the chance to get it out."

She remembered the fire in his eyes when he made her promise to download the information onto the web, no matter what.

The laptop loaded and never connected to the internet made it as clean as a computer could get. She packed it up and hid it in an adjoining barn in a home made Faraday Box, at Weir's insistence, because the box would protect the computer from any electronic or magnetic sweep. The thumb drive she put in a safety deposit box at Second National Bank in downtown Culpeper as a backup.

The plan was to wait. Then take the computer to an internet café in Northern Virginia and download the information to *Wikileaks*, the *Washington Post*, the *New York Times* and for good measure to a public forum hosted in Switzerland.

By then Weir told her, the downloads would have been detected and tracked by the NSA. "Get the hell out of there as fast as you can," he'd said. "Wipe the computer with a magnet and smash the hard drive. Then, dump it in a river. Do it before you get home."

Later, as she thought about how much John Weir was risking in order to save his family, and his country, she prayed, *"God help him. Help me to do the right thing."*

CULPEPER COUNTY COURTHOUSE

"All Rise!"

Chairs scraped and benches groaned as men and women stood for Judge Stringfellow to take the bench. The tall austere man, his long black robe signifying the awesome power he welded from the bench, mounted the steps to the center Judge's high backed leather chair.

When he sat, the bailiff ordered, "Be seated", to the accompanying cacophony that sprung from the century-old wood benches.

"Good Morning." The judge said to no one in particular. He looked down at the docket, then over at the prosecutor's table. "Is the Commonwealth ready to proceed?" he asked.

"It is your honor," Binford replied standing.

"Then let's get on with it," the judge growled casting a glance at the seven men and women seated off to the side in the audience. For purposes of confidentiality, the members of the special grand jury had already been selected and informed of their selection, with the result that the judge would not need to call their names aloud as he would have had to if they had been on a regular petit jury. Having the clerk swear them in as members of the investigating body, giving them housekeeping instructions and then appointing a foreman, he told the bailiff to escort the group off to the jury room.

"Mr. Binford," the judge said after they left the courtroom, "seeing that there is nothing else on the docket, I will ask the clerk to swear in your witnesses as you need them. In the meantime, I will recess from the bench."

"All rise!"

Stoically, Weir watched the judge leave the bench. "This was it," he thought to himself. A trite phrase, but one that summed up so well what it was that Binford was about to do. His career looked to be in a shambles. His personal reputation also on the skids. Since his meeting at the Gainesville Starbucks almost two weeks ago, he had heard nothing more from Conyer Somerfield, but he heard plenty from the *Culpeper Dispatch*. The paper was on a rampage with its daily stories about the Ellis case, leaked details from the bar complaint, and unsigned blogs on the newspaper website calling for his removal. Now the paper reported with blaring headlines the formation of a group to do just that--remove him from office. And making matters even worse, the stories from the Culpeper paper were being picked up by other newspapers across Virginia -- including the influential Richmond Times Dispatch. Binford had already begun to get supportive emails from friends across the state -- well-meaning but also proving the wide spread distribution of the story.

Meanwhile, Somerfield had filed an appeal to the Virginia Court of Appeals on the subpoena for Weir and Sims. Of course it was well publicized, and Somerfield made the appropriate remarks about Binford's abuse of power in his motion, all of which Dorcas Snider repeated almost verbatim. Binford, unable to comment, could only watch events unfold.

The removal petition had surprised Binford. The group formed online, and then began meeting at the local library. Petitions floated around the community, being pushed by family members of former defendants and political opponents. Binford realized that, after ten years, a prosecutor was bound to have rubbed some people the wrong way--it was the nature of the business--but even so he had been taken aback by the vitriol that slithered through the stories, letters to the editor and blogs online.

Perhaps the blogs were the worst. They seeped such evil that it was difficult to understand why the *Dispatch* allowed them expression on its website, and it was even worse when Dorcas Snider began to quote them in her stories.

Kate held him that morning and cried. In a matter of weeks their world had crumbled. And all of it wrong. So very wrong.

"Good morning." Binford said as he entered the cramped jury room. He knew three of the men in the room and one of the women looked familiar. "As you know, this is a special grand jury," Binford continued as an introduction. "That means you are an investigative body. Normally, I would not be in the room with you, but the rules are a little different in this setting. I bring witnesses in to question. You can also question the witnesses after I finish. You may also ask that other witnesses be brought in that I haven't suggested. At the end of the process, you will decide whether you will recommend to the court if any further action need be taken. I will, in all likelihood, ask you to consider recommending that several criminal indictments be issued. But that is up to a majority vote from you. Any questions before we start?"

"How long will we be at this?" Jack Brownlee asked with a hint of impatience. "I've got a farm to run." Binford knew him to be a man of few words and even fewer friends. He scowled at the remainder of the group, his short cropped salt and pepper hair ringing a shining bald head.

"This could take some time," Binford replied. "You need to set a schedule for meeting. I'd suggest once a week. It will take a while to get all of the witnesses here, and you may want to hear from more."

"You mean until we do what you want to get yourself out of this mess," Brownlee growled. He leaned back in his chair and stuffed his hands deep into his tan Cargill work pants.

"Now, that is enough Jack," Ralph Moore the foreman said. Moore turned to Binford, "We'll listen to the witnesses you have lined up today, and then decide what we will do after that. First though, tell us what's this all about."

In a few short sentences, Binford told them about the deaths of Ed and Pat Wood, their death and the questionable investigative reports. Their job, from his point of view as Commonwealth's Attorney, was to decide whether or not the reports had been doctored and then to decide whether John Weir should be indicted for felony forgery of a public document and perhaps obstruction of justice. There might be other charges as well, Binford told them, but the first order of business, he suggested, was to listen to the findings of Sheriff Carter who was waiting outside to be sworn in.

None of the jury had any idea of what their purpose was until Binford told them since the proceedings of a Grand Jury are secret by state law. Even the subject of inquiry is normally secret. Now that they knew the gravity of their charge, their faces took on a more serious countenance. Even Jack Brownlee seemed less agitated.

"Ok. Call in the Sheriff," the foreman said.

When Binford ushered in the Sheriff his brown uniformed bulk filled the doorframe. "Morning," Carter wheezed as he squeezed into the too small wooden chair at the table's end.

After a few questions establishing Carter's, name, position as sheriff and the like Binford dived into the meat of the matter: "First things first," he said. "Did you receive a report from the FBI regarding a murder suicide in Culpeper County?"

"Yes, I did."

"Do you have it with you now?"

"I have the original in the evidence room, but this is an exact copy."

Binford took the proffered document from the Sheriff and handed it to the foreman. "Please mark this as exhibit one and pass it around the Grand Jury," he instructed and pointed to a pen and a stack of small square stickers with "Exhibit No." printed in the upper portion.

"I call your attention to the signature at the bottom of the document. What does it say?"

"John Weir."

"Did you ever confront a John Weir about this signature?"

"I did."

"And what did he say?"

"Wait a minute there, Mr. Binford," a hostile Jack Brownlee interrupted. "I'm no lawyer or anything, but I know enough from *Judge Judy* to know you just can't go asking people to say what other people say. That's hearsay."

"Hearsay is allowed in a grand jury proceeding," Binford told him. "In fact you might not even hear from some of the people that you may decide to recommend charges against. This is all normal and proper. Please go on, Sheriff."

"Humph…doesn't seem fair to me," Brownlee fumed. "We ought to hear from this Weir fellow as to whether or not that's his report. Lot of funny lawyer business if you ask me."

"He acknowledged that it was his signature and his report," Carter said, settling his bulk more firmly in the chair, and readily providing the photographs of the crime scene when Binford asked for them.

"Where were these photographs represented to be taken?" Binford asked. He glanced down at the copy of the same sad photos he had seen earlier in his office. The jumble of bodies looked pathetic and forlorn. And again, Binford was reminded of that meeting with the Woods in his office. It was then that he had mentioned the Federal Reserve and the Warrenton Training Center, the very place the FBI report said the murder suicide had taken place.

Except. Except that the crime scene photos which did not match the tree line at the Warrenton Training Center, a detail Binford was determined to pursue at the proper time.

The remainder of the day was taken up with an autopsy report and testimony from the medical examiner who conducted the autopsy.

The grand jury decided to meet a week later and, in the meantime Binford, and Sheriff Carter were to get topographic maps of the murder-suicide scene as well as blown up photos. Binford planned on having a photographic forensic expert testify then as to his findings regarding Carter's photos and the photo's provided in Weir's report.

Afterwards Carter slapped Binford on the back as they walked downstairs to Binford's office.

"Good job, my friend," he said.

"Have you seen the papers?"

"Hells bells, yes I've seen the papers. You can't let that get to you Mordecai. You know I've heard more than one old prosecutor say that you haven't really done your job if you've stayed in office more than two terms. How many you had? Three?"

"Yeah, working on my third. But, Sheriff, what a way to go out." Binford said referring to the controversy surrounding the Ellis case as well as Somerfield's appeal.

"Mordecai, all of you attorneys are just a bunch of hyenas. No offence. Hell, I like you --but I know exactly what you are. You're an attorney. A fancy name for a hired gun. So, don't go whining to me about losing your position. You'll just set up practice on your own and do private work. Probably make a bundle. I'll still just be an 'ole country sheriff."

"Easy to say, Sheriff. Easy to say."

"You just keep plugging, Mordecai. Let's see where this takes us. I suspect though at the end we're going to see a recommendation for John Weir's indictment," Carter said flatly.

"Could be."

"And when we do, then maybe we can find out what those boys over at the Warrenton Training Center are trying to hide."

"Doubt that Sheriff. It will just be a regular criminal case. How would I be able to get documents or access to the Warrenton Training Center? It's federal property. We're skating on the edge as it is regarding jurisdiction."

"Well, I never liked that Weir fellow. He didn't lie very well. He knew he was lying, and so did I. Nasty business for a law enforcement officer to get into--lying. At least we can put a stop to that stuff." Carter puffed from walking the corridors in the courthouse.

"By the way, where is Weir?" Binford asked.

"He and the Mrs. are both gone. I've been watching the house, but there ain't anyone there. Kids aren't in school, either."

NSA HQ--FORT MEADE, MARYLAND

"Mr. Sims; I'll get right to the point. Our instrument package on Mars has picked up several anomalies that I think you need to explain."

Sims shifted uncomfortably in his seat. He was used to speaking and appearing at the Group 929 Campus in Fairfax. His station was, after all, the main project of Group 929. But, this was altogether different. Rarely had he met the National Security Advisor, the head of the NSA, and he had certainly never been in the conference room attached to the National Security Advisor's personal office. Normally, this would be a career enhancer, but this clearly, was not that sort of meeting.

Sims had known by the tone of his summons the day before this meeting that, whatever it might be about, would probably not be pleasant. A vague sense of unease developed in his mind as he thought of the operation at Mount Pony. The weapons' shipments were troublesome, particularly now that Weir was missing.

"I don't know what you mean sir," Sims said, making an effort not to appear as nervous as he felt, and aware that he was failing miserably.

"Let's review what we have found," the National Security Advisor replied. "Then, perhaps you can shed some light on the situation."

As if on cue, an aide came into the room, and as a projector rose from the table center, the lights dimmed and a screen appeared from behind two wood cabinet doors that folded back in accordion neatness.

"First, our Mars Orbital hi-rise camera picked up these images on a flyby of the suspected base area," Sims was told as several images from different perspectives showed an explosion on the surface. A dust cloud in a second image lifted above the surface in the classic mushroom shape belying a hot air bubble roiling into the colder atmosphere.

"Second set of images, please."

Several photos, from a shifting angle reflective of the orbiting vehicle's movement around the Martian sphere, showed lines of blurred objects.

"These, we think, are the aliens on the surface in a formation of sorts."

Another photo showed a similar blurred image but in two pieces.

"This looks to be a casualty," The security advisor said laconically. "Next set please."

New images flashed on the screen.

"This was more puzzling to my advisors," he said as a long shadow appeared to cross the red landscape. "But two things have cleared it up. This next image looks the same but it is in fact about 500 kilometers behind the first set of shadow images. They seem to be headed in the same direction. Now look at this next thermal image from the RAD package on Gale Crater."

An eerie ghost like image projected two cigar shaped mechanical objects moving towards the camera. In the first, a number of hot objects left a thermal signature. In the second image, farther away, two thermal sources burned red.

"Mr. Sims, I have my own sources within Mt. Pony," the security advisor said as the lights switched on and the projector retreated back into the conference table. "So, tell me, what the hell is going on in your project? Why is the center short ammunition and weapons? Why is your Security Chief missing, and why do I have advisors telling me we have a rogue mission gone bad and coming for our most important asset on Mars? Why is *Curiosity* the seeming target of these two craft?"

"I don't know what you are talking about, sir," Sims said automatically, a bead of sweat rolling down the side of his face.

"Oh, I think you do. I think you do," his interrogator said quietly, hunching his shoulders and fiddling with a pen. "I'm not mincing words with you, Sims. I suspect high powered weapons --and someone who knows how to use them --have been transported to Mars under your watch. Now, my advisors tell me that evidence points to a targeted move towards Gale Crater--where *Curiosity* sits. Why would anyone want to get to Gale Crater? Not the aliens. These things are travelling about 50 mph. The aliens could do it in an instant if they wanted. How, I don't know but I know transport between Earth and Mars takes two days. So, that leaves something else. You and I both know we transported a JPL engineer last year when he stumbled upon some unfortunate images. He never returned. He knows *Curiosity.* Put it together, and it's my opinion that someone is going to *Curiosity* for one reason: to communicate with earth, someone with a working knowledge of our rovers. So, unless you lost the JPL engineer I am assuming he is still up there and somehow involved in this effort to get to Gale."

The room grew deathly quiet.

"We cannot allow that to happen." The National Security Advisor said. "You are to jam any communication attempts from whatever it is heading to Gale Crater." The National Security Advisor stood up straight and pulled his French cuffs out to better exhibit the gold cuff links under his blue pin stripe suit. "If you fail Sims, if Breakout occurs-- I have specific EO2 authorization to dispense with unnecessary personnel to prevent embarrassing evidence from leaking out. This is from the President himself. You will be unnecessary if our operations are disclosed. This gives you motivation. Perhaps more than most, wouldn't you say?" The national security director scowled. "I've ordered that all *Curiosity* feeds be redirected to the Warrenton Training Center for scrubbing before retransmission to JPL. Don't screw this up."

Sims left the office determined to make sure nothing came out of *Curiosity* without his explicit authorization. *Nothing.*

CHAPTER 20

"BREAKOUT WILL OCCUR. THE QUESTION IS WHEN AND TO WHAT EFFECT."
    --TRANSCRIPT FROM A JUNE 20, 1972 DISCUSSION, RECORDED IN THE OVAL OFFICE, REGARDING NSA ACTIVITIES BETWEEN CHIEF OF STAFF H. R. HALDEMAN AND PRESIDENT NIXON. LATER ERASED AND REDACTED UPON NSA DIRECTIVE."

--EXCERPTS FROM THE PRESIDENTIAL BRIEFING PAPERS ON THE ROSWELL INCIDENT.

MARS--HESPERIA PLANUM: TRANSIT DAY 7

Cho shifted uncomfortably on the skimmer floor, his back arched against the curved side. But no matter how much he moved or changed positions, the uncomfortable sensitivity to confinement remained - not to mention the increasing bloodlust that roiled like an angry storm inside him, twisting and bursting outward, coiling inwardly, consuming what it closed upon.

He needed it so bad, so very, very bad.

And yet, despite the raging lust he held an equally strong tsunami- like emotion. He loved Leotie. It surprised him that he did so and with such intensity. He wasn't sure when he began to feel the attraction --- it just happened. But, he knew he dare not let her know how he felt. In the confines of the skimmer a relationship like that could go wrong so fast and there would be nowhere to get away. And then there was the other thing. Sometimes, what he felt for Leotie and "the need" seemed to merge.

Was that so wrong?

Cho knew, deep in the core of what made him human, what made him a man and not a beast, he knew that the merging created something so horrible that he could not bear to think of it. He could not plumb the horrors such a confluence contained.

And yet, there it was. Something he had avoided until now, in the bright sunlight of his mind--ugly and writhing but nonetheless real, nonetheless urgent, and nonetheless true. Better to confront it, he thought for the first time. Better to drag the awfulness out into the open.

Then, Leotie touched him, and electric current sparked along his body.

"Are you alright?" she asked.

"Fine. Just hungry," he told her, wiping beads of sweat from his forehead, uncomfortably aware that Stover was watching both of them.

"Aren't we all?" Stover said. "What I wouldn't do for a big ole pastrami sandwich. Or maybe some Arroz con pollo. You ever had Cuban food, Cho?"

"No," he replied, distracted by the buzzing in his head.

"Really? I thought I heard you say earlier that you'd eaten a whole roast pig Cuban style--what is it called? Lechon Assado? In fact, I think you used those very words. I remember, because I love whole roast pork."

"No. Well maybe. I might have had it." Cho's head hurt with the swirling need and the DEA agent's probing.

"You know the only place outside of Cuba to get good Lechon Assado is Miami. Ever been there?" Stover asked casually.

"No," Cho said, concentrating now. What was this man getting at?

Stu and Howington glanced at each other with a knowing look. Stu had caught Cho. He knew the man had been to Miami and, more importantly, Cho apparently didn't want anyone to know.

But Stu knew. And Stu had a good idea why.

As the skimmer continued on its unending course towards Gale Crater, the group slept in shifts, each taking a turn at the controls so that the craft could get there as quickly as possible.

Cho avoided Leotie in a strange dance of shifting seats in the confines of the craft. She noticed, and it hurt her, but somehow Cho's actions only seemed to fuel her interest in him.

Once past the flat Planum, they entered the cratered uplands of Terre Cimerra. On the far edge of upturned hills, rocky outcrops and multiple craters, Gale Crater announced the entrance into another lowland geographic feature on the far side of Cimerra. Like a bull's-eye, the large circular crater, 96 miles in diameter, with a huge uplift in the center and isolated on a flat plain, demanded their attention during sunrise -- the crater jutted above the landscape, catching the reddish rays before the surrounding flat territory. It was because of that characteristic that 19th century astronomer Walter Fredrick Gale first spied the brightly lit object on the darkening plain.

Reznik watched the horizon incessantly, whether on shift driving the skimmer, or standing behind the seats and looking through the forward observation bubble. Using dead reckoning and sunrise, he felt confident that they would see the central mound known as Mount Sharp long before they left Cimerra.

And he was right. Just as the astronomer Gale had first seen the crater so did Howington as he piloted the craft towards the rising sun.

"Reznik! Wake up!" Howington shouted to the sleeping engineer who, instantly awake, stumbled up towards the front.

"There?" Howington asked, pointing to a brightly lit mountain top in the dark distance as Reznik cried, "That's it!"

The remainder of the group, with the exception of Cho, crowded forward to see the long awaited sight of the mountain, brightly lit in the dark night.

"Hate to rain on your party folks, but we need to make another pit stop," Reznik said as they marveled at their destination. "We need to tank up on water again. I don't know what's under Gale Crater's floor. There is some thought it might be a salt brine rather than fresh water. I don't know the capability of the filtration system and don't really want to take any chances it won't work. We'll stop before we leave the Cimerra highlands."

"Roger that," Howington said.

Cho sat in the back by himself, watching everyone crowd around the front, while he wrapped his arms about himself and willed himself to ignore the need that raged within.

"Did you hear?" Leotie said excitedly, coming to sit beside him. "Gale Crater! We're halfway there, Cho. Halfway home."

"Home?"

"Well, home for Mars. You sure you're ok?"

"Yes. Just tired. I need to eat."

Reznik looked back and replied, "Quit your complaining Cho. You know, for someone so quiet, you sure put a damper on everything. Things are looking up. We might not die until we get to *Curiosity.*"

Reznik landed the skimmer in the shadow cast by a deep crater, the last before they moved downward toward Gale. Permafrost lay feet beneath according to Reznik. And while the others took a much needed stroll in the rocky crater floor, Howington, Stover and Reznik bustled about the skimmer platform watching the apparent extraction of water from the energy beam that punched down to the surface.

"I tell you I don't have a clue how they do this," Reznik fretted. "We knew there was water on Mars, but this method of extraction is at a subatomic level. I see no other explanation. When extraction completes, the surface remains undisturbed."

"What about nanotechnology?" Howington asked. "Could it be that what we see are nanoparticles retrieving the molecular compounds to be combined within the skimmer?"

"Possibly. Possibly." Reznik mused as he began to walk around the craft inspecting the exterior. "This is so advanced. I feel like a Caribe native looking at the *Santa Maria.* You know they described Columbus' ships as having wings. That was the only way they could describe sails. They used what they knew to describe something entirely foreign to their thought. I think we're easily falling into the same trap here. It could be nanotechnology. It could be some sort of sub atomic gathering system, or it could be something we don't even know about. I've had that feeling about this whole experience."

"Well, I know one thing," Stu said, "you are spot on when you say those aliens we met could not have built this, much less invented it. How do you explain that?'

"I think there is some sort of central command that controls all of them. Those things are a type of organic, inorganic construct to get the work done. And I might as well tell you my other theory."

"You got a million of them," Stu said.

"Yeah, well after a year in the freak show, you don't have much else to do but theorize," Reznik replied. "If you really want to know, I think that somehow they combined earth based DNA with inorganic nanoparticles to create the ETs we see. I think some combination of crab and praying mantis. The AI directs them as well as runs the mechanicals of the base.

"AI?" Howington asked.

"Artificial intelligence," Resnik replied.

"Why people?" Stu asked. "What the hell do it do with us?"

"It's pretty obvious. The base and everything else is engineered for human interface. They use people to do what the organic/inorganic construct cannot. But, I don't have answers to everything," Reznik snapped.

To break the tension, Stu pointed at Leotie and Cho walking off into the distance. "Those two are going to have to get a room soon," he said, chuckling.

"Oh leave them alone," Rebecca said joining the group while she watched Hunter and Heather run in circles around a boulder. "What they have is the only good thing going on up here-- the only human thing worth having."

"Yeah, what is that? Sex? Because I sure haven't seen any of that in awhile," Reznik replied with a nasty edge to his voice.

"No, you idiot. No. They're in love. I'm not sure they know it yet but it's easy to see if you watch them. He's afraid to admit it. She knows it and is waiting for him, being a stupid man, to figure it out on his own."

"You sure seem to know a lot," Reznik sneered.

"Men," Rebecca replied as it that explained everything.

"In the end that's what makes us all human," Rebecca continued. "It's what gives us purpose-- our love for each other and, laugh at me if you want to, but the capacity to love anything at all. This is a crazy messed up world we live in. To love in the face of such evil --especially here-- must be a gift from God to make life bearable. I think that concept gets lost in the static the world throws at us. So, I say leave them alone and pray they find something good in a hopeless place like this."

"How long till we get to *Curiosity*?" Howington asked Reznik, uncomfortable with the emotional edge Rebecca had brought into the conversation.

"We're just on the edge of the highlands. This is the last big crater before Gale. Probably 200 kilometers away before we hit the western crater wall. I'd guess half a day at the most. Then the problem will be locating the rover."

"We'll just follow the tracks." Stu said.

"Maybe we will, and maybe we won't," Reznik replied cryptically.

An hour later they trundled back into the skimmer. "All aboard!" Reznik imitated a train conductor. "Next stop Gale Crater!" Once the door slid closed and the atmosphere returned to the cabin, everyone removed the confining pressure suits.

"You know, I've never asked you, Reznik," Rebecca said. "What do the aliens use these skimmers for?"

"I've been on one a couple of times," he replied absently, concentrating on maneuvering through a boulder field inside the crater floor from which they had just lifted off. "It was filled with containers. The aliens seem to use the skimmers for transport for them and the containers."

"Containers? That's the first time I heard that," Howington said.

"Well, we haven't exactly been formally introduced either," Reznik said sharply.

"Who knows what they use these things for," Reznik continued. "The trips I stowed away on went from the base to the greenhouse we're heading to after Gale. They unloaded the containers there. I got out, but didn't get far from the skimmer. I didn't want to get left there."

"So why do you think that's the place for us to hole up?" Stu asked.

"Well, first of all it's not that hell-hole we left half blown up. I don't care how stupid those things are; you noticed they figured out how to use a laser against us at the end. I don't care to find out what else they might bring out. Secondly, they're growing edible plants at the green house. I saw them. And quite frankly, we can't eat a pure protein diet all the time. The human body was meant to eat plant material as well. Besides, I was sick of the place," he added, grinning, "needed a change of scenery."

After they had travelled through the bottom of the crater, inched up its eastern wall and angled over the jagged crater rim Gale rose majestically in front of them, its huge crater walls forming what looked like a perfect circle. Within, Sharp Mountain rising above the crater walls caught the fading evening light, twinkling in the darkening Martian sky.

"Beautiful isn't it?" Leotie said, awestruck.

"Is that snow on the peak?" Howington asked.

"Could be," Reznik said. "But not water. Probably dry ice. Carbon dioxide. Or it could be a crystal residue left on the rocks."

They were just beginning to drop down the other side of the crater wall when Howington said, "Don't you think we've been cautious enough, Reznik? We've had nothing from the base come after us. Let's just skip the ground hugging and take a high altitude straight shot to Gale. I'm tired of this creeping along the ground."

"I don't know. I've never seen these things get any higher than a couple hundred feet, a thousand tops. If this runs off of magnetic repulsion we might be too far away from the propulsion system's power source. There's a lot of variables."

"Damn man lets go for it," Howington insisted.

"I'm sick of this stinking can," Stu added.

"The sooner we get going the better as far as I'm concerned," Cho said.

"The enigmatic Cho speaks," Reznik replied, clearly surprised. "If Cho wants to go, then I'll give it a try. You really want me to gun it, Cho?"

"If it will shorten this trip, then yes; I say turn this thing loose."

"Wait a minute!" Rebecca said. "Don't I get a say? Is it dangerous?"

"Too late lady; everything here is dangerous," Reznik said, pushing the controls forward to increase speed and lift.

Like an old horse that was used to plodding along, the skimmer jerked forward taking on new life pushing everyone back with the acceleration as it zipped forward.

"Yeah baby!" Reznik exclaimed when the skimmer moved away from the crater wall, the land that dropped beneath them increasing their altitude exponentially as they raced towards the fast approaching Gale.

"Damn, how fast are we going?" Stu asked.

"Who knows? Fast enough!"Reznik exclaimed.

At this altitude, the group got a better view of the landscape below. The cratered highlands hid long vistas. Now they could look beyond Gale to the vast alluvial plain that stretched west and north.

"What's that?" Hunter asked pointing to a bright mountain jutting up to the left.

"If I'm not mistaken that's Elysium Mons," Reznik told him. "It's a volcano that sits out all by itself."

With the increased speed and altitude Gale Crater was moving quickly towards them. A trip that could have taken hours took thirty minutes.

"Ok, we've got to think about putting down." Reznik said. "I want to reconnoiter on the ground before we hunt down *Curiosity*." He pushed downward on the controls, and the craft moved accordingly. They drifted downward and slowed. The crater wall advanced, and then they crossed over into Gale itself -- the crater walls descending thousands of feet to the floor below.

"This is where *Curiosity* put down," Reznik said. "Do you see the heat shield?" He pointed to a small metallic shell glinting on the ground. They passed over it. He slowed the craft until he saw an area that looked to be disturbed by retrorockets and accented by what looked like car tracks that led away towards Mount Sharp.

"This is it," Reznik said. He landed the skimmer yards away from the disturbed dust.

No one noticed the small red instrument light that winked on as the craft settled.

FORT MEADE, MD--NSA HQ

The national security advisor digested the latest uplink from *Curiosity* as it sat on the heights of Mount Sharp.

"We can't just shut the thing down!" he shouted into the telephone. "That would create bigger problems. Announce a glitch. Shut down the feed temporarily if you need to. I don't want any footage of that landing getting out."

Slamming the phone down, he turned savagely to the Group 929 Chairman sitting in the room with him, "What I wouldn't give for just one Hellfire missile on *Curiosity*. Problem solved. And, need I say it again; you make damn sure Sims knows nothing is to come out of that pile of junk on Mount Sharp unless he vets it first. You'd think I've made it clear enough already, but I'm beginning to think he's lost control down there."

The National Security Advisor adjusted his cuffs with a vicious jerk, "We are not going to have a breakout under my administration. But if we do, well I assure you I won't take the hit alone. You're downhill from me Group Chairman. And you know what they say about what rolls downhill."

CULPEPER--BINFORD RESIDENCE

"How could something like this happen so fast?" Binford asked his wife Kate.

"It's the world, Mordecai," she said in the early morning darkness. "It's the way the world works. You're the watchman at the wall. Your job is to fight evil. The world tries to take watchmen down."

"BINFORD FACES RECALL PETITION," the headline of the *Dispatch* screamed, and a second story was headlined: "RUMORS OF GRAND JURY REVOLT". Inside on the editorial page an op/ed piece, written by a resident called for Binford's resignation. He had looked at the blogs online. It was as if a volcano of innuendo and hatred had erupted spilling uncontrolled across the newspaper's web page. All of it spelled political and professional doom for Binford.

"Are you going to continue with the grand jury today?" Kate asked.

"I've got no choice, Kate."

Once she was alone in the kitchen, she prayed, "Please God-- help us." And then, lowering her head to the table, she sobbed. She could not understand what had happened to them over the past month. She had encouraged her husband to do the right thing, but she had never considered the cost. *How could God allow this to destroy the life she and Mordecai had so painstakingly created? To what purpose did it all serve?*

FEDERAL RESERVE--MOUNT PONY

"Do you understand, Miss Burke?" Sims said. "All feed from Mount Sharp is to go through me first before being released to JPL. I'm picking you as the choke point because you seem the least busy out of the bunch in that friggin control room right now."

The two sat in a conference room deep underground at the Federal Reserve. The meeting had been cordial and businesslike.

"But why? It's just boring data from the surface," Burke asked innocently.

The question electrified the room.

"I want no lip from you Burke!" Sims shouted, spittle flying from his mouth. "You will do exactly as ordered, or I swear you'll never see the outside of a federal prison again. Or worse. Don't forget Burke. We can ship you up anytime we want. Anytime I want," he said threateningly.

"I understand, sir."

"You damn well better, Burke. Let me hear you say it."

"All feed from Sharp Mountain goes directly to you before being released to JPL."

In a psychotic change of mood, Sims smiled broadly. "That's the spirit, Burke," he said affably. "Sorry about that little outburst. We are all under a lot of pressure right now. Budgets and things like that. Nothing for you to concern your pretty little head with. Just make sure you follow my orders. That's all I ask."

Chilled by Sims' outburst then immediate change of mood, Burke could only respond woodenly, "Yes, sir. No problem, sir."

"Could be a big promotion in this for you Burke," Sims said rising.

"Yes, sir."

"Oh, and by the way, we'll be monitoring all of your work. Just standard procedure. Thought I would warn you, so you don't download anymore of that music you like. What's it called?"

"Reggae" she replied shell shocked at the turn in the conversation.

"Yes. That's right. And the obscure little band you seem to favor is called *Jahguar*. Right? Out of Tampa?"

"How do you know that?" she asked, chilled.

"Just want you to know that the NSA tracks everything and everyone. *Everyone.* Got it? There's nothing anonymous going on here."

GALE CRATER-- TRANSIT DAY 8

The landing in Gale occurred just as the sun set, they having used the night to rest and plan again what would happen once the squat car sized *Curiosity* rover was sighted.

"How do we know they won't just shut down the feed from the rover?" Howington asked Reznik.

"Seriously, I don't think JPL is part of this whole conspiracy," Reznik said.

"Dude, you're talking about the NSA," Stover said. "They've got their hands in everything. Even the CIA-- the agency that no one talks about-- doesn't have half the clout the NSA does inside the beltway."

"I can hack the rover," Reznik told them.

"You keep saying that," Howington said impatiently. "But how? Is there some sort of keyboard on the damn thing?"

Reznik smiled. "Nope. I got something better." And, with that, he pulled out a smart phone.

"A phone? Are you insane? You actually think you're going to phone home?" Stu exclaimed.

"I could. But no. This isn't any phone. This is a JPL Hadron milspec communicator. Solar powered, no less."

"A what?" Stu asked.

Reznik grinned, "It's a glorified phone that JPL issued. We used it to communicate directly with the rover mockups during troubleshooting. Theoretically it should work on *Curiosity*. I'll patch in to the correct receiving frequency, work off a sideband, and walla, I'll be in. And by in I mean in *Curiosity's* motherboard and by extension JPL's communications net, and again by extension the internet."

"Damn man, you don't fool around. Theoretically-- of course." Stu said deadpan.

"Of course," Reznik replied. "And if that doesn't work, then we just stand around in front of the cameras and flip 'em off."

"I know sign language," Leotie chimed in.

"Ahh! Everyone knows that kind of sign language," Reznik replied, almost giddily. "It's called redundancy in NASA parlance. Love it. We can use good old Anglo-Saxon hand communication. Then you can sign it out just in case they don't get the message back on earth. Love it!"

"Whatever dude," Stu said. "As long as it gets us out of this place."

"How did you get a communicator up here?" Howington asked, clearly puzzled.

"I don't know. I think they were in such a hurry they didn't give me a thorough going over. I'm eating a Big Mac in Pasadena and then, the next thing you know, I wake up, in this God awful place. I think I caught the train just as it was pulling out of the station, so to speak."

"What about being exposed to the Martian atmosphere?" Howington asked.

"It's summer. So believe it or not it can get quite warm here at the equator. As long as I keep it out of the shadows, we should be ok. Hopefully it's as hardy as those guns you brought. And if not then we use plan B."

"Plan B?"

"Like I said. Flip 'em the bird!"

Early the next morning, before Reznik and Howington took the controls, they ate a celebratory extra ration. "We'll just follow the tracks as best we can," Reznik said nodding towards the spotty trail left by *Curiosity* as it meandered across the Crater floor toward Mount Sharp. The trail was old, that plus the action of wind and the bare rock made the double parallel tracks hard to follow.

Reznik settled in, grinned, then pushed the lever forward.

Nothing happened.

He jammed it forward again.

Nothing.

"What the hell?" Reznik said.

"Not working?" Howington asked worriedly.

It was then that they noticed the small red light on the display panel. Reznik busied himself trying to understand what had gone wrong. At one point, leaving the craft, along with the others, to see if it were refueling in the same manner it got water, but he found nothing to indicate recharging activity.

"Sometimes things just break." Reznik said dejectedly, after half the day had elapsed, and they had regrouped inside the skimmer.

"It's obviously something to do with propulsion," Howington said. "The rest of the craft seems to be working."

"Yeah. Obviously." Reznik snapped.

"Now what?" Rebecca asked.

"Only one thing," Cho said.

"Uh oh. Another pronouncement from the silent one," Reznik sneered.

"We need to walk to the rover." Cho's statement landed flat and ugly in the middle of the group. Awful to contemplate. Awful in its implications. Awful in its logical sufficiency.

"He's right." Stu said reluctantly.

"What, and die out there?" Rebecca grimly asked, clutching Heather.

"Die there. Die here," Cho said, slouched against the wall. "Not a lot of difference, but at least we're still trying."

"Trying to do what? Die? I'm not trying to die!" Rebecca replied whirling to face him. "Between you and Reznik, you'd think that's the only outcome from of all this. I'm all for trying to get out of here, but I'm not for some sort of unspoken macho suicide pact."

"Every action creates new possibilities," Cho told her patiently. "To do nothing only prolongs the current status. The current status is we stay here and starve. We need to change things. Walking to the rover changes the equation. We might still die. But then, who knows what we may find. And if nothing else, if we are successful, we stop this terrible thing from happening to anyone else--even if we do die. At least our deaths will count for something greater than ourselves."

"What if I don't want to go? What if I don't want to subject my kids to a walk to nowhere?" Rebecca replied hotly towering over him.

"We all should go." Reznik replied. "There's safety and redundancy in numbers. The more of us that go the greater the chances we make it to the rover."

"What about afterwards? What? Do we just sit there?" She spit out.

"No," Reznik said. "If nothing else, we walk back to the skimmer and hope it repairs itself, maybe get a drink of water, watch the sunset, and then if need be, then we die. At least we could do *that* with a little style and without all the female histrionics."

GALE CRATER--TRANSIT DAY 9

As soon as the sun's rays splashed against Mount Sharp's summit, the group exited the skimmer, ambling in a line behind Reznik and Howington who were looking for clues as to the rover's progress across the crater floor. "We know it is going up Mount Sharp, and I guarantee you it will take the slope to the right. That thing isn't made for steep ascents." Reznik assured them.

One lucky find came during preparations for the expedition. They had never explored the skimmer for materials they might strip from it to use on a trek across the surface, but while banging and pushing on the resin-like side panels, Leotie popped open a compartment none had seen before to expose a small plastic shell with a diagram of a tent on the outside.

"Hot dog! Look at this!" Stover exclaimed when he saw it. "This is an emergency geodesic dome. We used them in the Navy."

"One more piece of evidence that these things were built for humans," Reznik observed.

Along with rations of water and food, they carried the three-foot-long capsule. Because they had the possibility of taking off their suits inside the dome, they now had the possibility to eat and drink. "Going to the bathroom is going to be a show though," Leotie commented grimly as they discussed how to use the contraption. All agreed not to open it because they did not know if it was reusable.

The flat alluvial plain quickly turned into a series of rocky outcrops and dunes. Always they followed the six wheeled track, noting when it stopped to drill into the rock or maneuver around a boulder or low rock outcropping. Mount Sharp, its layered structure becoming more and more apparent as they drew closer, looked like a multilayered cake. But the peak, as tall as the tallest mountain in Europe, looked rocky and foreboding.

After five hours of fast marching, Howington called a halt. "No use for us to wear ourselves out," he said. "Remember, no water unless we can open these suits up," he warned.

"I want to be on the slopes by evening," Reznik said. "It'll get cold down here. If we can gain some elevation and shelter in a crevice, we'll have a better chance at surviving the night."

"Surviving?" Stu asked. "Who said anything about surviving? How about just sleeping? Surviving sounds a little grim."

"Make no mistake. It's going to get cold tonight. I don't know how the suits or the shelter will handle the freeze," Reznik replied.

When the trail grew too faint to follow, the explorers milled about seeking another until eventually they gave up.

"Look we know it's going up the mountain," Howington said. "I say we just head up that spur to the left. We'll probably pick up the trail there."

"Things break, Howington, just like the skimmer. There's no guarantee the rover even made it up the mountain." Reznik replied.

"I'm willing to take the chance. You said it was already at the base when you were abducted. Seems to me it would be up there by now. And if it had failed, someone one here would have heard about it."

"Ha! You people have no idea what is going on in the space program," Reznik snorted in disgust. "Much less about the rovers. I'd bet *Curiosity* could have blown up in a nuclear malfunction, and not one of you would have known about it."

"I would have known about it," Cho said.

"Just what is it that you do?" Stu asked Cho.

"I never said," Cho replied.

"My point exactly," Stu said reflectively. "An interesting comment."

"Ok, Stu. Enough," Howington cautioned.

"Up the mountain it is," Reznik concluded. "We can use the elevation to look below. If *Curiosity* is beneath us, we should see a metallic glint in the light."

Turning left and heading for a spur that projected out from the towering mass, they were able to begin the ascent in an hour. Without saying it, each noted the absence of tracks.

"There is a lot of wind in the elevations," Reznik said to no one in particular as an explanation for the lack of evidence from the rover's ascent.

One foot after another. One gasping breath after another. The suits gripped in places unused to chaffing and, in the process, created blisters that popped, burned, and bled. In time each felt the effects of dehydration as tongues began to rasp against teeth and tissue, creating an agonizing silence of misery. Heads throbbed as blood, deprived of hydration, thickened and sluggishly streamed through already abused arteries and veins.

Cho in particular suffered. He walked in a nightmare of living flesh. All around him, breath and blood screamed for release. Behind the suits, walked release. He avoided Leotie, not confident he could trust himself in this weakened state. And he wondered what he would do in the tent at night. If he could last that long. And that man Stu seemed to know exactly why Cho was in the United States. Certainly, he knew about Miami. Cho felt it as surely as he felt "the need" pressing in on every pore, puncturing his skin in a thousand points of misery. How long could he resist? How long could he fend off Stu's probes? How long before he hurt Leotie, the one person who mattered more to him than life itself?

And Cho reasoned, between blood soaked fantasies, perhaps that was key: someone who mattered more than life itself. How could he live without her? And why was that? Because, he understood in a flash of insight, she was good and her presence created good within him. And maybe that was the key to unravelling the horrible quandary in which he found himself trapped. Start with the good, he reasoned, and extrapolate from that principle. Leotie was good. Love was good. The fact that they were here, together, hard as it was to understand, was good.

Being marooned on Mars, Cho realized with a shock, was the best thing that had ever happened to him. Even though the circumstances were horrible, they were, in the final analysis, a place where good had blossomed. And that, disturbingly, defied all the laws of logic.

Up, up the mountain they clambered without any sign of *Curiosity*. Reznik assured them the lack of tracks was disquieting but that, between wind and rock, not surprisingly, they may have been erased.

"This is the track I would have picked for the rover," he said over and over again. "And I know they landed on the side JPL wanted to climb. It's not like they would have circled the bottom. It was always about getting up into these sedimentary layers for the planners. That was always the goal."

At last the sun began to set in the west, and through the reddish atmospheric haze, they saw the oddly small sun shifting lower into the sky. Under Reznik's direction, they scouted out a protected crevice in a rocky outcrop and, with trepidation, they popped open the canister. Out slid a grayish rolled fabric which they worked together to unroll, exposing a tag which, once pulled inflated a geodesic dome just as the canister portrayed. A long tube popped from one side, unlike the drawing. It had a Velcro like door flap.

"Anyone notice this seems to be made of the same stuff as our suits?" Reznik asked. "And I bet that's the airlock. Give it time, and I think we may have a pressurized atmosphere in there. Otherwise, what is the point of the thing?"

Reznik was right. One after another, they crawled into the dome. It was a tight fit, but they all made it inside. Stu ventured to test the pressure and atmosphere by cracking his hood enclosure. When his eyeballs did not pop, he yanked the hood back. "Thank God!" he cried. "It's good. Break out the water. I'm dying of thirst."

An added luxury of the survival dome, as they came to realize, was a polarized window which, by accident, faced west. Sipping water and eating the last of their meager jerky rations, they rested and were able to watch the sun slip beneath the dark Martian landscape.

"I don't think I could ever get used to this view," Rebecca said while she held Heather and Hunter, stroking their heads in the fading light. "It's so different and yet so similar to something we would see on earth. I love the reds and purples, but there's nothing comforting in them."

"Not much of anything up here comforting," Stover said.

"It is beautiful, though," Rebecca said absently.

"Tomorrow we find *Curiosity*," Howington said. "There's comfort in that."

The group lapsed into silence, each contemplating the shifting sunset before them.

"May I make a suggestion?" Cho interrupted the shared moment of reflection.

"Oh no. This usually isn't good," Stover snapped.

"Shoot," Howington replied.

"Someone should be outside the dome to take watch."

"What? All night?"

"No, in two or three hour shifts."

"I don't know what to think sometimes," Reznik said. "Why do you always have to be right about the most inconvenient things?"

"I'll take first watch," Cho said stoically and suiting up took his leave through the double door airlock, but not before holding Leotie tightly against him and kissing her long and hard until there was nothing left but desperation, nothing left but baseless hope for tomorrow, leaving the young woman breathless and stunned.

"Well, that certainly was a surprise," Reznik said, once Cho exited the shelter.

"Only to you, dumbass," Rebecca said with a smirk. "My husband John would have done the same."

Once outside, Cho looked at the unusually bright sky, the stars stabbing his retinae with white and blue photons, lovely and deadly at the same time. The constellations looked familiar, but somehow they were skewed just a little by the different perspective given by the Martian orbit. Skewed and off center like everything else that touched this evil place, he thought to himself as he paced around the tent. One of the two misshapen moons cruised above, casting an eerie reddish glow back onto Gale Crater and the highlands beyond. He knew what he had to do. If he did not, then more than just one would die. It was better to kill one. It was better to kill one, and let the expedition get to the rover, and tell the world about what the Americans had created here. Better that one die. Cho knew "the need" was ready to burst through the walls he'd constructed to stay sane. *"The need" would be satisfied.* At a molecular level, he understood this as much as he hated it. It would take life. It must.

He toyed with satisfying "the need" during the next shift. The man named Stover was set to take his place later in the night. It would be so easy he fantasized, so easy to pull the helmet off, to bash his head with a rock, to see his brains ooze out and freeze in the deep Martian cold.

Oh yes. He was so hungry. Blood spurting now, would not be wasted. No, not at all. He could drink it like a fountain from an arterial flow--like an artisan spring its life giving properties would cascade into his mouth. He imagined the warm fluid slippery and thick at the same time.

NO!

Without thinking, Cho had started moving towards the airlock to take all the flesh he needed, to satisfy "the need" in a way it had never been satisfied-- but in a fashion he only dreamed about. He had been moving in this direction for years; he could not deny it any longer. Oh yes, he had thought about it. The forbidden fruit is the sweetest. He remembered the women walking in the park in Culpeper during his last episode. That new flesh, that new experience had tempted him mightily. So sweet. So forbidden. And here it was now, in multiples, waiting for him, almost as if God had placed him here for that very reason. Involuntarily, he reached for the airlock Velcro tab. This was his purpose: to slash and cut and relieve life of its mortal shell.

NO!

Cho stumbled backwards, cartwheeling to keep his balance. No, he could not trust himself anymore. With a sob, he ran off into the night, away from the one he loved and would not hurt. Could not hurt and live. Away from people with whom he had shared food and water and laughter. Away from the evil that lurked within, implanted within, corrupted within. Away from that thing he never wanted to become again.

He ran stumbling up and down crevices, over jutting spurs and mounting heights, always upward wanting nothing more than to be lost amidst the canyons and alien rocks. He feared knowing how to get back to the shelter, to warmth, to her. He could not kill himself. But maybe the cold and the need itself would do that for him. He would sacrifice himself for her. For her and her alone. Leotie.

How could it be that finally, after a lifetime, he had found love, which he must, for her sake, abandon? And she would never know why. Could never know, because if she did, she would know about the monster inside him. He could see her recoil in horror at the awful thing he could become. And that would be worse than death itself.

Flailing, he tripped into the void, hands grasping for hope long lost, down and down and down and over a crumbling cliff shining red in the alien moonlight.

And, at the rocky bottom, Cho found release--and redemption.

GALE CRATER--TRANSIT DAY 10

"Cho's gone," Howington announced to the group at sunrise.

No one had noticed until then, because Cho had never tagged his replacement during the night while they slept like the dead.

Leotie, numb with sadness, cried silently while the remainder decided what to do.

"We can't go searching for him," Reznik said at one point in the debate. "We don't have time."

In the end, Howington and the remainder agreed. Exhaustion, lack of food and dehydration spelled out for each in a language that none could ignore that time was short and precious.

"Maybe we will find him on the way up," Rebecca suggested hopefully to Leotie who merely nodded and woodenly put on her skin suit.

The morning ration exhausted their food supply. The water, too, was down to a few gallons carried in makeshift containers that Reznik had scrounged from debris left about the base. In the end, not knowing how to deflate it, the group also decided to leave the tent up, and the water inside, because there was no way to drink without a pressurized environment.

"At least the shelter warmed up last night," Stover said.

"Another mystery," Reznik commented.

"Well, mystery or not, today, we'll tell the world what is going on up here," Howington said to buoy their spirits. "Lead on, Reznik!"

At first they saw Cho's tracks, but lost them while traversing a rock scree. Stumbling and scrabbling, they worked up the crumbling mountain, their sweat disappearing into the nanotechnology of the suits. But once gone, their bodies craved for liquid replacement. Feet stumbled. More than once someone fell to be helped up by the others.

In the late afternoon, Hunter saw something glint in the sun.

"Mom. Why is there a car up there?"

"A car? Where?" Rebecca asked.

"Wait a minute, what did he say?" Reznik said, jerking around to look at the diminutive suited figure.

Just beyond the plateau edge above them, sunlight refracted off a gold surface. Then, in the shadow the eye could just perceive a squat car sized platform with a periscope like mast jutting upward. It was from that mast that the gold light shimmered and arrowed out in a glancing glimmer, almost by design, catching the young and sensitive retinae within Hunter's eye.

"That's it!" Reznik whooped as, summoning up the last remnants of energy, they pushed forward to what was, essentially, a flat platform with instrument packages attached at various angles and in the center a mast topped by what looked like binoculars. The binoculars were, in fact the stereo cameras *Curiosity* used to take photos as well as maneuver across the alien terrain. As prearranged, the group angled themselves so as not to be in view of the mast cameras which were luckily pointed toward the crater floor.

"We don't want them to see us until they hear from us first," Reznik had explained earlier. "Otherwise, someone might try to shut the whole thing down."

Reznik did not call attention to the fact that their little skimmer, some 10,000 feet below, shimmering silver on the russet rock crater floor, was in a direct line with the mast mounted stereo cameras. Instead, he pulled out his communicator.

"Ok, let's do this thing." Howington said.

"I may not even need to open her up," Reznik said, after reviewing the information he saw on the hand held instrument, and a minute later added, "They haven't changed the codes since I was last with JPL."

The remainder of the group stood around watching him, absorbing the breath-taking view from Mount Sharp, and marveling that they stood next to a vehicle that had been launched from the good old USA, symbolized by the American Flag emblazoned on *Curiosity*. No matter what it was the government had done to them, Howington realized, he still loved his country. He still loved what that collection of stars and bars stood for. Sometimes the country got it wrong, he thought, but usually its leaders still tried to do the right thing. He hoped his faith would not be misplaced after Reznik downloaded their message. He needed America to do the right thing so the madness would stop.

"I'm in!" Reznik exclaimed as he began to text.

CULPEPER -- WARRENTON TRAINING CENTER

Nora Burke, along with Sims in the role of supervisor, watched the readings and images coming in from *Curiosity*. When the skimmer came into view, she managed to turn the mast, but before the order to turn punched all the way to Mars more than eight minutes of evidence showing the vehicle, settling onto the Crater floor, arrowed back to earth. She punched a command to indicate a malfunction in a transmitter on Mars. An unexplained glitch that NASA and JPL worried about for hours before it mysteriously fixed itself. The mast, by then, had shifted so as to exclude the skimmer. The skimmer video, the real image, was stored in NSA vaults, but nowhere else. Later, upon orders from Sims, she reoriented the mast to the skimmer on the floor so that they could watch the Martian castaways.

Later, she saw the small group leave the craft. Again, the imagery never made it to NASA although concerned officials at Group 929 and at the NSA watched with growing horror as they picked their way across the Crater floor.

Then, the group was gone. Even the HiRise cameras trained on the area from orbit could not pick up their progress.

And then, during her next shift the following day, Nora saw that the craft's communications package had been accessed, although she did not actually see the physical opening of a compartment. She saw the data streams change and redirect as they opened to an outside data point. Someone was entering the rover's communications net.

And, although she knew that Sims would never understand that, she changed the data to show all systems nominal when the information package transferred to NASA and JPL.

Was Weir there she wondered? Had he made it? Was this the signal for her to do her part of their agreement even if before Weir's arrival back on earth?

GAIL CRATER--TRANSIT DAY 10

"Ok, remember," Reznik said. "Once I transmit, we all move in front of the camera. Leotie, you said you could sign. Then do it. Sign SOS. Sign who is here. Sign where we are going afterwards. Make sure you sign that we were abducted by the NSA. That ought to bring down the house. End it by saying that we are waiting for rescue from the Aires Project." He looked around the group. "Ready?" The group signaled thumbs up.

Reznik pushed the send button on the communicator, and a packet of information entered the rover's communications net, which in a high speed burst, shot up to the orbiting Mars Global Surveyor, a prepositioned satellite which forms part of NASA's deep space communications network or DSN. Like a rubber ball, the packet then retransmitted to earth. Radio waves travel at the speed of light, and since the distance between Mars and Earth being about 150 million miles, it took Reznik's message eight minutes to transmit to the receiving station nearest the radio beam--Canberra, Australia. From that huge dish mounted in the Australian outback, the message retransmitted to JPL in Pasadena. Normally. But, under the NSA preprogramed redirect protocol, which Sims had instituted, the packet of information went to the Federal Reserve, using the antenna farm at the Warrenton Training Center as the uplink, and from there to Nora Burke's monitoring station deep under Mt. Pony.

After waiting ten minutes for the message to cascade to earth, the group moved in front of the camera and Leotie, front and center, signed the message:

"SOS. We are humans abducted from earth by the NSA. Stranded on Mars. SOS. My name is Leotie Thunder. Cho Tsing, Ginger Wentworth and another Chinese National died. Surviving besides myself are...." Leotie named the remainder of the abductees. Then, she repeated over and over *"SOS"*.

"Did you tell them where to find us?" Reznik said, once he saw the repeated pattern for SOS.

"No. I forgot."

"Women! Crater Teisserenc de Bort! " he exclaimed.

"Do it again!"

She did.

For a time, they milled about the rover, inspecting its workings, listening to Reznik describe how he had actually been in the ready room with it back on earth. And, then, there was nothing left to do but sit next to their talisman from earth, emotionally exhausted, stunned at this contact with the home they feared they would never see again.

"Now what?" Stover asked no one in particular.

"I guess I was hoping for some sort of reply," Rebecca said. "I know that's stupid, but that's what I wanted."

"Unless the thing starts to move, we won't see a reply," Reznik said. "And what would they say? 'Stay there, we're coming.' I don't think so."

"Ok. We've got a long slog back to the tent. Then, after that to the skimmer." Howington announced. "Leotie sign the crater name and SOS one more time. Then, let's go. We're burning daylight, and I don't want us to be caught out at night without shelter if I can help it."

"What's the point?" Stover asked. "We'll never make it back."

"There's always hope," Leotie said. "If we keep trying." Remembering Cho saying much the same thing inspired her to keep moving.

"I forgot the most important thing!" Reznik announced. He maneuvered himself in front of the cameras after Leotie had finished signing, stood at attention, saluted, then flipped his middle finger at the cameras.

"Let's go!" Howington ordered.

The group stumbled downhill without even looking back at *Curiosity*. The last burst of exhilaration had drained them. All were working on their final reserves; the dehydration, the short rations, the stress, the exhausting climb had all taken a toll. Rebecca was the first to stumble and, falling was unable to get up. Depriving her own needs for that of Heather and Hunter, she had depleted the last of her energy reserves. Stover picked her up and slung the woman over his shoulder. The one third earth gravity made the burden lighter. But he grunted with exertion, none the less.

"We don't leave anyone," Howington said.

"Except, it seems, for Cho," Leotie said bitterly.

"We'll keep looking, but we had to get to the rover or we were all dead, including Cho," Howington replied evenly.

Young though they were, Hunter and Heather too were beaten down by the conditions. After more slogging, abruptly sitting down, convulsed with sobs, Heather refused to go on while Hunter slumped to the ground, unresponsive. In the end, it was Leotie who carried him, Stover carried Heather.

Having already lost the trail, they staggered on, hoping somehow in the glaring sun to come across their refuge tucked in a crevasse, even if it proved to be their final stand in this hostile environment, which all of them, now assumed, although they did not say it, would be their final resting place.

"Do you think they got the message?" Stu grunted to Reznik, as he stumbled over an uneven rock outcrop.

"Who knows," Reznik gasped.

FEDERAL RESERVE--MOUNT PONY

Nora Burke saw the transmission even though she had, under Sims direction, halted all inbound communications after NASA released a public information bulletin that *Curiosity* was rebooting, a public service announcement that barely rated a mention on *The Huffington Post*, let alone the main stream media.

The missive from a man named Reznik mentioned Steele as having been left behind. He did not mention Weir. And then, there were the unmistakable figures moving within sight of *Curiosity*. The sign language was unmistakably human, of that she was sure, doubly so after that final, defiant salute. It was a fully human and uniquely American gesture--of that, there was no doubt.

And so, this was it. This was the moment that Nora had both dreaded and known would happen. It was one thing to recite poetry and feel noble and pray after having not done so for so long. It was another thing all together to accomplish what she and Weir had planned. She had watched what happened to Wikileaks founder Julian Assuage and NSA analyst Edward Snowden when, having exposed the truth, they had been hounded, and in the case of Snowden, hunted to a Russian airport after which NSA agents scrambled his mind irreparably.

Nora knew she would be in worse trouble than Edward Snowden. The NSA was too insidious, too powerful, to just prosecute her, to just scramble her mind given the scope of Group 929's projects over the years. She would probably just disappear. Her mother and father told she had died, or even worse, told she died a traitor.

She had so wanted to make her parents proud.

Is Weir worth it? Is exposing a completely legal and authorized project to hostile public scrutiny the right thing to do?

But then she thought about the Bible verse she had read that very morning:

An appalling and horrible thing
Has happened in the land:

The prophets prophesy falsely,
And the priests rule on their own authority;
And my people love it so!
But what will you do at the end of it?

How true, she thought. A horrible thing had happened here at Mt. Pony. But, we love it so. We love the science. The knowledge. The power of secret things. But just as Jeremiah asked: what will you do at the end of it?

And Nora knew the right answer. As hard as it was she knew what was right, even if it meant death and dishonor, for what was life and honor worth in the midst of this universal corruption. But, there was a higher goodness that we were all answerable to--even if only in secret. John Weir, in his tortured confession of wrongdoing had showed her that. And the Bible she had reopened, turning pages not touched for years, reminded her of the same thing. In the end, what will you do, the prophet had asked Israel, and had asked her again this morning.

She programed the straight feed from *Curiosity* for release to JPL, NASA and for her own amusement, the NSA public web portal. Then, without hesitation, Nora Burke entered the release code--sending information, that most potent of weapons, into the wide internet.

And, with that push of her one finger, Nora Burke changed the world-- one woman, one soul, one light in a world covered in dark, signaling to other souls thirsting for truth and flickering in the night.

Afterward, she drove to Rochelle where the boxed clean computer waited. Driving further south, she stopped at a coffee house in Charlottesville, connected to the internet, and downloaded John Weir's confession to the world about the Wood couple, his part in the cover-up, his culpability in killing the two innocent travelers from Ohio, the documents that showed the depth and complexity of Group 929's operations, the reality of abductions to an alien planet 150 million miles away with government complicity and cooperation. And finally, she downloaded Weir's detailed description of his personal quest to find his family on Mars.

Then, Nora Burke kept driving. She didn't know where. But, she intended to drive as far away from Madison, Virginia, and from the world she knew there, as she could. Because, unless she did, she knew the wolves of vengeance would tear her apart without mercy.

CULPEPER COUNTY COURTHOUSE

Sheriff Carter waited for Binford at the top of the stairs at the Circuit Courtroom. The grand jury being slated to meet within the hour, Binford had subpoenaed a profiler from the Virginia State Police to testify about the characteristics of murder/suicide crime scenes in a last ditch effort to get the grand jury to buy the claim that the investigative report was erroneous at best, and doctored at worst.

The fact that neither Weir nor Sims would testify did not help matters. But, in Carter's mind, it was not critical to the grand jury process.

It was the recall effort that worried the sheriff. Every law enforcement official makes enemies. Add to that the general dislike of attorneys that seems to infuse the public, and he could tell Binford was in real political trouble.

The grand jury was not immune to the public discontent created by the news coming out of the *Culpeper Dispatch*. And their discontent had boiled over at the last grand jury meeting. Binford had never said anything to the sheriff about it. He hadn't needed to since Carter had his own deputies posted outside the jury room for security. They reported everything to him that they heard through the doors. There were no secrets in a court house; he made damn sure of that.

Some members of the grand jury had threatened to walk out at the last meeting. One deputy reported that someone in the room, he wasn't sure who, had said words to the effect that Binford was just using the process to save his own neck and the grand jury member even suggested that they investigate Binford for abusing the whole process. He had referenced the Defender Council's attorney, Roland Sprague, as a source for his information.

Carter heard Binford's steps coming up the stair case.

"Morning Sheriff," Binford said.

"Morning. It will get better today."

"Yeah? How?"

"Just got a feeling."

"We'll see," Binford replied despondently.

The two heard footsteps running up the three story staircase.

Deputy Grimes, at ninety pounds overweight, never ran. His red puffing face appeared at the bottom of the second story landing.

"Sheriff! Mr. Binford! You haven't seen the news have you?"

"Do we look like we have time to be loafing around watching info babes on the news?" Sheriff Carter responded.

"You're going to want to see this before you go in the grand jury room. It's on all the cable channels."

"Hells bells! I told you Binford, I bet they found Weir," the sheriff said, slapping his companion on the back as they followed the deputy to the bailiff's room on the first floor.

CULPEPER, VIRGINIA--WARRENTON TRAINING CENTER

Sims turned off the television.

He had read the news reports online and seen the cable news for most of the day, his secretary having discretely left him alone in the office after he told her he would take no calls. And yes, that included the President. "Tell them I am ill and will return their calls tomorrow." He wrote in an email to her.

When his cell phone began ringing, he turned it off.

It was The Gotterdammerung, the twilight of the Gods. The end of all things. Breakout. A breakout that no brushfire operation could ever hope to contain.

He knew that the things that he had directed to be done had been for the good of mankind. But, he also knew that no one would understand nor condone the extremities to which he had been forced to go.

A creature of Pentagon politics and inside knife fighting, he knew the blades were already out and waiting for him; the months of congressional hearings and recriminations, the federal grand juries, the civil suits, criminal prosecution and the personal insults stretched out before his mind in a burning and desperate battleground, not unlike the no man's land between barbed wire trenches in World War I.

No, he thought; he would not end it like that. He would not endure being judged by those, who, unlike him, knew nothing about what was at stake. Knew nothing about the new morality this crisis had created. No, he would not be judged by piss ants like that idiot sheriff and his lackey prosecutor.

No. He was above it all. His morality was shaped by something bigger than that of Weir and the sheriff and the prosecutor. He had fought an adversary from another world-- unknown but for the insatiable demand for more specimens. Ordinary morality did not--could not-- apply to him or to the program he directed from the Warrenton Training Center. But he knew that argument would die just as the program itself had died on one television station after another, one computer feed after another.

It would only be a matter of time now before he would hear a knock on the door. And, on the other side, there might well be a smiling man with a Beretta M9 in his hand. Or, he thought, a service processor to hand him a piece of paper that meant the same as death--a subpoena from some political body or another.

It was ignominious. He would not subject himself to such a process. He should receive a medal. Not the recriminations he knew that ordinary men possessed of ordinary morality would heap upon him. Like that piss ant prosecutor and the idiot sheriff.

No. He was above all that. His only regret was that he could not take care of that turncoat Weir. This was all Weir's fault. All of it.

Reaching into his top desk drawer, he took out a chrome plated 1911 .45 caliber, put it in his mouth, and pulled the trigger.

GALE CRATER --TRANSIT DAY 11

"What's that?" Steele pointed downward toward a metallic shell on the ground. He and Weir, who both after much meandering in the skimmer, found Gale Crater early in the morning, guided by the red summit of Mount Sharp.

"Never mind that. Look ahead," Weir said, gesturing towards a long cigar shaped craft sitting on the dusty plain, "It's the skimmer. Put me down next to it while I put on my suit."

"I see lots of footprints, but no activity in the front bubble." Steele reported as they settled next to it.

"Get suited up. I want over there as soon as possible," Weir said.

The two men depressurized their skimmer, then walked over to the grounded craft. Both men called over their radios, but got no response.

"We have a problem," Steele said.

"What's that?"

"We can't just depressurize the skimmer. What if they're inside without suits? We'll kill them."

The two men pounded on the craft's side before mounting onto the bubble itself and looking inside.

"I don't think anyone's home," Steele said to the distraught Weir as he peered through the front observation port.

"There are tracks leading away." Weir said.

"I think they walked towards Sharp," Steele said decisively.

"But that makes no sense."

"If the skimmer broke down, it does. We'd have done the same thing."

They got back in their skimmer and followed the trail. Soon it became apparent that the tracks all lead in one direction.

It was Steele who saw the first body. And then, behind they saw a silver suited group huddled against a rock wall on the side of the mountain. Neither man noticed any movement. Both saw the two diminutive suits held by a third suited figure-- but neither man dared to acknowledge the meaning of the trio.

"All right. I'm putting down just by that crater. We can pull everyone inside then re-pressurize." Steele said.

"Roger that."

The skimmer settled, they called through the suit radios to the others on the ground, but got no response. Weir ran to the trio first. He gathered up the inert childlike forms in both arms and sprinted back to their craft, where he gently set them down, before running back for the third inert figure.

"Who are you?" Steele heard Reznik croak over the suit com net.

"It's Steele. Where are you?" Steele asked as he dragged another inert form to the skimmer door.

"Stupid. I'm the guy all by himself waving at you," Reznik managed to rasp through parched lips.

Steele ran to the moving man, who was the first body they saw, and carried him back towards the skimmer. "Did everyone make it?" he asked Reznik as he sprinted across the dust.

"No. Cho didn't make it."

"We've got everyone in by my count," Weir said. "Pressurizing."

They waited the short time it took the craft to fill the cabin with oxygen. Weir crouched next to the three forms he first brought in.

When the indicator light for cabin pressure turned green, he ripped off the helmet to see Rebecca, her lips parched and dry. Her eyes flickered.

"John," Rebecca whispered. "Hunter? Heather?"

He turned and checked each, removing helmets, feeling for a pulse.

"They're all suffering from dehydration, but they'll be fine," Weir finally told her.

Steele and Weir gave each survivor a sip of water. Then more.

Rebecca caught John's sleeve as he moved about to help the others.

"Come here," she rasped.

He leaned down to her face. With a passion that had built up over the long days of stress and uncertainty, she pulled him down to her lips. He kissed her gently, then pulled up.

"I knew you'd come," she whispered before pulling him down to meet her lips again.

Weir's world collapsed to that one moment. The most important moment. The moment when he knew she was going to be alright, that they would be together-- in spite of all that could happen in a place as warped as Mars.

Later, with everyone hydrated and squeezed into the skimmer, Steele proposed they angle back down to the grounded craft to check on its propulsion system. "Perhaps it repaired itself like it refueled for water," Reznik had suggested.

Steele maneuvered the craft up and took a wide lazy circle of the site where they found the party. The group had never made it to the tent, having missed it in the climb down. He piloted up and saw the silver shimmer in the morning light.

"There's your tent," he said. "Anything you want from it?"

"The water containers," Reznik replied.

They settled near the tent, depressurized, and Weir opened the shelter to take out the containers. On his way back to the skimmer, he was surprised to see a slight figure walking hesitantly away from the parked craft, as if looking for something.

"Leotie?" he guessed aloud. "Why are you out?"

"I haven't given up on Cho," Leotie replied. "I thought you might understand that."

Once back in the skimmer, Weir told Steele to make a search for the missing Cho.

"Bloody waste of time, if you ask me," Steele whispered in response.

"I could have said the same about you," Weir replied.

"Quite right."

He flew a standard circular search pattern. After an hour, Steele said, "He's not out there. I'm sorry." With that he banked the craft back towards the grounded skimmer.

"Wait! What's that?" Leotie said from the side window. She pointed down a crevasse that was hidden from most angles in the sky.

Guided by her direction, Steele angled toward the large opening. Deep in the shadows, a shaft of sunlight reached the floor and reflected, revealing a shiny silver form.

"Cho," Steele said simply.

They landed, and carried the broken body into the skimmer.

Leotie gently opened the helmet to see Cho's busted and bloodied face. Teeth protruded through a mangled lip. His cheek sunk unnaturally inward. She bent down to kiss his blood caked forehead.

And it was warm.

She leaned closer and felt a slight stir of breath from his nose.

"He's still alive!"

"No way," Stover managed to mumble.

"Let's get this suit off of him and check his injuries," Weir ordered. "Steele, get me some water. That's probably what he needs most."

The two men, both trained in military field dressing, worked over the broken Cho. He woke slowly taking sips of water.

"He'll live," Weir pronounced when they finished. "It was the suit that saved him. That and the one-third gravity. Even so, it was a close call. He'll need someone to nursemaid him for a bit."

"I don't think there will be any problem there," Howington said, looking at Leotie.

She didn't notice. Cho was alive. And that was all that mattered.

As for Cho, as battered as he was, knew there was a freedom he hadn't felt in years. The coiled snake, always there before, had disappeared. He looked at Leotie and knew that, somehow, the evil implanted within so long ago in San Diego was gone. He was free. Through his misshapen mouth he tried to say something to Leotie.

She noticed his effort and bent down to hear his voice, her ear next to his bloody and mangled lips.

"I love you," Cho whispered, straining against the agony of ripped flesh and broken bone. Straining against all that, because he knew it was the most important thing he could ever say.

Ever.

GALE CRATER--TRANSIT DAY 12

They stripped the grounded skimmer of what they could and spent the night on the Crater floor. As the red sunlight illuminated Mount Sharp in the early morning, Steele gripped the controls of the skimmer in each hand.

They had a long trip and not a lot of provisions. They had water. They had a little food. But more than that, they had hope. And that was the most precious staple anyone could have. He pushed the levers forward and up-- lifting the skimmer vertically off the sandy crater floor. He turned and looked at Reznik.

"Where to, you bloody scoundrel?" he said roughly but affectionately.

"Teisserenc de Bort," Reznik said. "Northwest over the highlands."

"And what are we going to do there?" Rebecca asked.

"Wait. Wait and get strong again," Reznik replied.

"And if they don't come for us? I mean if earth doesn't come for us?" she asked.

"Well then," Steele replied with a grin, "we'll grab one of the bleeding alien ships, and bloody well go home ourselves."

GARY CLOSE

EPILOGUE

MARS: PRESENT DAY PLUS FOUR THOUSAND YEARS

Gaius Marius put on his protective zip suit, feeling at sixty five as nimble and elated as a teenage boy on his first date, fumbling with excitement, impatient for the helmet to latch into place. According to the theoretical equations upon which the whole project was based, today was the day the universe shifted. Today was the day life could start anew. Today was the day his son might get a second chance at life.

And although he didn't feel any different, according to Cato's time theory, the shift would happen today. Not everything in the universe would shift; in fact the shift would be so slight, that very little -- if anything -- would change. Shifting the inertia of the entire universe required a huge amount of energy, more in fact, than the universe contained-- making time travel impossible. Unless-- and here was the beauty of Cato's theory-- unless one only folded a tiny strand of the universe and did not travel through time but only traveled along a single "string" of the universe.

As the chief investigator for the project, it was Gaius' honor to take the lead vehicle to the site. Gaius reflected on the past fifteen years of the project. First, there was the gathering of resources, political and material. Then, there was the education and culling of the proper scientists and engineers which, with the present state of human genetics, had been no mean task. How could one even consider a life form human and competent to perceive the world as it really functioned if it were handicapped by a mixed genetic blueprint? Frogs. Cats. Corn. Fish. Fungus. That and more swirled within every living thing.

Really, who knew what sort of DNA one carried until the dreaded Ignus test revealed the truth?

Of course, pure was a relative term he mused as he adjusted the honorific insignia on his shoulder, then attaching on his left chest the

Ignus Test Symbol. The pure flame of a leaping fire, intertwined with the DNA double helix, indicated to the world his genetic purity-- even though he knew that his genes carried splices from a particular nasty form of fungus. But, except for outbreaks, easily controlled with medication, he suffered no real effects from the contamination, allowing Ignus to grade his DNA pure.

But others were not so fortunate; their contamination so much more visible, sometimes so that it was best to eliminate the mutation. Often the gene splicing was so severe, that the mutation could not live far beyond a few painful breaths. Other times, it grew outwardly until it overtook the original form -- be it a human or a tree. He still feared that manifestation in himself and checked carefully for any indications that the fungus had spliced into more of his DNA.

But, all that would change. Today. All, because of Cato's Theorem.

Cato's Theorem, built on an ancient truth sometimes called the theory of relativity. But that theory limited understanding to such a degree, that for many, it was almost useless. It did, however, offer a glimpse into the elastic nature of time. Honorius Cato developed time theory to its full potential. The rules were simple. The First Maxim: time travel was possible, but into time already created. How could one travel into something that did not exist? One folded the universe itself so that two time strands touched, two strings of the fabric of the universe touched, thereby making it possible to transfer material across the tenuous connection between the present and the past. The Second Maxim of Cato's theory postulated that time travel could only occur once on a particular time strand or string. In other words, someone from the future could only travel once from Day x to Day y. Forever. The strand once used could not be reconfigured again. And here was the real mind bender, once one travelled back in time the future did not exist. Therefore, there could be no return because there existed nothing to return to--the future had yet to unfold. The time strand itself ended. The third Maxim: organic material cannot survive time travel. The fourth Maxim and the one that constrained Gaius until today: the effects of time travel do not manifest until the tension between the inertia of the existing universe, and the changed universe becomes so great that the fabric of the universe itself snaps into the new configuration.

Like an expandable band, he had it explained to him once. The band stretches until a limit is reached beyond which the fabric snaps reconfiguring itself into two pieces rather than one. The fifth and final Maxim: the limit to time travel ended at approximately 4000 years. Why? Who knew? It just was.

Fortunately, Gaius mused again as he had often during the past few years, for Project Genesis 4000 years in the past brought them to the edge of the thing they were fighting. For it was 4000 years ago, according to their genetic calculations, that man first tinkered with the biosphere's genetic blueprint. They knew, for example, that the leading edge of the tinkering came in the form of genetically modified foods. Animal genes and plant based genes had been intermingled to boost food production according to archeological evidence and according to the mutation rates recorded in the genes themselves. Add to that the advent of nanotechnology and chaos ensued. Now, the very air and soil on earth teemed with genetic snippets attached to duplicating nanosplicers all swirling about unrestrained in an increasingly toxic stew. In biology, Gaius' field of study, there is another maxim: once released into the biosphere, life, any kind of life whether natural or manmade, finds a way, like water finds a way, to reach its level of stasis. And for life stasis is to live and replicate.

Of course, devastating wars, failing civilizations, and climate changes, had all but erased much of the electronic and paper history man was wont to use in those times --leaving the men of Gaius' time much to puzzle and guess about. It was accepted fact though, that 3500 to 4000 years ago, man began splicing unrelated genes into the food system. And once spliced, life as the maxim predicted, found a way.

But the past, twisted and forgotten, became revered. His own name reflected that fact. During the Renaissance some 500 years ago, Latin, upon its rediscovery in the peninsula once called Italy, grew into a vehicle for nation building, learning, and culture around the globe. Gaius always suspected the adoption of Latin was a primal yearning for a younger and more vigorous life--a life before the awful mutations.

Once launched, the Genesis project created laboratories, transport, nanotechnology, three dimensional manufacturer devices, and the most advanced artificial intelligence developed to date for oversight of the vast project. Then, they shipped it all four thousand years into the past, the year then called 1948, to operate independently and produce the fruits he hoped to harvest today.

It was the Genesis mission to gather pure DNA from earth: plant, animal, anything and everything, but especially human. Ironically, it was the gathering of human DNA that sparked the whole project. Gaius still remembered vividly the day they uncovered a temple in the desert next to a great salt lake in North America. The religious cult there had baptized literally hundreds of millions of people into the faith, and later, stored snippets of their DNA in the baptism ceremony. The DNA was corrupted, but the Mormons, as they called themselves, left a genetic roadmap for the future. And Gaius, then, conceived the notion that they could go back in time to collect specific DNA to help the living of his generation. Including his son.

His son needed a new sequence of DNA only found among the Cherokee. The problem was a total lack of uncorrupted DNA of that particular sequence. It existed in the past. Later, he learned it existed in one particular Mormon baptism. A girl named Leotie Thunder.

The project gathered DNA; using a spliced nanomachined organism to do the work in the labs and structures they sent back. The project picked crabs and insects as the most viable life forms for use on Mars and programed the AI accordingly. Saucer craft, and later other craft transported the material between the storage facility and Earth.

Genesis had to use humans for some of the tasks in the past. There was no getting around that facet of the program. The project used off the shelf technology in the labs and transports--all of which were configured for human use. The decision was a process of budget and working with what they knew. Besides, Gaius had decided early in the planning stages, if one sacrificed a few humans to save humanity it was not a bad thing. He wanted to be humane and did all he could to program that directive into the project. They would return the humans undamaged and programmed the AI accordingly. But in the final calculation, he had decided, if there were mistakes and humans died that was the price that had to be paid to save humanity.

Mistakes would happen. Gaius knew that. It was the nature of all projects that things would go wrong. But, he had confidence that the AI would correctly control the contingencies that arose. And perhaps it was selfish on his part, he acknowledged that, but Gaius also felt that if the project inflicted a little pain on the past; so be it, the past deserved a little pain after what they had unleashed on his time, his world, his body, and most importantly, his son who suffered a fatal genetic infection. It was a rough sort of justice, but justice nonetheless, in Gaius' estimation.

He nodded to his assistants as he walked out onto the Martian landscape. There in a line stood a convoy of specially equipped transports ready to gather the pure DNA in containers buried in vast vaults under the Martian ground. They picked Mars so as to be undisturbed by human activity during the collection and afterwards.

Gaius mounted up into the tube shaped transport, the Genesis project logo emblazoned on its side, a pure double helix depicting human DNA. In the cabin, he watched the pilot ready himself to start the procession. The man wore a headpiece specially outfitted with readers to decipher the cascade of information conveyed by microscopic bundles flashing from the instrument panel. The readers looked like a multifaceted insect eye. That was all Gaius could ever think when he saw the contraption in use. Gaius had used a reader, but he found it distracting from the real landscape beyond, so as much as possible he declined its implantation.

"We are ready, Chief Inspector," the pilot said, turning towards the back.

"Proceed." Gaius responded, and the transport, along with larger and heavier transports behind, mounted up into the thin Martian atmosphere, levitating by using the magnetic field of Mars itself for power and lift.

The Cato Theorem was so precise about predicting when the universal snap should take place that Gaius had decided, perhaps out of pride, or from a certain amount of showmanship, to position himself at a spot where they could see the snap take place. Again, he had been assured, there could be no danger if they remained removed from the actual storage area.

Of course, the wiser course of action would have been to wait and observe from Martian orbit and send robotic scouts in first. But Gaius was tired of waiting. He had, after all, waited all these years, and now he wanted to be there, to insure his place in the history books as an image of the man standing on a crater rim and watching the shift occur, in real time. The shift that saved the world.

Having glided smoothly away from the Genesis Industrial Compound, they sped, in an hour, two thousand kilometers away across cratered and windswept landscapes, to the mountain in which the storage facility was planned. Perhaps the next project, Gaius thought absently, would be to harness the awe inspiring technology of genesplicing and nanotechnology to Terre form this world. Make it a paradise for men to live and thrive as they would do again on earth.

The pilot circled the old volcano with its attending alluvial slope off to the east. Then he landed gently on the ground. The transports lined up behind.

Gaius took leave of his pilot. He stepped out of the transport and walked up the crater that gave a view of the mountain side where they planned the storage facility to be located--four thousand years in the past.

"All systems are nominal," someone announced over the com net.

"We have initial differential indicators," another man said, interrupting Gaius' thoughts about what he would say for the recorders.

"I copy and concur. All systems nominal." The pace was now picking up.

"Energy field flux detected."

"Affirmative."

"Transfer flux beginning."

"Light shift detected."

Gaius could not contain his excitement. This was the beginning of a new hope for him, for his son, for the world. Fresh, uncontaminated DNA, ready to reinvigorate the polluted and corrupted biosphere he and the rest of the humanity endured.

And then, the universe snapped with a single shimmer of the landscape, and Gaius realized that something had gone horribly wrong.

Gaping holes sprang from the mountain side. Craters, where none had existed, opened before him, exposing bits of twisted metal and composite resin.

Shocked, Gaius turned back to the transport.

"Take me to the lab facility." He said tersely to the pilot.

"Where is that, sir?"

"Take me to the top of the mountain!" Gaius snapped. "Tell those transports to stay put until I see what is going on. And turn off the recorder now!"

After the craft had moved up the mountain and settled at a large gaping hole, Gaius got out, followed by the pilot and the remainder of the crew. Five of them stepped into the cavern's maw.

"This was the reception laboratory." Gaius said picking his way through the dust and rock filled cavity, seeing more signs of the laboratory he had helped design. But all of it was blasted and burned. And, what was not destroyed, was ravaged by the searing winds that Mars was so good at creating.

"What happened, sir?" the pilot asked.

Gaius looked about astonished. To him it was clear what had happened. Someone or something had destroyed the complex. "Let's walk a bit more," he replied, not willing to speculate aloud.

He led the way into another a large cavern, scored by explosions and projectiles, hearing behind him the exclamations of the others as they saw the chipped and broken walls and pointed out the blackened char marks left even after four millennia.

It would take more investigation to find out what happened here, of course, but Gaius was pretty sure he knew. Last month, archeologists had uncovered an underground facility in an extinct volcano cone located in an area once called Culpeper. The chief investigator there, a friend, had put a lid on the artifacts they'd found, because, most jarring of all, the archeological team had uncovered several struts from an early specialized saucer specimen gatherer. In the plan created by Genesis, the first saucers robotically collected insect and animal specimens for nanotechnology treatment, making it possible to trace the exact manufacturing date of the saucer based on the identifying information packet magnetically imprinted in the material recovered during the dig.

Gaius feared that perhaps the wrack and ruin of time had hidden a period of contact between Project Genesis on Mars and humans on earth. The literature did not describe any such encounter, but then they knew so little about the past. How would he feel, he wondered, as he contemplated the ruins about him, if some unknown entity were taking people for experimentation and sampling? What would he do in response? It was a question he had never allowed himself to contemplate, until now.

He shook his head. Perhaps, they had time to send back corrective measures to prevent whatever befell the project here. But a deep disappointment and depression settled on the old man.

Humanity's last hope, the biosphere's last chance, his own son's future, lay in ruins at his feet. And the weight of time, the weight of dashed expectations, settled deep into his soul.

THANK YOU FOR READING

BREAKOUT

THE ROSWELL LEGACY

PLEASE LEAVE A REVIEW OF MY BOOK
ON AMAZON AT
WWW.AMAZON.COM/DP/B00N7OQAFY

GOOD, BAD OR INDIFFERENT,
AMAZON LOVES REVIEWS.

WATCH FOR NEWS ON
THE FACEBOOK PAGE
"BREAKOUT: THE ROSWELL LEGACY"
FOR THE SEQUEL.
MIND THE CRICKETS!